Sons of **Mercy** and **Justice**
A TRANSYLVANIA STORY

G. KEITH PARKER

AND

LESLIE PARKER BORHAUG

Cover photo illustration with the McGaha Chapel by Sarah Borhaug
Library of Congress Control Number: Pending
ISBN: 978-1477450222
Published in the United States of America

Dedication

To those many persons whose names will never, or rarely, be said or remembered and yet helped lay the foundation for the mercy and peaceful justice in the Appalachian Mountains of Western North Carolina, especially in Transylvania County, this book is affectionately dedicated.

"And what doth the Lord require of thee but to do justly, and to love mercy, and to walk humbly with thy God?" Micah 6:8

About the Authors

Leslie Parker Borhaug is the award-winning author of a silver 2012 Independent Book Publisher Award for her novel, *Unchained* (2012), which she penned under the name LB Tillit. Combining her passion for teaching, North Carolina history and writing she wrote three award-winning books with her students which embrace Transylvania County's local history: *Behind Closed Doors of the Allison-Deaver House* (2003), *Lake Toxaway… Back in the Day* (2004), and *Brevard Standing Alone, North Carolina's First Integrated Football Team, The Untold Story* (2005). Borhaug lives in Brevard, North Carolina.

G. Keith Parker, Ph.D., has published articles and books in the U.S. and Europe in history, theology and depth (Jungian) psychology, including the award-winning *Seven Cherokee Myths: Creation, Fire, the Primordial Parents, the Nature of Evil, the Family, Universal Suffering and Communal Obligation* (2006). Parker is Vice President of the Transylvania County Historical Society Board of Directors and he lectures often at college, church and community events on local and Cherokee history. He resides in the Dunn's Rock Community south of Brevard, N.C. where his family has lived for over two hundred years, also the setting of the book.

Table of Contents

Illustrations

Major Actors in the Historical Story

Jesse and Candace Hightower McGaha- Parents of James Crawford McGaha and siblings

James Crawford McGaha, 'J.C.' or 'Craf' or 'Crof'- Man of mercy and hospitality, Confederate Civil War Veteran, father of V.B. and siblings, husband of Harriet

Harriet Shipman McGaha- Wife of Craf, mother of V.B. and siblings

Volenus Bunyan McGaha- 'V.B.' or 'Bunyan', son of Craf and Harriet, sheriff and revenuer

Jessie Geneva Allison McGaha- wife of V.B., mother of Reba and Leslie

Rose Thrash McGaha- second wife of V.B., mother of Jacksie

Epiphroditus, McGaha-"Epi," brother of Craf, husband of Nancy Guice

Nancy Guice McGaha- wife of Epi, part Cherokee

Polly McGaha Fowler- sister of Craf, married to Tom Fowler

Tom Fowler- neighbor, brother-in-law and close friend to Craf, part Cherokee

Gerdi Sumi- Swiss immigrant, visitor

Andrew Jackson Loftis- 'A.J.' or 'Frosty Jack,' neighbor and friend of Craf, craftsman, contributor of land and labor for Little River Chapel

Margaret Loftis- wife of "Frosty Jack" and contributor of land for Little River Chapel

Jackson Gillespie- Trustee of Chapel, sawmill owner, family of famous Gillespie gun makers

Walter Raxter-Trustee of Chapel, helper in building, member of large Samuel Raxter family, husband of Laura Ashworth Raxter, contributor of land for Dunn's Creek Baptist Church

Laura Ashworth Raxter- wife of Walter, first postmistress and one who named community of See-Off, healer, mother of many

Rev. Elijah Allison- father of Jessie Geneva McGaha, popular Baptist minister, land-owner, slavery opponent and Union Civil War Veteran

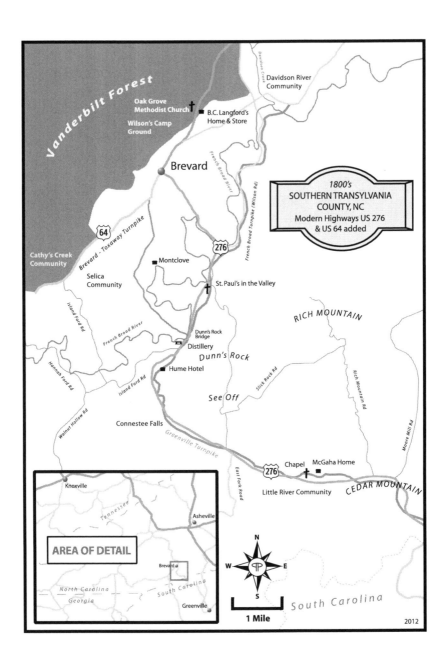

Introduction

Dunn's Rock, that granite cliff overlooking the Upper French Broad valley in southern Transylvania County, North Carolina, lends its name to the once thriving rural village and surrounding township, reaching almost to the South Carolina border in the days of early European settlement. Dunn's Rock community also was the site of an earlier ancient Cherokee settlement they called "Connestee."

The writer Frances Christine Fisher Tiernan, who wrote under the pen name Christian Reid and gave the Western North Carolina mountain area the name "The Land of the Sky," wrote in Appleton's Journal in March 1877 an article titled "The Mountains of North Carolina." Her perspective of this Connestee/Dunn's Rock valley was as follows:

> This queen of mountain-valleys lies twenty-two hundred feet above the sea, and has at this point an average width of two miles. The three forks of the French Broad - two of which rise in the Balsams and one in the Blue Ridge - meet at its upper end, and the united stream flows, with many a winding curve, down the emerald plain. Framing the broad fields and grassy meadows are forest-clad heights, and yet beyond rises the blue majesty of the grandest peaks in Western Carolina.

> To fully appreciate the charm, which fills every detail of this picture, it should be viewed from the summit of a cliff on its eastern side known as Dunn's Rock. The elevation of the hill, which rises abruptly in this castellated crag, is probably is not more than five hundred feet above the level of the river, but the river is one which lingers in the memory in colors that no lapse of time can dim. While it is easier to find more extended views, it would be impossible to find one of greater fairness.

The earliest European settlers who followed the Cherokee into this area in the late 1700s also appreciated its beauty, both from above and below, and made their homes above the Rock in a community that would be later named See Off, and below in the Dunn's Rock community proper. They built the turnpike through the valley and over the mountain to Greenville, South Carolina, following the previous Cherokee trading paths.

From the valley below, Dunn's Rock captures symbolically two opposite perspectives, one more dynamic and moving, the other more solid and stable. The former image is that of the bow of a mighty ship plowing westward and northward to face the ocean of Blue Ridge Mountains beyond. The latter image is that of a mighty iron anvil, a solid and stable abutment, too heavy to move.

Most of the early local Cherokee moved on westward to escape the European settlers' diseases and conflicts, or were forcibly removed. The few who remained integrated into the tide of settlers with whom they became identified. Two distinct groups of European settlers were identified shortly after most Cherokee left. First were the early pioneers who sought to build permanent homes and to find many different means of survival in a beautiful, but harsh, environment. The image of the anvil captures the hard working context of their lives. Secondly, several families from South Carolina, especially Charleston, eventually followed the earliest settlers, building summer homes to escape the heat and malaria as well as to participate in the beautiful mountain life. Most had made their fortunes or were simply successful business folks who made repeated trips into the area. Their many contributions to the Dunn's Rock and surrounding communities were complementary to that of the "local" folks for the most part. In many ways, they were also a positive, dynamic force in the community.

This story is basically about two men, their wives and extended families from the first group of permanent settlers mentioned above. It could be about many other men and women but it has to be limited by necessity. A story about the lives of James Crawford McGaha ('Craf', or 'Crof' to some) and his son, Volenus Bunyan McGaha (called 'Bunyan' and 'V.B.', but sometimes tagged with the nickname 'Venus') and their families can be told because some of their descendents have preserved many documents, articles, and records and have done extensive genealogical record searches. Without their life-long appreciation of family history and willingness to share with me, this telling could never have happened.

A word of caution is needed for my history and genealogy colleagues. Although this work contains much researched historical data and many correct family references, it is by definition an historical fiction. It contains constructed dialogue and a few fictitious characters to carry the story. In addition, it includes a few old undocumented stories from the Civil War and Reconstruction era, some of which were heard from my (Keith's) great-grandmother, Laura Ashworth Raxter, and grandmother, Hettie Raxter Cantrell Powell.

Most newspaper articles and letters woven into the text and in the appendices are authentic except in the text where they have been re-typed for legibility. The pictures are authentic as well. A note about use of local dialect is appropriate. Our years of living in Germany and Switzerland helped us appreciate not only their use of local dialects but also our own local Appalachian dialect with its long history reaching back into Old England. It is not just some "bad English" as is often claimed. In order to keep the story readable, the use of local dialect is limited, but the reader is reminded that most characters would have normally spoken with a heavy local dialect. Under some circumstances the story characters, however well-educated, will lapse into their dialect or "mother tongue." The same is true today.

Additional information and acknowledgements are found at the end of the story and in the appendices.

G. Keith Parker
Connestee/Dunn's Rock

Leslie Parker Borhaug
Rich Mountain

1

Summer 2012

Daddy always told me stories. I guess that's why I love this land. I guess that's why I loved the sound of Mammaw's Appalachian drawl when she picked me up at the airport warming me like her biscuits and apple butter. I guess that's why one day I'm going to make sure I live here surrounded by the mountains of North Carolina. I didn't grow up here, but my Momma and Daddy did. They sent me back, away from the big city and the noise, at least for the summer, as they did every year, away from the speed that consumes the lives of those who can't take time to stop and talk about their nanny goat giving birth or how big the rainbow trout was that they caught Sunday.

I was born here, so I can always claim to be a local, even without having to turn my fingers into "faingers," although I often wish the change would naturally spill off my tongue. But ten years ago, when I was six, I was thrown into the car along with Barney and Elmo when Daddy's plant shut down. He and six hundred others had to scramble for work. Mammaw said Daddy made thin paper for Bibles, so I figured they'd just made enough Bibles and didn't need any more. Took me years to realize that cigarette paper had made and broken Ecusta, the name locals called the paper mill long after the name had changed to Glatfelter. I didn't really care about the reasons. All I knew was we were leaving Mammaw and Pappaw behind.

At sixteen I was happy to be back with Mammaw, even if it was just for the summer. Pappaw died four years ago and Mammaw still missed him something bad. Momma figured having me with her would do Mammaw good. Daddy missed his mother and worried about her, so sending me was as close as he could get as to coming himself. I knew it would do Mammaw even more good if everyone came home. But that wasn't going to happen.

Pushing away the thought of the impossible, I shook my head and focused on being with Mammaw, at least for now. Here I was back in Mammaw's guest bedroom that was mine for the summer. I quickly opened up the little window and could hear water falling over the nearby dam that created a small swimming lake for the Sherwood Forest community where Mammaw lived. The fresh air quickly helped clear the musty smell of the orange and yellow handmade quilt carefully draped across the four-poster bed. The room, so tiny, gently encased the massive bed as if holding a treasure within its four walls. In the corner, a skinny, somewhat distorted mirror hung on the outside of the only closet. I could see the reflection of my shoulder length brown hair streaked with the blond highlights Momma quickly put in before I left. She had insisted she could fit me in between her customers. She wanted to make me look all "hip" before I left- her words, not mine. But the mirror showed my shorts and T-shirt were ready to explore these mountains, rather than make a fashion statement. I laughed at the picture of Daddy as a high school senior that was proudly displayed on the nightstand. I opened its little drawer and dropped in my prepaid wireless phone and my wallet. Mom had given me an extra twenty dollars to buy more minutes to call her and Dad, but I knew that if I carried the phone around the minutes would be gone before tomorrow. And, besides, I was here to spend time with Mammaw.

"Millie, is everything okay?" Mammaw found me sitting on the bed looking at Daddy's picture.

"Yes, Ma'am." I smiled up at my grandmother. Her round arms pulled me close. Her large soft breasts cradled me like a baby. "I'm home," I whispered into her ear, smelling her perm she must have had done just before I got here.

1844: James K. Polk is elected as the U. S. President; Baptists split over slavery issue; Violence erupts in Philadelphia between native-born Protestants and immigrant Catholics.

Little Man with a Big Heart

"You reckon it'll stay like this?" Craf feels small as he sits on a large flat rock that spreads out like a warm blanket in the middle of the field. He has a Gillespie rifle to his left and his younger brother to his right. The rock gives not only room to sit but also provides a view of the hogs and sheep they watch. He loves Rich Mountain. The fields, he'd been told, were cleared from the surrounding woods by Indians as hunting grounds high above the valley. The Blue Ridge Mountains rise in front of the youngster, already smaller than others his age, an inconvenience he was beginning to care about. He can't believe that at age twelve, when all other boys are really growing up and building out in muscle, he hasn't even reached five feet. Although Epi is a year younger, his legs stretch out past Craf's feet and offer an unwelcome and tangible reminder.

"What do you mean by 'stay like it is'?" Epi glances briefly at the North Carolina mountain skyline, leans back and lets his entire body soak up the warmth from the smooth rock. He closes his eyes and adds, "If'n you mean them mountains, hit's a stupid question! 'Course, they'll be there!"

Craf doesn't look at the smirk on his brother's face, but focuses on the large boulders towering in the distance, rock faces that had been standing long before his grandfather moved the McGaha family to these parts. Craf is aware that as a child of Jesse and Candice McGaha, surviving in the Southern Appalachian Mountains has not been easy. They have had to attempt farming with more forests than fields and more animals than crops to feed them. Their animals could scour the woods find mast enough, but must compete with wild animals for the acorns, chestnuts and other natural forest food. As fields are cleared, more grass eventually provides the hay for getting through the harsh winters of snow and cold. More corn and wheat are added as fields are cleared.

Craf questions whether he should continue the conversation with his brother who always seems to find Craf's questions somewhat annoying. But Craf can't help himself, "You reckin maybe we will always be here?"

Craf glances at his brother who opens one eye, "What in tarnation you talkin' about?"

"I don' mean you and me." Craf quickly scrambles to explain himself. "I mean the McGahas."

"James Crawford McGaha," Epi shakes his head as he rolls over with his back to Craf. "I think you've been thinking too much again. That's a question for Pa!"

Craf looks at his brother's back and sees the worn cotton shirt begin to pull at the seams. His older brothers, Joseph and William, handed their clothes down to Epi before they reached Craf. Craf laughs at the thought of getting what was left of this rag. But he stops his thoughts, thankful for the hard work his mother has put into making and mending the clothes. He smiles as he remembers her face as she gathers his younger sisters, Eliza and Polly Ann, around her while she swings a piece of cotton cloth in front of them. His mother, thrilled the cotton is already woven, begins to measure their height to begin sewing two matching skirts to be worn by her girls for years.

"I guess Pa would just tell me Grandpa brought our family to these mountains and we aren't intending to move on." Craf, gently nudging his brother with his foot, stands up because they have been sitting idle long enough.

Epi sits up and starts to stand, not questioning that their time to rest is over. Work calls and they all must do their part to sustain the family. He reaches his arms over his head for a good stretch and yawns, "Where 'bouts is them hogs?"

Craf looks around and realizes he's been looking at the mountains more than where the hogs have wandered off to. "Pa will kill us if we lose one animal!" Craf yells back over his shoulder as he runs across the field toward the woods where he last saw the hogs looking for mast. He sees some movement just behind some rhododendron bushes, and takes off in a run. As he leaves the open fields with his brother behind, he comes to a sudden stop. Too many branches are moving and Pa's words come rushing back to him, "Son, watch out for panthers! There's been a lot killed in these parts, but some still roam these mountains." Craf knows his father's words are true, because on some nights he can hear their wild, eerie cry breaking through the night. He sometimes wakes up, afraid something or someone was dying. Suddenly, Craf is aware that he has doesn't have his rifle strapped over his shoulder and he slowly begins to step backwards.

"Craf, what you doing?" Epi stands right behind his brother holding the water pouch and rifle Craf had left behind. Although he is relieved his brother was wiser than he was to bring the rifle, Craf doesn't speak, but points at the moving bush. Epi lifts his eyebrows and carefully pulls the gun to his shoulder. "You reckin it's a panther?" he whispers with excitement. He begins edging forward. Craf grabs his arm and motions for him to move back. Epi, although taller, listens to his older brother and follows him back into the clearing. "Come on, Craf, let's go kill us a panther!"

Craf shakes his head, "He hasn't done anything to us. Why should we?" Craf only hesitates a moment before looking at his brother who hasn't spent as many hours with Pa hunting game. "Now if he'd attacked us, we should have shot him. But Pa said that we hunt for food." The mysterious animal is quickly gone.

Epi looks longingly over his shoulder, but knows Craf's mind is set, so he moves on. He's seen Craf care for animals and hesitates regretfully for a moment before killing them. Epi never questioned his brother, but today seemed extreme.

It takes nearly two hours to get the hogs and sheep into pens and the dogs on overnight guard duty. The two boys know the walk down the trail through the woods to the McGaha home will take another hour, so they head down the mountain.

Ever the admirer of his brother, Epi is often confounded by his questions. On the way home Epi quizzes his brother, "James Crawford McGaha, how come you git so worked up 'bout animals? I never thank about such stuff."

"Well, Epiphroditus McGaha, do you mean 'think' or 'thank'?" Craf punches his brother on the arm.

"There you go again, correcting me. You knowed what I meant. 'Sides, sounds th' same to me."

"No, Epi, I was not correcting but just thinking that we ought to be thankful for all we have, even if we work hard for it. Besides, I am working hard to learn English reading, writin' and speakin', I mean speaking. Maybe I can be a teacher someday."

With a loving shove, Epi joshes his brother, "Well, I reckon that's all right with me. Don't reckon you'll ever be much with workin' timber or really hard farmin', bein' the runt you are!"

Craf knows he is quite small for his age, but he works hard with his parents. The rest of the way is walked in silence as Craf reflects on his own motives. Why is he so sensitive to God's creatures of all kinds? Is it because he is so tiny? He had always been so much smaller than any other kids his age and even those much younger. Does he also feel he needs protection?

But he says to Epi as much as to himself, "I do have my muscles and mind together. I can handle a pretty good sized sheep, hog or goat by myself. I can chop wood to match anybody and pull my weight on the other end of a cross-cut saw with any grown-up."

Epi grabs his brother around the neck, rubs his head and laughs, "I reckin we'll see."

Summer 2012

"Millie! Wake up!" Mammaw's voice startled me. For a minute I couldn't remember where I was. The sound of the water reminded me quickly that today I would get to swim in the lake. Memories flooded back of all the summers spent cooling off, catching newts and making new friends on Trout Lake.

"I'm awake," I yawned as I sat up. I noticed Mammaw was dressed and not in her usual morning purple zip-up-the-front bathrobe. I frowned a little. "Where are we going?" I asked.

"Well," Mammaw glanced down, looking almost ashamed. Then she steadied her eyes on me, "Honey, we're not goin' anywhere. I'm goin' to work." She didn't miss a beat. She quickly turned and headed out the door as she continued, "Since your Pappaw died I tried to be peaceful, but last year I just had enough of tryin' to figure out what to do with myself. So, well, the Dollar Tree's been boomin' since the economy took a dive, so they were happy to hire me since I'm flexible with my hours. It gives me a little extra spendin'. . . ."

"What?" I followed her as she walked into the yellow kitchen and plopped myself into one of the two bar stools she had managed to crowd around a small, new raised kitchen table. "I thought we were going to spend the summer together? Oh, NO! Don't tell me you've lined up a babysitter." The horror in my eyes made Mammaw suddenly laugh out loud. Her belly jiggled until I couldn't help myself but laugh too.

"Honey," she managed to finally breathe. "You're sixteen. Your parents already agreed to you being on your own while I'm at work."

"You mean they know you work?" I took a sip of the small glass of orange juice that Mammaw had poured for me along with placing a couple of warmed up biscuits on my plate. I started to reach for the apple butter suddenly much more aware of the growl that started to emerge from the pit of my stomach.

Mammaw gently touched the top of my head. "Your parents were afraid you might not want to come if you knew you'd have to spend some days on your own. They really wanted you to come regardless."

"Well," A couple of crumbs fell out of my overstuffed mouth. "Then they don't know me very well." I swallowed, looked at Mammaw and smiled, apple butter smeared all over my lips. "I wouldn't miss summer in Transylvania County."

A deep sigh rose from within Mammaw, as if she'd been worrying a long time. Relief swept over her and I just knew another big-breasted hug was coming at me. Coming from her, I'd take one any day.

1844: Samuel F.B. Morse sends the first telegraph message, "What hath God wrought!"; Annexation of Texas fails in the Senate because of slavery issues and fears of war with Mexico; A New York hotel offers the first private bath in an American hotel.

The Big Question

It is not far behind the barn and Craf is on the other end of a crosscut saw, the day that he approaches his much beloved father, Jesse, with the toughest question of his young life, worried that it will bring their first major conflict.

"Let's take a break son," Jesse exclaims. "My shoulders and back shore need it. I reckin ye need it too. I'm plumb amazed that you can outlast your Papa."

They sit down on the log and sip the still cold spring water from a clay jug, Craf wishing his father had bragged on his strength to Epi.

"Epi tells me you are askin' a lot of questions. That's good an' I'm impressed with your hankerin' to learn."

Wiping the sweat from his brow, Craf thinks this is the time. "Well, Papa, can I then ask you one?"

"Of course, you oughta know that you don't have to ask for permission. What kinda question do you reckin' I kin answer?" Jesse takes the clay jug from Craf and lets the cool water ease both his raw throat and the aches in his arms while he cradles it.

"Well, Papa, it is a tough one and I don't know how to ask without a-makin' you mad."

"Ah shucks. You're my boy. Go ahead." He sets the jug down on the flat rock by the log where they sit.

In a nervous voice, higher than usual, and suddenly shaking, he responds cautiously, "Well, it's about the slaves. Don't it bother you to keep them like you own them?"

Jesse picks up the jug again and begins to turn it in his hands, seemingly studying it. "Now son, we treat 'em lots better'n any of our neighbors and for certain better than many big plantation owners down there in South Carolina and Georgia. They got a good life here with us-uns."

"I know that. But you are my teacher and you teach from the Bible." Craf stands up and faces his father, as if for the first time. "You have always said that God loves all people the same, or something like that."

Jessie is startled by his small son suddenly eye to eye with him. "Son, they was slaves in th' Bible times. Some of them traveling preachers remind us of that. Maybe we can ask one of 'em when they come this-away again." He pats the log next him encouraging Craf to sit down again.

Craf can't move. His chest feels tight as he sees his father's eyes narrow. "Papa, please don't do that. Some of those preachers have no learning in the Bible and can't even read." Craf lifts an arm and points south. "Worse yet, some are paid by those big plantation owners down in South Carolina to stir up people to protect their rich way of life. That is not who we are. We may be simple folks but we can think for ourselves."

Jesse sets his clay jar down hard and they hear a crack. He asks firmly, "Well, what 'bout some of them teachers or preachers from Furman Institute that come up from South Carolina? Ye seem to like 'em and love to listen to 'em." Jessie slowly rises to tower over his son. "Is that where you get these questions? Are they a-settin' you against your Papa?" His body trembles as his voice grows louder.

Suddenly Jesse realizes he is getting upset both with his son and worse yet with where the questions seemed to be going. He says abruptly, "That's enough for today. Get back to the house to your chores. You know it is time to milk and you are twelve years old, practically grown."

Craf feels himself run by the back porch, then off to the barn, buckets in hand but with a heavy heart. Has he pushed his father too much? But these things bother him. He loves Big Jake, Mae and their son, Joe. They are like family and yet, something is wrong with this whole picture. It bothers him that most folks say because "everybody" says it is right to own other humans, that makes it so. Worse yet, many say that slaves are simply animals and thus can be bought and sold and treated like animals.

As he squeezes the first stream of milk into the bucket he remembers when he was about eight he had been on a long trip to Charleston with his father. There he had seen the slave market where black-skinned humans were brought off ships, chained, beaten and sold like cattle. And they were mistreated worse than any animals they had at home. The trip home in the wagon had been even longer for he could not sleep or eat. Nightmares plagued him for many nights until they finally climbed the Jones Gap road and reached North Carolina and home.

Craf finally listens to the sound of the milk filling the bucket as both hands capture a good milking rhythm. He wishes he could hide here in the barn and not face his father, perhaps not face the rough Appalachian Mountains with the harshness of both man and beast.

Summer 2012

It didn't take long for me to throw on my one-piece Speedo once Mammaw pulled out of the drive to the Dollar Tree. I quickly put the dishes in the dishwasher, grabbed a bottle of water, an extra biscuit just because, and let the screen door slam behind me.

Trout Lake was only two minutes up the road. Once I reached the open space I wrapped the towel I had grabbed around my shoulders. I had forgotten how cool it was first thing in the morning. I hurried onto the tiny wooded dock that jutted out in front of a lone swing set. The sun was starting to touch the tip of the dock so I placed myself strategically on the edge and turned my face to soak in the first warm summer rays. As I felt my body warm up, I slowly let one toe touch the cold mountain water. Soon both legs were slowly moving the water in front of me. Small waves rippled away and were eventually lost chasing each other over the small man-made lake.

"So, you're back?" An unfamiliar voice startled me. I turned to see who the heck would be scaring me like that. A tall tow-headed boy stood in front of me.

"Kevin?" I'd recognize the bright blue eyes and almost white hair anywhere. "Sounds to me like your voice finally changed."

"Thanks for noticin'," Kevin's face suddenly turned pink and I suddenly became aware that I might should have kept that thought to myself. He walked over and plopped down next to me. "Thought you might not come this year. Turnin' older and all."

I had spent most summers seeing Kevin play on the lake. Sometimes we swam together, but most of the time he kept to himself. When his older brothers joined him they'd let me join in a game of Marco Polo, but alone he was happy to just keep to himself. So I was a little surprised to find him on my dock, so near. I looked at him cautiously, as if I'd never seen him before, "Well, I can't miss all this. You know the trout would miss nibbling on my toes."

Kevin smiled a little. His pink shade hadn't quite faded. He glanced around nervously. "Well, Millie, things have changed here a little since last summer," he almost whispered.

I was thinking a lot must have changed for Mr. Keep-to-Myself to suddenly be so friendly. I finally threw my towel off and jumped into the water, splashing water all over the place. Kevin was freaking me out just a little. I mean I was happy that he was friendly and all, but come on, what was up with getting so close?

He looked at me like I had hurt him, jumping in when he was trying to tell me about whatever was new. "What did you do that for?" He was wiping off the water as if the drops were fire ants crawling up his arms.

"I want to swim. Is that a crime?" I tried to smile, but Kevin was looking around nervously. I felt a little sorry for him so I swam back up to the dock and put my arms up on the warm wooden planks, resting my chin on my very white arms. "Okay, Kevin, what's changed?"

He looked at me from where he was now standing and with a coolness in his voice I had never heard he stated, "We got Mexicans movin' in."

My stomach lurched slightly. "Are you kidding me?"

"No, I'm serious." He had a smirk that scared me a little. "Seems more and more are comin'..."

"No!" I stopped him, pushing off from the dock, just so I didn't have to be so close to him. "I mean are you kidding me that you even care about that... that somehow that it's a bad thing in your eyes?"

The pink was getting brighter in Kevin's cheeks. This time anger steadied his eyes. "What are you sayin'?"

I swam right back to the dock, pulled myself up and wrapped my towel tightly around my bathing suit. Then I returned his gaze with equal fierceness. "I'm SAYING that I THOUGHT you were from HERE."

1844: Mormon Leader Joseph Smith is murdered by a mob; Brigham Young is chosen to lead the Mormons; Anesthesia is used in dentistry, childbirth and surgery with much skepticism from many doctors.

The Dream

Jesse looks to the sky. The clouds threaten to produce a good storm. Maybe it will be nothing, like yesterday, charging the air to make it harder to breathe. He tells Candice he might spend the night on the mountain since he has heard of neighbors losing sheep, hogs and cattle to big cats, 'painters,' recently. Besides, he needs time to think about several things, and hopefully get away from the heavy feelings stirred up by Craf's questions.

He gets his walking stick, his Gillespie rifle, his pouch of bullets and powder horn and heads for Rich Mountain to check on the sheep and hogs. He needs time to think anyway. The dogs were good to stay and watch the animals, but often a bear or painter would take out one or more dogs, especially to get to the sheep. He has tried leaving a slave to watch but they are too frightened of the wild animals and feel more secure closer to the houses and barns. But mostly they need to be near each other; he respects that. He realizes he had been more sympathetic with their plight than most of his neighbors were. They sometimes tease him for being "too good" to both his slaves and animals. But he just ignores it.

His trip to Rich Mountain is not an easy one. Craf has really upset him. Anger makes the heavy air even harder to inhale. He would never have asked such impertinent questions of his father at age twelve. As he walks his feelings envelop his entire body. He stops for fresh air. Anger he has never felt also stops him and he can't take another step. How could he lose his temper? How could he show such poor judgment in front of his son? He is really a good boy and very sensitive. Is he too sensitive? No, he reckoned not, for he has some of his mother's traits.

Taking a deep breath, he tries to let the smell of the thick rhododendron soothe his body, but the familiar mountain air only seems to smother him. Slowly, Jesse moves again up the mountain trail with his mind spinning. He leans heavily on a rotting log and whispers to the growing silence, "Craf is right little for his age and maybe he is just a-trying to make up for that. But boy, is he a smart young-un and hears ever' word when they read anything, 'specially from the Bible. He talks on an' on with them Furman folks that come through th' mountains, a-preachin' and a-teachin'." He waits for a moment, wishing for a word of assurance or reason, but only silence pushes him to face the worn path and finish his journey to Rich Mountain.

As he steps over a small stream, Jesse suddenly kicks the water. "Damn them teachers an' preachers!" His strange cry is answered only by the continued trickle of the stream. Why did they say it was good to ask questions? Now Jessie wonders if it was such a good idea to let those educated men spend the night with the family, along with the drovers. Pain grows in his chest as he remembers all of those evenings when his family listens to their stories about what goes on in the outside world, especially the rising tensions over slavery and other things in the struggling states of their new land. But Craf, after they leave, would practice their speech and especially their grammar. He always wants to learn. And Jesse realizes his son is absorbing more that better English.

Jesse reaches a cleared piece of pasture land and sees that the storm clouds are passing. He can breathe easier now. He smiles at the thought of Craf when some of those jack-leg preachers claim authority straight from God on about every topic and how Craf's questions stir them up to no end. They would often criticize him, even as their host, for letting a young whippersnapper question their so-called authority. He never saw that as so bad, and actually enjoyed Craf's challenging their egotistical ways. So why should he disapprove when Craf questions him? He is the boy's loving father, not some ignorant preacher or traveling snake-oil salesman!

It is a clear, comfortably cool summer night on Rich Mountain as Jesse settles down for the night. Jessse drops off to sleep, but finds little rest as he tosses and turns. There is a young boy about twelve in some kind of church, asking questions, tough questions, of the preachers and teachers. The boy's father is upset that he would do this and tries to take the boy away. But he is somewhat paralyzed by the situation, realizing the profound nature of the questions. He finally relents, listening, and learning from the boy. And then he realizes that, while still in the dream, he is the father. Craf is both the son and the teacher.

Jesse awakens sweating in spite of the cool morning, absolutely shaken by the dream. His cold biscuit breakfast is hard to swallow as he tries to rationalize the dream away. Then, as he looks toward the mountain tops and the morning fog still sleeping in the valley below, he smiles. "Craf!" he mutters. He almost curses again but he can't. "What kin I do?" He raises his voice to the sleeping giants, Toxaway, Pilot, Pisgah. Even the rock faces on Cedar Rock look like strange eyes staring back at him and whispering, "You know."

By now he is drooping, bent like an old man. Jesse hangs his head but for a moment. Then he straightens his back and slowly stands up, ready to head back home on the long trail through the woods toward the Little River Turnpike. Tears flow. He does not try to stop them.

Thoughts of human life, human dignity and slaves as persons, all torment him, especially when he realizes that his twelve year old son thinks about them more than he does.

As he walks the final bend of the footpath he stops short of the cleared yard in front of the house porch. "I'll do it!" he says to himself, "I'll set free them slaves."

Jesse knows he will have to face the consequences of his decision, but he feels an inner freedom he has never known. A divine peace calms his fears. The divine love that he has counted on for years relaxes his body and the fears of being a pioneer settler, fears of Indians, fears left from the Walton War and fear of simply surviving in the wilderness and providing for his family, amazingly dissipate with the freedom he feels when he knows he has to do it -- to set his slaves free, and to do so in love.

Jesse takes in a deep breath of the mountain air he so counts on to sustain him. Finally arriving, he takes his first steps into the yard, the first step into his home, the first step into a place that will never be the same.

Summer 2012

"What is that supposed to mean?" Kevin's eyes were staring me down as I started to walk away. He was obviously surprised with me not supporting his disgust with Mexicans moving in, but he also didn't like me being irritated with him. He ran up to me as I passed the swing set. Kevin quickly jumped over a swing and landed in front of me. "Millie!"

I stopped. Not because he told me to, but because I heard something in his voice. Like a please… well, almost. He would never admit it, but it was there. So, I looked at him. He was holding the swing's chain and suddenly sat on the well-worn blue plastic fabric.

"I meant that I thought you were from here." I was trying to figure what he wanted from me. "You know, a mountain person."

"A mountain person?" Kevin suddenly grunted. "That's kinda stupid! What? You think I'm some dumb hairy back-woods mountain man that lives off the land?"

"That's not what I meant!" I was feeling the heat rise. I saw Kevin start to nervously look around again. His glare returned and I could see it was time for me to leave. I turned my back to him and started to walk away. I heard the rattle of the swing behind me and Kevin running the other direction. I turned around and yelled after him. "I mean from HERE! These mountain people! The ones that made this place what it is!" He didn't hear me. As I watched him disappear into the woods on the other side of the lake I whispered, "The ones who made this my sanctuary!"

1844: Charismatic preacher William Miller's prophesy of the Second Coming of Christ on October 22 fails after many followers had given away their property and were dressed in sheets, waiting on hillsides or in cemeteries; Foes of slavery thwart Texas annexation.

The Decision

Craf heads in for dinner. He's finished his chores for the day and is looking forward to his Ma's cooking. He tries to wipe out of his head the memory how he rattled his Pa yesterday. Yet all day long he'd seen his Pa drop his eyes and avoid looking at him. He asks himself if Pa is disappointed in him and his eternal, infernal questions.

The kitchen is warmer than usual. The familiar smells of cornbread and greens elicit a deep growl from the pit of his belly. He smiles, knowing he will soon be satisfied, but stops in the doorway to the eating room. The table is full of his favorite fixings and almost every chair is taken around the big table.

Craf quickly pulls off his cap and smiles awkwardly at Jake, Mae and Joe who have joined the table with Epi straddling the corner of the table. His sisters, Polly and Eliza, are propped up in the laps of older brother's

Joseph and William's. Craf wonders why he was not told the family slaves would be joining them for supper. Was his Pa trying to make a point, trying to prove how good he is to the slaves?

Craf sits next to Epi and their Ma comes in with fresh cornbread still in the hot iron skillet. Not looking her normal cheery self, she too does not look Craf in the eyes. Craf is sure they must really be angry with him. Craf glances at Epi who simply shrugs his shoulders. His older brothers also give him a blank stare. No one seems to know what is going on.

"How are you, Mae?" Craf asks awkwardly, trying to break the tension. It is clear the slaves also have little understanding of the sudden invitation. She can't seem to answer so she cautiously smiles in response.

Suddenly the door from the kitchen opens again and Jesse walks in. His head is held high as he hooks his hat on the wooden peg in the wall next to the chestnut cupboard.

He walks right up to his wife, who is sitting with her head slightly lowered. Craf wonders what is going on as he watches his father gently place a hand on his wife's shoulder. The answer soon comes.

"I got somethin' real important to tell ye. It affects us all. Please hang in there with me whilst I try to get it out. I done gone an' decided-- an' Candice agrees with me- - to let go th' slaves."

There is nothing but silence. Craf doesn't know if his chest will burst from shock, fear or pride. His eyes dart from his pillar of a father to the dark figures sitting across from him, half hoping Mae, Joe and Jake will jump up and down for joy.

But Craf sees fear in the eyes of the soon-to-be-free slaves as his father continues. "Jake, Mae, Joe, just as soon as we can get th' right papers fixed all legal you-uns is all free to go as freed folks."

Craf watches his father squeeze his mother's shoulder. He must have calmed her fears earlier and this subtle communication is assurance for them both.

Big Jake responds in a shaky voice, "But Massa Jesse, how you gonna work this farm, clear more land, care for th' place?" Craf sees sweat begin to bead on Big Jake's forehead.

"Jake, I ain't your 'Master' any longer so please call me 'Jesse'. If'n you want, you are free to stay on but only as paid, hired hands or tenant farmers just like lots of our kinfolks do here in these parts. But you are also free to go. I know from th' letters we've read for you that you got free kinfolks in the north askin' you to come. Take time to decide, but we gotta get them papers done afore word gits out. I'm a little scared 'bout what some other folks might do."

"As for th' place, we got younguns growin' up an' a whole passel of kinfolks and neighbors a-helpin each other. I reckin our own teenagers, Joe and William, will be right glad to come home from their 'prentice work. You know how it is, come plantin' or harvestin' time, everbody helps everbody else."

Tears fall everywhere when the implications become clearer. Young Craf is in shock, yet deep down inside so very proud of his father. He knows his father is taking a stand for what is right. Only time will tell what might come of it.

It is not long before Craf hears from the neighbors. Most simply respect their decision and say nothing. Some, however, talk about the danger, how this will feed into the minds of other slaves and cause dissension if not an uprising. Craf simply listens. He is proud his father has made waves, ones that don't stop rippling. From Cedar Mountain, down Jones Gap all the way to Greenville and north to Cathey's Creek, Brevard, Hendersonville and even Asheville, word gets out soon that some of the McGahas have released their slaves who have gone north.

Craf smiles to himself when he hears that the folks in South Carolina who are not happy about the McGaha decision still keep coming to the immediate area of Cedar Mountain, nearby Flat Rock and Dunn's Rock to build summer homes to escape the heat of the low country. Although they do not agree with the McGahas, they feel they are not in conflict since they have left most of their slaves in the low country doing the work of the plantations and bring only a few household slaves for their seasonal visits.

Although Craf is proud of his father, he knows that tensions over slavery are building and the ever-increasing visitors to the mountains are easily polarized over the issue. But since the McGaha clan is small at this time, no major public issue is made. It has been their own choice and they do not push it on others.

Summer 2012

I stood there alone on the bank of Trout Lake, sorta glad that Kevin was gone, but totally confused. One minute he was friendly, much friendlier than I'd ever known and the next he was evil incarnate. Possessed! That's what I finally chalked it up to in my never ending superficial explanations for the unexplainable. Heck, I didn't even really know the guy and after this day was not intending to.

I headed back to Mammaw's not really feeling like swimming anymore. Didn't know if Wacko would show up again, so I decided to leave the coolness of the lake and return to the mustiness of my room. That didn't last long. I had to get outside, so I grabbed a Mountain Dew out of the fridge and headed down Robin Hood Lane. The sweet cool Dew tasted like summer and the further away I got from Trout Lake the more excited I got! I couldn't believe I was allowed to be here on my own. I mean, I had never much explored this area beyond Trout Lake without my family. We'd always headed to the tourist locations and to float down the Davidson River in an inner tube or eat ice cream at Dolly's, but today I would search for something new.

At the bottom of the hill I reached the small concrete bridge that we crossed every time we entered the community. Instead of crossing it I headed to the bank of the stream. The Little River was one of the reasons there were few houses actually built right along the stream... When it rained it flooded. Always thought it somewhat crazy how this water turned into some of the most beautiful waterfalls in the county.

I took off my flip-flops and waded in the stream looking for any sign of fish. I was startled by a sudden splash not five feet from my legs. "What the heck!" I jumped out of the water looking for the source of the unexpected and annoying interruption.

"So sorry! I'm so sorry!" A voice yelled from behind a bush that obviously needed to be cut back. "I didn't see you." A head finally appeared with long black hair and skin like clover honey. Her smile made me think she was trying to show off every one of her perfectly straight white teeth. I couldn't help but smile back.

"That's okay!" I jumped back into the water and headed downstream toward her.

The girl, who looked about my age, reached out a hand to pull me up on her side of the bank.

"What were you trying to do? Smash a fish? Have you never heard of a pole?" I giggled hoping she would think my lame joke was funny too.

But she just kinda looked seriously at me for a minute. Then she smiled ever so slightly. "Actually, I was trying to kill a snake."

I felt the blood drain from my face. Then she just about punched the fire out of my left arm as she yelled, "Just kidding!"

I couldn't help but laugh as I rubbed my slightly sore arm. "I'm Millie," I finally managed to breathe.

"You can call me Elli." The girl held her hand out officially to me.

As I took her hand I frowned just a little. "What do you mean I can call you? Is that not your name?"

Elli showed me her teeth again, "Oh it's really Eleadora Alverez Antonio. But around here it's easiest with Ellie Alverez." She looked at me and smiled, "I'm guessing Millie is short for something too."

I blushed just a little. "I guess I'm happy my parents don't really call me Camilla Florence Fowler." We both laughed until I could swear I just about had an embarrassing accident.

1850: Millard Fillmore becomes the U.S. President after the death of Zachary Taylor; California becomes a state.

The Cherokee Question

"Papa?" Young Craf McGaha and Jesse begin one of their many walks up the path leading to Rich Mountain. Craf has grown more in wisdom than in body, but is always proving he can work as hard as anybody, pull his end of the crosscut saw, do even more than other eighteen-year olds. But he still loves to dialogue the best. His dialogues and debates with any and all travelers set him aside from most other mountain neighbors who prefer to keep to their own folks, except to listen to the disturbing news that comes with the flatlanders.

"Yeah, son?" Jesse stops as they are passing between the gigantic, square, granite outcroppings some folks call "house rocks." He knows his son is still proud of him for freeing the slaves. And now Jesse looks forward to his son seeking times to be alone with him out on some mountain, to take a break and learn about life and its injustices. Jesse knows other tough questions bother Craf, even at age eighteen when most young men are sure they know it all. Jesse is relieved that his son is no longer reluctant to ask.

Craf scans the giant rocks as if trying to remember something. "Papa, I was about six years old when those troops rounded up our Cherokee neighbors and friends." Craf looks at his father. "Why could we not do something? How could that happen?"

Jesse looks at his son, almost hiding a smile. He looks around to make sure they are alone, even though they are in deep woods amidst the massive boulders.

"Craf, you shore ask hard questions. Bein' as we're out here with nobody around, I reckin I can talk a little about it, but you gotta promise not to talk or ask questions when anybody is around, even folks ye think might agree with you."

"How come? And why can't I ask something of the educated folks from South Carolina?"

Jesse places his arm around Craf's shoulder and gives him one hard squeeze before he lets go. Craf is slightly surprised by his father's sudden show of affection, but fiercely aware that his father worries. "'Cause, storm clouds is a-brewing all over this here land about people of color, be they red or black or brown or yellow. You never know where someone stands or what they'll tell somebody else. We already had nosy folks asking too many questions 'bout us because we let our slaves go. Thankfully the Hefners, Gillespies, Rabbs an' other neighbors ain't 'bout to tell anything to strangers 'bout th' McGahas."

Craf watches his father begin to head on down the path away from the fortress of boulders. He quickly catches up to him. "What about my question? What about the Cherokee?"

Jesse slowly shakes his head. "Well, you know the troops rounded most of them up back in '38 and put 'em in stockades, eventually driving them like cattle out west to Indian Territory. About a fourth died on the way. Th' stories told by both th' Indians an' soldiers who had to do it was so bad I get sick hearin' 'em. There was no mercy."

Craf listens carefully as he looks back at the huge rocks wondering if the Cherokee also stood in awe there before or even if they had cleared some of the fields the McGahas now used on Rich Mountain.

Jesse continues, "It makes no sense. When Andy Jackson was President he set it all in motion to send 'em away as 'lesser' beings. It was all illegal. Even the U.S. Supreme Court said so, but he just asked where their army was!"

Craf, now agitated, cries out, "But why? What had they done?"

"Son," Jesse quietly responds, "They stood in th' way. Some called it progress. Some called it greed. Some said God intended for white men to rule an' conquer all, something about a 'manifest destiny,' whatever that ought to mean."

Craf listens without interrupting. He knows his father is digging deeper than usual, but doing so willingly. Becoming the teacher Craf longs for, Jesse continues, "Our first leaders like Washington and Jefferson, thought we-uns could all live together and, whenever them Indians learned 'bout our 'civilized' ways of farmin', metal workin', millin', tradin', an' so on, we'd all be just good citizens and neighbors." Jesse slowly lifts his arm and draws an imaginary line through the dense forest. "The gov'ment drawed up a lotta boundaries 'tween settlers an' Indians, one even running right through here where we sit now. But they never held."

Jesse drops his arm and continues on the path, but he doesn't breathe in the rhododendron's scent as he usually does, instead he holds a steady gaze on the path ahead. "So, Craf, I reckin what they 'did' was exist, and be successful for the most part. They got 'civilized,' according to white folks, and got right effective in farmin', millin', ferryin', metal workin', blacksmithin', weavin', and about every trade you can imagine. An' as farmers workin' with all animals they was really good. Over in North Georgia they was far more prosporous than th' white neighbors, creatin' all kinds of tensions an' jealousy. And a few even got rich, like Chief Vann over in Georgia, who had a big plantation with slaves."

Craf's eyes grow larger. An Indian owning slaves! He finds himself suddenly standing still. Before he knows it, his father is disappearing ahead of him beyond a pine tree with branches that showed signs of ice damage from last winter. He runs to catch up and hears his father half grunt, "Worse yet, thanks to Sequoiah, they had developed their own writin' and newspaper. Most Cherokee learned to read in their own language practically overnight."

Craf, now breathing harder, realizes his father has picked up the pace. "Oh, is that who you meant when you were teaching us at school about the importance of reading and writing and how it would help us as individuals and groups of folks everywhere?"

Jesse glances at Craf and smiles. "Glad to hear you remember something from some of them classes, son. But then you was always the best student."

Craf and Jesse walk on in silence. The familiar path to Rich Mountain begins to lull the two men into a rhythm broken only by the occasional crossing of a stream. Craf follows behind his father as he has done since he was a boy, but finds himself suddenly stumbling and bumping into the back of his favorite teacher.

Jesse looks back at Craf briefly. He waves for Craf to walk next to him as the path widens slightly. Jesse almost whispers, "More scary for lotsa white folks, 'specially in Georgia, I hear, was that the Cherokee had their own government modeled after ourn, with different branches, and even a Supreme Court. Then gold was discovered on Cherokee land, or said to be, an' white folks decided they had to be removed." Jesse stops. He and Craf have reached the fields. The Blue Ridge Mountains suddenly rise before them like sleeping giants. Jessie almost sighs, "But I really reckin everybody just wanted the Cherokee land, their beautiful farms, mills, ferries, cattle, their gold and whatever."

"But Dad, if the politicians could not stop this and in fact set it up, why did the preachers and teachers not stop it?" Craf follows his farther to the same rock that Craf remembers sitting on years ago with Epi.

Jesse sits down and Craf joins him, but in spite of the warm sun he feels a slight chill as his father continues. "Some tried, son, and went to prison for a-sidin' with th' Cherokee. Some was missionaries that lived amongst the Cherokee and taught 'em many things, includin' matters of faith. But if'n you remember our talks about freein' the slaves a while back, not all preachers and teachers is the same, though they may carry the same book in their hands. Unfortunately many was -- an' are -- opportunists."

"What is that?"

Jesse pauses for a minute. He finds a dead branch nearby and begins to break it into small pieces. As he chucks wood, one piece at a time, toward nothing in particular he continues, "These is folks that grab any opportunity to turn thangs aroun' for somethin' to help themselves. For 'xample, some will preach or teach somethin', supposedly from th' Bible, in order to get folks to chase off somebody else in order to take a piece of land or farm or business so that they can then claim for it themselves. And worse yet, when they claim it's from the Bible, too many folks think that it must be from God."

"Like slaves?"

"Yep." Jesse chunks the last piece with such force that Craf almost backs up. "But when anybody - - not just preachers -- sells his soul for power, money or prestige, you better look out!"

Craf grabs a dead branch on the other side of the rock and quickly hands it to his father. "You just might want one more piece of wood to throw." Jesse looks at his son before they both laugh and Jesse tosses the whole branch back at his son. They take advantage of the relief and lie down on their backs.

Craf knows his father is tiring, but he just can't help asking one more question. He has just one more- -one that he knows is somehow painful for his father. "You seemed intent on my being quiet about the Cherokee thing. I have the impression there is something more than just all the slave tensions of these days, the storm cloud a-brewing all over our land."

Jesse props himself up on an elbow and faces Craf. His closeness makes Craf fiercely aware of his father's graying temples and weather worn skin. "Son, for very practical reasons we-uns try to protect our own." Jesse sees his son frown, so he continues, "You know the Guices and th' Fowlers. You may know some others nearby and down Little River, on Big Willer, and over in Cathey's Creek who are part Cherokee." Craf feels a tightness grow in his throat as he pictures Nancy Guice, a friend he and Epi often meet in the fields. Thoughts of her family add to his discomfort. As his father continues, Craf becomes all too aware that they are no longer talking in generalities. "Them folks live in fear for their lives, not just 'cause of the 'white folks is superior' talk all 'bout us these days, but also for fear that them troops or other gov'ment agents are gonna come to take them to Indian Territory. Many of them hid out and got relatives still hidin' in th' mountains further west from here."

Craf is silent. Jesse raises his body slowly off the warm rock and reaches down to offer his son a hand. As he pulls Craf up, Jesse tries to smile. "You might get a chance in your lifetime to see some changes, but in the meantime, just don't bring it up to the Blythes, or McCrarys or others who got a few Cherokee in their family."

Jesse knows it's time to check on the hogs and sheep before they head back into the woods. He heads down the field but suddenly turns with a trace of a smile on his face. "And you know your young buddy Tom Fowler?"

Craf, slightly confused by the seeming change in subject, remembers the ten-year old friend from church meetings who follows him around like a puppy, also asking questions. He thinks, however, that Tom is really sweet on his little sister Polly. Then a light goes on. He asks, "He's Cherokee?"

"A quarter. Their fear is real, based on the terror of th' past and present." Craf is surprised that he had not heard this from young Tom before but realizes why he might have not told him, since he might hope to be Polly's man someday down the road. And Epi, too, is sweet on Nancy. Craf smiles to himself, looks like one day he'll have a bunch of little Cherokee kin. He is happy for Epi and doubts he himself would be marriage material as short as he is.

Craf raises his voice to his father as he emerges from a brief break behind a bush. "Sure, I'll be careful and keep those questions to myself."

Awkwardly, Craf stretches to his full five foot three height and hugs his dad around the waist. "Thanks, Papa."

2

Summer 2012

"How was your day, Millie?" Mammaw raised her voice so I could hear her as she fried up some summer pork chops. The microwave beeped and I started to pull out the potatoes. She smiled at me. "Thanks, honey. Just add some milk and butter and start mashin' them." I grabbed the beater and started mashing and beating the potatoes. Mammaw's finger soon found the white mess and a huge glob of mashed potatoes disappeared between her lips. "Needs salt!" She grabbed the shaker and poured, whipped, tasted and smiled. "There. Perfect." She looked at me and narrowed her eyes ever so slightly. "Well, how was your day?"

"It was fun and sorta weird." I grabbed some plates and started setting the small kitchen table.

"Well, go on. Tell me what happened." Mammaw was still smiling, but I could see just a little worry behind those tired eyes. I still couldn't believe she had a paying job. Hoped it was the distraction she needed, but I wasn't so sure.

"I made a new friend and scared off an old neighbor." I smiled at myself for being able to be so precise. But the look in Mammaw's face showed me she wasn't having a precise answer. She wanted the whole story. So I told her. We ate, I talked, and she listened.

"Mammaw, you are awfully quiet!" I finally said after I had very little response.

Mammaw put her fork down and looked straight at me. "Well, Millie, I'm not sure what to say. Looks like you know what you stand for and you're not afraid to say so."

"You say that like it's a bad thing." I felt my stomach turn, just a little.

Mammaw reached across the table and gently touched my hand.

"No, honey, that's never a bad thing. But, I just think you should be careful not to judge Kevin too harshly."

"What? He's the one judging!" I felt my face get red.

"Is he?"

1850: *California becomes a state; The Fugitive Slave Law is signed, giving federal jurisdiction over runaways and punishment for any who help.*

Cherokee Secrets

"Hey, Nancy, can we join you for some vittles?" Epi McGaha calls out to the young woman already sitting on their favorite rock, as he and Craf walk across the Rich Mountain pasture.

"Si Yo . . . Sorry, I mean hello, Epi. Do set down." The seventeen year old Epi claims a piece of the rock a couple of feet away from Nancy. As the young Cherokee's eyes sparkle, she offers Epi some cornbread, but he is more interested in satisfying the growl in his stomach with his own ham biscuit. Craf sits down next to his brother and laughs to himself that she responds with a Cherokee greeting but he says nothing, not wanting to insult Nancy.

Once again, Craf and Epi make sure they have a good view of the hogs and sheep. With an occasional glance at Nancy, Epi nervously chows down on a piece of cold ham and biscuit. Craf ignores the subtle exchange and seems to have more urgent matters on his mind as he asks, "Can you tell me more about Cherokee ways with animals?" He is excited to have Nancy almost alone, with no one judge their conversation, except Epi who was used to Craf's incessant questioning.

"I told you before, Ma says I am not to tell the old ways. It will git me and her in trouble. They's lots of folks that see us as too different." Nancy's bronze hands nervously smoothe the wrinkles on her blue apron." 'Sides," she adds with much anxiety, "It was only twelve years ago they done drug th' Cherokee out west. Ma says since I am only half Cherokee, I'm to be 'white' or they might come back fer us-uns."

Epi takes a big swallow and says, "Let her be, brother, she don't need more trouble. Some folks talk right bad about Indians."

"Thanks, Epi." Nancy sends him a thankful glance before he returns to his ham biscuit.

But Craf can't wait. "Nan, I promise not to say a word to anybody, even to tell that you talked to us. But there are some things I've heard that I need your help with."

Nancy looks at her young friend. She knows that his word is good. "If you put it that way, I reckon we could 'chaw' a little bit." She has long heard about young Craf's constant worry about all animals and how they are treated. His love for dogs, she has heard, is because they protect the most helpless, like sheep and hogs.

Craf knows that Nancy is giving him a gift by answering, so he carefully chooses his questions. "Is it true that Cherokee apologize to beasts afore they kill them?"

Nancy puts her cornbread down. She seems to take in the Rich Mountain beauty, gathering strength from the rolling hills which are unable to hide the towering peaks of age-old mountains in the distance. She draws a deep breath and says, "As I understand, it ain't that simple. Ma says they gotta saing the right songs first and say the right things afore and a'ter, thankin' them for giving their life. So I reckon it is kinda like a 'pology cause it's respect for your kin."

"What? Respect for kin?" Craf interrupts. "I was meanin' animals, like deer or bear." Epi stops chewing for just a minute, wondering what Nancy means, too.

A whisper of a smile crosses the young half-Cherokee's lips, "Yep. Most Indians that ain't apple Indians yet, and still hold to old ways, feel awful close to all animals and even to plants. The old, old Cherokee stories had little difference between humans and animals. My folks would saing the right songs and thank 'em."

Craf can tell she is proud of her mother being full Cherokee, scary as it could be these days. It's Epi that frowns just a little when he asks, "What happens if'n you forget the songs or don't do it right, or don't apologize or say thank you or whatever?"

Nancy turns her fingers into ridged claws and pretends to go after Epi. "That's when you git bad joints, Epi, or arthritis or other pains as punishment." Nancy laughs.

Epi quickly rolls out of her way and, trying to whisk away a growing smile, he quickly asks, "And who are 'apple Indians?'" trying to show that he is paying attention.

Nancy folds her hands back in her lap and giggles, "Red on th' outside and white on th' inside!"

Epi smiles at her as she immediately tries to cover the red on her cheeks.

Craf, still noting that Epi is sweet on Nancy, tries to pull her attention back to his questioning by pointing northwesterly. "Nancy, didn't I hear about some feller over yonder, some giant with slanted eyes or something, also a-settin' in judgment over folks who don't treat the animals right?"

Suddenly Nancy freezes. It is as if a different young woman sits on the rock. Craf knows he has gone too far. "Hold on, Craf. I done said too much. I'm in trouble if'n Ma finds out I've been a-talking 'bout these things. And I'm really scared to talk about HIM. Ma says some white folks say he was the devil and not to talk about him, lest I'm overheard and get in trouble with th' preachers." She faces the Blue Ridge Mountains rising from the valley below. Her dress stretches tightly across her broad shoulders. Time for a new one, Craf thinks, just like the rest of us. He glances at the worn holes in both knees of his pants. He glances at Epi who is glaring at him. Epi nods towards Nancy and mouths, "Fix it!"

Craf's voice is quiet and gentle, "I really 'preciate you a-telling me what you did. I really do. I worry 'bout God's creatures and how folks abuse them. This helps me see that the Cherokee had some better, more 'Christian' respect for them than most of us white folks."

Nancy slowly turns her head to face the boys. She smiles at how small Craf is next to handsome Epi. She knows they are her friends. She looks around as if to make sure they are alone. She almost whispers, "Ma says the Creator just wants us to respect His creation and give thanks, that's all." Nancy wants her friends to see a broader picture. "But don't go a-thinking all Cherokee is the same, or all white folks. They's good and bad in ever-body and in the last years, Ma says, most of the old ways is lost. Some Indians kill just to trade hides, or get money or whiskey, just like some of the whites. No respect or 'pology or thanks." Nancy faces the mountains this time to search them out, listening for a whisper, a promise that all is not lost.

There is a long silence. Epi slowly moves to sit next to Nancy, almost touching her, but not daring to break a sacred moment. Craf scrambles after him and sits on her other side. He wraps his wiry arms around his legs pulling them tightly to his chest. "I'm sorry. Sorry for some of the ways my folks brought here." Craf hopes she can understand his passion for the many animals they have on the farm and his desire to protect them from man and beast.

Craf suddenly feels a gentle shove. Nancy leans in toward him and then over to Epi. Quickly sitting back up she gently blushes again. "Me too, but don't forget I'm half white so I feel the same. We kin give thanks for so much good that did come with some of th' bad."

Epi interrupts, his chest about to burst from the presence of this mysterious, beautiful girl next to him, "Well, um, I reckon we'd best head back a-fore all our creatures is et and thanked over by wolves and wildcats!"

All three laugh heartily as they notice that the animals are beginning to wander into the woods in search of mast, plentiful this year. "Thanks, Nancy," Craf says, as he heads towards the woods. Nancy jumps up and begins to run off to follow her hogs in a different direction. Craf does not notice the shy, smiling looks Epi and she exchange before she disappears into the forest.

Craf loves it that there are still a few Cherokee around, especially Nancy's family, the Guices. He knows that her mother is full-blooded and is so thankful that she trusted them enough to share what she had learned from her mama.

Summer 2012

Mammaw saw I wasn't recovering very well from her taking sides with Kevin. I stayed in my room sprawled across the orange and yellow quilt letting its musty smell flood my senses of happier times. She knocked on my door and when I didn't answer she came in to sit next to me. "Honey, I'm sorry if I upset you." Mammaw gently pulled my hair out of my face. "It's just that there are so many things you will never understand about Kevin and the whole Carp family for that matter."

I raised my body up to sit next to her. "I wasn't meaning to judge him. He just made me so angry!"

"I know, honey, but let's not let his words ruin your summer. Okay?" Mammaw smiled and I couldn't help but feel like a child again, where anything Mammaw said meant everything would be okay. I couldn't help but return her smile and nod.

Mammaw looked out my window and whispered with a girlish grin, "There's still a few hours of daylight. How about a trip into town?" Mammaw's reintroduction of Brevard consisted of taking me for a walk down Main Street. It was fun to see "busy" according to Mammaw. All I could think was that she doesn't know what busy really looks like. Hanging out at the mall a block away from the two bedroom house I grew up in was busy. Trying not to get hit by the speed-of-light shoppers in the parking lot was busy. Brevard was not busy.

As we walked down Main Street I asked Mammaw about the "Do not sit on sculptures" sign in front of the red brick courthouse. Beautiful iron sculptures of an elk and a red wolf stood sentry in front of the courthouse along with several other woodland animals scattered throughout downtown Brevard. A smile rose up from somewhere deep. She just looked at me. "Millie, I guess the folks here are just tryin' to bring some of the spirits back. Help us remember who once roamed this land."

"No way, Mammaw!" I gently shoved her and she almost bumped against the stone wall in front of the courthouse. "That's just weird."

Mammaw just smiled. "Is it?"

1854: Smith and Wesson invent the revolver; Passage of the Kansas-Nebraska Act, which allows the new Territories to decide the slavery issue brings about much violence; The Republican Party is formed in Wisconsin on the basis of their opposition to slavery; The Know-Nothing Party has its convention and opposes immigration as well as denying voting rights and officeholding for anyone who comes from a family that has lived in the U.S. less than fifty years.

The Little Giant

Craf McGaha is making a name for himself as a hardworking, farmer, carrying on the family tradition but also with a natural skill for business. He makes trips to Greenville each week, hauling meat and produce to eager restaurants and schools. His own desire to learn pushes him to also trade for books and eventually surveying instruments. It is only natural that he learns that needed skill. When the community asks Craf, the eternal student, to become the local school teacher he willingly accepts, feeling proud he can follow in his father's footsteps. With only three months of school, he can keep his other tasks going, especially working on his house and expanding his growing surveying business.

The rough grains on the plank still need to be sanded down, yet Craf is proud of the tough skin on his hands, earned from working on his own first house. He grabs another plank and begins to hammer a nail with determination. He laughs to himself as he thinks of how he has had to prove himself over the years. Although he is older and more mature, he is hardly taller. Yet, he knows his passion to be fair to all and to be merciful to man and beast alike increases his stature in the minds of people who otherwise might not take him seriously due to his small size.

Craf has ample opportunity to get news from all over, with the Alison lodge receiving guests in Cedar Mountain, as well as the Hume Hotel in Dunn's Rock down the mountain below Connestee Falls, and talk of a hotel just across the Little River in Loftis. The news disturbs him deeply for it sounds as if war is imminent. Even his many friends and relatives are torn apart with opposing opinions. And some of the traveling preachers are not always helpful, although some preachers are calling for peace and working together.

Also, some open air meetings, Craf tells himself, are worth the get-together with neighbors and travelers. He is eager to hear more news. Taking a break from his labors, he looks forward to worship. The brush arbor meetings in the fall provide such opportunity when the crops are gathered and the many drovers are returning from South Carolina, having sold their stock and purchased household goods. The wagons come up from Jones Gap, drawn by horses, mules or oxen and head across East Fork. One simple sign at Jones Gap lets the travelers know when such a meeting is being held for week or two week at the popular Preacher's Knob on the well-used Lyon Mountain Road over into Cherryfield. Locally, word is passed around in churches and post offices.

"Amazing grace how sweet the sound," Craf clears his throat as he begins to lift his voice again. He looks around at friends and strangers worshipping together. He glances over at the animals that pull the wagons, tired from pulling the wagons up the mountain from Greenville. He knows that meeting at Preacher's Knob on the Lyon Mountain Road near East Fork will allow the families from across the ridge in Jackson and Haywood counties to still make it on back home in a day or so.

As they finish singing, most who are gathered sit down to listen to current preacher, the traveling Methodist circuit rider, one of many Craf has shown hospitality to in his home. He is pleased with the turnout. He is never quite sure how many drovers will stay as they pass through. For the most part, these folks are common farmers, hardworking folks wanting to head home with the fruits of their family labors for the year: coffee, cloth, tools and the like. Craf can relate to them. But he believes the cool autumn day and good music make it welcoming for some good preaching and music. Of course, Craf almost laughs out loud as he watches the families socialize quietly with an occasional glassy-eyed nod in the preacher's direction as if they are really listening to him.

After an hour, Craf stands up and decides to stretch his legs. He walks over and leans against the brush arbor he helped construct the day before. He is pleased that the quickly constructed shed, where brush makes do as the roof, doesn't give against his weight. The preacher smiles at Craf as he continues to preach from underneath the arbor. Craf lets his eyes wander once again out into the crowd. He notices several young men are not looking at the preacher. Their heads are all turned. Craf follows their gaze and finds himself looking into the eyes of a beautiful young woman. He quickly looks away and shakes off the encounter as an accident. He thinks she must actually be looking at the preacher since he is standing right next to him.

Craf forces himself not to look again, but wishes the preacher would hurry up and come to a stopping point. However, Craf is all too aware that it is not always clear in such meetings when there is a break, except at meal times. Folks come and go, check out the outhouse or their wagon or stop a dog fight, most often when the preacher is on a sensitive subject.

Craf finally decides to take a break himself. He is sweating in spite of the cool breeze. Craf heads down to the spring for a drink. He kneels and dips his hands into the fresh clean mountain water. He lets his hands touch the rich soil under the water. Suddenly he hears a heavenly voice. "You are Craf McGaha, right?"

He first looks up to the sky and then toward the top of Preachers Knob as his heart jumps. Is it a word from the Lord or an angel sent down by the Lord? He wonders if he's been to one too many a preaching. Then he turns around to see her, the woman whose eyes had captured his only minutes earlier. Craf stumbles backwards, sitting down hard on the bank. Not wanting to let her know that the dampness seeping through the seat of his pants makes him feel like jumping up, he tries to pretend that he meant to sit down.

"Yuh, yes, I reckon I am." Craf is suddenly very aware of the dirt on his hands. He tries to wipe them on his pants, only leaving a worse mess on his clothes.

A tall, beautiful woman stands there smiling. "Reckon you are? You not sure?" She slowly passes by the now very red-faced Craf. She carefully lifts her skirt ever so slightly so she can kneel by the spring. Craf tries not to look as her ankles peek out at him. Something stirs inside him and he can't help but keep staring at this young woman who is now drinking from the same spring.

Craf clears his throat. "Of course I am. And who might you be?" He jumps up so he is finally looking down on her.

After what feels like a lifetime, the young beauty reaches out her hand as if asking to be pulled back up to her feet. She smiles as Craf awkwardly pulls up a woman a good head taller than himself. "I'm Harriet Shipman and I have heard a lot about you."

Craf quickly lets go of Harriet's hand, looking around to make sure no one is watching. "You have? What have you heard?"

Harriet drops her hands to her waist and carefully straightens the folds in her skirt. "That you are very smart and ask questions to learn all you can. That you like to help folks and beasts just from the goodness of your heart. And lots more."

Turning crimson Craf responds, "I don't know what to say."

Harriet quickly puts him at ease. "You needn't say a thing. Just come sit with me and my family at our wagon for lunch." She starts back to the gathering.

Craf is still flabbergasted and blurts out, "But what about all those boys and men a- staring at you?"

Harriet stops and looks back at the little man. She smiles, obviously holding back a laugh. "Well, it ought to cool them down just to see you with us."

Craf does not remember much about her parents or the meeting or meal or the rest of the sermons or music. He is absolutely smitten and overwhelmed that any woman would pay attention to him - and such an exceptional one at that!

For many days after the encounter, the work that Craf does is driven by something new in his heart and body. Jesse and Candice watch with humor and great interest as their little son bumbles about like a man in love.

Having met Harriet's family at the brush arbor meeting puts Craf more at ease when he comes a-calling at the Shipman house on a Sunday afternoon.

Harriet's father comes out first to see who is coming. "Why it's young Crawford McGaha. Come up on the porch and set a spell young man."

"Don't mind if I do, Mr. Shipman." Craf settles into one of the two rocking chairs with Mr. Shipman in the other.

He can hear giggles from unknown children inside. The men sit and talk about raising and selling cattle, hogs and sheep, cutting timber, the weather, about guns and ammunition and about changing times. All the while, Craf tries to catch a glance or two beyond the door which is cracked slightly.

After about an hour, which seems an eternity to Craf, Mr. Shipman calls out, "Harriet, how about coming out here and talkin' with this feller? I don't thank he come out here to chaw the fat with the likes of me!"

A red-faced Harriet immediately steps out the door, having been just inside awaiting her cue.

Her father looks at the two and Craf is suddenly tongue-tied. Mr. Shipman says laughingly, "Here take my chair, Harriet, and talk with this shy young feller. I done checked him out and he's a good-un." Harriet shoots her father a hard look as he disappears into the house, closing the door behind him.

Finally, alone on the porch, they can talk freely about the smallest and yet biggest things.

It was when Craf asked her one seemingly insignificant question that Harriet knew where he might be headed. "I'm going to Greenville tomorrow with some hogs and need to pick up a new flat iron. The handle is so busted on one of mine I can't fix it any more. It was a hand-me-down." Craf looks at Harriet and raises his eyebrows ever so slightly almost as if trying to cue the young woman.

With a lump in her throat, she queries, "What are you askin'?" Craf notices Harriet try to hide a smile.

Craf shifts nervously, rocking a little harder than he should. "Well, I saw an ad in the Greenville paper for an iron where you put hot coals inside, instead of just heating on the stove top."

Practical, men stuff, she thinks, but he is headed in a serious direction. "Do whatever you think is best, Craf. It sounds very interesting and practical to me."

Craf gives a sigh of relief as if a most important question was already answered, yet she thinks he wants to say more. "Was there something else, J.C. McGaha?"

Craf gives her a funny look. Only his mother had ever called him J.C. He swallows hard.

"Well, er, uh, yeah. Will you go out to Pretty Place with me next Sunday afternoon, weather fittin'?" Craf knows that asking to take her to the breathtaking view of South Carolina from the mountaintop is asking for more than just an outing. He hopes Harriet knows it too.

"I'd love to," Harriet answers almost before he is finished. Craf slows his rapid rocking to a gentle pace and smiles.

"Do I need to ask your folks?" Craf looks anxiously at the closed front door, any moment expecting her pa to jump out and forbid Craf from courting his daughter.

"I'm a grown woman and it ain't needed." She smiles back and the talk returns to the weather, but Craf can hardly wait until Sunday.

Although Craf does not want to leave, he knows he should not outstay his welcome. As he leaves he feels so light-hearted he practically leaps upon his horse. He turns to find Harriet smiling at him. He returns her smile. "See you next Sunday, then." A small frown crosses his brow as he continues, "I'll bring a wagon, if that's all right with you. I don't have access to a buggy right now."

Harriet, who has walked out next to his horse with him, gently strokes its mane. "I'd be honored to ride in your wagon with YOU, whatever you've been hauling in it!" She laughs and he is thrilled as he rides off giggling like a little kid.

The following Sunday Craf arrives with his wagon, all washed and cleaned. His mother had accused him of scouring it with lye soap so it'd not smell like hog manure.

Harriet's parents stand on their porch, smiling as the two ride away on the bumpy wagon. "Make sure you get back afore it gets dark!" one of them cries out as they round the curve, but Harriet doesn't turn her head to see Craf's flaming red ears.

The trip to Pretty Place is as beautiful as the weather that day, but the glow of both young folks is prettier yet. Small talk is made with long periods of silence. Harriet notes that Craf seems to be focusing on driving and yet she knows he is preoccupied.

When they arrive they are both overwhelmed by the sudden bird's eye view of South Carolina. They can see the mountains taper off into hills which roll into the distance infinitely, making them fiercely aware they are on the edge of the Blue Ridge Mountains. They stand in awe even though both have visited there several times before with their respective families, sometimes for Easter sunrise services.

She speaks first. "Craf, this is the purtiest place on earth, I reckon. Edge of South Carolina, ain't it?"

He seems relieved in the practical question which he can answer. "Yep. We're looking east as you know, right into the prettiest part of South Carolina, the so-called 'Dark Corner' but you'd never know anything about the troubles down there from up here. It looks like heaven from where we're standing." Craf suddenly looks at Harriet and, with a subtle smile, decides to make a transition as if it were natural, "Speaking of heaven, Harriet, will you marry me?"

Harriet returns Craf's look and raises her eyebrows. "Are you kiddin?" She leans into him as close as she can get and whispers, "You better not be!"

Craf can almost taste her breath. He reaches out to pull her the rest of the way into his arms. He whispers back, this time his lips almost touching her neck. "Never in a thousand years would I joke about that."

Harriet lets her body melt at the feel of his breath. She smiles. "Of course I will. I'd love to marry you and make our life together."

For the time being, nothing more is said. The beauty of the moment and the discovery of touch are matched by the surrounding scenery. If there are bumps in the rough road on the way home, they are not noticed at all.

Summer 2012

I shuffled into the kitchen and ate some cold cereal. Mammaw was gone already. She had come in and kissed me goodbye, but I couldn't be bothered to get up and eat with her. I loved Mammaw more than anything, but right then I was enjoying sleeping in.

The window was open and I could hear the water from the dam. My body wanted to take a swim, but my mind was not ready to face Kevin. So I threw on my shorts, a spaghetti strap top and flip-flops and rambled down to see if Ellie was around. She told me her mom and dad owned the Mexican restaurant across from Sherwood Forest, so I thought I'd just head that way.

This time I walked across the small bridge over Little River. The water was pretty low and I knew that all of Transylvania County was wishing for some rain. My memories of summer were always flooded with afternoon rains everyday when we would swim anyway, in spite of thunder rumbles in the distance. But today the sky was blue and I was already getting hot. I walked along the Greenville Highway for a few hundred feet before I stood in front of El Capitán. The OPEN sign was dark. I suddenly thought I was the stupidest person around. It was only ten o'clock in the morning. Of course it was closed.

I was thirsty so I checked my short's pocket for any change and found two crumpled dollar bills that looked like they'd been washed a few times with the shorts. I walked over to the gas station that was next to the restaurant. A blue Dodge Ram truck, with several bags of kitty litter and a pail with a sponge mop sticking out the back, was parked in front of the diesel pump, but no one was around. I figured the owner was inside. I pushed open the glass door which was hard to open. There was some sort of rubber attached to the bottom that looked like it needed to be replaced. The cold, frigid air conditioning just about took my breath away, but it was a relief from the growing heat outside. I headed to the refrigerators at the back of the store. I almost knocked down a couple of bags of chips as they stuck out into the narrow aisles. As I picked out the biggest Gatorade I could get with my minimal cash I heard something I hadn't heard since third grade. "Hey, look it's your girrrrl friend!"

You can imagine how absolutely shocked I was to find two tall guys, probably between eighteen and twenty years old looking straight at me, each holding a bottle of charcoal lighter fluid. They looked a little familiar. Then it hit me they looked like Kevin, except one had red hair and the other looked like he'd had his nose broken one too many times. I quickly looked the other direction and tried to go down the only other aisle. Well, that was a BIG mistake. Kevin was standing in the aisle, looking like he was hiding from either me or the two others. He looked at me and quickly looked away; his cheeks matched his red ears.

I frowned slightly and tried to walk around him. But, no, his dumb brothers came running up behind me. "Well, ain't you gonna say hi?" Broken Nose shoved Kevin.

Kevin held up his head and with a toughness that scared me just a little, he looked straight at me. "Hi, Millie, what're you doin'?"

"What's it look like I'm doing?" I held up my Gatorade and marched right past him. I paid the lady at the register. She brushed a long strand of red hair out of her face and gave me a very quick are-you-okay glance. She put her hand briefly on a cordless phone clipped on her belt telling me help was one send-button away. By the look of her tattoo sleeve I figured she'd have no problem jumping to my rescue on her own. The thought made me smile and I just grinned at her and mouthed, "I'm okay." As I crammed the change in my pocket I shoved the door open like I was a linebacker.

I started to walk back in the direction I had come earlier when I heard Kevin again. "Wait, Millie! Wait up!" I looked around as he came running at me. I turned and kept walking. Finally, he caught up with me. "Hey, what's the hurry?"

I just couldn't figure him out. Kevin was nice one minute and then something scary the next. Right now he seemed almost desperate. "I just want to get home," I finally said, maybe a little kinder than I intended. I took a big swallow of the cool Gatorade, pretending I was a little more relaxed than I really was.

"Well, maybe I could walk you?" His eyes pleaded. He glanced over his shoulder and then back at me. "Please?" That's when I heard the Ram. Its heavy diesel engine revved loudly and in a moment it pulled up beside us. I took another sip.

"Well, comin' with us?" Redhead called.

Kevin looked at me. I guess it was just something I couldn't explain. Maybe it was what Mammaw said the night before, but somehow I just couldn't stop myself. "Looks like Kevin's gonna walk me home."

Kevin's eyes thanked me. "Suit yourself!" Broken Nose yelled as they left us in the dust.

1854: Lawyer and politician Abraham Lincoln calls for the emancipation of slaves; Recluse Henry David Thoreau publishes Walden *and is also jailed for failing to pay taxes that support the Mexican War; "Babe" Cooper builds his federally approved distillery in Dunn's Rock Community, a few yards north of the Hume Hotel.*

Sex Education

The smell of hay and sour milk soothe Craf as he walks up to his father a few weeks after his proposal to Harriet. Craf settles in near his father as they milk the cows. Jesse looks at Craf and sees his son struggle for words. Jesse says nothing for he knows Craf will figure it out; he's never been one for holding back. Soon Craf poses a strange, yet obvious, question to his father, "Papa, you 'member when we went to Greenville to that feller to see if we could afford one of the mules he produces?"

Jesse stops for one second and glances towards his son. He answers, fearing where this is going. "Shore. What 'bout it?"

"Well, I was wondering how that worked out?" Craf tries to lighten his voice to make the question seem matter-of-fact.

"What worked out?" the sweating Jesse asks, stripping the last milk from the cow he is milking, wishing there were at least two more gallons so he could focus on the streaming milk and not this long-feared question.

An equally sweating Craf clarifies, "You know. How a jack can do it with a mare."

Jesse hears a cough outside the barn and remembers that his wife, Candice, was to go to the hen house to get the eggs. She must have heard part of the talk. Jesse suddenly smiles to himself.

It doesn't take long for Jesse to clear things up for Craf and with the milking and talking done, Jesse tactfully sends Craf on an errand for firewood and carries both buckets of milk. He notices that Candice is still in the hen house so he peeks in to see what is taking her so long

Candice is livid! Never has he seen her so angry. "I just can't believe it, Jesse McGaha! How in heavens' name could you be so stupid?"

"Now hold it, honey. Try to calm down, please." Jesse places the milk pails on the ground and reaches to calm his wife.

Candice just turns her back to him. "How can I? Our little boy, now a grown man with such a small size to get over, a-thinkin' of marriage to a wonderful young lady and YOU try to escape a man-to-man talk 'bout sex by talkin' 'bout little donkeys and big horses breedin' to make mules! ARGH!!" She grabs the eggs from the hay and places them so forcefully in the basket that Jesse is surprised they don't break. Suddenly she stops and turns to face Jesse to continue her angry roll, "Well, I know who th' jackass is in this marriage! Am I just the mare?"

Jesse is silent. He tries not to laugh at his livid wife who has stirred up so much hay that pieces of straw are stuck in her hair creating horns to match her temper. Slowly he asks, "Did you hear our talk from start to finish?"

Candice drops her eyes pretending to look at the back of her hand. Embarrassed as much by her anger as by her confessed answer, she says, "No."

"Well," Jesse calmly continues, "He asked me 'bout donkeys- - or jackasses-- an' horses from our trip to Greenville when we was a-thinkin' about a-gittin' a mule from the breeder."

"Oh. Well, how did you answer?" Candice sits down on the only crate against the hen house wall.

"I answered his question and said basically, 'Son, it just comes naturally an' size don't matter. Nature takes care of that, just like with all them animals you've seen a-breeding'." Jesse starts to walk around in front of his wife like a rooster as he retells his proud moment with his son. "Then I went on to say, 'It's the same for people. God created human bein's in such a way that it just comes naturally when two people love each other.'"

A repentant, hesitant Candice asks, "And what did Craf say?"

Jesse reaches out his hand and pulls Candice to her feet. "He smiled and said, 'Thanks, Papa. That's a big help.'"

Candice lets Jesse pull her into his arms. "I'm sorry Jesse. I shoulda figgered you'd rise to the occasion and do what's best for our son."

Jesse gently pulls the hay out of his wife's hair. "That's fine, my love. I know your mother love wants the best for him. You're like a mama bear protectin' her young!"

Candice looks at her husband and smiles. "Right now I feel more like the jenny, a- brayin'!"

The two lovebirds, Craf and Harriet, work hard through the summer and into the fall on what is to be their home, motivated by a deep love and hope for the future. Craf is thrilled that she has the strength and energy to help him and his occasional work team.

By the time the house is finished the corn needs picking and the apples need to be harvested. Animals need to go to market in Greenville. There is no time for a wedding and Harriet is getting tired of the ride each evening back to her parents' place.

Finally, on December twenty-first, Craf McGaha and Harriet Shipman are married with much joy and celebration. Folks are in a Christmas spirit and most can gather inside the new house by the fire to escape the cold winter day outside. They marvel at the amount of work the couple has done and how Harriet's feminine touch has smoothed out Craf's rough handwork.

With the brief but cold holidays behind them, the young couple enjoys their own nest. The wedding, now a memory, still makes Craf smile as he pulls Harriet closer to him under the quilt his momma gave him only three weeks ago. The cold January nights have been a welcome excuse to spend more time under the covers. Craf gently takes his wife's hand in his and is comforted to feel her draw in closer. He laughs for a moment which causes her to prop herself up on one elbow. "What you a-laughin' at, Mr. McGaha?"

Craf props himself up as a mirror image, "Well, Mrs. McGaha, I was just thinking that I can't believe you married me, considering . . ."

"Considering what?" A playful smile crosses Harriet's lips.

"Considering we didn't do much courtin'. Mostly going to church and then there is the matter of your helping me finish this house." Harriet sees Craf's playfulness is gone. She knows he feels guilty for all the months they spent doing hard physical work.

"Well, Craf," she responds warmly, "I reckon we were a-doin' the best kinda courtin' the way I see it. Like birds, we built our nest, twig by twig. And now we're lying in it." Harriet drops back down to snuggle under the covers and draw up close to her man. "Besides, when th' hammer hit your finger instead of the nail, I saw a side of you I'd not see out a-ridin' to Pretty Place."

Harriet feels Craf's warm breath and feels him kiss her gently. "You know that circuit riding preacher talked Sunday about not being "unequally yoked" referring to not trying to put a mule and donkey or big ox with a small calf into a double yoke. I was just thinking about my being so small and you being so tall. What a team we are!"

Harriet laughs with him and returns his kiss. Craf is pleased she is not so sensitive about his size. He feels his wife draw him in to her as she whispers, "You know, my little man, when I first heard stories about you, I thought you must be ten feet tall. Now that we are together in this wonderful yoke I know you are even taller! You are my little giant!"

Summer 2012

"What was that all about?" I asked Kevin, after his brothers' truck roared away from the gas station next to El Capitan and disappeared down the Greenville Highway toward Brevard.

Kevin didn't answer at first and I wondered if he was going to answer at all. Then I saw him kick a stone out into the street. "Nothin' really. It's just my idiot brothers. They think they are all that and I just didn't want to go with them." Kevin glanced at me for a second and I knew he had told me one big fat lie. But his look also said, don't ask me, please. I thought, "What do I care? As long as Kevin isn't a wacko, then I'll not get into his business."

"Okay." I just pretended that what he said made sense.

We started walking back toward Sherwood Forest when Kevin suddenly smiled and yelled at me. "Hey, Millie, I know a fun short cut! Come on!" He darted across the road and headed across the Sherwood Forrest Golf Course. I knew Mammaw told me I was not to walk over the course, but I didn't have anything better to do so I looked around first to make sure no one was playing golf at the moment. I found myself running after the tall blond boy like we had been best friends for years. I kept hearing Mammaw's voice telling me not to judge Kevin. I guess that made me somehow trust him.

It didn't take long before we were on the bank of the Little River. I smiled remembering my encounter with Ellie yesterday and found myself looking back over my shoulder to see if she was anywhere around.

"See here!" Kevin was reaching into the same big bush where I hadn't seen Ellie the day before. He pulled out a plank that looked like it had been intentionally place there. He placed it across the Little River and for the first time I saw Kevin look almost proud. "Come on. Let's cross." He went across first and I was thinking we probably could have just jumped from one side to the other, but heck, what's the fun in that. So I followed him across.

He grabbed the plank and hurled it through the air. Doggone if that sucker didn't just land smack in the middle of the same bush. "Wow! You've done that before!" I smiled.

Kevin turned slightly pink and his smile faded, "Not really!" Big fat lie number two. I couldn't figure why he kept doing that.

"Oh, well!" I punched him ever so lightly on the shoulder. "I guess you are just great at thinking on your feet." I handed him my almost empty Gatorade.

Kevin's smile returned as he grabbed the drink and gulped down the rest in one big swallow, "Yeah, I guess you're right."

We walked up the road in silence with nothing really to say. Somehow, I wasn't freaked out by Kevin anymore. I think I felt more sorry for him than anything. It didn't take long before we were at Mammaw's. "So, Kevin, you got your swimming shorts on?"

"What?" Kevin looked at me like I was a pervert, but then I saw the light go on. "Yeah, I do."

"Great! I'll go change quickly and we can swim. That is if you want to!" I looked at him and smiled.

"Yeah! I want to." Kevin smiled back.

"Good." I turned and headed into the house while Kevin headed toward Trout Lake. Suddenly I yelled back out the door, "Kevin, do you want a Dew or a Dr. Pepper?"

Kevin smiled. I could actually see his teeth. "I'll have a Dew."

1855: Kansas has two governments, pro- and anti-slavery; Henry Wadsworth Longfellow publishes "The Song of Hiawatha"; Berea College for Appalachian Mountain youth is founded in Kentucky, the first in the South to be coeducational and racially integrated.

The First Baby

"Harriet, do you reckon he will make it?" Craf worries deeply and feels helpless. Their first baby, Little Mitchel, has blessed their home late in 1855, but has not seemed healthy from the start. The two new parents gently move back and forth in their rocking chairs in front of the fire as Craf is holds the baby in his arms.

Craf looks at his first son and realizes that his accomplishments mean little compared to the desire for his son to live. He knows he makes a difference in his community. As a teacher, he acts on his convictions about the urgency of learning for all the mountain folks. As a surveyor, he helps lessen tensions between neighbors by helping sort out confusions about boundaries. And since school is only three months of the year he, like his students, can keep the farms, the grinding mills and other businesses going. But all of this fades in importance as he looks at their young son and worriedly looks into the eyes of his young wife.

Harriet reaches out and gently touches the hand of her little giant. "It's in the Lord's hands, Craf. He is a gift and we'll do the best we can." In a voice mustering up as much positive energy as possible she gives Craf hope. "See if Nancy Guice can give us some of her mother's medicine. She knows some Cherokee healing ideas. Just don't tell anybody."

Craf smiles as he responds. "My love, Nancy and Epi have been married three years now and have a young-un. Better to call her Nancy McGaha. She's real family- - always has been since we all grew up together." He touches Mitch's weak body and continues, "But asking Nancy for help is not a bad idea."

Harriet is surprised that she has forgotten to use the correct surname. She senses a little jealousy in her own mind of Nancy's striking beauty and the bond Epi, Nancy and Craf have had since childhood, but she says nothing. Her real worry is their son.

Craf suddenly stops rocking and looks into the eyes of his wife. He leans in as close as possible and confesses, "I've been a-wondering 'bout somethin' else."

"What is it?" Harriet frowns slightly.

Craf speaks so quietly Harriet has to bend closer to him to hear. "You reckon this has anything to do with my bein' so little? Ought we not have more children?"

Harriet takes Craf's free hand in hers as she resumes her rocking. She smiles gently. "Now Craf, hold back with your worry and guilt. These things happen and you know how many young-uns just don't make it in this life. Just because little Mitch seems small does not mean anything. We can only pray that God will give him long life and mostly give us many more to play with him! You have work to do as a good father and in making more babies!"

Once again a red-faced Craf realizes what a wonderful wife he has and what a unique mother she is. He utters something that shocks even himself, "And how soon?"

3

Summer 2012

"So did you have a better day, Millie?" Mammaw looked at me from her overstuffed couch and then quickly glanced away, pretending to be busy with watching TV, although the sound was on mute.

I plopped down beside her. I threw my arms around her, or at least as far as they would go. "I am so sorry, Mammaw. I was such a butt about Kevin."

"Millie!" Mammaw pretended to be upset by my choice of words, but I could see her smile grow. And then she nodded, more for herself than me. "I guess you were . . . a butt." Then I heard Mammaw giggle like a little girl. That's when we both started laughing until I just about peed in my pants. It felt good to see Mammaw smile and just have fun.

Once we stopped laughing I stretched out next to her on the excessive variety of yellow, red and orange flowers of the pattern that covered the couch. I put my head in her lap and she gently stroked my hair as I told her the events of the day. "So, you were right, Mammaw. Kevin isn't so bad. It's his brothers that freak me out."

Mammaw sat silently for a moment still stroking my hair. At one point it felt like she was making little braids and then undoing them. Finally she said, "The Carp brothers are well known around here." I just listened. Today I was going to let her explain instead of jumping to conclusions. She finally continued, "The two older brothers Junior and Roy have always been on the rough side. They're nothin' like their momma. Tempy and I have known each other since she and your daddy where kids." Mammaw's eyes had a twinkle in them. "When they were in school Russell Carp was the most handsome boy the girls had ever seen. He was rough and wild, but that just made him more attractive, much to your father's dismay. Your daddy had a little crush on Tempy, but she only had eyes for Russell."

I smiled listening to Mammaw talk about Daddy. "What happened, Mammaw?"

"Well, Russell had his eye on Tempy too, and it didn't take long before Russ Junior was on the way and Tempy dropped out of school." Mammaw suddenly sounded more matter of fact.

"That sounds so cliché." I snickered a little. "I guess he married her at the end of a shotgun?"

Mammaw stopped stroking my hair. "This is not funny, Millie." I was silent again. Obviously I couldn't keep my opinions to myself when I needed to. "Tempy and Russell did get married, but not until Roy was on the way a year later. They just decided to move into Tempy's parents' place and she worked odd jobs while he worked construction."

I decided to ask a question. "So then they moved to Sherwood Forest?"

"No, they still live in the same home, just over the knoll on the other side of the lake. They are just outside the community boundary." Mammaw was finished. She gently shoved me to the side and got up to go to the kitchen.

I was totally confused. "But I thought they lived in Sherwood Forest because the boys have been swimming at the lake since I can remember."

Mammaw looked back at me with a gentle smile. "Tempy cleans house for some of the homeowners, and has for years. Her children have been welcomed by the community to swim. But now..." Mammaw suddenly caught herself.

"But now what?" I jumped off the couch and followed Mammaw into the kitchen.

Suddenly Mammaw looked old again. "Nothin', honey. Just times change and well, you know, the boys are wilder than ever." Mammaw saw the confusion in my eyes. "Not Kevin. He has his mother's good nature, partly because he was born seven years after the other two and stayed her baby for so long. But Russell has raised the two older boys with the same wild streak he had."

"Well, it can't be that bad. You told me yourself not to judge." I smiled.

Mammaw looked at me, holding a frying pan very still. "Listen to me, Mille! I want you to be friends with Kevin. Heaven knows he needs a good friend. But stay away from Junior and Roy. Do you understand?"

Mammaw's look scared me. I whispered, "Yes Ma'am."

1855: Prohibition movement gains in New York State stopping the sale, but not drinking, of alcohol; Brigham Young proclaims that a single drop of Negro blood renders a man unfit to enter the Mormon priesthood; On election day in Louisville, Kentucky, members of the "Nativists" or "Know-Nothing Party" riot, burn buildings and kill Irish and German immigrants.

The Visit

The Little River soothes Craf's aching feet as he wades up and down this small river that has at times wreaked havoc during heavy rains, flooding the open spread of land used today for an open air church meeting. He observes Harriet sitting on a quilt making cooing sounds at Little Mitch whose legs and arms flail as he reaches up to his Momma. Craf is thankful that his son seems to be healthier. Craf misses spending time with his own father, Jesse, and the long talks they used to have as he was growing up, so when he heard of today's gathering he took the opportunity to see his father.

Jesse sits on the bank of the river enjoying the sight of his grown son splashing though the cold mountain water like a child. He knows Craf has a need to talk. "Another one of your hard questions, my boy?" Jesse asks.

Craf looks at his father and smiles. He is pleased that his father can still read him even after so much time away. "Not really, Papa. It has more to do with what you learned from your Papa."

Jesse picks up a stone and tosses it at the opposite bank. "'Bout what?"

Craf wades down to his father and sits next to him, still letting his feet dangle in the water. "About religion. I mean about Bishop Asbury who came through these parts in his time."

Jesse frowns slightly, finding the question a little odd. "I' m not sure I know a lot. The Loftises across the Little River know a lot more."

Craf joins his father in tossing stones. "Not really him but what he did and what he set up." Craf suddenly waves towards all the people gathered in the clearing, socializing and saying their goodbyes after listening to a traveling preacher deliver his message from an old tree stump. "Why do we not have some place to meet so we can have more regular preaching and mostly teaching? People are so torn asunder by all the slavery and war talk and we do welcome so many itinerant preachers from everywhere and from every church into your home and mine. It just seems about time for a church of our own."

Jesse stops throwing rocks and looks at his son. "Well, you may not know 'bout it, but some of our neighbors did set aside land for a Methodist church back in 1848." Jesse points to a small hill that slopes gently ahead of them. "See that small knoll? That's where we hoped to build a church, but the tensions you mentioned seemed to block it and then I heard too that some other tensions within Methodist leaders arose 'bout that time, or maybe a little afore then."

Craf stares at the piece of land and frowns. He can't figure out what would could possibly stop them from building a church. He guesses, "About whether Methodists were still answering to the Church of England and King?"

Jesse laughs a little and stands up to stretch. "Oh no, that was took care of with the Revolution. Methodists is clearly American and, in fact, the largest Protestant church in the country." Jesse's face becomes serious again as he looks at his son, revealing an old familiar pain. "The problem was, briefly put, over whether Bishops could hold slaves."

"Oh! No!" Craf stands and forcefully throws the rest of his stones in the water. "Like the Baptists!"

Jesse gently places his hand on his son's shoulder. "Son, the storm of our days affects all of us. And I reckon your idea is right. Findin' a spiritual solution is far better than takin' up arms which is what's a-being called for all over. The camp meeting' and arbor revivals is great, but they seem to be a-draggin' an' some is bein' misused to push an agenda."

Craf almost whispers, "Like slavery."

"Unfortunately. Don't lose your ideals or your great idea, my boy." Jesse heads toward Candice who is waving at him to join to help her with packing up.

"Thanks, Papa." Craf sighs as he watches his aging father wade back across the Little River and head towards the dwindling crowd.

Summer 2012

"Is Ellie here?" It was eleven o'clock a.m. and I was determined to find Ellie today. Maybe spending some time with her would keep me away from the Carp family. I couldn't get Mammaw's talk about them out of my head.

"Si!" A round faced woman gave me a friendly smile and a wave of her hand which told me to check out a back room.

"Ellie?" I peeked my head into what was obviously the overflow room, but was now being used to entertain and keep all of the children as occupied as possible. The TV was blasting and several bottles of soda and bags of tortilla chips covered the tables. Ellie's face lit up as she saw me. She jumped up from one of four soft arm chairs and said something to one of the younger kids who immediately pounced for the desired seat.

"Hi, Millie!" Ellie walked up to me. "What are you doing?"

"I didn't mean to disturb the excitement," I smiled, "but wondered if you could hang out with me today. Maybe you want to go swimming in the lake?"

For just a minute I saw a strange look I could not recognize. But it disappeared almost as fast as it appeared. "I'd love to do something with you. But maybe we could hang around here and hike some of the trails out back." Ellie looked at me with pleading eyes. "Mom and Dad don't let me hike them unless I have someone with me. What do you think?"

"Why not? That's something new." The air felt hot and heavy today and I really wanted to swim to cool off, but I was trying to get to know Ellie better. What could it hurt anyway?

"Great. Let me see if Mom will let us take some water and some food." Ellie disappeared from the room and I was stuck watching Sesame Street in Spanish. The younger kids didn't even seem to notice I was there. I finally walked out of the room toward where I thought Ellie might be talking to her mom. That's when I heard a lot of Spanish in very loud voices pouring from the kitchen door. Finally Ellie pounded through the door with a plastic bag of some food and water. She had an irritated look on her face, but when she saw me she quickly put on a smile.

"Let's go!" Ellie then yelled something to the kids and they all responded back without letting their eyes leave Elmo and Big Bird.

"What was that all about?" I asked Ellie as we headed toward a path that started behind her family's El Capitán restaurant.

"Nothing really." Slight irritation rose in her voice. "Mom and Dad don't really like me taking off much. They worry about me. That's all!" Ellie looked at me with the same look Kevin gave me earlier. She was begging for me to drop it. So I did.

1856: James Buchanan wins the U.S. Presidency on a fourth try, defeating the first Republican candidate, John C. Fremont; Increasing violence occurs between pro- and anti- slavery factions; U.S. Senator Charles Sumner, an outspoken abolitionist, is severely physically beaten in the Senate by U.S. Representative Preston Brooks of South Carolina.

The Road and Refuge

The breeze offers a refreshing break from the warm days. Harriet and Candice finish cleaning up from a rare Sunday lunch they have shared. The two women open the front door and decide to sit on the front porch for a spell. They settle in around the scrap-wood table that Craf dragged up onto the porch once Harriet moved in. Little Mitch bounces up and down on his Grandma's knee as Harriet pours four glasses of cool sweet tea.

Candice nudges Harriet to look out in front of them. Both women suddenly start to laugh, startling Little Mitch. Craf and Jesse are both pacing back and forth in front of the home. They glance up and point at the roof line and back at the barn. Craf says something to Jesse who in turn shakes his head.

Finally Harriet can't help but laugh out loud. "What in heaven's name are you a- doin'? In case you forgot, this is your home. You're a-lookin' like you ain't too sure 'bout somethin'."

"I reckon Craf ain't so sure 'bout a few things!" Jesse answers Harriet as the two men head up to the porch to join their wives.

Craf frowns at his father and turns to his mother. "Ma, I was telling Papa here I have been taking in traveling folks and their animals, like you did. I'm thinking about building a bigger stockade, and several pens, and maybe a kind of sleeping barn or shed."

Candice takes a sip of ice tea and looks at her son while she watches her husband shake his head. "How come you wanna grow your place bigger, Craf? Don't you have 'nough for your own animals?"

Craf takes a glass of tea from Harriet who nods at him to continue explaining. Craf knows Harriet feels the same way he does about wanting to help the many drovers and their livestock who come along the road in front of their home. It is a compassion borne of identification with these, their own people. After letting the cool tea soothe him he continues, "Of course, but I want to make a kind of rest stop for tired mountain families and their animals so they can save their sparse money for the Greenville Turnpike and other places where they have to pay."

Jesse tries not to let his agitation show. "You mean you figure you'll put 'em up for free? You gonna feed them too?"

Craf knows his father is concerned, but he gives his father a smile and hands him the last glass of tea. "Sure, why not? We are blessed with enough and why not share? Anyway, they come in the fall months and most carry some food with them."

Jesse finally settles on the top porch step. He gulps down the tea so quickly his wife is slightly embarrassed by the liquid beginning to trickle off his chin. He wipes his mouth on his sleeve and then looks straight at his son.

Craf settles on the step next to Jesse. "Papa, the drovers are hardworking, mountain folk, just trying to survive and support their families, just like us. The cost of the toll roads is almost too much for most of them, even if they pay with a hog, or turkey or cow."

Craf sits across from Harriet on the porch railing and continues, "I was a-readin' that our State legislature set up the Buncombe Turnpike Company over around Asheville and that just made matters worse for the smaller farmers." Harriet and Candice just nod their heads and allow Craf's thoughts to pour out. "In the past they could-a driven over Hendersonville or Flat Rock to the South Carolina markets. The paper says the thousands of animals from Tennessee and Kentucky flooded the Turnpike from October through December."

Jessie nods his head. "You heard 'bout Jim Smith's toll bridge, ferry and cattle stands as well as other inns for drovers. Smith has even bought enough land in the Asheville area for growing corn to feed the thousands of animals, charging well for all the services."

"Pop, he is of your generation and I have no problem with his becoming the richest man around. But I think of the little farmers who cannot even begin to pay all those fees."

Jesse begins to see his son's concern for the small farmer. "Craf, Smith ain't the only feller making sacks full o'money 'round Asheville. And they still use lots of slaves to do the work."

"Yeah, I heard about that and that they are working on a railroad. Dad, I really don't need to try to make a lot of money. I just want to help the drovers that pass through."

A cautious but loving Jesse says, "Craf, I reckon it's all right but it don't sound like good business. So long as you know what you are a-doin' and ain't neglectin' your family, you may as well give it a try. Just be careful."

Summer 2012

"Where are we going?" I asked Ellie as we took off into the growing heat. I was happy to spend some time with her away from the Carps, but still wished we could have taken a dip in the lake. We followed a path that cut around the back of a storage unit and led us to an old road running parallel to the Greenville Highway. The road was dirt and needed some grading pretty badly, but from where we were standing you could go left or right. I could tell there were a couple of houses along the road, some old and some recently remodeled. One had a truck and a trampoline as close to the road as you could get, so I figured this was pretty much a long driveway.

"Let's go this way." Ellie led us to the right and we followed the driveway along the fence that acted as security for a storage unit. We passed a small yellow house with a couple of T-shirts drying on a pair of folding chairs. A curtain in one of the two front windows moved slightly and then suddenly the door flew open.

A young Hispanic boy wearing nothing but black Addidas soccer shorts came out and leaned on the front porch post. "Where do you think you're going?" He had to push his shoulder-length jet black hair out of his face.

"None of your business!" Ellie yelled at him and finished with a few words in Spanish. Then she leaned close to me, "That's my idiot brother, Rai. He's always in my business. He's just fourteen, but thinks he's my big brother."

I glanced back at Rai who kept watching us. I awkwardly waved, but the half-naked boy just nodded once and kept watching, so I turned my head to pretend we were on an enjoyable hike.

We reached the end of the road and headed down to a little path that led us along the highway until we picked up what looked like the same road we were on earlier. "Wow, that's a little weird." I stopped and pointed behind me and then up the road we were on. "It almost feels like we are on the same road we were just on."

"We are!" Ellie smiled. "It's really cool. It was the old turnpike before the Greenville Highway was built." She picked up pace and started running towards what looked like the entry to a camp. "Come on. The old turnpike goes this way."

I followed Ellie and we passed through an open gate that looked like it had recently been unlocked since the key was still sticking out of the lock. I could see horses on our right and a barn in the distance.

"Should we be doing this?" I wasn't at all up for trespassing.

"Don't worry. I know the groundskeeper, Charlie. He told me I could come in any time." She stopped and looked at me. I gave her an I don't believe you stare. She laughed at me. "No, really. It's true! Where else do you think I learned about the turnpike? It's not like I'm from here." I smiled at her joke and I felt a little better, but I figured I was just a guest and I could play ignorant.

We passed through a beautiful archway of pine trees growing over the old turnpike. Ellie suddenly jumped up on a pile of stones. I noticed the stones were actually an old wall that made a ninety-degree turn and headed off to the left. "Some wall, huh?" Ellie sat down on top of the wall and waved for me to join her.

As I climbed up the carefully laid stones I saw how the dirt behind the wall backed up to the top of the wall and then spread out into a flat open area. Once I was seated Ellie opened her bag and pulled out lunch. She had a Styrofoam container with two soft tacos. She offered me one and I gladly took it. Unfortunately it was a little spicier than I like, so I grabbed one of the two bottled waters. Ellie laughed at my increasingly red face. "Sorry, I didn't ask if you like jalapeños."

Once the intensity of the peppers faded I offered Ellie the rest of my taco and she, of course, was thrilled. "I bet you did that on purpose, just so you could get more food!" I teased.

"Sounds like something Ellie would do!" said a deep rich voice behind us.

"Charlie!" Ellie practically jumped into the arms of a very old black man. His white hair was pulled back into a pony tail and his matching beard was neatly combed. The overalls he wore showed signs of fresh paint. It seemed like all his teeth were smiling at the beautiful Ellie. She turned and pointed at me as I still sat on the stone wall. "This is my friend Millie Fowler."

"Fowler you say?" Charlie never stopped smiling. He looked up to the sky like he was remembering something from long ago.

"Yes, sir," I answered looking up to see what Charlie was looking at.

"I remember a Fowler. Could play a mean fiddle!" His dark eyes looked at me as if he knew me from somewhere.

"My Papaw could play." I smiled. "You must be talking about him. Did you know a Bill Fowler?" I found myself jumping to my feet and joining Charlie and Ellie.

"Billy was a good man!" Charlie looked at me and I knew they must have been friends.

"Billy's son, Robert, is my dad," I said proudly.

"Ellie, it looks like you picked a good family to be friends with." Charlie patted her head gently. I noticed there was a wave of concern in the last pat that lingered.

Ellie suddenly became defensive. "Don't I always?"

"Sure you do," Charlie lied.

Ellie quickly changed subject. "Come on, Charlie. Tell Millie about this wall."

"See how the wall is basically a holding wall?" Charlie pointed to the flat area that was being held back by the wall. "There was a family that had their homestead here and housed people traveling through from Greenville, or on their way to Asheville." He pointed to the road that came right up to the wall. "I'm sure Ellie told you it was the old turnpike. So they built their place easily accessible for people to stop."

"Sorta like a hotel?" I was curious now and felt like I was somehow standing on holy ground.

"Not like a hotel," Ellie helped. "Like a gathering place, a spot to rest and socialize. Right, Charlie?" She put her arm through Charlie's arm.

He patted her hand. "That's right, Ellie, since they didn't ask for any pay. Really made this a popular site." Charlie and Ellie walked around the open space where a home once stood. "At least the wall still stands to remind us of its existence."

I suddenly heard the rumble of a truck engine, closer than I expected. I turned around to see the blue Dodge Ram thundering up the road. It stopped with a vengeance in front of the wall and dust just about choked me. I could see Junior and Roy were in the front and

Kevin was trying to go unnoticed in the back seat.

I felt Charlie's hand suddenly on my wrist. His touch was gentle, but it said clearly, " I've got this." The deep voice spoke with authority, "Boys, can I help you?"

Junior, who was driving, had his window down and his red hair looked like it could use a washing. He spat some brown liquid at the base of the wall. "Just out lookin' around. Got a problem with that?"

Charlie's voice remained calm. "Actually, I do. This is private property."

"Well, Mille and the little Mexican don't live here!" Roy almost sounded like a whiny girl. I could feel my blood bubbling.

"Well, they are friends and have been invited." Charlie remained calm, but continued to hold onto both of us.

Junior looked coolly at the old black man. "So, old man, you sayin' that friends can stay?"

Charlie remained silent. He could tell that Junior was trying to trap him. We stood there and waited for what would come next. Charlie refused to answer, but I couldn't keep my mouth shut. "Why don't you go on and leave us alone? What do you want anyway?" Charlie gave me a pained look. It said I didn't know my place. It said I didn't know the way it's done. It said I wasn't from here. I knew at that moment I had made a mistake.

At that the two older brothers jumped out and took my challenge. They quickly scrambled up the wall and stood face to face with the three of us. Junior immediately got in my face, the smell of cat pee almost choking me. "You think you're tough?" This time I shut up. "If it weren't for the fact that you're Kevin's girl I would teach you a lesson." I heard a gasp from Ellie.

"What? Do you want attention too?" Junior walked over to Ellie who was shaking. He ran his grease-stained finger up her arm.

"You stop that now, son!" Charlie's voice was firm, without a trace of fear. "You need to head on down the road."

Junior stood face to face, very close. "You talkin' to me, old man?

For shore I ain't yore son." With one swift push Junior shoved Charlie to the ground. "If I got business with a little Mexican girl then it ain't none of yours!" He grabbed Ellie, who swung at him with her free arm.

I started to grab Junior from the back, but found myself smothering in Roy's armpit as he hooked his arm around my neck. I couldn't see much but it was only a second before I heard him. I couldn't believe it. Kevin's voice screamed, "STOP IT! I SAID STOP IT NOW!" He was swinging a huge flashlight he had grabbed out of the back seat. He hit Junior on the arm and Roy let go of me out of sheer shock.

"What the hell, Kev!" Junior held his arm like a hurt puppy.

"I said stop it!" Tears were flowing down Kevin's cheeks. He wouldn't look at us. He simply stared at Junior in defiance. "You want to give Ma a heart attack? You know you can't get away with this. Just stop it before anyone gets hurt."

Junior looked at us and nodded for Roy to get in the truck. As Kevin turned toward the truck, Junior locked the doors. "No! We know where your loyalties are." Junior's red hair was plastered to his face in sweat. He looked at me with disgust. "She better be worth it!" The Dodge took off leaving the four of us standing by the remains of the old stone wall.

1856: A Richmond, Virginia paper warns that fundamental social and economic differences between the North and South may lead to civil conflict; William Walker, with his private army funded by Cornelius Vanderbilt, declares himself "President" of Nicaragua but loses ground to Central American armies.

The Visitor

In the years when he already has a few drover families as guests, Craf has developed some close friends who are deeply appreciative. Most of all they enjoy the spiritual discussions in his home or in the yard. Often there is a circuit riding preacher from the Methodists or Baptists or even Presbyterians or Episcopalians.

And so it is that the McGaha way station expands even more, right on the Turnpike. A stone wall rises to four feet to keep cattle and passing travelers out of the yard. The small wooden gate with its partially woven, upright wooden cross-beams and diagonal braces, however, seems to welcome those who would enter.

The large log house, called by most a lodge, welcomes many visitors and is home to the many McGaha kin on their way to somewhere else. The sapling fences around back extend into the distance to accommodate various animals.

As the visiting drovers come and see a need of repair or more room, they head for the woods to cut more fence saplings to contribute at least something to help around the place.

Once, even though Craf protests, some even see that the massive roof with its wooden shingles needs repair, and insist they will fix it.

But not all who come are so kind and helpful. It is Harriet who first notices that occasionally a man is riding with the parties returning home but has few belongings and talks very little. One fall evening about dusk, she sees a strange man taking notes as others speak around the fire outside. He's wearing more formal "city" clothes, causing Harriet to believe he is obviously not from around here.

Harriet pulls her husband up onto the porch out of earshot of the others. "Craf, I think that man is spying on who says what."

Craf puts his arm around her. "Now, honey, we have to be hospitable to all who come through."

Harriet doesn't like him patronizing her and pushes his arm away. She can't help herself from pointing at the man. "But why is that man here? He clearly does not belong with the group. Look at his clothes. And he has not introduced himself to anybody." By now Harriet is not only frustrated with her husband but is nervous and shaking.

Craf senses her anxiety and wonders if she is worried about Little Mitch or is simply overly protective. Or is she pregnant again? He knows Harriet has been feeling nauseous almost all day. Nancy is staying with them a few days and he hopes her visit will help. She did bring herbal medicines from her mother. He smiles to himself at the possibility of another child, but right now he needs to calm his wife's fears.

He gives in to her intuition and says, "Of course, if he makes you uncomfortable, I'll simply ask him who he is and why he is here."

As he turns to move along the porch toward the steps, he feels her grab his arm. He turns to look at his wife who desperately wants her husband to understand. "Thank you, Craf. Maybe part of hospitality is not just caring for sheep, but also making sure no wolves are in with them."

Craf squeezes Harriet's hand as she eases her grip on his arm. "Gracious! You are worried. I'm going right now."

As Craf reaches the bottom step he hears Harriet's voice. "Do make sure somebody else is around."

He trots back up the steps and kisses her quickly on the cheek. "No problem. Everybody is around the big fire a-jawin'. I'll ask there." He can feel her body relax just a little.

Craf finally heads into the yard where about twenty men and women sit around the fire. Harriet sits in one of the rocking chairs on the porch and soon Nancy joins her, leaving young Mitch inside to rest. Both women rock in silence as Harriet watches her husband mingle with the small crowd.

As always, discussions envelop the visitors. Sudden bursts of laughter or shouts flicker with the flames. At a break in the discussion, Craf addresses the man Harriet is worried about, sitting a little back from the rest. With a smile the gentle, short man walks over and extends his hand to the stranger. "Excuse me, sir. I don't believe we've met. I be Craf McGaha, host of this party. And who might you be?"

Standing quickly, avoiding Craf's outstretched hand and moving toward the fire, as if on cue, the blond-haired man of about thirty years addresses the group more than Craf. "I, sir, am an honorable member of the South Carolina group of true Christians who wish to see our land kept pure and clean." The talkative group becomes awkwardly silent as they become aware of the sudden oration. "We call upon all people of faith to make sure this land is purified and not diluted with heathen, lesser creatures of color, any color. God gave this land to the superior white race and God intends to keep it that way!"

The visitors slowly shift themselves away from the stranger and some look to Craf with wide eyes. Craf is beside himself. "Stop! I asked for your name and you give us a sermon of hate. Who are you and who is this group about which you speak? " Craf glances to the front porch and sees his wife and Nancy suddenly rise and stand shoulder to shoulder.

The tall blond man stands taller as he announces his name. "My name is Reverend Joseph Schmidt, called of God and led by His Holy Word to see that all people keep their place in life. My task is to proclaim this vital word and collect those who will stand up for what is right. In other words, to cleanse our darkening society."

Craf moves in closer to the "reverend." He will not stand for this display of hatred on his land. "So, you are here recruiting?"

The Reverend Schmidt pulls out a shiny black Bible and waves it in the air. "Only giving the true word in the hopes some will hear the call."

The visitors continue to watch, now intrigued with where Craf is taking this discussion. Craf firmly asks, "And the notes you are taking, are they only to identify those who might go along or those who might not? In other words are you spying here in our mountains?" A few yells rise up from the others who are now becoming enraged.

An angry Schmidt attempts to go on the offensive to avoid being defensive. "There, on the porch. It is almost dark outside, but I see you have no scruples and allow a woman of color in your house!"

There are several moments of silence. Nancy does not budge and Harriet puts her arm around her. The crowd, collectively holding their breath, watches Craf, to see how he will handle this strange, aggressive man.

Craf gently speaks as if changing the subject, "Reverend Schmidt, you say you are a man of God?"

"Yes, of course." Schmidt raises his chin with pride.

"Then," Craf slyly asks, "you know your Bible?"

By now the man is uncomfortable and it is clear he does not, but must claim such in front of this group, "Yes, naturally."

Craf, choosing his words carefully and avoiding more obvious biblical references to race, says, "Then you are aware that the Italians played a big role in the biblical times- - in fact the Apostle Paul went to Rome and later wrote letters to Rome called letters to the Romans."

Shaking and quite unsure of himself, Joseph Schmidt responds, "Everybody knows that."

"And everybody knows also that Italians are a little more dark-skinned than other Europeans, yet are great Christians, at least the Apostle Paul thought so. He himself even claimed to be a Roman citizen!"

"Oh," a dizzy Reverend Schmidt weakly utters as he backs out of the group, quickly saddles and mounts his horse, and rides toward Jones Gap and Greenville. The rest of the group starts laughing at the speed with which the stranger leaves. It doesn't take long for them to settle in to discussion again. Craf speaks to them for a few moments, but then heads back up the steps to the two women still standing on the porch.

As Craf approaches, it is Nancy, with tears freely flowing, who speaks first, "Thanks for defending me. Not ever-body woulda done 'at."

Craf simply says, "You are family, a McGaha also with a rich Cherokee tradition of your own. You are one of us."

Craf turns to his wife, expecting a warm embrace, but is surprised to find Harriet is quite upset, not by his comments to Nancy but by what she had heard. "Craf, did you just tell a lie to that man and in front of this group? Does facing such a man, however filled with hate, call for a blatant lie?"

Craf is silent for a moment replaying the discussion. He then smiles, "What lie?"

"You said that Nancy was Italian."

Craf turns back to the smiling group and yells loud enough for all to hear, "Did anybody here hear me say that Nancy was Italian?"

One man, Webb Parker from up in Gloucester and occasional drover, stands up and walks closer to Craf and the two women. Harriet can see he is smiling and trying not to laugh, "Nope, you just told 'bout Italians in olden times. You didn't even point at her. You set a kinda trap and he done stepped right in it. 'Sides, I don't think he really knowed his Bible. He was a bluffin' and trying to scare us."

Harriet begins to laugh, then Nancy, then Craf. The entire group breaks into boisterous laughter, enough for poor Reverend Joseph Schmidt to hear way down the turnpike in Cedar Mountain.

Summer 2012

Charlie's dust-covered hand gently touched Kevin's shoulder. "You done good, son!" Roy and Junior's attack had just happened, but the whole thing felt surreal. I couldn't believe I had just been in a fight. I looked at Ellie who was trying to hide her tears by fixing her pony tail packing up our lunch trash. I ran over to Kevin and stood in front of him. His tears still flowed and I could see a pain in his eyes I had never seen before. But he didn't look at me.

"It's not over, Charlie!" Kevin whispered. "You know it." He turned away from me and looked into the old man's eyes. "It's never over." Kevin buried his head into the old man's shoulder. I was confused. It seemed to me that they knew each other well.

Charlie embraced him, gently patting his back. "It will be. It will be. One day. You just keep doing what is right."

I awkwardly patted Kevin's back feeling sorry for him too, and yet grateful at the same time. I wanted to say something, but what could I say? Finally, I uttered, "Thanks, Kevin. You were amazing."

He looked at me and tried to smile as he gently punched my arm. "You weren't so bad yourself."

I noticed a small sigh from near the wall. Kevin turned his head and for the first time looked at Ellie. Kevin's lightness was gone and was replaced with a deep sadness mixed with fear. Ellie only briefly glanced at him and then hung her head again pretending to clean up what was already neatly stashed away in the plastic bag she had brought.

"This is Ellie!" I tried to be light and introduce the two, but Charlie cut me short. He shook his head telling me introductions were not necessary. I stood there like an idiot waiting for someone to say something,

Kevin finally looked my way again and shoved the flashlight in the back of his pants. "Well, I guess I better get walkin' home. See you later, Mille." He nodded at Charlie and quickly glanced again at Ellie, who did not return the favor.

1857: Financial panic occurs and almost 5,000 firms go bankrupt; Texas Rangers are formed to deal with violence in Texas; President Buchanan's inaugural speech calls for tolerance of slavery to preserve the Union.

Joy and Birth

Craf is proud they built the house so large intended for guests for it is soon needed for newborn children as well. Baby Julia enters the McGaha home with enough energy to cheer them from the very first day. Little Mitch sits in a little rocker of his own that Craf has built for him in anticipation of his little sister. The boy rocks slowly mimicking the movements of his father. With Julia at her breast, Harriet reaches over with her free arm to pat her glowing husband's arm. "Well, here we are off on our family pilgrimage. You now have a daughter and son who need you."

Craf gently reaches to touch the tiny toes sticking out from the hand-quilted blanket. "I know, I'll do my best but all babies look so small and helpless that it kinda scares me." Little Mitch runs over to join his father. He tries to reach up to the baby's toes. Craf finally lifts the boy up to help him accomplish his mission.

Harriet smiles at the two men in her life. "Craf, that is why I love you. You reach out to so many and try to show mercy knowing that it doesn't always work. Every child is a gift of God but not all make it," she says, not realizing how prophetic she is. "You provide a good home and lots of love, just like you love all those folks who stop over."

Craf whispers to his wife, "I know all that but I still feel anxious in these times. And I love you, love of my life. You really understand me and tolerate my funny ways." Mitchel finally settles on Craf's lap as Harriet tucks the baby's tiny toes under the blanket to keep them warm.

Summer 2012

"I'm so sorry." I desperately looked at Charlie hoping that he wouldn't run back to Mammaw and have me sent home on the next airplane. The whole fight was so bizarre that I really couldn't figure it out.

Charlie tried to smile, but I could tell it was for show. "Millie Fowler. Some things you just don't mess with. And the Carp boys are one of those things."

But that wasn't enough of an answer for me. I followed Charlie as he helped Ellie get up and watched him gently wipe some of the tears off her face. "How can you just let it go? Should we do something?"

Charlie looked at me and was not smiling. "Oh, trust me. I will! Nobody pushes me down or attacks Ellie without consequences." I followed behind him as he started to walk with us back towards Ellie's house. "I'll report it. We'll all be interviewed and then it's just a matter of time before the boys dig themselves a hole they can't get out of anymore."

Then I heard Ellie speak for the first time since the boys arrived, "Let's just hope they do it soon."

1858: Revival meetings increase across the land in uncertain times; Abraham Lincoln declares, "A house divided against itself cannot stand"; Minnesota becomes a state.

Joy and Help

Craf and Harriet keep their hospitality waystation, bearing the ever-increasing news of national tensions as best they can. Great joy arrives, however, in the form of twins, Wiley and Sally Sarah in 1858. Mitch and Juliet are thrilled in the arrival of a little sister and brother, a playmate for each as they see it.

Craf worries that four young children are too much for Harriet to care for. "Should we ask some of our family to help out with the kids from time to time, Harriet?" The worried Craf stands behind his wife in the kitchen as she kneads dough.

She doesn't look at her husband but continues to turn and push down the flour mixture. "Craf, I can handle it but maybe from time to time just find someone to come when I have to wash clothes and cook for the visitors. Then it is a lot. You do a good job with keeping wood for the fire and water from the spring."

Craf can see the tension in her shoulders as she continues to work the dough. He knows she is being gracious, but still he will not accept her answer. "I hear that the Summeys have a cousin who has emigrated from Switzerland, a young woman who came over just a few months ago and is trying to settle in and improve her English. Maybe we could ask about her for some help."

Harriet turns around and gently pushes a strand of hair away from her face leaving a small steak of flour across her forehead. Somewhat in resignation and with obvious tiredness in her voice, Harriet responds, "Whatever you think is best, my love."

So it is that Gerda Sumi comes to stay with the McGahas and to make friends with Nancy Guice McGaha who is checking on Harriet and the children from time to time.

Sitting on the front porch one fall afternoon, Nancy asks, "What do you miss most from your old country, Gerda?"

Gerda struggles with her English in response, "De mountains, I guess. Alps we call them. Und mountain farmers or peasants- - they work so hard mit cows and cheese. Dann, I miss the orchestra too!"

Nancy is surprised and asks, "Are you saying the farmers have an orchestra?"

"Oh nein. De cow bells. Everywhere cows, goats und sheep, dey all have bells. Near und very far, dey ring mit such clear sounds. The farmers can know where alle de cows are by da sound. Like an orchestra. Sometimes on Sunday de farmers play Alpine horns up there. So beautiful."

Nancy's curiosity cannot wait, "And your mountains, the Alps, are they as beautiful as ours here?"

Gerda, whose English seems to have improved with practice and confidence in the relationship with Nancy, replies, "Mountains are like men und women. Each hat its own beauty. The Alps can be overwhelming, exactly like dese here. With white snow - oder clouds und contrast mit a very dark blue sky – is all so beautiful. But dann when snow und stones - and the mountain itself comes down, it takes everything, houses, villages, trees, people. Dat ist terror."

Nancy responds to her sharing this memory of the Alps, "Sounds like the respect our folks here got for our mountains. Sometimes in the spring we get what we call a "mountain freshet." Creeks get to be rivers and take trees, homes and people, whole mountainsides. Sounds like we both have a love of, and fear of, our mountains at the same time."

Gerda is enthusiastic in her "Jawohl! Oh, yes!"

Summer 2012

That night I didn't tell Mammaw the whole story about the fight along the old turnpike. I felt like a liar, but I knew I was in way over my head. I did tell her that we ran into the Carps and that they harassed us, but that Charlie took care of it and was going to report it.

Mammaw seemed pleased that I had met Charlie and started telling me stories of Charlie and Pappaw. For the first time that day I felt safe. I let the flowers on the couch cradle me as Mammaw laughed through the memories. Finally she slapped my leg and jumped up. "It's been a long time since I pulled it out." She headed into my bedroom.

"Pulled what out?" I could hear her shuffling through my closet. She finally returned with a big grin on her face. There in her hand was the oldest looking fiddle I had ever seen.

"Your Pappaw used to play this almost every night." She gently fondled the strings smiling at the images that only danced through her mind. Then sadness filled her eyes. "We never could get your daddy to play. He thought it was too old-fashioned."

I knew Daddy was more into sports in his day. I'd heard he was pretty good at basketball, but I always teased him saying there was no way he had ever been good since he had such a gut on him now. "Maybe he will play one day." I tried to cheer her up, but it seemed sorta lame.

"Well, it's been in the family since the early 1800's." She sat down on the couch next to me and held the fiddle in her arms like a baby. "But I guess there isn't anything much sacred anymore."

I knew Mammaw was hurting and I wished more than ever that my parents had been able to come. I gently took Mammaw's hand in mine. I could feel her wrinkles, but they felt soft and warm. I really didn't know what to say, so I didn't say anything.

1860: Lincoln is elected U.S. President; In Charleston, S.C., James L. Petigru responds when asked to direct someone to the local insane asylum, "The whole state is an insane asylum!"; South Carolina secedes from the Union.

The Loss

It is Saturday afternoon and it seems strange to Craf to walk into his parents' home and find his parents sitting at the dinner table with no food on the table. The air feels thicker than normal and the faces of Jesse and Candice are drawn into a weird distortion. Harriet is with him and has left Gerda to watch the young children. Craf's sister Polly Ann and her husband Tom Fowler are present, somber-faced.

The announcement is blunt and shocking. Jesse looks at his son with water pouring from his eyes and nose. He wipes his face on his sleeve the best he can. "Well, y'all. I hate to have to tell but we done lost Epi today."

A shocked Craf breaks in, "What do you mean?"

"He was a-workin' some timber over on Hurricane Creek and a big chestnut twisted back and kilt him," Jesse says softly as Candice reaches to hold his hand.

Harriet reaches to hold Craf's hand but he is holding his hands folded, looking so shocked that he cannot respond. Harriet settles for touching his shoulder, feeling a deep trembling begin to emerge from her husband.

Harriet, allowing her tears to flow freely, looks at Candice and asks, "What 'bout Nancy? Does she know? How is she?"

Candice stands and reaches for Harriet who lets go of Craf to embrace her mother-in-law. "Her ma is with her," Candice sobs. "She's asked Tom

Fowler and some of the Raxter men to bring him home for cleanin' up and a service." She looks at Harriet and her eyes are wide. "She come by to tell us-uns herself."

Suddenly Candice breaks off, sobbing uncontrollably, so Jesse continues for her. "We asked what we could do. We'll all be working on that. But we told her she's always a McGaha and one of us."

Silence fills the room as they all realize Craf has not spoken. Jesse stands and tries to embrace his son, but Craf remains with his hands folded tightly, staring at the floor. "Craf," Jesse shifts the topic, "Kin you write to Joe down in Alabama to let him know? Tom Fowler said he'd like to tell your brother William. Nancy said she'd write your sister Eliza down in South Carolina."

The flat, "Yeah," response from Craf seemed out of character, but they all know how close he and Epi were.

Craf gets up abruptly to leave and Harriet says, "You go on home, Craf. I need to stay here a while to help your Ma and Pa." But Craf does not answer.

Candice gives a weak protest but Harriet raises her hand, "No discussion. Folks'll be coming from all over and bringin' food and a-visitin'. You need to be free to grieve your son Epiphroditus too."

Jesse and Candice shed tears of thanks as they watch Harriet take off her sweater and place it neatly over the back of a chair. Craf is gone before they finish their brief exchange. At the barn he unhitches the wagon and puts a saddle on the mare. It is out of character for Craf to ride a horse at a gallop in the woods but he pushes her toward Rich Mountain, to the very rock in the field where he and Epi had spent so much time together.

They say you could hear wild animal screams for hours from Rich Mountain, like a painter or smaller cat.

4

Summer 2012

It was Saturday and Mammaw had the weekend off. This meant we could finally spend the day together. She suggested we go into Brevard, since she said it looked like I needed a change. I wondered what she meant by that, but I guessed she was referring to my increasingly subdued behavior. I really was mellow and less excited about being here since the Carps wacked out.

Charlie ended up coming by the house with a sheriff's deputy and then, well, needless to say, Mammaw was a lot more upset about the incident. The nice detective said they would file a report and in the meantime we'd have to get a lawyer to get a restraining order placed on Junior and Roy. If we did then they couldn't come near Ellie, Charlie or me. This made Mammaw relax a little. They were also being fined for trespassing on the old camp property. Mammaw was fiercely aware of my insistence that Kevin should not be included in the restraining order, but it seemed that Charlie had already made the point. But the whole thing was a little more than I could handle, so I hadn't want to do anything for two days except lie around, check the TV and spend endless hours on the internet. I even called Mom and Dad several times a day, using Mammaw's phone. They suggested I come on home, but I couldn't. I guess I wanted to somehow rebuild my sanctuary. I just didn't know how.

We climbed into Mammaw's Metallic Maroon Monterey Malibu. I loved to say that, "Mammaw's Metallic Maroon Monterey Malibu." I repeated it until Mammaw just told me to basically shut up.

"Can't we call it something else?" Mammaw slammed the door and started the engine. "Or you'll send me to an early grave." I laughed. I mean really laughed for the first time in a while.

"Okay, let's call her Big M," I teased and Mammaw nodded a whatever you say, Millie nod. I could tell her mind was already somewhere else.

"Why don't we stop and see if Ellie wants to join us?" Mammaw reached over from the driver's seat and squeezed my hand. "I think it would do you two good to get together again and do something fun." Ah, so that was it. Mammaw was already trying to fix my bigger issue.

We were at the entrance to Sherwood Forest and I knew that turning left meant we were going on into Brevard and right meant we were picking up Ellie. As we turned right I sighed a little. I hadn't really faced Ellie since I couldn't keep my mouth shut, but Mammaw just patted my knee. That same pat told me it was going to be okay when she took me to the doctor's or when I was nervous about flying on my own. That pat always ended up being right. Things did seem to somehow work out.

I saw Ellie was already standing outside waiting for us. I looked at Mammaw, slightly confused. She smiled at me. "I called ahead."

"Mammaw!" I was definitely frustrated. How could I face her? I knew she would hate me. But when I saw her as we pulled in, she was smiling and waving. I heard Mammaw unlock the back door and as soon as we came to a stop Ellie jerked the door open and jumped into the Big M.

"Hey, Millie! Hi, Ms. Fowler. Thank you for inviting me." I couldn't believe how excited she was. I figured she must not get off the mountain very often during the summer.

"We're happy to have you join us, my dear." Mammaw turned the car around and we pulled back out onto the Greenville Highway and finally headed toward Brevard.

I looked out the window as we drove the curvy mountain road. In a few places the trees were cut away revealing the impressive mountains as they stared back at us. Their overwhelming beauty was quickly whisked away as we turned yet another curve. About fifteen minutes of curves opened up into a straight section in the valley and generally followed the French Broad River for a part of its journey. The last seriously tight curve before the straight stretch looked down on the eternally flooding river. I always loved this curve the best. On the right towering above us was Dunn's Rock. The huge rock face of the mountainside always made me feel like I was entering a gateway to the community I loved. On the left was a building that Pappaw told us was a pre-civil war federal distillery and was also a mill. He said it had a huge water wheel and a stream was diverted from the mountain through a wooden sluice over the road to hit the wheel which then emptied then into the French Broad River. I thought it must have looked funny with a wooden contraption suspended over the road with water pouring through it.

I missed Pappaw's stories. Mammaw always made feel at home in Transylvania County, but Pappaw always made me see the Transylvania that had once lived and breathed long ago, the people whose blood still flowed through my veins.

1861: Abraham Lincoln is inaugurated as the U.S. President, after the Pinkerton Detective Agency foils a plot to assassinate him prior to taking office; Jefferson Davis is Acting President of the Confederacy; More southern states join the secession.

The War

A loud, irritating horn sounds in the distance "What's that noise?" Harriet calls to Craf who is working on a broken gatepost. Craf is already looking in the same direction down the road. They both know it's about the time when Al usually arrives in Cedar Mountain to bring news along with mail. Each appointed day that the mailman arrives in Cedar Mountain, increasingly larger crowds await not only the opening of his precious pouches but also his words on the latest news. Postmaster Thomas himself reads the newspaper to all present, and, if requested, individual's letters from relatives in Charleston, Columbia, Philadelphia, Greenville or Brevard.

Craf looks at Harriet and she immediately understands he will be following the noise. As Craf jumps on his horse he wonders why Al would be blowing a horn, something he has never done. He had no idea the mailman even had a small horn with him.

Craf soon finds himself closing in on a small crowd. The past several months had been full of growing concerns. The crowd was always asking: "Ain't these thaings just paper lies?" "Do you reckon we'll have war?" "Will them Yankees attack us?" "What on earth will that Lincoln feller do?" "Is it true they is gonna blockade our ports?" On and on they asked questions no one could answer and they could only share in their fears. But today the crowd is almost silent as they watch the mailman approach, still blowing his off-key horn.

Craf notices that Al's horse looks exhausted, as if it had been run most of the way up the mountain from Greenville and Travelers Rest. A chill envelops his whole body as they all hear Al's cry. "War! War!"

Like his horse, he, too, is panting painfully. He cannot speak. No telling how many stations he had given the news to this day. Craf helps him from his saddle and pushes the crowd back to give him air. He asks if he might open the mail pouches and the mail carrier nods approval.

Hoping the slight shaking in his hands is not visible, he takes the Greenville paper from Al and hands it to the local postmaster who reads the headlines aloud. "Fort Sumter Attacked: Long Awaited War Has Arrived."

Craf can no longer hide his shaking and sudden urge to retch, so he walks away to his horse, crying softly to himself.

Harriet, who has not moved from the porch sees him coming, sitting so strangely in the saddle. She knows something is wrong and runs to meet him at the gate.

"What is it, Craf?" Harriet looks up to her husband who is still on his horse and she grabs his boot. When he doesn't answer she begins to shake his leg until he looks at her, tears already flowing down her face.

The one, long-dreaded word creeps out of his down-turned mouth. "War."

Summer 2012

"Millie?" I felt a nudge from Ellie as we sat on the courthouse wall waiting for Mammaw to come out of the bakery. "You haven't said very much."

I shoved her back a little trying to will myself to relax. "I'm okay."

"Liar!" Ellie got up and headed to the War Memorial standing directly behind us. She leaned up against the Vietnam side and looked towards the bakery down the road, obviously hoping Mammaw would hurry up.

I took a deep breath and jumped up and walked toward her. I could hardly look at her. "I'm sorry." She didn't say anything. "I really feel awful for what happened and feel it's all my fault." There, it was out.

Suddenly I heard a huge laugh. "Are you kidding me?" She grabbed me around the neck and pulled my ear up to her face. Then she whispered, "The secret is that no one blames you. Except for maybe being stupid!" I shoved her away playfully.

"How can you be so light about this?" I asked her a little more seriously then I intended to.

Ellie sat back down on the wall and pointed to me to join her. As I settled in beside her she started to speak. I heard just a slight crack in her voice, but she smiled to cover the darkness rising from within. I almost didn't dare look, but I had asked. She finally spoke, "It's not the first time. The Carps have made our lives hell more than once." I suddenly looked horrified. She laughed, just a little. "Don't worry only close calls and lots of harassment." The smile faded. "But that's bad enough."

I could just barely hear myself ask, "And Kevin?"

Something changed. A softness, maybe. Her lips quivered ever so slightly. "No, not Kevin." She smiled at me. "Never Kevin."

I couldn't imagine how life must be for Kevin. He had loyalties to his brothers, yet he also found himself standing against them.

1861: Fort Sumter is attacked and surrenders to the Confederates; South Carolina had seceded the previous December; Congress authorizes three new territories: Dakota, Colorado and Nevada.

The New County

Life would never be quite the same at the McGaha hospitality house.

Guests continue to come, but conversations are usually muted and cautious, especially about the war and family loyalties.

There are, of course, more private conversations with close relatives and others from down the Little River with the Jones, Huggins, Loftis families and down into Crab Creek community, especially with the Hamiltons, and others. Mill days are especially good times as they wait their turns to have their corn ground.

But mill days have slowly changed. The mills on Mill Hill, either at the Connestee Falls end or at Babe Cooper's distillery, along with Samuel Hogsed's on down the Turnpike had been popular for most neighbors. Now the Moore Mill on the Little River below Triple Falls in Buck Forest gets increasing use by some locals who want to avoid many of the summer residents, who are slaveholders and proponents of war.

It is breakfast time on May 20, 1861 when Craf announces to Harriet at breakfast, "I need to go to Brevard."

"How come?" Harriet puts her fork on her plate leaving the last bite of scrambled eggs untouched.

Craf, aware of his own unfinished breakfast continues, "A big meeting has been called about organizing into a county of our own, apart from Henderson and Jackson Counties. We hear that the State already approved it a coupla months ago. The justices of peace are calling for a county court. If it works out, they should elect a sheriff which, Lord knows, we really need. I reckon there will be other decisions, too."

Harriet takes a sip of her coffee as she listens to her husband. She is proud of Craf's desire to be part of the decisionmaking. "Craf, you taking your dad with you? The McGahas, like the Hogseds, Raxters, Loftises and others, have been around here a long time and done a lot. Your ideas need to be heard. Don't be shy."

Craf tries to take another bite. A little cautious, he responds, "Naw, I don't think it's a good idea to take Papa. He is so nervous about all the tension. I'll fill him in when I return. Besides I might need to spend the night with some of the Hogseds at the foot of the mountain if things go on more than a day. I'm not sure how good the Dunn's Rock Bridge is these days and

I might have to go upriver to Island Ford to cross. Too many uncertainties."

Harriet, sharp as usual and knowing her husband well, responds, "Sounds to me like the uncertainties don't just have to do with shaky bridges!" She starts to stack the finally empty plates and silverware.

Craf quickly grabs his coffee cup before she takes it. "I reckon that is so. And, I know- - I will be careful and not speak out too much as if I were home."

So it is that Craf McGaha, solid citizen of Henderson County, North Carolina rides his horse from the upper Little River community in Cedar Mountain, north on the Johnstone/Greenville Turnpike past Connestee Falls Mill, into the lower Dunn's Rock/ Connestee community. As he reaches the foot of the mountain he feels uncomfortable because no one is there to collect tolls from travelers passing through. He rides around to the Hume Hotel only to find no one there. Dunn's Rock seems to look studiously down upon the deserted hotel, normally a bustling gathering place for church groups, the Masons and others mixing with the tourists.

Craf nudges his horse ahead to Babe Cooper's Distillery just beyond the hotel.

Finally he finds a worker trying to repair the flume to the giant overshot wheel. Water awkwardly spills over the sides as a young man furiously works at patching a growing crack in one plank. "Hey, don't reckon I know you. I am Craf McGaha. Who might you be?"

The young man, startled at hearing someone else, almost falls off the already unstable ladder. "Oh, mister, you shore scared me. I ain't from these parts. I just come up from Greenville to help Babe Cooper fix that sluice. It's a-leakin' right bad."

Craf looks at him and the leaky sluice then looks around one more time and the ominous quiet of the usually busy community bothers him. "Where is everybody? No toll takers, no hotel folks, nobody waving from their porches."

By now the young man has come up to Craf's horse and is stroking its mane. "Mister, ain't you heard? Big meetin's in Brevard. Lots goin' on. Dem Yankees done started war and we-uns got to defend ourselves."

Craf refrains from correcting him or debating who started what, but does state, "I understand the meeting in Brevard is just to start a new county and set up a government."

The young man, feeling corrected, stops stroking the horse and avoids further discussion. "Whatever you say, mister. I got work to do." He turns and heads back up the ladder.

Craf rides the few feet past the distillery and, turning left to the French Broad River, decides to walk his horse across the shaky Dunn's Rock Bridge, which has been recently strengthened with angling poles bracing against upriver water pressure and floating debris.

The trip from Dunn's Rock Bridge into Brevard is not far. Within a few minutes he sees the large, beautiful estate called Montclove overlooking the river. He is almost overwhelmed with contradictory emotions, and he is wondering why he feels so good and yet so bad when he looks over there. Craf is confused by such feelings. The Montclove folks from South Carolina really formed a kind of seasonal colony in these parts. Not only that, they are all church-going Episcopalians and nice folks.

He thinks, "They even started their own church right over there back in '56. They met first right there in the shed outside Montclove, the Johnstone summer home, then built their St. Paul's-in-the-Valley across the river in Dunn's Rock, right by the Turnpike. They are such good neighbors."

Craf calls out into the stillness of the valley, "Lord, help me out with this. These are your folks as well. And from time to time their minister came to preach or teach to our community when we had not gotten a circuit rider for some time. I hear they even helped out the Methodists, the Cathey's Creek Baptists and the Presbyterians at Davidson's Creek."

As he turns to look back toward Dunn's Rock he realizes he has just ridden past the beautiful home of Rev. Hankle, the Episcopalians' first rector. Craf knows he helps so many Methodist churches and even preaches fairly regularly at the old Oak Grove Methodist Church in Brevard.

Symbolically suspended between these two homes of helpful, loving Episcopalians he struggles to resolve the conflict of his good and bad feelings. Then it hits him hard. "Oh Lord, of course. The Johnstones, the Humes, and most of these fine folks are also slave holders!"

Craf doesn't know whether to laugh or cry. He has had mixed feelings most of his life and tries to give everybody the benefit of a doubt and not to judge others. He chuckles at his thoughts and moves on toward the little community of Brevard. He remembers vividly his childhood talk with his Papa years ago about releasing their own slaves.

By noon Craf guides his horse down a slight slope into a wide valley with farm land stretching before him. The Valley Store is already welcoming several men and other folks are gathered nearby under the shade trees in the Oak Grove, visiting, full of lively talk. Excitement fills the air. Expectation of something coming is palpable.

Craf soon joins the men who have started to pull in closer to the store hoping to take advantage of the little shade the porch casts. As Craf leans on the porch post he glances toward the barrels stacked against the front of the house and takes note of the transformation B.C. Langford's home has undergone. Is now looks more like a store than a home.

The growing number of spectators settles down as they turn toward a group of the slightly graying men who are all awkwardly wearing their woolen suits in order to appear as stately as possible. Craf smiles to himself, thankful he left his one woolen jacket at home. Craf understands these men are the justices and their attempt to be most solemn is working. Craf hears nothing but the occasional neighing of tethered horses. It seems there are more than a dozen justices in front, but three seem to be the leaders and spokesmen.

The justices stand on the high ground by B.C. Langford's store in order to be visible to all. They explain every legal and procedural detail carefully. Craf and others find themselves overwhelmed at times and the justices repeat often in order to assure clarity.

A few times the justices call for a quick recess, quickly running to the outhouse or into the grove to relieve themselves, but also giving the men time to think about decisions that need to be made. By the end of the day they have affirmed the name approved earlier by the North Carolina Legislature--Transylvania, "across the forest."

Craf and others congratulate Robert Hamilton who is elected as sheriff, the county's first. In addition, the county elects a county clerk and some other officers. Committees are set up to propose a county seat and to divide up places for needed buildings. The justices hope they will be able to report proposals in about a week.

Then, just before dark, the new clerk of new Transylvania County announces, "Please come back tomorrow for the rest of our work. We must decide on schools, roads, bridges, taxes and one other vital item. And we'll need to meet over in Wilson's Camp Ground across the way, beyond the Oak Grove Methodist Church. We'll find more water and facilities there." Trying to find humor in the situation, he adds, "The Methodists were always good in providing for necessities." No one laughs.

Craf is very aware of the growing darkness. He was not sure how all this was going to work when he arrived and he has learned a lot today. It is called a 'court' for legal decisions, yet it seems like a community meeting with a program for order. The justices are fair. Not so bad. He would like to go home, but something inside, his gut maybe, tells him he should come back. It is then that he decides to come back the next day, so he crosses the river to see if Samuel Hogsed can put him up for the night.

Summer 2012

I couldn't believe how relieved I was that Ellie wasn't ticked at me about not keeping my mouth shut when the Carp brothers were trying to pick a fight. By the time Mammaw came back to us with some fresh bread we were laughing at, well, nothing really. It just felt good to laugh.

Mammaw piled us in the Big M and we headed down Jailhouse Hill to the four lanes which passed Brevard College, Ingles' grocery store and then ultimately opened into as much of an open valley straightaway as you can get in Transylvania County. We passed McDonalds on the left and soon Blue Ridge Community College on our right. I looked at Mammaw as I got more excited. "Are you taking us where I think you're taking us?"

"Well, if you are thinking ice cream at Dolly's then you're right," Mammaw smiled. Ellie and I screamed like little girls. It wasn't long before we turned left and stopped near the gate to the Pisgah National Forest. Dolly's looked like an old building that had been added onto a few times to include a few more vendors, but it was the ice cream that made Dolly's famous.

We walked up three steps onto the wide porch to reach the window where we placed our order. I loved their cookies and cream and Ellie didn't hesitate to order their famous banana split. Once Mammaw grabbed her pistachio in a cup we headed to one of the stone tables that sat out in the open. Ellie and I plopped down and noticed Mammaw standing and looking at us.

"I'll let you girls sit here and I will join my friend over there." I mindlessly looked up and saw a skinny woman who looked about my parents' age. Her blond hair was pulled tightly back in a single ponytail and she wore blue eye shadow. She was not smiling, and looked oddly pale, especially with the baby blue T-shirt she wore. She glanced at us strangely and then quickly looked away.

"Okay, Mammaw. She looks like she could use a friend." I looked at Ellie, but she suddenly looked a little pale too. She was staring at the woman and leaned into me. "Do you know who she is?"

"No." I looked at Ellie and was confused.

"She's . . ." Ellie was interrupted as a second huge banana split was placed down between us on the table. We both looked up.

"Can I join you two ladies?" A very pink Kevin stood awkwardly before us. He stared back at us and when we didn't answer he just sat down. Ellie and I scooted over a little to give him space. Ellie frantically looked around and I knew she was looking for the Dodge Ram. Kevin smiled at her gently, "Don't worry they ain't around." He nodded toward Mammaw's friend. "Ma wasn't about to bring 'em into town."

"What are the odds we'd find you here?" I said loud enough for Mammaw to hear, knowing very well there were no odds. She glanced at me and smiled.

"Millie," Kevin tried to explain, "Ma and Mrs. Fowler are friends. I think they were figurin' we'd better try to start over again." Kevin was still trying too hard.

"You, figure?" I tried not to sound too sarcastic, but well, I just couldn't help myself.

Kevin shook his head a little and started to stand up. "You're not helpin' here much, Millie."

I grabbed his arm. "Sorry. Please stay. I was just frustrated with Mammaw, not you." I looked at Ellie. "We want him to stay, right Ellie?"

Ellie barely whispered, "Of course."

Kevin settled in and we all awkwardly started a conversation. It wasn't long before I noticed Kevin every so often reach out and touch Ellie's hand. At first I thought he was just being nice. But then I realized Ellie did not flinch or pull away.

1861: Jefferson Davis moves the Confederate Capital from Montgomery, Alabama to Richmond, Virginia; Virginia and Kentucky proclaim neutrality in the Civil War; The first telegraph message is sent across the continent.

A Higher Decision

Craf welcomes the cool morning mountain breeze as he gathers with the same crowd from the day before. Neither the early start nor the new location has kept anyone from being present. The cooler temperature allows for more people to gather closer to three justices who have already resumed their positions and air of importance. Apparently they have been selected from the dozen or more to carry on and can use the Camp Ground preacher's platform to their advantage. A couple of rows of old weatherbeaten wooden benches complete the feel of an outside church and offer relief to several older men gathered, already claiming a spot to sit.

Craf feels a sense of pride as the second day of Transylvania County Court gets off to a good start with the group moving quickly through the issues of schools, roads, bridges, and even taxes. It seems that most communities had been meeting before and had suggestions for their locality.

Some offer subscription schools that pay for themselves; they only need books and a teacher.

By mid-morning the crowd becomes slightly restless as they begin to discuss taxes- - of course, a volatile issue. Craf knows that all of the planning and then ultimately implementation of a new county will have to be paid for. He is curious to see how the subject will be handled. Finally one of the justices reminds them, "No, remember you are no longer Henderson County or Jackson. You do not pay their high taxes. And we now have our own Robert Hamilton as Sheriff so we have our law close at hand. We must pay for peacekeeping!"

There is a moment of nodding and understanding, but from the back someone calls out, "And what of us pore folks? What if we can't pay for roads and bridges?"

The justice's response is gentle and clear, "We are planning for alternative means like other counties, like our neighbors in Jackson County." Spotting one of the Parkers from up in Gloucester, near the newly proposed county line, the justice points to him and all heads turn. "Brother Parker, you are in the part of Jackson bein' given to our new county. How did you folks do it over there?"

The heavyset bearded man tucks his hands in his overalls and raises his voice. "We put in some hard labor, a-buildin' roads and bridges, so many days a year. We sweat our taxes out!"

The crowd roars in laughter, releasing a lot of tension. The relief is clear to all. Most do not realize that in the future if they do not do their required sweat equity for taxes, they will be answerable to the county authorities.

The crowd begins to disperse as it seems the planning has come to an end. Craf is feeling good and thinks he will mount up and go home to let folks know they are now in a new county without having to move. As he unties his horse he suddenly hears the newly charged Sheriff Hamilton fire his ancient ball and cap pistol into the air, a profoundly symbolic gesture considering what is to come.

The crowd quickly gathers back around. By now the noon sun has caused some to find shade under trees and brush arbors. Once Hamilton has everyone's attention he puts his gun down. "Now hear up all you citizens of Transylvania County, North Carolina!" the Sheriff with his shiny new badge declares. "Let us hear from Mr. Francis W. Johnstone, a member of our honorable court here. He has important news for us." All faces turn to look at one of the justices who steps away from the other three.

F.W. Johnstone quickly steps up on a large stump near the preacher's platform and, after slowly and carefully surveying the crowd with an intense stare, he pulls out some papers. Following a pregnant pause, he addresses the gathering.

"My fellow Carolinians, fellow patriots of this God-given land. News has reached us over these days that Harpers Ferry has been seized by Virginia and Fort Sumter has surrendered. Seven states have seceded from the Union and others are following in the next days. The Yankees want to take away our rights, our homes and businesses, our way of life. They are aggressors, denying us what God has given us."

After a long pause for effect, he pulls out a telegram and waves it before the crowd, saying loudly, "Just now our mail courier rode in from Greenville with a telegram from our Honorable North Carolina Governor Ellis! Just yesterday, May 20, in the year of our Lord one thousand eight hundred sixty-one, as we were giving birth to this county, our leaders in Raleigh voted to join our sister states and to secede! Welcome to the Confederate States of America!"

Craf is already at the crowd's edge as pandemonium breaks out with shouts, screams, whistles and yells. He had heard the word 'hysteria' somewhere, but has never seen it before now. He hides behind his horse and empties his stomach. He leans his head on the soft side of his horse but then vomits up all the wonderful Hogsed food.

He holds to his horse and prays, "Oh Lord, let this be a bad dream. Please let it not happen. I see only darkness. Can you bring light? If it is true, help me to find the right way." Hoping it would somehow help, Craf barely whispers, "Amen."

As if the first announcement were not enough, an assertive Johnstone calls for quiet with the help of an inexperienced Sheriff Hamilton. A second shot rings out bringing the crowd to attention. "There is more. Governor Ellis has called for 30,000 volunteers to stand against this invasion from the North. We could form a company of militia from right here in Transylvania."

Craf wonders if his sweating is due to the warming sun or the intensity of the crowd. He fumbles for his water bottle, so lovingly woven over by Harriet, and lets the water soothe his thirst. He forces himself to watch the crowd resume their cheering. He wants to jump on his horse and ride home, but he knows that it would make him look like a traitor to these men, his people. So he watches the court members draw back into a whispering huddle behind the preacher's stand in order to try to take some action on the Governor's request. They finally face the gathering and the clerk announces, "This court hereby orders that each man who volunteers will receive fifteen dollars and will be subject to orders from the Governor."

To Craf's surprise the crowd is now stirring about, murmuring and definitely not cheering. The court quickly huddles together again, looking Craf thinks, very much like three school boys whispering. Craf slowly walks within ear shot.

"What is wrong?" asks Johnstone. "Are we missing something?"

Craf hears an intentional cough from the nearby Sheriff. He, too, is within earshot and is trying to get the justices' attention. The cough works because Johnstone makes eye contact with him and he invites Hamilton to join them. The cautious new Sheriff walks over to say, "They are worried about their families. Many will fight but they are hardworking farmers for the most part and have no one to care for their families."

Johnstone seems slightly confused. "Can't their slaves do most of the farming?"

Sheriff Hamilton, a little sarcasticly, responds, "Mister, you don't seem to understand. There are very few slaves in Transylvania, and most of them belong to you South Carolina folks who bring your household servants."

Johnstone, not sure if he should be offended, begins to unbutton his vest. The clerk interrupts and offers a proposal to the others on the court. They agree and he then faces the crowd to announce, "Upon further deliberation the Court should supply support for the families of volunteers who may be in want of necessities."

This seems to please the worried families but the Court has another immediate problem: where could they get the money they just promised? They have no taxes collected and no functioning local authorities . They quickly authorize their chairman to go to a bank in Asheville to borrow $1500 to pay the Transylvania volunteers.

As the day fades, Craf finally feels free to head home. As he passes the Johnstone home he now remembers that it is Captain Francis W. Johnstone who lives there. He will lead Company E of the 25th Regiment of North Carolina Volunteers. His earlier intuitive feelings become clearer now as he goes on, passing homes and businesses of those who feel God is calling them to not only keep humans as slaves but also now to break up the Union.

He soon begins his ascent up the mountain as he passes Dunn's Rock. He pauses halfway up the Greenville Turnpike to look over the peaceful and magnificent view of the mountains, his home. He knows his home will never be the same as he replays the images of his many friends and relatives at the gathering. He can still see them cheering and signing up with the North Carolina Militia. His heart is heavy.

Summer 2012

"The water is too cold!" Ellie was sticking her little toe in Trout Lake. Kevin and I were laughing at her and calling her a wimp. We had finally managed to get her to go swimming with us. I guess the restraining order and Mammaw's little trick meeting at Dolly's had done us some good. Ellie relaxed enough to go swimming with us without constantly looking over her shoulder. It had been a good two weeks now since the attack and summer was finally starting to feel like the summers I remembered.

"Come on, Ellie! Just jump in!" I yelled as I let myself float in the cool water. I looked up at the sky and was thrilled to see some clouds start to form. Maybe we would start having Transylvania's famous afternoon thunderstorms that cool the air.

Suddenly I saw Kevin run up behind Ellie and shove her in. Ellie screamed as she flew into the lake, but the scream sounded more like excitement than anything else. "Kevin! I'll kill you!" Ellie smiled. Kevin leaped into the air and landed a cannonball as close to the two of us as possible. As soon as his head poked back up from under the water he was met by bombarding splashes from both sides.

We played hard for at least an hour before we heard some rumbling off in the distance. We willingly climbed up onto the small dock, exhausted.

"Looks like we're goin' to have an afternoon thunderstorm," Kevin said to no one in particular.

I reached for my towel and dried off as best I could. "Mammaw will be happy to get some needed rain for her little garden."

Ellie wasn't paying attention. She seemed suddenly very intent on the other side of the lake.

"Ellie, what's wrong?" Kevin noticed her change in behavior too.

"Did you see the movement?" Ellie pointed to a section of the lake where an old tree had fallen into the lake, pulling up the dirt and roots behind it and leaving quite a hole in the bank. The uprooted base created a perfect hiding place.

Kevin and I stood still as we watched two figures emerge from behind the base and climb out as far as possible onto the tree. They stopped short of actually getting in the water.

"Junior and Roy! I should have guessed," Kevin whispered.

"Hey Kev! I see you and your girlfriend are getting' real comfy with that Mexican!" Roy yelled.

I looked around hoping some other Sherwood Forest residents would be joining us for a swim, or taking their dog for a walk, but then I remembered the looming storm. No way anyone would be heading this way.

"What do you want?" Kevin yelled. Ellie was quickly drying off and frantically looking for her flip-flops.

"You gotta come with us. We've got some work to do," Junior yelled. "Don't forget who feeds you!"

Kevin was silent for longer than I expected. I gently touched his arm. "Kevin, are you okay?"

"Do you need me to come and get you?" Junior turned toward the bank indicating that he was okay with coming over to us. As he started toward us I could see Roy grab Junior's arm. The two older boys seemed to suddenly be arguing about something until I could finally hear Junior yell at Roy, "Damn it! If I want to go and get my ungrateful brother there ain't nobody gonna stop me!"

Kevin suddenly took off in Junior's direction. "Just shut up, Junior. I'm comin', I'm comin.'"

"Kevin!" I yelled. "You don't have to go!" I thought I was being helpful, but once again I was wrong. For just a moment Kevin glanced back at us. I could feel the first drops of rain fall and I suddenly felt chilled as Kevin's eyes told me to back off.

1861: President Lincoln declares state of "Insurrection" not war; West Virginia votes to secede from Virginia; Kansas becomes 34th State, slave-free.

The Sad Report

It's getting dark and Harriet decides to walk to the turnpike for the fourth time today to look down the dirt road to see if Craf might be coming around the corner. Little Mitchel comes running after his mother with Julia, Wiley and Sarah toddling not far behind. Harriet smiles at her four young children all piling onto the rock wall. She quickly reaches over to embrace Wiley who thinks his mamma is there to catch him flying through the air. He jumps into her outreached arms. As soon as she puts him down Sarah yells, "Me, me," and flings herself at Harriet as well.

It is young Mitchel who breaks the merriment. "Is that Pa?" Harriet follows her son's pointing finger to find Craf coming with sagging shoulders and his head hanging low.

Harriet quickly sends the children back inside and tells Mitchel to fetch a big glass of cold spring water. Mitchel doesn't argue and taking one last look at his father, heads for the water.

Harriet meets her husband just as Mitchel returns. He quickly hands the glass to his mother accidently spilling some cool water onto her. She doesn't reprimand him, though. She just nods for him to go watch the younger children inside.

Harriet hands the water to her husband as he slowly dismounts. "Take this and sit in the rocker on the porch. Let me put the mare away."

Craf says weakly, "No, I'll do it. It's my job and besides I've done no work for two days."

"Honey," Harriet firmly says, "It appears that whatever you've been through was more than two weeks of hard work. Sit down. I'm a-doin' it."

She returns from the barn relieved to find Craf covered with giggling children loving on and playing with their father. However dark the world looks, this is God-given light for him. To some degree his prayer was answered.

With the kids soon in bed, Harriet joins Craf on the porch, making a simple, loving suggestion, "Tell me about it." She reaches out and gently takes his hand. He returns her gesture.

Craf reiterates most of the events in Brevard with considerable detail. Harriet reaches for a quilt to wrap around her shoulders to warm her from the cool night air. Refusing to go inside she continues to listen to her husband. He, too, doesn't want to move until he has finished. He finally confesses, "I worried about my feelings as I went by those places. I prayed for God to help me with them. I can't sit in judgment on anybody."

Harriet replies, "Now, Craf, don't be so hard on yourself. The way I understand it, feelings are feelings. It's what you do with them that matters. And I have never heard you passing any judgment on anybody, even folks who have slaves. You have your convictions about what is right and wrong and you try to live by them. You love people. You have a bigger heart than anybody I know."

His burden is suddenly lightened. Craf is thankful for the darkness so his wife doesn't see the few tears that manage to escape. "What would I do without you? You can lift me up when I am down. How did I ever deserve such a gift? I reckon I didn't ever. It's just grace!"

With a faux stern face Harriet says, "There you go! Bringing theology into this! But that's fine 'cause it goes both ways - you are my grace-gift!"

Craf shifts into a fake stern face and voice and says, "There you go talking theology. And you a woman! Wait 'til I tell them jack-leg preachers when they come through!"

They break into laughter, the first in weeks. It isn't long before they leave the darkness of the porch to find themselves under the same quilt finding relief and release in their love.

5

Summer 2012

"I don't get it!" I paced back and forth in the kitchen like that was somehow going to help me stamp out my frustration with Kevin. Why did he let Roy and Junior ruin our afternoon at the lake?

"Millie. Will you please stop pacin' and help me dry these dishes?" Mammaw slung the hand towel at me as I reached for the big pot from the spaghetti dinner we just finished.

I dried and put away the big pot, awkwardly shoving and clanging the rest of the pots in the same space until the noise was so awful that Mammaw finally put her hand on her hip and gave me a what the heck look. I stopped shoving. "What? I'm just putting the stupid pot away."

"Don't take your anger out on me, or the pot for that matter." Mammaw wasn't laughing.

"But Mammaw, why did Kevin go with those idiots? He stood up against them just the other day." I couldn't help it anymore. I started to cry, just like that. I felt like such a baby and my emotions surprised me. Why did I even care? Mammaw dropped her hand from her hip, came over to me and put her arms around me. I managed to sob, "It's like he doesn't care about what's right or wrong. He let them bully him."

I felt Mammaw stroke my hair. "It's not as easy as that. Remember Roy and Junior are Kevin's family. Right or wrong that counts for a lot!" She lifted my chin and made me look into her eyes. "And besides, you really don't know who he is protecting."

1861: President Lincoln signs into law the first income tax to pay for the Civil War: 3% from those making over $800 per year; Yale University grants the first American Ph.D. degrees; Matthew Brady and team start a photographic record of the war.

The Mail

Craf stands with the rest of the Cedar Mountain folk as Postmaster Thomas once again reads the news. Like many of their kin, friends and neighbors, Craf and his family try to go on with life as best they can, keeping their opinions to themselves, eagerly meeting the mailman for news from Greenville, be it in newspapers or letters, it is all bad.

On this day Craf notices the mailman rest and water his horse away from Postmaster Thomas and his reading of the news. Craf leaves the crowd and gently approaches. "Al?" The mailman is slightly startled, but quickly recovers and smiles at Craf's familiar face. Craf sits down on the grass beside Al. "I been a-wantin' to ask you, remember that day in May when you rode into Brevard at the founding of the county?"

Al shifts ever so slightly. "Of course, how could I forget it?"

"Well," Craf notices Al gets up and seems suddenly more attentive to his horse, "Harriet was here that day, but Postmaster Thomas told her you rode right through here and never stopped. How come?"

"Now, Craf," Al finally looks down at the mountain man sitting on the grass and answers somewhat condescendingly, "If you were in Brevard, you should know why! I had that telegram from the Governor of North Carolina to get to Brevard!"

"Al," Craf jumps up, briefly, intentionally knocks the grass off the back of his britches and walks up to Al. "You did not have to tell anybody here about the telegram, but did you not have regular mail for many of us?"

A sheepish Al responds, "I reckon, but you-uns got it all the next time."

Craf places a heavy hand on the mailman's shoulder. "Al, I've known you a long time. Tell me, what is going on?"

Almost in tears he responds, "Ever thang is upside down in Greenville. The Confederates control 'bout ever-thang and I was told not to stop here 'cause they'd heard too many folks was on the wrong side."

Craf turns Al to face the farmers and mountain folk still shaking their heads and mourning as they drink in the words Postmaster Thomas pours from the paper. "Look around you, Al, do you see any blue uniforms? And lots of our kin are wearing gray uniforms. Most of us are trying to provide for our families and stay out of the way."

Al shakes his head and pulls away from Craf's touch. "Craf, I know that, but them folks down there don't. 'Sides, they think 'bout everybody up here is ignorant, illiterate and dangerous."

A small laugh escapes from Craf. He tries to fight the familiar need to prove himself, but he just can't help it.

His anger pushes him from his practiced teacher's tongue into his local dialect. "Next time them folks commence 'a-talkin' like that, ask 'em how come we-uns git so much mail here if'n we can't read, and tell 'em how we-uns here treat you-uns and others that come through these here parts. They're not to fergit the lodges and hotels for Greenville and Charleston folks that give 'em lodging. I ain't askin' for praise, but tell 'em 'bout my puttin' up for free a lot of the beef that lands on to their tables and in their fat bellies!" Craf is suddenly aware how angry he is and, slipping back from his mother tongue into a more accepted English, apologizes to Al, "I'm real sorry. Please don't say anything. They will believe what they want to. I'm sorry they are so hard on you. Just do the best you can. You are our lifeline to the world out there."

Al looks at Craf. He suddenly looks paler than before. "Craf, there's one more thang."

Craf is suddenly worried that his friend is sick. "Are you okay?"

Al walks over to one of the pouches on his horse. He pulls out a poster rolled up tightly between his fingers. "I wanted to hand it to Postmaster Thomas kinda like I'd about forgot. I just couldn't bear seeing you-uns readin' it."

Al walks past Craf and into the crowd. He hands the poster to the postmaster who immediately nails it to the bulletin board.

As Craf and the others gather to read it, a tightness grows in Craf's chest. The poster announces that President Jefferson Davis will soon get the conscription law, requiring every able-bodied man to report for duty to fight for the Confederate cause.

Craf turns to see the back of Al's hanging head as he and his horse strike out northward, down the Greenville Turnpike towards Brevard.

Although he lives close by, the walk home feels forever. He pulls Harriet out onto the porch immediately. He almost can't bear the look of horror on the face of his eternally strong wife. She finally whispers, almost as if cursing, "It looks like that death angel will come back, not just for young-uns this time."

Craf cannot find any words of comfort. "It may or may not mean death, but it sure does not mean life!" After a silence while both ponder the same question, Craf finally speaks. "Harriet, I just can't do it."

Harriet hopes he is thinking what she is thinking. "Do what?"

"Leave you and the kids. I don't know what to do." Craf thrusts his head into his hands as he rests his arms on his knees. His fingers comb frantically through his thinning hair. He suddenly looks at his wife, feeling very much like a trapped animal. "I hear already what they are doing to men who will not go -- and their families and farms. You go at gun point!"

Harriet tries to comfort her husband, but feels frantic herself. "I knew that. We've been spared this long. Can you just hide out?"

Craf suddenly stands, runs one hand down over his short beard and looks at his wife with a fierceness she has rarely seen. "Try to understand, when they set this up, they will enforce it with troops or some sort of home guard. I reckon I could hide out like an animal, but that just isn't right and there is greater danger for you and the kids. That is not an option for me." Harriet's gentle giant storms off the porch and yells over his shoulder, "I've got to pray about this." Without looking back he heads off into the woods. Harriet does not follow. She knows he is heading for Rich Mountain or Panther Mountain to spend time on a smooth rock where he will call to the mountains for answers he knows won't come easily.

For a few days Harriet watches Craf work the land harder than ever. At dinner his silence upsets the children, but Harriet simply tells them their Pa isn't feeling well. Harriet knows Craf is anything but a cowardly man and he has to make a decision before some of the so-called "recruiters" round him up. Everyone has heard bad stories of how they treat able-bodied men and their families who have not come forward. As much as anything he has to protect his family.

Harriet is particularly worried one day when Craf is gone longer than she expected. When he finally arrives home he finds her in the kitchen bending over a large wooden bowl. She is attempting to make some biscuits, but Craf sees they may not even rise because she is kneading the dough too vigerously and for too long. He knows she is actually letting out some emotion and he watches her pull herself together as she turns to look at her husband who is attempting to embrace her. "I'm sorry I've been gone so long, Harriet. I've been talking to some of the Hamiltons, McGahas, Cantrells, Blythes and others down at the Moore mill. Some of them are signing up with the Union and really are against slavery. Our own relatives, Volney Hamilton and his brother Joseph and two of his sons have already joined the Union forces, along with the beloved Baptist preacher Reverend Allison. Most families are split. And I wonder how our new Sheriff Hamilton will deal with it being as many are his relatives. "

Harriet takes a deep breath and wipes a wisp of hair out of her face leaving some flour on her cheek. "Craf, what have you decided? Are you going with them?"

Craf shakes his head and sits down at the table. "No, my heart is with them but I fear that in order to protect all of you, I'll be forced to go with the Confederates. It's like I don't have a choice."

A little less aggressively Harriet pats the dough flat and grabs a tin cup from a nail on the wall. Turning it upside down she begins to cut biscuits. "I was afraid that would happen. We are surrounded mostly by Confederate sympathizers, and Brevard, our new county seat, is a hotbed of folks pulling for Jefferson Davis and Robert E. Lee. I just heard that ole Babe Cooper knocked some holes in the rock walls of his distillery in case the Yankees come either way on the turnpike."

Craf looks a little shocked at the information his wife has gathered. "Harriet, does Babe have cannons too?"

A little smile emerges from Harriet. "Nope. I guess he thinks Robert E. Lee will give him a couple just to protect good whiskey!"

Craf smiles at her attempt at humor during such a hard time. But the lightness is fleeting. "Harriet, you know that some of my close friends from these parts will also be shooting at me, at us. I just hope it does not come to that. Few families are not split. It's clear some McGahas will be on both sides."

Harriet washes her hands in the basin and wipes them clean on her apron. She kneels before him. She folds her arms and rests her head in his lap. She feels him touch her head and whispers, "I'd hate to be a mother sending sons off to war, fearing they will be killed, possibly by close kin."

Craf lifts her chin to find tears have replaced the smile. The flour is now a messy white smudge. "Well, my love, we can be thankful we are not. I will promise you I'll come home as soon as I can, back to you and our children. And if I make it home alive, we'll build that little church we've been talking about since we first met."

With tears still flowing, Harriet tries to smile. "Ha! You have been thinking about that long before you knew me. Don't tell me that all those times you were providing hospitality for drover families, travelers, and circuit riding preachers of all faiths, that you were not playing church!"

Craf tries to wipe his wife's face, very aware that she is taking in every touch as if it were their last. "I guess you are right, Harriet. You usually are. You have insight into these things better than I do."

That evening Craf holds his wife tightly after he hugs each child longer than usual at bedtime. He whispers in her ear, "I must leave before daylight to head for Brevard." Putting his hands on her cheeks, he looks into her eyes and assures her, "My love, do not worry. Try to keep the farm and garden going. We've a lot of kin and good neighbors who can help. Be very careful of strangers." Harriet can only nod. She feels sick and hopes that it is only from her worries, yet the nausea feels overwhelmingly familiar. Sadness fills her as she pushes away the thought of having to bear this worry without her husband.

Finally, in July, 1861, the name James C. McGaha is added to the Muster Roll of the Transylvania Volunteers 1861, led by Captain Francis W. Johnstone. In July, 1862, the Brevard Confederate soldiers march to Waynesville to join the 62nd North Carolina Infantry Company.

Summer 2012

"Hello? Anybody home?" I could hear Kevin's voice float through the screen door. I was sitting on the overly floral couch and was looking at Pappaw's old fiddle. I had pulled out the worn case this time. It was pretty beat up but it would still open and close. Mammaw had told me I could examine it anytime I wanted to, but I hadn't really felt like it until then. I really had no intention of going anywhere that Wednesday. I was tired of Kevin not standing up to his brothers and I didn't feel like seeing Kevin or even Ellie. I just wanted to hang out at Mammaw's. As I gently turned the fiddle over to admire the maple on the back I heard Kevin again. "I can see you, Millie. I know you're in there."

I didn't look away from the fiddle as I yelled, "Door's open!"

"Wow! Is that yours?" Kevin took no time at all to sit down on the couch next to me and reach for the fiddle.

"Hey, careful! It's my Pappaw's and it was his dad's and his dad's, or something like that." I looked at Kevin to see him looking in awe. I smiled. "Cool, huh?"

"Can I?" Kevin held out his hand to the fiddle.

I looked at him and there was a look of confidence that screamed at me to trust him. I finally held the fiddle out to him like I was offering a sacrifice. "Okay, just don't break it."

He smiled at me, almost like he was saying be quiet little girl. He took the fiddle and placed it up to his neck like it belonged there. He reached into the case and pulled out the bow. His fingers suddenly began to move like they were remembering a familiar dance. The sound was terrible, but Kevin kept a serious look on his face and concentrated on something only he could see and hear. He twisted and turned knobs and screeched out a few more notes. That's when a huge smile suddenly crossed his face. "Are you ready?"

I snorted, "To stop being tortured? YEAH!" That's when it happened. Kevin paid me no attention and suddenly the room was filled with unbelievable sound-- no, it was music.

I can't really explain it, but I was suddenly with a different person.

Kevin's eyes were closed like he himself decided to check out while this new Kevin possessed him. I sat completely still as Kevin finished one song and moved into the next. Some I recognized like Amazing Grace and I'll Fly Away, but the rest were new to me. The last song in particular, seeped into my gut. It was despairing and full of such sorrow that I felt tears well up.

Suddenly silence filled the room. It almost hurt. The old Kevin was back as he sheepishly put the fiddle and the bow back into the case. His cheeks were beginning to turn pink. It suddenly dawned on me that I hadn't said anything the whole time. "Oh, my God, Kevin! That was unbelievable!" I jumped up and practically shoved him off the couch.

A huge smile washed the pink away. "You really think so? I done wrote the last one!"

"You're kidding! I can't believe how great you are. You should like study this or something. Or, hey, maybe you can be like a performer in one of those symphonies." I was jumping around the room like I had just discovered gold.

"Hang on there, Millie," Kevin stood up to help put the fiddle away. As we walked into the back bedroom he helped me put the case back on the top shelf. "You know I cain't do that. I got to watch out for Ma."

I suddenly thought about Mammaw's comment. Kevin is always thinking about someone else and here I go always getting ticked at him for not standing up for himself. So even though I thought he should run away and become a big fiddle player, I shut down my first gut reaction and just smiled. "Kevin, I guess you've got to do what you've got to do."

Kevin smiled at me. "Thanks, Millie. I know that's not really what you're thinkin', but I'll take it." This time I could feel my cheeks burn, but just as I was about to give a rebuttal Kevin became excited. "Hey, I got a good idea. Go grab Ellie and meet me up at the big rocks in about a half hour."

"What? Where are the big rocks?" I was not sure what the heck he was talking about.

"Ellie knows." Kevin was already shooting out the screen door. "Half hour."

"Great! So much for staying home." I yelled to the disappearing figure. As the silence grew I could still feel the sorrow Kevin shared through his music.

1862: President Lincoln's third son dies; Over 23,000 from both sides die at Antietam. The Gatling gun is invented; The Ironclads, Monitor and Merrimac do battle.

The Death Angel

Harriet rocks gently in front of the cold fireplace. It is late spring and there is no need for wasting wood. She reaches out her hand to stroke Craf's empty rocking chair. She places a small notebook on her lap and begins to write.

My Dear Craf, it has not been a good year for the McGaha family as for most families. Like many, our kin, friends and neighbors, we go on with survival as best they can, keeping our opinions to ourselves. But we still eagerly meet the mailman for news from Greenville, be it in newspapers or letters. It is all bad.

Harriet pauses dreading the real news. She finds strength from within and continues.

My dear husband as if the reality of war is not enough the death angel has come a calling. Little Mitch has died. I know you feared this when he was a baby, but it seems he never overcame his early weaknesses. Then four-year old Wiley passed.

I gave birth to a beautiful baby girl, Hattie, who only lived a few days. No one knows if it is the consumption or what.

Harriet can almost not continue. She rocks for a moment before she goes on.

I have been very fortunate to have many folks help in various ways caring for Juliet, now five, and Sally Sarah, now four. The two girls are doing well, although they miss their brothers terribly. My sweet Nancy, even as a widow, has been by to help. I don't know what I would do if I didn't have her and your sisters and brother. That is right my dear husband. Eliza, Polly Ann, Joe and William have all been taking turns with household chores for some time. When it comes to crops there is not much difference since they usually helped us anyway with planting and harvesting. Sometimes a younger McGaha nephew or niece will stay some days to do the milking, and watch the cattle, sheep and hogs.

Harriet wipes her eyes and runny nose on her handkerchief.

It is a good time to have so many relatives and friends. Craf, I feel our hospitality for others has come full circle. I long to help in return, but I have so little I can give.

I miss you my Gentle Giant. I do hope this letter finds you.

Before Harriet signs her name she tenderly kisses the paper.

Summer 2012

The rocks were huge. It felt like we had discovered a secret fortress deep in the woods. Ellie said they were known as High Rocks or House Rocks. I was a little jealous that she knew so much more about this community than I did and was about to ask her why that was the case when Kevin came through the path in the forest we had just emerged from. His smile was so big he looked like he was about to burst. I could see a dark brown long duffle swinging on his back.

"Come on." He waved to us as we followed him into the woods along a well worn-path leading away from the Cedar Mountain community. The rhododendron smell mixed with the growing humidity, now that afternoon showers had returned, and almost made it hard to breathe.

"Where are we going?" I asked as I stepped over a small creek.

"You'll see." Ellie was also ahead of me and she turned and cupped her mouth as if whispering. "It's really beautiful." I looked at the two of them trekking ahead of me and thought they looked awfully comfortable, like they'd done this hike a million times, and maybe even together.

I soon got used to the sudden rises and dips of the hike through the forest, really enjoying the memories of earlier summers flooding back. Mom and Dad loved to hike these mountains. We would drive up to the parkway and hike Black Balsam where we stared down on the vast mountain ranges over a picnic lunch. I knew we weren't on that hike, but the memories made me suddenly miss my parents.

"We're here!" Kevin stood proudly where the path opened up into a field. I didn't even know there were fields this high on any mountaintops. It took me a minute to realize Ellie and Kevin had already climbed over a fence and walked to a smooth flat rock that allowed them to take in an unbelievable view. I realized we were actually staring back at the Blue Ridge Parkway. I quickly joined them and sat down between Kevin and Ellie.

"This is unbelievable!" I couldn't stop staring at the continued rise and fall of the mountains which were gently spotted with an occasional home. Off to my right I could actually make out Mount Pisgah rising slightly above the other peaks, of course accented by its famous TV tower.

Suddenly I heard the beautiful sound I had heard earlier in the day. I hadn't noticed Kevin pull out a fiddle from his backback. The fiddle was newer than Pappaw's, but the same melodies poured from Kevin's fingertips. I looked at Ellie to see if she was as surprised as I had been earlier, but was a little disappointed to find her stretched out, eyes closed, with her hands behind her head just soaking up the sun and the music.

I looked at Kevin to say something to him but found his concentration so intense that I also settled for no conversation and let myself be filled with intense sensory overload.

1863: President Lincoln signs the Emancipation Proclamation freeing all slaves; Many bloody battles occur; The Gettysburg Address is given by Lincoln.

The August Furlough

"Hello?" Harriet quickly hangs her apron on the hook behind the kitchen door. She hurries into the living area to greet the stranger coming through the door, maybe another hungry wanderer who needs shelter for the night. Her mind is scrambling to think what she can cook up since she just finished cleaning up the kitchen later than usual. She spent more time with Sally Sarah and Juliet this evening and thought the dishes could wait. Any hint of a cold or a cough sends Harriet spinning into a mother worry time, knowing that her children are only a gift for a short time. Sally Sarah's recent cough made her drop everything.

"Harriet?" A familiar voice barely whispers.

"Oh my God! Craf!" Harriet rushes to her man. His frail body feels unfamiliar in her hungry arms. "Why, Craf, you're nothin' but skin an' bones." She tries to smile but the weariness in his eyes is beyond her comprehension.

"Harriet," he whispers more to himself than her. He squeezes her hand as he tries to return her smile.

"I'm here. Just set yourself down." Harriet leads him to his rocking chair. Pulling up her rocking chair beside him she takes his hand in hers. They sit. Silence is all Harriet receives. No war stories. No glory. Just her husband, but this is all Harriet needs right now. It is then that Harriet sees a piece of paper in Craf's other hand as he barely reveals it. He doesn't look at his wife for fear of seeing her disappointment when she reads that he is only on a brief furlough.

"So I reckin this is how it is," Harriet finally breaks the silence with strong feeling in her mountain accent. "They send soldiers home half broken and starved fer us women folk to fatten back up and send back out to fight and git kilt." When Craf doesn't answer, she just scoots as close as she can and decides to breathe in and savor every minute she has been given with her gentle giant.

Summer 2012

I could hear the rumble, just a faint memory at first. It's like that first smell of a twig of pine that makes you think of Christmas. Thunder rolling is Transylvania in the summer, a heaviness more like a huge washcloth that moves in to cover you up, scrub you down and then move on, somehow leaving you refreshed, in spite of its harshness.

"Let's go." I heard Kevin jump up and begin to pack his fiddle tightly away, almost like tucking a baby neatly into its cradle.

"Already?" I whined, not wanting the moment to end.

"Yes, already!" Kevin wasn't very happy with my reluctance. "We need to get back before the storm hits and it looks like we may not make it." He pats his bag gently. "I really don't want my fiddle gettin' wet."

"By the looks of it," Ellie gently shoved Kevin, "your fiddle will be dryer than any of us." Ellie then took off running into the woods yelling , "Of course, my Momma will ground me if I come back soaking wet again." There was just something to that again that began to make me wonder more than ever if Kevin and Ellie had been friends for a long time, something I just didn't get, considering my first disastrous encounter with Kevin this summer.

As we rushed through the forest at a pace I was not used to, I could feel the storm moving in. The thunder began to be accompanied by a loud clapping and bright light. The two were still more than twenty seconds apart, but I knew that we were getting ready for the ultimate drenching. The faster we ran and the louder the thunder got, the more my heart raced with excitement. Small droplets began to cool my body, caressing my forearms and face.

I found myself blindly following the two bodies running ahead of me. Suddenly I was racing up a little hill along a seemingly old dirt road. I could see El Capitán at the base of the little hill and wondered why we weren't headed there. Just as the heavens opened up and rain pelted down I head Elli, "In here." I was standing in front of a very old wooden church. It was built on what looked like stilts made of three wide stones that held the church up about every three feet. Kevin was already climbing in one of the three windows on the right side. He quickly pulled Ellie in and reached his arm out to me as I just stood in the rain and gawked. "Well, are you comin'?" I grabbed his arm and he pulled me in onto one of the pews made of the widest single boards I'd ever seen.

"Where the heck are we?" I finally said as I looked around at the very simple sanctuary. There were pews all the way up to the front and two long pews then faced the rest of the benches with a small wooden pulpit standing between them.

"Welcome to McGaha Chapel!" Kevin smiled as he stretched himself on a pew, letting the drops of rain drip from his head onto what seemed to me sacred ground.

1863: Pro-Confederate Quantrill's Raiders strike a Kansas town, killing 150 people with the help of Frank and Jesse James as well as the Younger brothers.

The Hume Rock Hotel

"Missus Jane, when Massa Robert come home?" Betsy asks. The daylight has faded and finishing off the evening dishes Betty and the other two slaves have a few moments with their owner who sits quietly at the kitchen table. The three slaves have been with Jane Hume since Jane and her husband Robert, who are part of the "colony" from Charleston, built their successful rock hotel in1849. Although they provide accommodations primarily for the summer visitors seeking to escape from South Carolina heat and disease, the Humes are also active in raising money and building the Episcopal Church in Dunn's Rock, St Paul's in the Valley. With more than twenty slaves, the Humes also manage more than eighteen hundred acres in the valley.

"Mr. Hume is gone to Charleston to raise money for our little St. Paul's church here. We hope he'll be home anytime." She is anxious, even though many folks on the turnpike stop to water their horses outside the hotel where the road crosses the little branch. Still she is fearful because she has heard of the horrible actions of the bushwhackers- their murders, raping, theft and burning. No one knows which side they might be on, but usually they are deserters or outlaws, taking advantage of the lack of home protection. The Humes and twenty-one of their slaves had left the war actions in Charleston thinking the mountains were safer. They have become year-round residents in their Dunn's Rock Hotel, called by locals, the "Hume Hotel," by others, the "Rock Hotel."

Betsy nods and tries not to let the growing darkness outside take control of her as she sees the worry in Mrs. Hume's eyes. All four women are suddenly still as they hear a gentle, quiet knock at the back kitchen door. They look at each other wondering who would be knocking. Guests use only the front door.

"Are you 'spectin' guests?" Betsy looks to Mrs. Hume for answers.

"No Betsy, we're closed for the season." She tries to smile reassuringly at the three women who have already found potential weapons- - an ax, a piece of stove wood and a kitchen knife. The knock is repeated with a little more urgency. "I'm sure it's just a neighbor in need." Jane Hume slowly cracks the door. She can barely make out the figure of a skinny disheveled man she does not recognize. His white face is pale against the outline of dark, stringy hair. "Who is it?"

"Ma'am?" The voice is a whisper.

"Who is it?" Jane repeats as she motions for the three slave women to stay close to her.

"Ma'am, you-uns ain't a-knowin' th' likes of me. I ain't a-goin' to hurt you-uns." He shifts awkwardly looking once over his shoulder.

"Well, Mister, what do you want?" She speaks through the crack in the door.

"Ma'am, I done snuk off frum th' other fellers who is a-campin' up Dunn's Creek." He steps back from the door.

Jane notices the motion and opens the crack a little more, "What are you doing here then? Why sneak off?"

As Jane opens the door another inch more, the light from the inside reveals the man is little more than a boy. He shifts nervously, keeping Jane on the defensive, although something about him doesn't seem right. He keeps his distance as he whispers as audibly as possible, "Cuz they's real mean, them fellers, an' they'd hurt me bad fur a-comin' here to warn you-uns." He starts to back off, trying to hide himself from the light.

Jane glances at the three women behind her, still clutching their weapons. She looks back at the young man, confused, "Warn us about what?"

The young man awkwardly steps forward so they can see the serious look in his eyes. He does not want to say this more than once, "You gonna git burned out tonight, 'bout midnight or earlier. You-uns better git gone real fast afore they, I mean we, gits here."

The man turns to go, but Jane, alarmed and therefore losing her caution, runs after him, "Oh my God! Where? How? What?" She finds herself standing vulnerably face to face with a stranger who seems to hold her future captive.

The young man is visibly shaken by Jane's closeness. He takes a moment to think. He finally points toward the mountain that gently slopes upward behind the magnificent rock building. "Jist, git up Mill Hill as fast as ye kin. Not up Dunn's Creek road. They's a-comin' that-a-way."

Trying to collect her composure, Jane Hume says, "I thank you Mr. whoever, for warning us and saving us. I am deeply indebted to you. What can I do for you?"

She tries to reach out and touch his arm, but he flinches away. She does not try again. But he does look her in the eye, "Jist pray fer Billy Boy who done got hisself in with th' wrong bunch." Silence fills the night air as Jane stands in the fresh fall breeze until the sudden sound of a horse galloping into the dark toward Dunn's Rock and the road up the creek.

Fear and a sense of urgency grip Jane as she realizes no help is anywhere nearby. She runs back into the house not bothering to close the door behind her and she grabs her family Bible, some papers, and a wrap for her shoulders. Collecting what they can, all four women rush from the Rock Hotel and scramble into the darkness. Before she crosses the little bridge on the turnpike and up Mill Hill, she turns to the three terrified slave women. "Quickly, run down Island Ford Road to your house. It's far enough away from the hotel that it looks like some other settler's home. It's around a curve and they should not be after you, but we cannot take a chance."

"But we ain't 'bout to leave you all by yoreself. We 'posed to be yore help." Betsy is in tears as she holds onto her favorite cooking pot and cutting knife.

Jane replies, "You are helping me if you get on home and out of sight. I'll be okay and just might have to spend the rest of the night down with you in the slave house."

"We'll fix up a pad downstairs fer you , Ma'am."

As a tearful Jane heads up the turnpike on Mill Hill, she wonders, "Why us? What have the Humes done to deserve this?" But she knows the answer may never come. She hears galloping horses stop at the foot of the hill. As she reaches the hilltop curve she hears a loud roar and turns to see flames leaping into the clear night sky, lighting up the face of Dunn's Rock as bright as day.

Now fearful the bushwhackers might ride up the same road that she walks, she steps into the woods below the curve, remembering the old Indian Cave nearby and a logging road connecting to Island Ford Road. Jane knows she is safer by taking Betsy up on her offer and gives up her desire to be as far away from the burning as possible. Before she gets to the cave between her and the slave house, she sees a kerosene lantern coming toward her.

"Missus Hume?" A shaky voice calls out. Betsy's husband, John, reaches out his large hand to pull her toward the cave out of sight from the turnpike above.

Grabbing his hand she allows herself to be pulled in closer. "Oh, thank God! Yes, I am here, headed your way down the branch. Just talk to me in whispers and put out the lantern, lest they see us." They hear horses riding up Mill Hill above them.

"Yes'um. Come this-a-way. You ain't far from our house. We done got you a pad fer th' night, if'n you kin sleep." In few minutes they sneak into the back door of the slave house.

After the obvious relief in Betsy's eyes assures Jane she had made the right choice, they all try to settle in, but sleep they do not, and all gather in the upstairs room of the tightly locked house. Looking out the window, they watch the glow of the fire and its reflection off Dunn's Rock until daybreak.

Summer 2012

The musty smell of the old church was more than a mix between old wood and damp summer afternoons. It wasn't unpleasant. It just made me curious about this building I had never noticed before although it stood so close to the Greenville Highway. I ran my fingers down the back of the pew I was sitting on admiring the very wide plank and tried to imagine how large the tree must have been.

"Cool, huh?" Kevin was now sitting up from his pew right in front of me. Ellie popped her head up in the pew in front of him.

I smiled at my two new friends who had pulled me into a Transylvania I had never known before. "Yeah, cool!" I agreed.

"It was built sometime in the late 1800s." Kevin was looking at the front of the church now where the small wooden pulpit looked lonely. "Something like that. . ." He looked at me awkwardly like he felt stupid for not finishing. He quickly disappeared again as he stretched. Then his voice spoke, almost as an afterthought, "Good place to get away from it all."

Ellie was still sitting up with her head facing me, but she slowly turned her head to stare out the window near her. The rain was beginning to beat down on roof of the small sanctuary and I could barely hear Ellie agree, "Yes, it is!"

1863: West Virginia joins the Union as the 35th State; Anti-draft riots hit New York City with the cry "rich man's war, poor man's fight."

Mail Time

It's November and Harriet pulls her shawl in more tightly around her shoulders as she gathers with others to hear the postmaster read the weekly newspaper. Her emptiness feels even greater since Craf's brief visit and Harriet feels that in some obscure way the weekly gathering is the one thing that makes her feel closer to her husband. The post office gatherings, however, are increasingly tense because families have loved ones in both armies and all equally hunger for word -- any word.

Harriet watches members from the Jones, Hamiltons, McGahas and other families as they gather close when Postmaster F.L.D. Thomas begins to read the Greenville newspaper. As his voice rises above the crowd Harriet has to hide a smile when she realizes the postmaster has "accidentally" pulled out a Knoxville newspaper. No one dares to interrupt as they hold onto every word as he reads:

Military News: On October 6 this year, a group of hardy mountain men from Henderson County, North Carolina was mustered into Captain Joseph Hamilton's F Company, 2nd North Carolina Mounted Infantry, Volunteers, United States Army, having been organized on October 1st. For obvious security reasons names of these brave men will not be made public, but it is stated that they are of the finest mountain stock and will surely serve bravely. Word is that many are related or close friends. This paper thanks these soldiers for choosing to fight to preserve the Union of our states.

There are no outbursts, no outcries, just sighs and a few tears. Joe Hamilton and many of his men are kin to many of those present. Even Transylvania's own Sheriff Robert Hamilton was kin to several including the captain.

Harriet can only wipe away her tears, knowing that her Craf had close friends, kin and neighbors who shared convictions and who were now declared enemies. She quickly steps over to hug Solomon Jones' wife, Mary, and Big Joe McGaha's wife, as they stand apart from the others, knowing their men were in this Union Army F Company. Harriet scans the faces of all who are present as they watch the postmaster finally read the Greenville paper. Some are relieved to have a distraction, but the pain and fear is clear, so the tears tell what words cannot.

Summer 2012

The pounding rain only lasted twenty minutes before the dark clouds rushed on to release their fury on another community in the mountains. In those twenty minutes Kevin remembered he had a pack of cards in his duffle bag and we played a round of Crazy Eights, the only game we all knew.

"Looks like the rain's stopped," Ellie stated the obvious. We were all reluctant to let the small adventure end, but I could tell Ellie was needing to take off. "I've really got to get back to the restaurant." She looked out a window closest to El Capitán, which stood at the base of the hill. "I know Mom's worried about what I'm doing out in the rain. . . especially since she thinks Millie and I went on a hike."

"And Kevin," I corrected her.

"Yeah, sorry," Ellie added awkwardly, "And Kevin."

Kevin stood up quickly to open the window we had all climbed in through what seemed only moments ago. Ellie followed him and she let him help her out the window as she waved to me. I waved back and suddenly she was gone. Kevin and I were alone. It didn't feel strange, though. I helped him gather the cards together and couldn't stop smiling.

"What're you smilin' at?" Kevin laughed at my stupid grin.

"Nothin'" I looked at this boy I hadn't wanted to be near a few weeks ago, "Actually. Thanks for taking me with you. I had a great time."

"Yeah, me too!" Kevin stood, slung his duffle bag over his shoulder and walked over to the window again. He held his hand out to me. "You coming?"

I took a final deep breath letting the musty smell flood my senses one more time. Then I let Kevin help me out the window. His hand was firm and strong. Suddenly I realized that I had not been angry with Kevin since he picked up Pappaw's fiddle. I felt myself turn slightly red and was hoping Kevin didn't see me. When he let go of my hand I awkwardly said, "Thanks," and turned to head down the hill.

"Wait, Millie," Kevin's voice yelled as he quickly closed the window and jumped down to follow me. "What's the hurry? I'll walk you home."

I felt myself blush again. "Okay. Sure." That's all I managed. But I looked at Kevin briefly and caught him smiling. "So what are you laughing at?"

"You're just funny, Millie." He laughed out loud this time. "One minute you're so calm and having fun, the next minute you're rushing off and getting all red in the face!" Then he punched me in the arm.

So he had seen me. Now I was embarrassed. I quickly pulled myself together and pretended to rub my arm as if I was hurt. "Now that's no way to treat your girlfriend."

It was Kevin's turn to turn red.

1863: The War Department orders draft of all able-bodied men aged 20-46 for the Union Army, unless they can pay $300 for a waiver; 35-inch Tom Thumb marries 32-inch Lavinia Warren as Showman P.T. Barnum watches; Nine Union Ironclads fail to take Charleston Harbor.

The December Letter

"Go on open it!" Candice nudges her daughter-in-law.

Harriet sits down in Craf's rocking chair, thankful that his parents have come over to help with the children today. Jesse is pacing nervously. "What're you waiting for?" His voice is slightly rougher than he intends it to be.

Harriet cannot keep her hands from shaking and she knows it is not from the growing winter chill. She looks at the neatly addressed envelope in her hand. Harriet gently smiles as she caresses the letters that form her name. For a moment her worries and wonders are suspended. Religiously she has been writing Craf weekly. At times she has had to pull from somewhere deep inside herself to keep the letters positive, a task growing increasingly difficult. As she looks at the letter she almost dares not open it, holding onto the moment full of expectation. Soon she gives in and lets the words unravel.

Marshall 1863
Madison County, N.C. Oct 15th

> *Dear wife and children. Again through the kind merces of our blessed savior I am permitted to let you know that I am tolerable well. Truly hopeing that this may find you and the children all alive and well. Yes I hope and pray that when I hear from you to hear that Sarah is well and all the rest for I haven't heard a word from you since I left you. The mail came here from Asheville a few minutes ago and brought me nothing. I will say to you that the day that I wrote to you last at Reems Creek Gen Vance gave orders to Harris to send 10 men on a scout to Paint Rock. Harris detailed me for one. We went to Paint Rock and got back here to Marshall this morning and found our Co. here. Gen Vance has moved his headquarters here. All of Woodfins calvary is here. There is I think some 400 mounted men here. They are fighting in Tenn rapid. The Yankees has run our men from Morristown to Limestone above Greenville. When I last wrote I thought we would go to Cherokee but we will not. We will go into Tennessee as soon as Woodfin gets all his men together. I think we leave here soon in 2 or 3 days. I thought I would get to drive a wagon*

but we will not have any wagons at all. I suppose we will have to carry all that we have on our horses. There is bush whackers plenty about Paint Mountain. We captured a negro while out on our scout. He belongs to a man in Greenville Tenn. We will keep him to cook and curry our horses. Still direct your letters to Asheville and they will follow me. We are now attached to Woodfins command. Just say on the back of your letters Mr JC McGaha in care of I.A. Harris Woodfins Calvary Asheville NC and I will get them. I want to hear from you all very bad as the children was not well when I left. Write often and tell me how you are getting along and whether Yewbanks moved or not. There is many things I could write to you if I had time but it would only make you uneasy and trouble you so I say to you that I am here in this war as you are aware among bushwhackers and many other dangers. I shall be in Tenn soon and if I don't come out you need not be uneasy. I may never live to come out and I may be captured. I cant get letters quick as we will be from place to place but write often. So dear wife all I can do for you is to say to you to do the best you can and take care of the children and yourself and remember the prayers of your husband is with you and your babes. Farewell.

JC to H McGaha

Harriet weeps and weeps when she reads the letter over and over. What has happened to her many epistles? Should she have mailed them at the Dunn's Rock post office? And now to hear he is obviously concerned for his life as well as for them is just too much.

"Well, Papa Jesse McGaha, what do you think?" Harriet finally asks the man so eager to hear, yet awfully quiet now.

He sits silently trying to compose himself, then responds, "He loves you. And the kids. He worries that you-uns is all well. I'm right relieved that he's headed for Tennessee. I had no idea that he was amidst them bushwhackers there in Bloody Madison. We can give thanks he is movin' away from them."

By this time, Candice has regained some composure and gently lays a hand on her daughter-in-law's arm. "Now, Harriet, we are a-goin' to help out 'til he gets home. And he will. I just know it. You just keep writin' them letters, a-hopin' some get through and do tell him we is a- helping you here."

Harriet returns her loving gesture by cupping her hand over Candice's, but she too can feel a slight shaking in the older woman's touch. For all parties present, the feared word has been spoken: bushwhackers. They sit silently, afraid of putting into words what they are all thinking. The burning of the Hume Hotel down the mountain in Dunn's Rock was a shock to all. These men are like animals and have brought havoc across the mountains, killing, stealing, burning, looting, raping, and committing every conceivable crime known to humans. Their neighbor, Phil Sitton, had been forced to make a big meal for a group of such villains, after which they laughingly thanked him by shooting him. Robert Thomas had been murdered over on Willow Creek in Henderson County and one visitor, a Mr. Peahuff, had been murdered and robbed on the road right there in Cedar Mountain.

Finally the silence is too great and Jessie can't take it anymore. "Damn bushwhackers!" Harriet and Candice can't cover the little smile that emerges from hearing Jesse express what they all feel. Jesse leaves the kitchen, trying to calm himself down.

"That's right, Jesse," Harriet yells after her father-in-law and finally tucks Craf's letter into the pocket of her apron. "Let us not forget that Captain Morris and his North Carolina 64th Regiment tried to protect us left-behinders from that killing trash of bushwhackers. Forget not that he sent ten men a-chasing them toward us and they got ambushed right down the turnpike from atop Dunn's Rock! One man was killed and most the rest shot all up -- right here in our own community!" By now Harriet is standing and shuffling to the sink to start peeling some potatoes.

Candice follows her and gets a pot out to set some water to boil. "I reckin' we can give thanks that it weren't as bad as over in Madison County, or Ashe or even Henderson County. What scares me most is them reports 'bout Kirk's Raiders, that band of Union soldiers destroyin' and actin' a lot like them bushwhackers." Candice sets the pot down a little too loud, bringing Jesse back into the kitchen to smile at the two women who are taking out their anxiety on pots and potatoes. As Candice slings potatoes into the water she continues, "Lots of folks askin' if he's got any control of his men. I heard that most of his men was outlaws or deserters."

Jesse finally reaches out to help his wife add wood to the stove. He tries to lighten the women's fears, "Let us just give thanks that Craf is a-movin' on to Tennessee."

6

Summer 2012

"Mammaw, I'm going to walk around outside and call Mom and Dad." The day before with Kevin and Ellie in the McGaha Chapel had been great, but I was missing Mom and Dad and was eager to talk to them. Convincing Mammaw to take me to Wal-Mart to buy more minutes for my phone had not been hard. She loved Wal-Mart. We never stayed less than two hours because she had to visit with all her old friends. Definitely not my favorite place since I didn't know anyone, but Mammaw looked like she could use some time away from work.

"Okay, Millie." She smiled at me and then waved at a short skinny old man with his hair slicked back and I could have sworn he was wearing his Sunday best. I had to bite my lip so I wouldn't laugh at the obvious flirtation taking place. Suddenly Mammaw was aware that I was still standing next to her. She blushed slightly. "I thought you were leaving?"

"I am." I started to leave and turned to smile at her with a teasing wave. I practically sang, "Have fuuuun!"

"Millie!" Mammaw was not amused.

As I walked through the automatic doors out into the open I was hit by a wall of heat that only a parking lot can offer. I walked over to Big M. and found a leftover napkin from our trip to Henry's restaurant this morning where we had eaten biscuits. It was one more place where Mammaw caught up with the other half of her friends. Using an old pen I found abandoned under the passenger seat I managed to write Mammaw a note that I was going to walk up the hill to The Allison Deaver House to make my call. I had memories of my parents taking me there years ago. I could still hear my dad saying, almost as if sharing a secret, "Millie, honey, it's the oldest standing frame house west of the Blue Ridge Mountains." I would hold his hand just a little tighter as we discovered room after room while breathing in the musty smell of old fireplaces. I remembered loving the shaded path leading from the end of Wal-Mart's parking lot right up to the back of the old house. Somehow that path seemed a perfect cool place for my call.

It was fun to talk to Dad alone since Mom was giving a lady from church a perm and couldn't get to the phone. I told him almost everything, but could tell he was slightly distracted. "Is everything okay, Dad?" I finally asked as the shade gave my body some relief.

"Millie, I'm fine! Looks like there may be more layoffs and I'm just worried some about that. But I always figure something out don't I?" I could tell he was really trying to be positive.

"Yeah, Dad! I won't worry about you," I lied. Before I knew it I had walked the entire path as it gently sloped up to the barn that was part of the Allison Deaver House property. As I hung up the phone I decided I might as well walk the rest of the way. I did worry about Dad and being here just made me feel closer to him. It was like I had walked back in time. The Allison Deaver House rose before me but not quite the sleeping giant I remembered as a child. The two-story building seemed to be showing off its recent coat of white paint. I started to move around to the front of the building to see the porch that stretched across the entire second floor neatly outlined by a red crisscross railing. Right smack in the middle of the porch there were red stairs that led up to the upper porch from the ground level's wooden porch. Three long stone steps lead up to it.

"Hello? Is anyone here?" I called out to the restored ancient house. I slowly climbed the stone stairs and saw a note on the tightly locked front door Open 12:00-6:00. It was already eleven and I thought maybe Mammaw could bring me back later. I suddenly had the urge to see if I could climb the red stairs to the second floor. I started up the stairs and was on the top step when I heard the roar of an engine in the parking lot close to the official entrance to the house. At first I didn't think anything of it but then I looked and saw a blue Dodge Ram pull in followed by a brown van driven by some dark-skinned man with his arm hanging out the window. I kept thinking he must have borrowed the van from his mom since the van clearly had a bumper sticker that read Proud Army Mom.

I found myself as flat down on the porch as I could possible lie. I felt my heart racing as I prayed that the red crisscross slats were thick enough to hide me. I could just barely see Junior pull up alongside the boy. I knew Roy must have been there because I heard Junior yell, "Shut up, Roy!"

The young man from the van was the only one who got out and he walked over to lean against the truck. I could now barely make out long black hair braided into neat corn rows. He was wearing a white tank top, contrasting with his dark skin. He was eye to eye with Junior and they spoke only a few words. Junior nodded and there was some quick movement. Without another glance the young man got back in the van and tore out of the parking lot.

1865: Lee surrenders to Grant to end the Civil War; Lee notices the dark General Eli Parker, a Seneca Indian who wrote the surrender paper, and comments, "Well, at least there is one American among us." Parker looks him straight in the eyes and says, "General, we are all Americans."

The Bushwhacker Murder

February 24

"Billy Boy! Get over there and knock on that door!" The young man wipes his forehead in spite of the February cold. He wants to take off his jacket, but knows carrying it is not an option when they try to make their getaway. "Here, boy! Here's some help for your job." The man he's been calling General for over a year hands him a bottle of whiskey. Billy Boy quickly welcomes the liquid fire to calm his nerves. He has long known General is far from any real general, leaning heavily on the booze for courage.

Billy Boy slowly climbs three stone steps to the front of a wooden framed home, larger than any house he'd seen since they burned the hotel. Billy knows he's here on his own doing since he helped General and the rest of his bushwhacking gang find out where young Captain James Deaver lives. Billy Boy discovered that Deaver worked in Hendersonville obtaining supplies for the Confederate Army and was about to be, like most, mustered out of the army. Billy Boy had also told General that the home belonged to the older William Deaver and his wife, Margaret Patton Deaver, who have accumulated thousands of acres in Transylvania County and are successful farmers and business people. General didn't seem to care and as Billy Boy starts to knock he tells himself he doesn't care either.

The knock is loud and clear and Billy Boy jumps off the porch missing the stairs completely and dives into the bushes in front of the house. In a slightly slurred voice General booms, "DEAVER! Captain Deaver!"

Billy can barely make out the weary, seventy-year-old William Deaver, formerly a militia Captain, as he steps out onto the long porch to see who is calling to him. The shot from General's gun is sudden and leaves Billy Boy temporarily deaf, watching in utter silence as the old man falls dead on the porch.

Billy Boy joins the handful of bushwhackers as they mount their horses and ride away laughing. They ride west to their campsite in the woods and celebrate with more moonshine whiskey. Once Billy Boy gets enough courage from the jug he asks General, "You reckin we got the right feller? He looked awful old to be in the Army."

The leader, still laughing, pats Billy on the back so hard the young man's head starts to hurt, "It don't matter none, son. We got us a Deaver and they's more of 'em. Like 'em houses and hotels we torched- - they's all rich folks that look down on the likes of us. But we is stronger and free-er! We got our own law. Them fellers, they thank they is law and sets up courts and sheriffs and officers to suit them and their friends."

By now, Billy Boy, not as whiskeyed up as the others, realizes the boss' need to talk a little more and boast of his exploits. "What you mean, officers and the like?"

General sits down next to the fire and takes another gulp from the almost empty jar. Then General stares at Billy and responds angrily, "Them Johnstones, for 'xample. High and mighty. Rich in South Carolina and here in the mountains. Ever-body calls 'em 'leaders.' Makes 'em officers in the Confederate Army and builds 'em big houses."

Billy Boy thinks he made a mistake, for the boss is really worked up, if not liquored up and there is no stopping him. General suddenly wobbles to a standing position by the fire now, speaking ever louder and slurring, "But they done had their comeupance last year over in Flat Rock."

Billy vaguely remembers a year ago when he was laid up with dysentery at his Momma's. General had mentioned what a good time they had had while Billy was gone, but that had been the extent of his boasting. Now General is ready and Billy, afraid not to ask when the boss looks at him for the response, finally asks, "What you mean?"

"Well, they was six of us and we told 'em we was hungry Confererate scouts. They took and fed us in the kitchen. We ev'n fooled around a little with the girls and got 'em to play the pie-ano fur uns. That there Andrew Johnstone he give us bread for the trip. We shore had 'em fooled." General empties the jar and then throws it into the fire.

"How come?" Billy Bow watches the fire hungrily lick the bottle.

"We got right to the door and I said, 'Are you ready? Draw!'" General starts to pace around the fire.

"What happened?" Billy tries to avoid eye contact in case General was intending to make an example of what happened.

Suddenly General loses steam and plops himself down next to Billy Boy, so close that he can feel the hot stink of the old man's breath. "It warn't like we figured. Oh, we did get that big Johnstone feller in the gut, but his boy, 'bout ten or eleven, come out with a pistol a-blazin'. His papa tried to shoot us but didn't hit nobody. That boy, Elliot was his name, he hit four of our boys! We lost good men that day, but that fancy 'Beaumont' place won't fergit us."

Billy is thankful for the cover of darkness which hides how pale he is. He doesn't want to ask any more since he remembers that he had heard the rest of the story, how the father had in fact died from the shot, but not until he had buried one outlier gang member in the yard where Elliot shot him and placed a stone devil's head over the grave.

Billy Boy decides it is time for a toilet break in the woods. His stomach violently empties not only the bad booze and bad food, but also the bad deeds he has done and has heard about. Looting and stealing was one thing, even burning the hotel was a test he thought he'd passed, but murder? No more! As the others laugh in the background at his youth and misery, he plots to sneak away from such a pack of animals to which he has so naively attached himself.

Summer 2012

By the time Mammaw got into Big M with a huge smile on her face, I had already torn up the note I had left her and was sitting in the front seat waiting. I had tried to calm myself about what I had seen at The Alison Deaver House before she got there, but as she started the engine she looked at me and her smile faded, "What's wrong?"

I don't know why I didn't tell her. Maybe it was because I wasn't really sure what I saw, maybe it was my fear of losing the rest of my freedom this summer, or maybe I was worried about Kevin. I looked at her and I told myself I wasn't lying; I just wasn't telling her everything, "I talked to Dad and he's facing layoffs."

I could feel Mammaw's warm chubby hand squeeze my clammy fingers, "Now, Honey, it'll all work out. Your Daddy's faced this before. He'll figure somethin' out." She reached up and gently touched my face, but I saw, for just a second, a hint of worry in her eyes too.

1865: President Lincoln is shot, the assassin is killed, and eight others are convicted; President Johnson has difficulties in rebuilding the country and begins Reconstruction in the South; Former Confederate President Jefferson Davis is captured in Georgia, disguised as a woman.

Homecoming

"Come and sit a spell," Harriet calls to Craf who is stacking firewood beside the house. She is thankful to have her husband home. Craf has come home, like so many -- tired, weary of war, and heartbroken at the destruction of limb, life and property. She sees in his eyes his thankfulness to be back in his beloved mountain home.

Craf hesitates a moment and looks at the pile of wood. He knows he's been driven since he's been home to work hard to make up for time lost, but his body isn't always willing. The warm spring day still promises cold nights and the wood pile needs to be replenished, yet his body's hunger for rest is greater. He turns to head towards his wife and the glass of cold spring water she holds out to him.

Over the last two weeks Harriet has learned quickly that Craf does not wish to talk about the horrors of war, only to give thanks that he could return alive and sound, although many would question the latter as he had lost so much weight. Being so small and slight anyway, his war experience has taken a toll on him physically. So Harriet settles in next to her husband in their two rocking chairs on the front porch, hoping familiar moments will ease his pain.

Sensing he should talk about something other than trying to get the farm going full steam she tactfully asks, "Craf, what about friends in your time away -- did you see any?"

Craf feels more comfortable with this line of questions and responds, "Actually, I ran into several besides the ones from Transylvania I signed up with."

"Any I know?" Harriet restrains her joy of finally hearing her husband engage in conversation beyond basic needs.

"A few folks who had stayed with us on their way to Greenville with stock. You might remember Webb Parker who came through with a few cattle and hogs." He gently touches her hand almost as if remembering how her skin feels.

Harriet smiles, but is careful not to scream with joy. So she tries to tease her husband a little. "Oh yeah. He was the one who bailed you out of that near-lie when that so-called preacher Schmidt was spying on us."

Craf pauses a moment, then a spark is lit, a memory caught and suddenly they both laugh, something they need to do again and again.

After they both catch their breath, Harriet squeezes her husband's hand. "Craf, can I ask something other folks are asking me? You don't have to answer if you don't want to." She hopes she has chosen the right moment.

"What is it?" he asks nervously.

Harriet carefully words her question. "We had a lot of neighbors, from all around, who came home before the war was over and hid out in the woods to be fed by their families. They worked their crops by night sometimes. One feller, or more, even hid on the ledge midway up Dunn's Rock so his wife could ease food over the top. Another hid in the cave below the Rock. Folks say bad things about deserters."

Craf breathes deeply and covers her hand with his free hand. "Harriet, please ask your friends, whoever they might be, not to be so hard on these men. Many did walk away disillusioned in what they saw and how it was going, especially toward the end when the conclusion was clear. Most were worried sick about their families and felt their greater calling was to protect them at home against the bushwhackers and starvation."

Seeking to lighten the situation a little, Harriet asks, "Did you hear about your ever- honest friend Samuel Raxter?"

A little apprehensive, Craf responds, "No, what?"

"Well, it seems he and Felix Rabb were stationed in Greenville and assigned scouting duty to look for deserters above Traveler's Rest toward Table Rock and Caesar's Head."

Craf interrupts, "Well, that's very close to home, just down the road."

Harriet declares, "That was the problem. It was too close to resist, so they slipped on home to check on things. But then they heard that the war had ended exactly when they got the orders to go on the mission!"

Craf says, "But what happened?"

"Well, your ever-honest friend feels he was technically a deserter and thus refuses his pension."

Craf gently laughs, "That is Samuel. Even though in his heart he did not desert, he refuses just because it looks as if he did, due to the timing." Craf pulls Harriet in close to him as they watch Sally Sarah and Juliet chase each other up the path screaming for their daddy to look at the turtle they found.

Summer 2012

"Hi, is Ellie here?" El Capitán was in the midst of the lunch rush. I had found Ellie's mom and expected to see the same smiling round face I saw a couple of weeks ago. But as I asked my question she started going off on me in Spanish. Of course, the only word I understood was "no", but the rest was lost. I wondered if she just didn't want me to bother her since she was so busy, so I took a quick peek in the kids' hangout room. With the TV blasting as usual I tried to get someone's attention. That's when I saw Rai get up and head toward me. I hadn't seen Ellie's brother since I first got here. I was thankful he at least had a white T-shirt on this time. But he still had that serious look on his face.

"What you want?" He was right up in my face and I stepped backwards so he could follow me out of the room.

"I'm just looking for Ellie," I said and then looked at his scowl, "but it seems to me that everyone here is pissed at something so I just better head on home . . . . See you!" I turned and shot out the front door as fast as possible.

"Wait!" Rai caught up with me and I found myself suddenly with his arm around my shoulders like we were long lost buddies, definitely creeping me out. I stood still as he whispered, looking around suspiciously, "So Ellie is not with you right now?"

I pushed his arm away and looked at Rai, suddenly aware that his family was not ticked at me, but at Ellie. "No," I said very slowly, "remember, I am the one looking for her."

Rai shook his head. "Stupid girl! She's gone again. She told our mother she was going to hang with you again today, but I guess she lied."

I could feel my cheeks burn slightly, "I guess she did." I couldn't believe she would use me like that. "I thought we were friends. I guess I thought wrong!" I turned and started down the road behind the restaurant.

Rai ran up beside me and his scowl was gone. "Hey, girl, just chill!" Rai tried to smile. "Bein' pissed at Ellie is my job!"

"What?" I was looking at a very handsome young boy who suddenly looked his age. He had lost the tough look and his eyes opened wide as if begging for a piece of candy.

"Look, things ain't that easy for her and," Rai nodded his head toward the restaurant, "sometimes it gets to be too much and she's just got to split."

1865: The Ku Klux Klan, a secret society opposing Negroes and Reconstruction in the South, is formed; General Robert E. Lee vows allegiance to the Union, to help free the slaves, and to help in Reconstruction; The Commandant of the infamous Andersonville, Georgia prison is hanged for the atrocities committed there.

Girl Talk

"I'm downright a-worryin'." Nancy sits next to Gerda on an old quilt now recently decorated with bits of cold cornbread and ham. The two women have decided to enjoy the crisp spring sun with a picnic. Their friendship has deepened through the war and the repeated efforts the two have made in helping out families in distress, in addition to the McGahas. Their Cherokee and Swiss backgrounds have paid off in combined knowledge for homemade remedies in medicine, gardens and simple survival in hard times. Today the two have decided to picnic at the tallest falls in Buck Forest and just visit as they did so long ago when Gerda struggled with her English.

"Vhat are you vorried about?" Gerda reaches for a slice of cornbread, slipping again in her English.

Nancy reflects, "Gerda, 'member back when we was first together and talked 'bout how unpredictable the mountains is -- these here and yore Alps?"

"Oh, yes." Gerda enjoys the cornbread, even cold. She secretly smiles to herself, proud that she can throw together a good cornbread just like the locals.

Nancy pauses. She picks up a piece of the cornbread and takes a bite, but doesn't relish it quite as readily. Her thoughts are with the Deaver family and the ruthless murder which still causes every citizen in Transylvania to think twice before opening the front door. "I've been a-thinkin' that durin' these here awful times we have had, how it is that even with the War done and over, how many strange thangs is still a-happenin'."

Gerda stops chewing and looks at her friend who is much too serious. She sighs gently knowing this picnic was supposed to be a relief, an escape. She confesses, "I do not understand."

Nancy does not look at Gerda, but takes in the beautiful waterfalls, as the water endlessly cascades without a worry. She breathes in the moist cool breeze suddenly dancing up from the bottom of the falls. Nancy pulls her shawl in close to keep away the chill. "Folks is a lot like the mountains. They can be downright beautiful, but I reckin, with the right pressures, they kin strike terror and total destruction. I reckin that is how come so many of our parents and grandparents come over to this here land. I mean to see the beauty part and hopin' the bad part was left over there."

With some sadness in her voice, Gerda responds, "True."

Nancy looks at her friend and realizes she has stopped eating. Their escape has become much too serious too quickly. She decides to change to a lighter topic. She rolls onto her stomach and looks up at her Swiss friend like a little girl. "So, Gerda, what do you reckin you do not miss -- nary a bit – 'bout your old country?"

Gerda is pleased to see Nancy's change in demeanor and without hesitation she responds, "The KKK."

Nancy suddenly finds herself uncomfortable on her stomach and her head seems to suddenly spin. The thought that the Ku Klux Klan might be at work in Switzerland would mean that other European countries might have this infectious movement against the so-called Reconstruction in America. Nancy sits up awkwardly and tries to grab a piece of ham. Had her old friend, a beautiful woman with blond hair and blue eyes been tied to the KKK before? She certainly could fit the stereotypical looks of a white superior being. She is not sure about her religious beliefs yet, but is she one of them? The cold piece of meat in her mouth seems to grow and Nancy just can't seem to swallow.

Gerda watches her friend in silence and wonders what is wrong. "Are you sick? Is de ham bad?"

Nancy just shakes her head and, throwing her shawl off, runs over to spit the well-chewed fleshy mass into the bushes. In the silence of the pregnant minutes, Nancy thinks, "Why am I judging her? I have only heard of men, not women, getting into those awful sheets and doing awful things to people they considered as inferior beings. Do women do that in

Europe?" Maybe this Swiss woman did feel superior, yet her intuition and observation told her otherwise.

She feels Gerda has come up behind her and is trying to wrap the abandoned shawl around her friend. As Gerda finally breaks the ice her anxiety regresses into broken English, "Vat is de matter?" Have I offended, pained you in soom vay? Perhaps, my English ist not so gut."

With some relief in the direct openness of one woman to another Nancy finally looks at her friend and confesses, "Yep, I was right shocked that you mentioned the KKK. I had no idea they was in Europe."

Still confused but searching, Gerda also confesses, "I do not know WHO you mean ven you say 'Dey' are in Europe. KKK has to do wit dat awful praxis in my former land, and many others in Europe, that, women are created by God for only three tings: KKK stands for Kinder, Kuche und Kirche; dat is children, kitchen und church!"

Gerda's eyes are wide and for just a minute Nancy stares at her taking in the true meaning when suddenly both women break into laughter and cannot stop for some time. Then they cry tears of relief and embrace in a hug that only a deep relationship brings.

The two friends return to their quilt and Gerda, wiping away the tears, confesses, "Now, you must know that not all men in my old country believe dat way."

Nancy, picking up the implication and Gerda's glowing face, asks, "Well now, be that one feller you kin giv' a name to?"

"Ja," Gerda gently nudges her friend sitting next to her, regressing to her mother-tongue, "Gerhard." Nancy smiles at her friend. Having lost her own Epi so long ago, she understands the longing Gerda must be feeling. Suddenly Gerda looks at Nancy with a twinkle in her eye. She pulls up her long skirt and Nancy sees a pocket Gerda has sewn deep within the folds. She reaches into the pocket and pulls out a very small red cloth carefully wrapped around a little flat object. The Swiss woman unfolds the cloth to reveal a picture of a dark- haired man with a serious look. "Dis is Gerhard." She gently caresses the picture, letting the red cloth fall onto her lap. "I vill go home to him someday soon."

"What in heaven's name is that?" Nancy points at the red cloth, noticing a white cross in the middle.

"Oh, dat's de Swiss flag." Gerda carefully collects the red cloth and gently pats it out as flat as possible. She looks at Nancy who is frowning slightly. "Okay, vat's wrong?"

Nancy carefully traces her finger around the cross on the flag. "You prob'ly ought to keep that flag tucked away in your skirts. The KKK emblem here in this land looks an awful lot like a copy of that Swiss flag."

"Vat?" Gerda frowns at her friend, obviously disappointed that something seems wrong with this treasure.

"Yep. A white cross on a totally red background. Except'n, the cross is in a circle and has got a drop of red blood in th' middle." Nancy tries to be matter of fact in order not to upset her friend.

Gerda shakes her head. "Nancy, I do not know who de KKK is? Who are dey? Vat do I need to know?"

Nancy suddenly feels awful, "I'm real sorry, Gerda, I thought you knowed. It's a bunch of folks who believe white Anglo-Saxon Protestants, is superior to all other races and gotta survive over 'inferior' races. And they do kill to get their point across."

Gerda, with eyes open in alarm says, "Liebe Gott! Oh, Dear God."

Nancy continues, "They go 'bout here and there a-preachin' hatred for folks not like them and destroyin' other races and religions, all in the name of God. They cover up their faces and clothes with white sheets so they cain't be identified whilst they is doin' terrible things. They is a real secret group, so folks ain't supposed to figger who's in it."

"Are dey here?" Gerda's looks around as she quickly places Gerhard back into the small flag, tucking him in safely for another time.

Once the picture is stashed away, Nancy briefly pats Gerda's shaking hand. "Not regularly. Sometimes they'll come up the mountain from South Caroliner to 'educate' us pore, ignorant mountain folk."

Gerda breaks in, "Where are these ignorant folks? I have not yet met dem."

"Welcome to the world of the Appalachian mountains and thinkin' in stereotypes. Ever since the settlin' of this area, folks has tended to picture ever-body as ignorant, lawless and uneducated. You can find some folks a-livin' here that fit such a picture, just like you can in every big city and open countryside in this here land."

Gerda nods, "Yes, even across de ocean!"

Nancy stands up to stretch. Gerda sees Nancy smile ever so slightly. "Some of these KKK people do come through from time to time. In fact, on the McGaha porch a couple of years ago Craf defended me against one feller who is most likely in the KKK now, in front of a crowd."

A puzzled look on her face, Gerda asks, "Why you?"

Nancy laughs and dramatically bows, letting her long dark hair cascade in front of her, "Ain't you seen that I be part Indian? I'm half Cherokee. Quite a few families in these mountains is blended with Cherokee and European blood. When them so-called preachers come in a-preachin' racial purity they got no idea how many folks a-listen' might be Indian or part Indian." As Nancy pulls her hair back behind her shoulders she smiles at the memory, "Most folks ignore them and walk away, but sometimes folks like Craf will speak up and speak from the Bible they so often misuse. Hard to believe some folks can be so ignorant 'bout the world, the Bible and other people. Yet they call all of us mountain folks ignorant!"

Gerda responds, "I'd love to have seen it when he defended you." Gerda breathes deeply in relief. "It is good dat ve don't have much of de KKK around here."

"Yeah, but," Nancy hesitates just a minute, yet she realizes her friend should know everything, "I hear that just down the mountain in South Caroliner, they got groups of people called the "Red Shirts" that wear red and really scare folks into votin' their way or not votin' at all."

A new worry crosses the Swiss woman's face. "Are they the same as the KKK?"

Nancy rejoins her friend on the quilt. "Yeah and nope. Them Red Shirts don't cover up their faces and is more open than the KKK, but they bring big public pressure in meetin's and in private. They is a-tryin' to reverse war results, or leastwise to bring the old ways back in and to 'keep the Negroes in their place.'" Nancy sees her friend still looks confused. "Let me put it this way. The KKK is a secret vigilante group, the Red Shirts is a open local militia group with resistance to the many changes done brought on by the Civil War. They is real active, I read. They do scare a lot of folks, both blacks and whites."

Gerda takes a deep breath and looks directly at Nancy. A little smirk is on her face as she tries to sound as official as possible. "Okay! So vat you are saying is I better be sure not to fly my Swiss flag, even on the national independence holiday August first, lest I am associated with the wrong crowd! And I am not to speak to strange men who speak to us like ve are ignorant, AND I'll not wear a red shirt!"

Nancy giggles a little, "And don't forgit yore blond hair and blue eyes!"

Gerda grabs Nancy's arm and looks around as if getting ready to entrust her friend with a secret. "Do not vorry. Should any one push me, I'll insist you and I are twin sisters. Dat ought to really confuse dem."

Summer 2012

I watched Rai walk back into El Capitán and just before he disappeared he looked back at me. He flung his hair to the side again with a jerk of his head and he tried to give me a quick wink; cool Rai was back. I waved at him in response and tried not to laugh at his embarrassing attempt to be older than he was. Yet, somehow, he wasn't quite as creepy. I looked down the road toward the Sherwood Forest entrance and decided I wasn't quite ready to go home. I was upset that Ellie would tell her family she was taking off with me and then actually not wait for me. I was confused and thought about Rai's words to not be so hard on Ellie. I tried to brush it off as I walked toward the other side of the restaurant and stood in front of the gas station. Since there was no blue Dodge Ram parked out front I figured I would go in to get a drink.

As I pushed the front door open as hard as I could, I almost bashed it into the side wall. Obviously the rubber at the bottom had been replaced. I looked up at the red-haired lady at the counter and could feel myself blush. "Dang. I'm sorry, I thought the rubber thingy was still broken."

"Don't worry about it, Sugar, everyone's pushed that door so hard, I think we shoulda just left it be, instead of fixing it." The tattoo sleeve arm-waved at me to move in a little closer. "Ain't you that girl that was in here some weeks ago with the Carp boys harassin' you?"

I turned slightly red. "Yeah, but that's over now." I lied, once again wondering what I was doing.

"Good!" She pointed at the refrigerators in the back. "You go git you a cold drank on me." I opened my mouth to object, but she just waved me on. "Go on now, girl. Anybody who has to deal with the Carps deserves a drank!" I couldn't argue with that so I walked to the back of the store and pulled out a Gatorade. I heard the front door open again and I froze for just a minute, but soon relaxed when I heard the woman laughing. By the time I reached the counter she was pulling off a lottery ticket and handing it to Charlie. I could feel myself smile as I watched the old man take the ticket and put it in the top pocket of his overalls like it was a treasure to keep for later. He turned and looked at me.

"Well, hello, Millie!" Charlie's perfect white teeth greeted me.

"Hey, Charlie," It was good to see him again. I could feel a little disappointment in the fact that Ellie was not with him, a thought that had crossed my mind. But, maybe I could ask him some questions without her around.

Charlie must have read my mind. "So, you want to walk me back to the campground?" I smiled and nodded. Charlie waved at the lady and I thanked her for my drink, but I wasn't sure she heard either of us because she was already headed to the back of the store to stock some shelves.

I could feel the breeze from the cars as they whizzed past us on their way down the mountain towards Brevard. Some pulled over slightly, others must have not seen us, leaving me thankful to finally step off the shoulder of the Greenville Highway onto the gravel road leading to the campground.

"What's on your mind, child?" Charlie's voice was gentle and I could feel his step move in time with mine.

I hadn't been called child in awhile, but coming from Charlie it was not a putdown. "I just don't get some things!" I looked at the man's dark eyes and with his smile gone he looked older than I remembered. He didn't say anything, obviously waiting for me to go on. "Where do you think Ellie is? I mean for the last four weeks we have been swimming and hiking and hanging out together."

"With Kevin?" Charlie asked quietly.

I looked at him and frowned slightly. "Yes, with Kevin. At least most of the time. Some days he couldn't make it. Said his idiot brothers needed him, but yeah, a lot with Kevin."

"So have you looked for Kevin today?" Charlie asked, but his voice remained very matter of fact.

"Well, no." Suddenly I felt like an idiot. I should have thought that maybe they went out without me for a hike since Mammaw and I went off to Wal-Mart this morning.

Maybe they just didn't want to wait. I smiled a little at Charlie, "Yeah, I guess they took off without me today. I was kinda late getting down here."

Charlie didn't smile, "Yeah, I bet they did!" I saw his eyes wander back towards the road. I saw, for just a minute a glimpse of fear, a moment so quick I almost missed it.

"Charlie? What are you not telling me?" I had to ask. There were times I felt like such an outsider along for a ride where I felt blindfolded half the time.

"Nothing that Ellie shouldn't tell you herself." Charlie's answer was forceful. I was slightly shocked and Charlie could tell it. He softened his voice and his dark hand touched my very white skin ever so softly, like Mammaw trying to calm me down. "Millie, Ellie will sometimes make poor decisions and you better believe I worry about her."

"Does this have anything to do with the attack?" I asked.

Charlie looked at me and didn't hesitate. "Yes." He continued to stare at me as if deciding to finish his thought. "Did you know that she begged her parents not to press assault charges?"

I felt a slight chill. "You mean against the Carp brothers, Junior and Roy?"

"Yes." Charlie suddenly looked very tired. We were next to the old wall again and Charlie leaned against it almost as if looking for strength.

"Why?" I moved in close and touched the old rocks that reminded me of the strength of the old wall.

"Why do you think?" Charlie knew I knew the answer.

"Kevin?" I barely breathed.

1866: Former slaves, but not Indians, are made U.S. citizens; The KKK spreads in the South; Indian attacks increase in the West and more forts are built; Whites riot in Memphis, Tennessee, killing over forty Negro victims, burning schools and churches; The Freedmen's Bureau of the War Department helping freed slaves find jobs, medical help, etc. is ended by President Johnson after only a year, saying that freed slaves should "advance by their own merits and exertions".

Rebuilding

"What's got you down? You seem to have a burden on your back." Harriet joins her husband who is sitting on the stone wall he built years ago to welcome drovers to his home. It has taken a full year for Craf, Harriet and the children to find some sense of normalcy, if the word could be used at all in the postwar rebuilding time, the so-called Reconstruction Period in American history. She knows Craf likes to sit on the wall and stare down the Greenville Turnpike in hopes of seeing the drovers who are slowly rebuilding their little stock and bringing them south. But most have had their hogs and cattle stolen or decimated by one army or another, if not by bushwhackers.

Craf doesn't look at his wife, but keeps his eyes steady on the empty dirt road. "Is it that obvious?"

Harriet knows Craf's recent trip to Brevard serving on jury duty has left him more frustrated than previous visits. "Something happen to you in town?"

Craf finally turns to look at Harriet. Although he looks tired and angry, Harriet is pleased to see some of her husband's old fire back in his eyes. "I'm unhappy with some of the decisions of our local leaders. They seem to make rash decisions when a charismatic speaker comes through town."

"So what has happened this time?"

Craf shakes his head. "They just let a contract to build stocks and a pillory. It should join the whipping post."

Harriet frowns at the picture of a somewhat barbaric downtown. "And just who is supposed to be punished one of those ways?"

Craf finally jumps off the wall and throws his arms in the air. "The argument was that they are for the drunkards, with so much whiskey being sold in Brevard."

A confused Harriet asks, "But wait, these are the same leaders who give out the liquor permits are they not?"

"Well," Craf starts pointing down the road towards South Carolina, "I don't think that was the real reason. Some Red Shirt from South Carolina convinced them that 'carpetbaggers, scalawags, and Freedmen's Bureau Racketeers' could be kept in line or at least scared away with such humiliating punishment."

Harriet asks, "Yankees and Negroes?"

Craf slowly rejoins his wife on the wall. "Unfortunately. This is not South Carolina and we can handle our rebuilding ourselves, in more civilized ways. It really gets me down."

Harriet sits silently next to her husband. She knows that she cannot solve the legal issues facing Brevard, but she wants Craf to cheer up. She gently nudges her husband with her foot as she lets it slowly swing from her side of the wall to his. "I saw a notice that there is a meeting in Brevard for Confederate War Veterans." Craf doesn't move, so Harriet continues. "Wouldn't you like to take a Saturday off to see some old friends?"

Craf returns his wife's nudge lovingly and finally looks her straight in the eyes. "My dearest, loving Harriet. Thank you for asking but no, I would not. Let me tell you why. My true friends are still my friends. Some of those fellers will wear their confederate uniforms and will want to tell of their war exploits, make themselves heroes, and glorify the war. They will pat themselves and each other on the back for surviving. They may or may not remember those we lost or killed on the other side. I did what I had to do."

Harriet doesn't respond. A tear silently falls as she is listening to her husband. "I am no hero, just a man, a creature of God called to be here with you and my family, to cultivate what we can in this community to bring peace, to fight as best we can for harmony in our world, starting here."

Harriet is deeply moved and stands. She brushes the dirt from the wall off her skirt and holds her hand out to her husband. Craf doesn't hesitate to join her. As they slowly walk up the path to the house they see the two girls playing on the porch. A smiling Harriet touches Craf's shoulder gently, then his face. "Craf you are some man that I married, one giant of a creature. Would you like to have another child?"

Quite startled and still pained by the loss of so many young children, including his son, he is at a loss for words. "Huh! What are you saying? I mean how?"

Harriet giggles at his red face and his not in front of the kids look. "Well, handsome fellow, if after so many births and breeding so many animals you don't know how, I guess I'll have to teach you again!"

Summer 2012

"Well, maybe I should hop up the path to Rich Mountain." Now that I thought Kevin and Ellie had taken off on a hike without me, I thought maybe I could see if they were on the same hike we went on the other day. I looked at Charlie who just shook his head at me.

"Child, you would be stupid to go alone." Charlie stopped leaning against the wall and seemed suddenly stronger. His old wise self was back and I didn't dare argue with him. "Why don't you just come over to the horse barn and help me give the horses some hay?"

Since it was more of a statement than a question I followed him until we drew closer to the huge horse barn that stood toward the end of the long pasture running along the old dirt road. The silence was killing me. "So, Charlie, how do you like your job?" Okay, lame question, but I had to say something.

Charlie answered without missing a beat. "I'm getting too old for this. I love the land, my boss and especially the horses, but I am tired." I didn't know what to say, so Charlie laughed and started to jog ever so slowly, "Don't worry child, I bet I can still outrun you." I smiled and pretended to race him, obviously letting him win.

Just as we came to the entrance to the barn we both stood still. I could hear the familiar sound. The sadly sweet notes dancing off Kevin's fingers made me suddenly smile. I looked at Charlie and screamed with joy, "They're here!"

Charlie looked slightly less overjoyed. "I guess they are." Charlie thrust the barn door open with one big yank. Leaning up against one of the piles of hay sat Kevin, totally absorbed in his fiddle, and Ellie waving at us as if she'd been expecting us all along.

1867: Alaska is purchased for $7 million; Reconstruction is enforced but resisted by Southern legislatures; Britain makes Canada a dominion; Nebraska becomes the 37th state.

A Wanted Child is Born and Named

"Please call me Charles," the guest insists. Dr. Charles Manley is not a regular visitor, but he is a welcome one to the household for he can answer many of the biblical, theological and historical questions they have saved up in the hope that another Furman University professor might make it up the mountain from Greenville. The visiting scholar notes immediately that the McGaha household is alive with excitement far beyond his casual visit. The girls are about to have a little sister or brother born. They are all engaged with their overnight visitor at the evening supper table about the coming birth. Even the parents-to-be, now in their mid-thirties, are caught in the contagion of anticipation.

"We are honored that you might spend the night with us. What brings you to these parts?" Craf asks, enjoying entertaining visitors again.

Manley enjoys a bite of molasses on the freshly baked bread. "Actually times are hard in South Carolina, especially in Greenville and at Furman University. Folks thought that the change from a college to a university in 1850 would also expand support, but as you know, we had to close during the war. But students are coming back in now and we badly need support. I am on my way to Asheville hoping to raise some money for the school."

Harriet, offering him another piece of bread, breaks in very apologetically, "I am sorry but we don't have any money to spare."

Grateful for the second piece of bread, Manley quickly puts her at ease, "I would not take it if you did! Please understand that I am going to approach folks in Asheville who made a lot of money in the war effort and who should be willing to let go of some for the cause of education."

Craf takes a bite of his own bread, "I'm afraid we are still rebuilding our lives here and have little to offer."

Manley shakes his head and assures the whole family, "Your wonderful contribution is allowing me to stay overnight for which I shall reimburse you. I insist. You have no idea how wonderful it is to experience the McGaha hospitality about which I had heard far and wide before I first came by."

Somewhat embarrassed, Craf responds, "Well, I thank you kindly, but we are just common mountain folk."

Swallowing his last bite the guest manages to muffle, "Mountain, yes. But in this age of tension, not so common. For years stories have come our way from people who were cared for, drovers and travelers of all sorts who had no money but were taken in." He wipes his mouth with the back of his hand. "In many biblical classes at Furman, teachers tend to speak of you folks when they teach about the words of Jesus, 'I was a stranger and you took me in.' "

Both Harriet and Craf are dumbfounded and red-faced. They cannot speak.

Professor Manley sees their embarrassment and changes the subject. "So, I note that you are about to be blessed with a child! How wonderful. Have you chosen possible names yet?"

Craf still cannot speak but Harriet awkwardly stands to clear the table, fiercely aware of her protruding stomach. "Well, we have some girls' names picked out but still struggle with boys' names." Pausing for a moment she faces the stranger with a serious look. She gently strokes her belly, "You see we have lost several children including our firstborn, a son Mitch in eighteen sixty-two. He was only seven."

Manley speaks with great compassion, "I am so very sorry. What a tragedy when any child dies. I had no idea, and so much of your loss during those awful war years, too."

Craf by now is more recovered and proposes, "Maybe you can help us as your 'payment' for overnighting which you insist on paying. Let me tell you what we have been discussing. We really want a child who will make it in this life. We are in our mid-thirties and fearful we might lose another as we did before. Any child will be a blessing for which we will be thankful. For some reason, we cannot settle on boys' names although we feel good about some girls' names we have."

"How can I help?" Manley has a sparkle in his eye, knowing very well where this is going and honored to be asked for input.

Harriet re-enters the conversation, "We have thought about the name 'Bunyan' but would like another name to go with it, should the Lord bless us with a son."

Manley smiles and says, "What about 'Volemus'? It is Latin and would mean that 'We really, really want this child.' It is a strong word, more than to wish for something. It has to do with 'will' and we use the basic meaning when we speak of God's will."

Both Harriet and Craf are in tears as she finds some paper and writes down the word, unwittingly misspelling it as 'Volenus'."

So, on a cold snowy February 22, 1867, a strong, healthy Volenus Bunyan McGaha enters the happy home of J. Crawford and Harriet McGaha, truly a 'wanted' child.

7

Summer 2012

Charlie thoroughly chewed out Ellie and Kevin for hiding in the barn. I hadn't seen loving, gentle Charlie that ticked at Ellie. He fussed about what would have happened if his boss man came and found them. He fussed. How would that look for Charlie? Did they ever think about anyone else? I just stood silent and watched Kevin and Ellie turn slightly red. Once Charlie had said what he needed to say he threw a handful of hay at each of us and told us to feed the horses. It wasn't long before Ellie cuddled up next to Charlie and whispered that she was sorry, but some awkwardness remained.

The day dragged on with us helping Charlie, beyond just feeding the horses. He had us clean out the stalls and lay fresh woodchips in the garden beds that marked the entrance to the camp. Although it was hot and muggy no one complained. We settled for some cold water and a peanut butter sandwich for lunch, courtesy of Charlie's mini-fridge in the barn. By three o'clock I was wondering if I had a dry spot left on me. I knew I would have to peel my clothes off when I got home. Charlie, smiling with satisfaction at the sight of us, exhausted and dirty, finally sent us home.

Kevin and I walked Ellie home along the road behind El Capitán. Once we said our goodbyes we headed to the front of the restaurant in order to start down the Greenville Highway towards the Sherwood Forest entrance.

"Where ya'll been?" Junior's voice sounded so matter of fact I hardly recognized him. He was leaning against the front of the gas station obviously waiting for Roy to finish pumping gas. Kevin and I just stood still, as if standing next to the restaurant, in front of a window, gave us an invisible protection. But that didn't stop Junior. He did not hesitate to slither over to us and circle around us like we were on trial. "Shoo, you two shore are dirty." Junior took one finger and ran it down the dirt on Kevin's arm. Kevin shoved his hand away. "What? You so sensitive? Been rollin' in the dirt with your girl friend?"

"Shut up, Junior!" Kevin shoved his big brother a little more forcefully this time.

Junior's smile disappeared. "You better watch it little brother." He grabbed Kevin's arm as he tried to shove him again. This time pain shot across Kevin's face as Junior pulled his arm up behind his back. Junior's lips were right up against his brother's ear. "I think you'd best remember you belong to me."

Suddenly there was a door slamming and to my horror I saw Rai come running around the corner with a broom. His hair was in his face and the one eye I could see was wild with defiance. "Get out of here, asshole!"

Junior slowly let Kevin's arms loose, but only because he was done with him. Rai just added a new look to Junior's face, a harshness that made my stomach churn. He lifted his finger and pointed, "Boy! You got yours a-comin'. Ain't no Mexican gonna talk to me like that!" Junior turned and headed to the truck.

"Rai, are you crazy!" I looked at him and then at Kevin. "Kevin, what's he mean? Is he going to hurt Rai?" No one said anything. "You've got to do something!"

"Like what, Millie?" Kevin was rubbing his arm. "Dad thinks it's all fun and boys bein' boys. Ma cain't handle any more stress. What the hell am I supposed to do?"

I looked at Rai, "You've got to tell the police!"

Rai almost laughed, "He hasn't touched me yet, girl. What do you think they can do?" The same wild look returned. "I ain't scared of two rednecks. They can bring it on!"

I frowned and grabbed the broom he was still holding. "Oh yeah, that's really smart and this makes you such a man!" I threw the broom aside and headed down the highway. "I'm going home! Maybe all the way home."

I felt Kevin run up behind me and Rai was yelling from behind, "YOU'RE WELCOME!" I didn't even turn to look, but I could hear El Capitán's door slam.

1868: Ulysses S. Grant becomes the U.S. President; Custer's 7th Calvary wipes out Indians at Washita; Documentation is done on the deaths of hundreds of freed slaves.

The Boy

Harriet picks up the little straw basket from the corner of the chicken shed, a chore that takes little thought. As she carefully begins to reach in to grab a handful of chicken feed she smiles and stands still as she hears Craf's voice next-door in the barn. "Now son, it's more than squeezing and a-pulling, it's being gentle with the cow. You talk with them in a quiet voice, maybe even thank them for the milk. If they finish their food first, then give them a little more. And always make sure your hands are clean. You don't want to hurt the cows with all they give us."

Harriet is proud that Little Bunyan is walking before he is one, toddler-talking nonstop and inseparable from his Papa Craf. Harriet is amazed at how her normally quiet, reserved man carries his son around and talks with him, telling stories. Often she worries that Craf will not heed her warnings about safety for their son. She continues to stand still to listen to the commotion next- door.

"Cow kick." Bunyan's voice makes Harriet smile as she wonders at his ability to remember what his Papa had obviously told him.

"Oh yeah, sometimes that happens. Usually something is wrong -- like they got a cut or thorn. We try to find out. But then some young cows can be just plain mean, so we have to be firm until they learn who's the boss. I hate to hit one, but sometimes it is necessary to get them to cooperate."

A smiling Harriet slips back to feeding the chickens, confident her son is in good hands.

Once Harriet finally leaves the coop, she meets Craf and their son as they awkwardly carry a pail of milk together without spilling it. Harriet walks alongside the comical couple and soon grabs her son up in her arms. He fights to get down, so she plants a kiss on his forehead and puts him back on the ground. Craf and Harriet laugh as the two older girls come running and start chasing their baby brother, who giggles with delight.

Harriet looks away from the scene and gently touches her husband's arm. "Craf, I wish you would not take Bunyan so often when you go over to Rich Mountain to check on the livestock there. It is more dangerous with all the wild animals about and you running around, trying to catch different stock."

Craf swings the milk pail to his other side and reaches for his wife's hand. As they continue to walk toward the porch he slowly feels her relax. "Now Harriet, maybe you're right. How about if I swing by the Hogseds or Raxters above Dunn's Rock? They love kids and always ask about a visit. I could leave him a little to play with their young'ns and cut over Slick Rock to Rich Mountain real easy."

Harriet squeezes her husband's hand and lets go as she climbs the porch stairs. She reaches out to receive the milk pail as Craf bends down to rest on the top step. She waves at Sally Sarah to come and carry the milk into the kitchen. As she joins her husband she just can't drop the subject. "That's fine, or some of your kin could also keep him a few hours. I know Rich Mountain is the prettiest place on earth up there and you can see forever. I know you want him to go and learn but he's just a child, not a grown man!"

Harriet notices her husband just nods and remains silent. Obviously the conversation is over. She could kick herself for appearing too overprotective to Craf so she just sighs. Not wanting to end the few minutes with her husband she decides to change the subject. "By the way, what was Frosty Jack Loftis a-bendin' your ear about last week?"

Smiling, Craf thinks fondly of his old friend, remembering when they were younger how Frosty Jack, as a teenager, would throw young Craf into the Little River which runs right through his Daddy's land. "Complaining about getting older."

Harriet knows Frosty Jacks hair is as white as snow, but he wears his nickname with pride. "You're teasing me, Craf McGaha, there was more than that, as worked up as you both were."

Craf leans back on his two elbows. Harriet relishes her husband's boyish excitement as he speaks with some enthusiasm. "Well, keep it quiet, my love. He asked about my surveying in these parts and all the property changing hands so much. But mostly he wanted to know about some talk from before the war about getting a place to worship. He said he wasn't getting any younger and he'd sure like to see that happen before his time comes."

Harriet has tears in her eyes, for she knows her little man with such a big heart is about to take on something that means a lot to him, not just to his friend and neighbor. She leans back too on her elbows, "Do you remember when we first met, what drew us together?"

Aware that she is awkwardly leaning back further than he is, he smiles, "My overwhelming height and good looks?"

Harriet sits up reaching over to tug on his beard and says, "There you go, teasing again. Seriously, we met at that camp meeting. All these years you have wanted some peaceful place to worship and try to bring split-apart folks back together. Admit it. And over these years as the guests came through and stayed with us, you encouraged faith topics to be discussed and welcomed visiting preachers. So, big feller, you ain't getting younger either! I think a church would be wonderful."

Summer 2012

"Millie, stop!" Kevin tried to touch my arm as I was cutting across the golf course. The looks from two old white men wearing matching white golf caps would have sent Mammaw into a fit, but thank God she wasn't there. I was so ticked at how Rai and Kevin didn't do anything about the threats from Junior.

"What?" I stopped beside the Little River for only a moment before I flung my tennis shoes onto the other bank and waded across, letting my filthy, sweaty calves enjoy the sweeping motion of cool mountain water. I stopped midstream, not ready to get out, and looked at Kevin, who hadn't said anything else. He didn't take off his shoes, but took a flying jump, landing easily next to my shoes, where he just plopped down to look at me. "Well. What Kevin?" I repeated.

"You can't go home." He paused. "I mean home home."

I stood, slowly feeling my toes go numb in the cold water. "Why not? This place is getting too crazy for me. It's not what I remember."

"What do you remember?" Kevin slowly took off his shoes and edged his toes into the clear water.

"Swimming without a worry, ice cream at Dolly's, walks with Mom and Dad talking about what it would be like to move back here. Friends and families going on forever about the weather and who will start as head coach at Brevard High." Tears started to flow. "Hot summer days where you stand out in the thunderstorm just to cool your body, a quick drive up onto the Blue Ridge Parkway, just because there's nothing else to do. Easy hellos as you walk by folks downtown that you don't know." I looked at Kevin who was almost frowning. "And most of all, feeling safe, feeling like there is nothing bad here, nothing that will take away my sanctuary. My childhood!"

Kevin slowly waded over to me. "Wow, I never knew I lived in such a place." I could feel a sadness in his voice and suddenly I could feel his song. I knew now where his melody came from, his longing for what I just described, a world I thought everyone in Transylvania experienced, but- - I was wrong.

1872: President Grant is re-elected in spite of bribery charges; 500 Klansmen are arrested in South Carolina; Gang led by Jesse and Frank James robs a bank in Kentucky.

The Church

"Can I watch?" Five-year old Bunyan jumps up to sit on a log rolled up to the side of the barn. The barn smells like wood chips and sweat, just the place he wants to be.

"May I," Craf corrects his young son, but smiles at the bundle of curiosity. Craf is more than happy to have his son be the mascot of the odd trio of men who are sweating away, intent on building their own house of worship right in their growing community. The Loftis family is donating land on a knoll right next to the increasingly busy Turnpike. Folks are excited about a real worshiping, healing community meeting place all their own. Craf fondly remembers his conversation with his father on the bank of the Little River years ago, looking up at the knoll, hoping one day they would have their own house of worship.

" 'Course you can!" Frosty Jack yells up out of a long trench that has been dug deep in the ground parallel to a large log. At fifty-six, A.J., "Frosty Jack", is the oldest and the most experienced woodworker with furniture and carpentry.

"Just 'cause you're the oldest doesn't give you permission to interfere with my parenting!" Craf laughs and throws a handful of wood chips at the white-haired man in the pit. He is thankful for the friendship he has with Frosty Jack and knows Jack needs him too. Craf knows that at forty, he may be small but he too is gifted with his hands. And he is skilled with draft animals that could drag the foundation stones from the river, as well as the massive logs to saw.

"Are you-uns goin' to play around or get to workin'?" Craf and Jack turn to the voice of a young man who is straddling the log that lies parallel to the trench and astride two beams across the pit. The two seniors are grateful they drew Walter Raxter into their confidence. He is their close friend, younger, with a strong back and work experience that belies his seventeen years.

"Looks like Craf here needs some woodchips flung in his face," Frosty Jack jumps out of the trench and offers Craf his spot. "I think it's your turn to be pit man." It has been hard work with one in the pit and one on top of the log, pulling the saw. Walter, the youngest, often volunteers for the pit since most sawdust lands on him, but they quickly learned that he was much stronger and could do more by being the top man and pulling the saw against gravity as well as guiding it while it cut on the down stroke. So Craf willingly takes his "sawdust-in-your-face" place in the pit. He is also proud to show off some in front of Bunyan.

It has taken nearly two years for them, working here and there when they could find time, to snake the logs from the woods and cut them into lumber. Craf and Jack both have set aside places in their barns where they could pull the logs onto a frame across a pit they'd dug. The times they could work at it were usually during bad weather and the barns offered not only protection but also a place in the loft for the lumber. And the sawdust was close to the stalls without hauling. Being a community effort, the church building project draws labor from many different families whose names will be on the final roll. But the three men are willing to be the core group and guiding inspiration.

Board by board, they slowly prepare the wood. Nothing tests their friendship and resolve more than the sawing of those logs. They joke about alternating between the barns in order to leave their anger and frustration in the other pit. Toward the middle of their efforts, they decide to have the last logs, especially the big ones, mill-sawed by Jackson Gillespie in nearby East Fork. The Gillespies are willing to help out for a church endeavor and have already been helping in several ways.

Frosty Jack walks over to sit on the large log where Bunyan has spread himself out to watch and he jumps up to sit next to the boy. He explains to Bunyan that the huge log they are sitting on is one of several of the largest logs that are saved for Jack's great handiwork -- the pews which he feels should be of solid boards, top and bottom. "They ought to be one, like we ought to be one together."

"Jack, what on earth are you a-talkin' 'bout?" Walter has stopped sawing to let Craf brush the sawdust out of his face.

Jack pats the large log as if he sees something inside he is itching to release. "Lots of folks are making pews with slats of wood nowadays. For me that's like so many individuals, kind of a-setting close but not together. We ought to be one in the Spirit!"

Craf laughs, "There you go preachin'! It's just wood. Give me something practical and leave that for the preachers who will come."

Frosty Jack is quick to respond, "Well, the solid plank I plan to put underneath every pew ain't just for strength but for warmth and to keep young-uns from a-crawlin' underneath too far!"

By now young Walter has climbed off the log and is homing in on his water jar. As more water hits his bare chest than his mouth he looks at Jack quite confused, "For warmth? What on earth can you be talkin' 'bout?"

Craf climbs out of the trench and heads for the barn door. He opens it to let some cold air blow to clear the growing stuffiness. As he turns to let the breeze cool his back he speaks before Jack can answer, "Some of the professors from Furman who come through a-teaching -- and I read about it and saw some pictures -- said that in the old countries those big cathedrals and little churches don't have heat in the winter, so they close in the pews, especially at the bottom, to keep down drafts. Folks just wrap up good. I hear tell that some in England and in New England are like boxes with little doors to let you in."

Jack shakes his head a little. "Now fellers, that fancy they ain't gonna be. But I hope to put together a nice little pulpit to go right behind the sinners' bench."

Walter, moving back to straddle the log, asks, "And just what is a 'sinners bench'?"

"Some churches call it a mourners' bench. I reckon you Baptists call it the altar where folks come to repent," Jack responds patiently.

Meanwhile, young Bunyan listens intently, soaking up the conversation like a sponge. Finally, he asks his burning question, "What about those men who did those bad things, like burning the Hume Hotel down the road and stole things and killed old man Deaver. Were they 'sinners'?"

All three grown-ups stop, looking at the child and the anger mixed with enquiry in his eyes. Finally, Craf asks, "Son, where did you hear about that?"

"Papa," Bunyan responds, "ever'body talks about it and how it is not fair that they got away with shootin', burnin', thievin' and other bad stuff."

Walter suddenly starts to fiddle with the handle of the crosscut saw and looks apologetically at Craf and the others and says, "I'm sorry. I reckon he musta picked that up at our place when he was stayin' with us some. So many Raxter and Hogsed kids runnin' around, they pass along a lot of stuff - 'specially what's fair and ain't fair. Sometimes it's just 'bout who got the biggest biscuit but other times it's 'bout how them bushwhackers got plum 'way with some real bad stuff."

Craf is thankful Harriet is not here, after worrying about Bunyan so much. "No need to apologize. Of course he would pick up some. I have been hesitant to say anything about the terrible acts of the outlaws who did so many bad things because I saw unbelievable actions by them during the war. Maybe I've been too quiet."

An inquisitive Bunyan jumps down and walks over to his father who is still standing in the breeze. Suddenly chilled from the cold breeze, he pulls in close to his father's legs, but looks straight up at him. "But what 'bout my question? Would this 'sinner's bench' be for the bushwhackers too?"

They all look at Frosty Jack and with their eyes call on his wisdom of years to respond to a deep question of this five-year old.

Waving the young boy back over to sit on the large log, out of the direct cold, Jack calls forth his understanding. "Young man, that shore is a good question. Yep, the sinner's bench, the mourner's bench, the altar for repentance, or whatever you want to call it, is also for bushwhackers. It is for anybody and ever'body who needs to repent and change their ways." Jack pauses for a minute. "Different churches have got slightly different words or meanings."

"Huh?" Bunyan seems confused as Jack goes on, quite aware that Walter is just as intent on a clearer explanation. "Well, you and your folks was at that camp meeting where they had a kind of altar or mourner's bench and asked folks to repent and come to accept Jesus into their hearts." Jack gently puts his arm around the young boy. "And for some folks it's more a private matter where you come to pray and ask forgiveness privately, or take communion."

A persistent Bunyan asks, "Would a bushwhacker come then to do any of those things?"

Jack shifts awkwardly, but his voice does not reveal any doubt. "Only if it's in their heart to do it."

Not afraid of how high the log is off the ground, Bunyan suddenly stands to his feet, now towering over all three men. "And if not, what happens? Do they get away with all they did?" Bunyan's eyes are fiery again.

Craf , the man of mercy, clearly hears his son of justice. He closes the barn door, leaving a crack for some circulation. He goes over to the log and takes his son in his arms. "Son, we always hope bad people will change their ways. Fact is, many do not. For that reason we have a sheriff and other law folks that try to keep such things from happening and capture those bad people who do them. Even in the Bible times they hoped there would be some justice. Someplace it says something like, 'Let justice roll down like waters.'"

A seed is planted in a young mind.

As the three men resume cutting the logs, young Bunyan's mouth is closed but his mind races with ideas of justice, even though it is not yet a functioning word in his vocabulary.

Summer 2012

My feet finally couldn't stand the cold water any longer. I hopped up on the bank and started putting my shoes back on. Kevin slowly got out and joined me. He hadn't said much, so I finally broke the silence, "Okay, Kevin, I won't go home home. I'll just go home, BUT I still think something's got to be done. I know Junior and Roy are your brothers, but it's just not right."

"I know," Kevin started, "But I don't know how." He still didn't look at me. His hair looked matted with dirt from the hard work Charlie had thrown at us and there was still some hay sticking to his shirt. I started to pick off the hay when he suddenly flinched. "Stop! That tickles!"

It was good to hear a giggle, so I poked him. "Really? Like this?"

"I said stop it!" Kevin tried to be serious. But I could see him smile. So I poked him again right in the armpit, and then I felt his arms suddenly grab me and fling me into the river. The shock of the cold water sent me jumping up gasping.

"Oh! You are so dead!" I grabbed his leg and pulled him in too. He came up out of the water gulping air and flinging water at me. It didn't take long for our fully drenched bodies to lie sprawled out on the bank.

He looked at me and asked with a big grin, "So, is that what you're talkin' about?"

"Yeah! That's what I'm talking about!" I was suddenly aware of how close I was to Kevin and became fiercely aware of a question I had wanted to ask him.

"What is it?" Kevin must have seen a change in my look.

"Can I ask you a question?" I propped myself up on one elbow. Kevin just nodded and looked at me sort of worried. "Why do your brothers keep calling me your girlfriend and you never correct them?" I paused. "Even I teased you about it the other day and you didn't correct me."

Ever so slowly Kevin's cheeks turned red. He looked away and became concerned with twisting the water out of his shirt. "I don't know!"

I wasn't about to accept his lame answer. "Yes, you do! Don't give me that!" I tried to keep it light but Kevin suddenly looked almost afraid.

"Look, Millie." He finally looked at me with eyes that begged me to understand more than he was going to tell. "It's just safer that way."

"Safer?" I was totally confused. "So, I'm not your girlfriend, but you tell others I am, so your brothers tease and harass you about it and somehow it keeps everyone safe?" The ridiculous scenario almost made me laugh, but the look on Kevin's face kept me from making a fool of myself.

His eyes were dark and serious. "Yeah, somethin' like that."

1872: The first Negro enters the U.S. Naval Academy; The first American woman to graduate from law school, Charlotte E. Ray, also becomes the first Negro female attorney in Washington, D.C.

The Methodists

"Your folks been connected to the Methodists for some time?" Craf asks Frosty Jack as they begin to line up the pews.

Jack pauses to make sure there is enough leg room between pews. He signals for Walter to help him nudge one pew slightly to the left. As soon as he is satisfied he looks at Craf. "Oh yeah. You know Bishop Asbury was through these very parts some years ago."

Craf suddenly sits down and then stretches out. "Was he that circuit riding preacher who rode all over our country, a-preachin' and teachin' and startin' churches?" Craf breathes deeply, also savoring this moment of being so close to completion.

Jack and Walter take a hint that it is time for a break and each finds his own pew. Jack sits in the one in front of Craf. "Yep. I read once that he done rode way over two hundred thousand miles and ordained something like four hundred preachers." Jack stretches out too and gently touches the back of the pew, proud of his handiwork. "He wrote 'bout his travel in a journal you kin buy. He was in Old Buncombe County up an' down the French Broad Valley. Kept going over to Mud Creek and even wrote 'bout coming up our Little River here! As I remember readin', it was 'bout 1803."

Craf asks, "Did he like our part of God's creation?"

Jack laughs, "Well, Craf, as I remember, he shore sounded like he did when he heard an' seen our purty waterfalls and clean world, different from where he'd been. Somethin' 'bout escaping all the filth, fleas, rattlesnakes and so on. He even wrote 'farewell western world -- for a while!'"

Walter interjects, "Guess he didn't meet our rattlesnakes and the fleas just didn't come out to greet him!"

Craf's retort is quick. "You mean two-legged ones?"

All are laughing when Jack shifts the topic, "I shore am pleased that so many folks from all around these parts is a-makin' this building happen. Hard to believe that so many Baptists, and even Presbyterians and Episcopalians been a-givin' some kind of help. Even folks that never went to church."

Craf's sits up and leans forward to rest his elbows on Jack's pew. Looking down on his relaxed friend, Craf's gentle addition comes forth, "That is the mountain way. Folks see something is needed and they do it. We help feed sick neighbors and care for each other's stock or hay or whatever. Everybody knows we need a church in our community and they pitch in."

Jack echoes his friend's observation and goes further, "Yep, that's right. And we all enjoy the camp meetings, the brush arbor gatherin's and even hearing the piles of different evangelists that ride through. But they is gittin' less frequent and, quite honestly, some of them preachers sound like they got the only truth and ever'body else is wrong."

"That," Craf adds, "is why we need something consistent like regular Bible teachers and some educated preachers."

By now Walter has started to line up the last pews, "And maybe some of our Baptist kinfolks over on Dunn's Creek headwaters need the same!"

Finally, the big day arrives, a celebration Sunday, dedicating the new church. It is an exciting time and folks come from far and near: from Cedar Mountain and Buck Forest, from Dunn's Rock/ Connestee and Dunn's Creek, from East Fork and Jeptha, and all the way from Brevard and Cherryfield. Even from Greenville.

Craf has chosen the same next-to-the-back pew as earlier in the week, now a spot that holds a fond memory of the final days of "the trio." And he notices Jack and Walter have done the same. Ready to enjoy the service, Craf is not pleased that people ask him to say something before the guest preacher from Oak Grove Methodist Church speaks, Waving them away gently, he cannot and will not, preferring to be in the background.

Aware of Craf's humility, but also understanding the community's need to recognize Craf, his good friend, Andrew Jackson Loftis, 'Frosty Jack,' rises to the occasion.

Jack walks to the altar, which he himself so carefully crafted, and he awkwardly pats down his hair. "My dear brothers and sisters, I thank all for comin'. My friend, Craf McGaha is tired out from his hard trip just yesterday to Greenville to get the last of the pressed glass you-uns all see in these windows. Did we have a hard time getting' them all put in afore today!" A few muffled laughs rise up to ease the awkward moment.

Jack continues without looking at Craf, for fear of faltering, "But you-uns all know him and that he really is shy 'bout talking to a big group of folks, always doing something for others without credit or praise. He done put that glass up so the light and love of God kin enter this little house of worship. And also enter our hearts."

Comments rise up and Jack hears, "That's Craf all right!" Craf feels a few pats from behind. He knows his face is red, but he sits still.

Jack continues, "You know too that for years he and Harriet have taken in not only strangers and friends but took in their beasts, giving refuge to all creatures that needed it. Although Margaret and I done give this little piece of land, Craf done give us inspiration to make this a spiritual way-station, a real light along this Turnpike and within our community."

More voices arise in agreement and Jack lets the crowd share their thanks.

As the noise subsides Jack shifts his eyes to look at young Bunyan. "Long afore that awful war he was burdened for people in need, not just folks who was hungry or poor or sufferin', but also for them with evil in their hearts, them that hurt others out of the evil in their own hearts."

Craf feels his son's hand touch his leg. Craf reaches out and covers it with his own.

Jack addresses the crowd further, with a rising confidence in his voice, feeding off the energy of the people, "We done seen the split a-coming long afore the guns was brandished, how all our families was torn asunder and Craf kept tellin' me that the only way to heal it was spiritual-- only God can bring us-uns all back together agin." Jack pauses and softens his voice. He finally looks at his friend. "So this oughta be a place without politics, without malice and revenge, a place where love and hospitality kin be found, where healin' of hurt hearts can be done." He pauses once more, holding back the rising ache in the back of his throat, "Thank you, Craf. Without you, this woulda never happened."

Five year old Bunyan finally climbs up into his father's lap and sees everybody looking at his father. Tears are pouring down Craf's face and soaking his beard. Bunyan puts his little fingers in his dad's long beard and says what he feels from his heart and from the hearts of others, "I love you, Papa."

Summer 2012

It was Sunday morning and Mammaw had to do an extra shift and open the Dollar Tree that morning. I told her I would be all right, but somehow wished we were going to church. I remembered summers with Mammaw meant church service at Carr's Hill Baptist until noon followed by potluck meals with so many pies and so much fried chicken that when we came home everyone would take a nap. This summer we'd been to church once and Mammaw knew it was something I missed, but she was constantly being called in to work because others weren't showing up.

I had her drop me off at the Sherwood Forest entrance so I could walk up to the McGaha Chapel across the street. I told her I would meet Ellie at the restaurant at noon and we'd eat lunch together, but I just wanted some time alone first. The whole conversation with Kevin about being his girlfriend when I really wasn't bothered me more than I thought it would. It wasn't like wanted to be his girlfriend; I just felt like I was playing a game that I didn't understand.

The old dirt road gently curved up under a canopy of tall pine trees, whose needles gave a carpeted feeling to the road. Once I stood in front of the old wood structure I could see El Capitán below with the gas station on the other side already busy with well dressed couples quickly getting gas before they headed down into Brevard for church.

I hadn't been there since Kevin pulled me through one of the windows some weeks earlier. As I stood on a large tree stump carefully rolled up under the same window, I checked to see if the window was still open and it lifted easily up with a gentle shove. I was really careful not to force it since the glass looked pretty old.

Using my elbows I awkwardly climbed into the room, wishing Kevin was there to pull me in, an entrance I remembered to be much easier. After I stood in front of the old pews and the wooden altar I walked over to the front and sat down on one of the side pews that leaned up pretty close to one of the other windows. I stretched out on the pew and found myself once again admiring the width of the pew back. It wasn't long before I heard a soft rain fall and the gentle tapping against the aged window panes soon lulled me to close my eyes. It was the first time ever I had felt such peace. Deep down I longed for answers to the craziness of my summer, but I knew that answers were obviously not meet to come my way. Only three more weeks, I told myself. I knew it would all end and I would go back to my huge high school where texting was the only way to be in touch with anyone and everyone, back where the smell of Mom's salon would let me know she was home, and where Mammaw and Transylvania were once again a memory.

As I opened my eyes, I became aware of the many carvings on the pews. At first I was ticked that stupid idiots would come in and tear up such a beautiful piece of mountain history. Then I looked a little closer. That's when I saw it. KEC + EA. It didn't take me more than a heartbeat to know that I was looking at Kevin Emerson Carp and Eleadora Alverez. I suddenly understood. I felt like such an idiot . . . I had sudden flashbacks of both of them knowing that there is a piece of wood in the bushes to cross the Little River, the familiarity between the two when they walked out to Rich Mountain, and finding refuge in the chapel, and, of course finding them in the barn. My head started spinning. Of course, that's why he beat off his brothers that day at the camp and that was why she didn't press charges. Not because they were friends, but because they were more than friends. I knew now, too, that I was Kevin's "girlfriend" to keep Ellie safe.

1875: The Whiskey Ring Scandal is exposed, implicating many, including President Grant's secretary; Out west the "Hanging Judge," Isaac Parker, executes 60 of 79 criminals on his gallows with the sign above announcing "Gates of Hell."

The Trackers

"Uncle Tom?" The beautiful sound coming from Tom Fowler's fingers as they dance across the neck of the fiddle make Bunyan hesitate only for a minute, but he knows he'll never get a word in if he doesn't interrupt. Bunyan loves that his uncle has some Cherokee in him even though he pretty much looks like the rest of the mountain folk, with a full beard, leaving only his twinkling eyes peeking through. The eight year old boy seeks out more time with Tom since new siblings have come into his life. Florence and Missouri demand Bunyan's share of Craf's attention. Bunyan figures that time spent away from the crying and fussing babies was time well spent, especially if it meant he could learn some Cherokee ways.

"Yeah, Bunyan?" The music stops abruptly, but Tom's gentle eyes show no irritation with the young boy. He slowly leans forward in the high-backed wooden chair - - his throne on the small front porch. "I reckin you be figgerin' to git out and track agin?"

Bunyan starts to jump up and down like a jackrabbit. "Oh, please, can we?"

Looking up at the sky as if contemplating the wisdom of the request Tom scratches his graying head. "Don't reckin' it'll be too safe bein' about dusk." Bunyan keeps jumping up and down with a pleading look on his face. Finally Tom stands up and slaps his leg. "Well, let's git, son." He suddenly pauses and tries unsuccessfully to look very serious. "Of course you best not jump 'round like that 'cause you're likely to scare off even the littlest ant." Bunyan stops and looks worried, but his smile returns when without hesitation the fiddle is packed away.

Tom immediately disappears into the thick brush only a few feet from his house with young Bunyan on his tail. The sweet smell of rhododendron and the thick canopy that the bushes offer make the young boy feel like he is walking through a magical kingdom. "Where are we goin' today?" Bunyan finally whispers after about twenty minutes of weaving through pockets of dense brush and following narrow paths, obviously traveled by few.

Tom stops and stares at the boy. "What did you just do wrong?"

Bunyan drops his eyes and whispers, "I spoke out loud." He looks back up to his uncle with pleading eyes. "I'm sorry. It won't happen again."

Tom softens his eyes and then gives his nephew a swift slap on the shoulder. "Let's go and see what animals lurk 'round our church in the evenin's." Then he winks and swiftly moves on.

With renewed excitement Bunyan follows. What could possibly come to the little wooden church at night? Bunyan wonders if some animals might take shelter under the raised floor. As they approach the building Tom waits for Bunyan to quietly decide the best location to lie in wait, an honor that Bunyan takes very seriously. He remembers the first time Uncle Tom let him be in charge and he did such a good job that they could have practically reached out and touched a doe.

Loving the heavy cover of the rhododendron bushes, Bunyan chooses a spot where the large leaves are the densest. He signals for Tom to join him and takes heed not to speak. Tom smiles at the young boy as they nestle in close together and begin their long wait. The silence surrounding them only gives Bunyan a stronger sense of adventure. He digs deep to keep his innards from jumping up and down, a feat he has mastered late at night lying in bed. As darkness completely rolls in, the moon begins to shine so brightly that Bunyan suddenly realizes why Uncle Tom checked out the sky earlier. If there had been cloud cover they would not be able to see.

Soon they find themselves watching a small raccoon as it climbs up the front steps of the church only to find the door securely fastened. Bunyan begins to turn his head to smile at Uncle Tom, when he suddenly feels the man's hand grab his wrist, a warning only used once before when they came upon a rattlesnake. Bunyan slowly turns his head to see where he might have not seen a snake when he realizes that there is movement at the church. A wide-brimmed hat hides the face of a man who stealthily maneuvers himself around the front of the church to the left side. He is carrying a heavy jug, hesitates briefly and then quickly places the jug under the church. Then as quickly as he appeared he disappears. Bunyan tries to look at his uncle, but only sees a dark mass lying very still. Just as Bunyan is about to break his promise and speak, he sees a second figure approach the church. This man is also unidentifiable due to an awkwardly cut canvas bag he has draped over his head. He doesn't hesitate as the first man did, but walks up to the same spot, grabs the jug and runs as quickly as he can back the way he came.

The two trackers lie still for a good half hour before Tom finally speaks, "We'll be a takin' the path home." He climbs out of the bushes and Bunyan follows. Play time is over and a heaviness hangs in the air.

"What were those men doing?" The young Bunyan catches up and dares to take his uncle's hand. He looks behind him every so often just to make sure they are not being followed.

Tom doesn't hesitate to hold the young boy's hand, although it had been a good two years since the last time they had done that. "Don't worry. I'm shore them bootleggers is long gone!"

"Bootleggers?" Bunyan began to feel a fire burn inside. "You mean they were a-hiding and swapping liquor under our church?"

"Shore looks like it!" Tom keeps a steady pace, and Bunyan finds himself almost running.

"Well, that jist ain't right!" Bunyan's slips into dialect as his fear is now clearly replaced with anger.

Tom still holds onto the young boy. "No, it ain't right!"

Summer 2012

I lay still on the old wooden pew staring at the carved letters KEC + EA and thinking about Ellie and Kevin as a couple. It was still too soon to meet Ellie and I really didn't want to see her or Kevin. I couldn't shake the feeling of being used. I thought that I had made new friends, but I was really more of a convenience. I stood up and headed for the window. I thought I might as well go on home and just call Ellie and tell her I felt sick. I reached the window when I saw a familiar hand lift the window pane. The almost white hair popped up before it was joined by a suddenly very red face. "Oh, hi, Millie. What are you doing here?" There was shuffling of someone else's feet below, obviously running in an attempt to hide somewhere.

"Well, Kev, I guess I'm just discovering that you and ELLIE," I yelled loud enough for the hiding body to hear, "seem to think it's fun to use me as your decoy!" Kevin looked like a deer caught in headlights.

"What?" He stammered, awkwardly climbing into the church.

I sighed and looked at him with a you've got to be kidding me look. I stomped over to the pew with the heart roughly scratched into it and pointed at it with my eyebrows raised. I stared at the young man who was starting to look like a three year old caught with his hand in the cookie jar.

"Oh," Kevin said flatly, "I guess that was stupid."

"You thank?" I did my best local drawl more easily this time, but it fell flat as something inside me felt sorry for the pitiful guy.

"Hey, Millie." Ellie was peeking in the window and Kevin went over and pulled her in, this time not letting go of her hand once she was inside. She looked at me and was not as pitiful as Kevin. "I guess we should have told you. But we were too afraid that you would stop hanging with us."

"And stop being your cover!" I put my hands on my hips and was trying to fight back the tears.

Ellie and Kevin were silent for a minute. They looked at each other and then back at me. When I couldn't take it any longer I started to walk towards the window. I was done. Suddenly Kevin touched my arm. "Don't go. You are right, we did use you as a cover, but not 'cause we planned it that way. It just happened."

I sighed and wiped away the tears that were starting to blur my vision. "Oh yeah, THAT makes me feel better."

"Well, it should!" Ellie was a little more factual about the whole thing. "Look, Millie! We never lied to you. We just never told you the whole thing. And when our parents were more relaxed about us hanging together because you were along, well, that made it even better. We did a lot of things together and I hope you still want to, but if not then that's your business."

"Wait a minute!" I could feel my face turn red hot. "Don't you for one minute make this something I should blow off!" I turned and climbed out the window. "This is YOUR issue NOT mine!" I looked in the window one last second before I jumped to the ground. "And shame on the two of you for vandalizing an historic church! You obviously don't care about your heritage!" With that I jumped down and marched indignantly back down the road under the pine tree canopy, hanging heavily in the growing humidity.

1875: Railroads now crisscross the nation; Alexander Graham Bell invents the telephone, a "harmonic telegraph," by accident; Pinkerton Detective Agents are unsuccessful in attempting to capture the Jesse and Frank James in their mother's home.

The Funeral

October 16, 1875 brings great sadness to the congregation and the entire community. Craf cannot believe the first funeral in the little chapel would be spent saying goodbye to a McGaha, much less his own mother, Candice Hightower McGaha. Even nature seems to be showing reverence as it begins to color the mountains with gold, red, and brilliant orange. Craf stands in front of the chapel for a moment waiting for his father so they can enter together. He breathes in the slight breeze and smiles at the beauty that surrounds them.

As Craf waits and listens to the muffled sounds of friends and family who wait patiently inside he cannot believe that ten years have passed since the awful war ended and yet times are still hard for many. He is grateful that through the years there has been joy and relief in the building of the chapel alongside the Turnpike and the Little River. It is a place where the community comes together and meets to worship, learn and have weddings and funerals. Yet there is no graveyard for the small chapel, so Jackson Gillespie, beloved neighbor and early Trustee for the chapel, has offered to make grave preparations and to transport Candice's remains to the Orr Cemetery over toward East Fork.

Jesse finally reaches his son, bringing Craf back to the dreaded day. "Papa, I'm so sorry." Craf tries to comfort his dad as they both finally stand in front of the open doors.

"Yeah, I know, son. We all are. She's in a better place and ain't hurtin' now." Jesse tries not to relive the last moments with his wife, but the tears are hard to hold back. He grabs his son's arm and squeezes it indicating he is ready to step inside.

But Craf hesitates for one moment and tries to speak with some authority. "You'll come to stay with us now?"

Jesse looks at his son and is grateful, but gently shakes his head. "Ain't no way. But thanks. I can make it by myself. I had to care for your Mama and got pretty used to fixin' vittles and cleanin'."

Craf returns his father's look and realizes there is no arguing, not this time. He simply whispers, "Okay."

As Craf begins to lead his father inside it is Jesse who hesitates this time. "One other thang. Whenever my time gits here, I want your promise you'll plant me next to your Ma over in Orr Cemetery. It's right purty an' I got to be next to your Ma."

"Course." Craf goes on, slightly ashamed that he has not prepared for this moment, "Sorry we don't have our own cemetery, bein' as McGahas are so many and a-growing."

"Son," Jesse replies, "It'll come in its own time. That's maybe your job someday. I just want to be laid down next to your Mama-- nowhere else!"

Craf realizes he has missed the point and needs to assure his grieving father, "Absolutely. I'll guarantee that whenever your time comes it'll be Orr Cemetery next to Mama."

Jesse manages a smile and breathes in deeply. "That's all I need to know. Thanks." He nods at his son and they both finally turn to face the open chapel doors.

8

Summer 2012

I somehow hoped that Kevin and Ellie would follow me and was disappointed that they didn't. I guess I had seen one too many soap operas and life really was more complicated and crazy than anything I'd seen on TV. At that moment the feeling of hurt was like a bad meal I just wanted to puke up because I knew I would feel better if I could just get it out. Suddenly the three weeks ahead seemed too long and I wanted to go on home. But I would never do that to Mammaw, so I decided to just shut my mouth and not say anything.

I walked onto the small bridge at the entrance to Sherwood Forest and leaned over the side. The Little River flowed without a worry as it had for generations. The thought of that gave me peace. I could picture my father and grandfather building dams and wading to cool off their hot and dusty feet. I was thinking of climbing down the riverbank and putting my feet in with the hope of restoring my initial love of Transylvania when I noticed a vehicle coming up close behind me. I didn't think much of it since Sherwood's residents came and went all the time, so I simply stayed to the left side of the bridge. I suddenly felt fear grasp my body as a brown van came to a stop next to me. A very dark arm was resting halfway out the window and a cornrow filled head smiled the biggest white smile I had ever seen. "Hey, girl! What cha doin'?"

I stood frozen, but managed, "Going home!"

"So you live aroun' here?" I notice that the young man looked older than I had thought he was earlier when he showed up at the Allison Deaver House. Now, close up, his skin wasn't that of young man's and I could see that his face had years of shaving. Yet, his tank top and nose piercing indicated a younger man.

"Maybe." I just stared.

"Damn! Am I that scary?" The driver started to laugh. "Ain't you ever seen a black man before?"

I frowned, slightly confused. "Oh, no, it's not because you're black." My face reddened.

"What is it then?" He lifted his arms and smelled his pits. "I know I don' stink."

I was trying to relax just a little. If he was going to try to sell me drugs then he wouldn't do it with the golf course behind me dotted with men and women brave enough to take on the heat. I finally tried to smile, "I just don't know you, do I?"

The young man nodded. "Fair 'nough." He reached his hand out the window, "I'm Eamon." When I didn't take his hand he just slowly pulled it back in to the car. He frowned slightly as if baffled by my behavior. Finally he sighed, "Okay, I'll leave you alone." As he saw me relax, he quickly added, "So, do you ever swim at Trout Lake?"

I stiffened again. "Maybe. Why?"

Eamon tried to be as casual as possible. "Just wonderin' if you ever explored the other side of the lake? Like found any old paths or anythin'?"

I frowned and my heart started to race again. What did he want? To find another way to get to the Carps to get his drugs? "Not really." I tried to be factual, without offering any info on the path the Carps used to get to the lake.

Suddenly Eamon was done with me. "Okay, thanks. See you 'round." He backed up, turned and then headed down the Greenville highway. I just stared at his Proud Army Mom bumper sticker.

1876: General Custer and his 7th Calvary Regiment are destroyed at Little Big Horn by Sioux and Cheyenne led by Chiefs Sitting Bull and Crazy Horse; "Wild Bill Hickok" is killed playing poker in Deadwood; Centennial Celebration of United States is held in Philadelphia.

Redmond

"I can't believe it's come to this!" Bunyan has never heard his father so upset. He slowly moves closer to the kitchen door and sees his father sitting at the table with his head in his hands.

Harriet continues to dry a pan that is clearly already dry. "Why on earth can't you believe it! He is a moonshiner and everyone around here knows it! He's probably one of them using our precious church to sell the devil's brew!"

"Harriet, you don't know that!" Craf looks up at his wife. "The Major worked mostly with his driver, best friend, and brother-in-law, Amos Ladd, and he worked out of the 'Dark Corner' over near Saluda on the North Carolina-South Carolina line."

"Well, I heard they had a warrant for his arrest for his moonshin' last month, but he didn't turn himself in, did he?" Harriet's hands were on her hips.

"But murder, Harriet?" Craf shakes his head. "I just can't believe Lewis Redmond murdered Al Duckworth! Not only his friend but a Deputy U.S. Marshall."

"What?" Bunyan walks into the kitchen where the smell and warmth of the wood burning stove still chases away the cold chill lingering on these March mornings.

Harriet gives Craf a look what you've done look, but Craf is not bothered by her notions of what a boy of eleven should or should not know. He motions for his son to sit and pulls himself together as much as possible. "Son, it's true. The way I heard it from family and local officers, Duckworth was supposedly trying to serve a warrant and stopped Redmond and Amos as they came off a hill on or near the East Fork area in their wagon. Since they knew each other, they talked and Redmond convinced him to lower his pistol while he read the warrant. We do not know what went through anybody's mind in such tense moments. A gun is on you. You may go to jail or get shot. Your family starves. Anyway, it seems that Amos passed a small pistol to Lewis who fired it at Al, hitting him in the throat."

"Papa?" Bunyan interrupts. "Why would anybody shoot a feller in the throat? Even an outlaw knows to go for a head or body shot!"

Craf nods in agreement and is surprised at his son's ability to consider all the facts. "My thoughts exactly. And that makes me think it was more accidental, like a struggle or a warning that went wrong." Craf ignores Harriet banging the pan down with more force than necessary. He continues, "We know that Redmond was an excellent marksman. In any case, Duckworth died from the shot. "

Bunyan leans into his father, "Are you a-sayin' it wasn't cold-blooded murder?"

Craf is pensive for a bit and then responds, "The story is a sad one. Both Lewis and Amos reportedly told someone that Al asked for water, there next to that creek. In such a short time there are already different versions of the story. Some say he died there, others say he died later. The real questions focus on whether he had on hand a valid warrant for Redmond or just claimed to have it."

"Do you know all this for sure?" Harriet finally says her piece. "What your Pa is not telling you is that what really happened will never be known and the stories around Lewis Redmond, the so-called 'Major,' will grow until we won't know who the man is anymore! And where is he now?"

Bunyan looked at his father who paused and shook his head. "No one knows!"

"You and I know that's not true!" Harriet tries to calm herself and walks over to her son. She wraps her arms around his back and steadies her voice. "Bunyan, the man is hiding out up in these mountains and it's for sure that he has people hiding him. It's just a matter of time till he's caught." She pauses and then turns Bunyan to look straight into her steady eyes. "Your Pa thinks you're old enough to hear this story, then hear this. Sometimes we have to make choices and pick sides, even if it's for or against friends and family."

Summer 2012

With Eamon gone I finally headed for the bank of the Little River. I sat down and pulled off my flip-flops and let my feet soak up the chill of the flowing mountain water. I stretched out on the bank letting my feet dangle. I couldn't wrap my head around Eamon and the Carp brothers. I wondered how much Kevin knew and if I should tell him what happened at the Allison Deaver House and here. But suddenly the old hurt came flooding back. I figured he already knew since it seemed like it was a summer of secrets.

"Millie? Is that you?" I could hear Mammaw's voice from the bridge. She had climbed out of the Big M and was heading down the small grassy slope toward me.

"Hey, Mammaw. You're done early?" I smiled. I could feel my chest burst with joy.

Mammaw was breathing heavily when she awkwardly sat down beside me. She reached out one leg for me to pull off her shoe and unroll the knee-high hose. I bore the whiff of sweaty feet as I fumbled with the shoes and the hose until both were off. Mammaw hiked her dress up as far as it would go without embarrassing me completely and eased her feet into the water. "Well, I got to work and they ended up not needing me today after all. They finally fired the no-show girl and hired someone who we all hope will be there on the weekends." Mammaw patted my leg and suddenly looked serious, "I thought you were meeting Ellie."

I couldn't help but let the tears flow, "She's not quite the friend I thought she was."

"Do you want to talk about it?" Mammaw asked as she watched her very white toes wiggle in the cold water.

I leaned my head into Mammaw and felt the weight of her arm around my shoulder. I whispered, "Not really."

1880: The U.S. Census shows a population of 50 million people with over 11 million immigrants in the last ten years; A major gold strike is made in Alaska; The first American woman receives her Ph.D. in Zurich, Switzerland as no U.S. school will give the degree to a woman.

The Naming

Unified as they are about the need for this house of worship, the folks of the upper Little River community in the Dunn's Rock Township cannot settle on an appropriate name for their beautiful little house of worship. For many months they struggle with a decision.

The Holdens and Rabbs try to convince them to go with something relating to their township of Dunn's Rock. The Fowlers lean toward something relating to nearby beautiful Rich Mountain. Some suggest that the name relate to the Loftis family who gave the land but the modest Frosty Jack will have nothing to do with it. Still others call for nearby Cedar Mountain to be in the name as it has become so widely known.

Sometimes with good humor, sometimes with tension, the debate goes on.

Finally, September 30th rolls around and F. M. Pressley, preacher in charge, has gathered the small but still growing congregation together. Everyone knows why they are gathered and yet Pressley wants to make sure everyone understands. "Dear friends, for months, even years, you have debated the name for your group. A decision must be made to register all the legal documents at the courthouse. After talking with W.C. Daly, your Presiding Elder, he and I agreed that we would meet today to decide and finalize our class list of members. Thank you for passing the word around!"

As the debate begins there is much of the same vacillating between names. After an hour the Reverend is exasperated with the lack of progress. He stands and commands attention. All look to Rev. Pressley as he speaks. "Brother Craf McGaha, I have noticed that you have not said much in this long debate. Can you share with us your thoughts?"

Craf stands slowly and pauses for a moment before speaking. "It seems to me that a more descriptive name could be used. Right now the only one I can think of goes back to when we were part of Henderson County and they called this area the 'Dividing Ridge' as part of their school strategy. Besides, the ridge that divides the south-flowing waters on Little River and north flowing waters of Connestee Creek and Carson's Creek is just down the Pike a bit."

Elder Daly laughs loudly and says, "Leave it to our own teacher and surveyor to provide that brilliant compromise!"

Craf gives a thankful nod, but remains pensive, "We can do that now, but let us all be open to the Spirit should another one come forth. My preference is simply that it is descriptive."

Rev. Pressley does not hesitate to grab the moment of opportunity and so it is that a document is made up.

1880
Class Book for Dividing Ridge Church
1. 1. M. J.C. McGaha   CL to S
2. 2. M. Harriet McGaha
3. S. R.W. Raxter
4. S Sarah S. McGaha
5. M. Susan Eubank
6. M. P.E. Keith
7. M. Susan Eubank
8. M. Harriet E. Sidney
9. M. Felix Rabb
10. M. M.A. Loftis
11. M. Jane Rabb
12. M. Nancy Summey
13. M. Nancy Galloway
14. M. Sarah A. Holden
15. M. Thomas Fowler
16. S. Sarah E. Holden
17. M. Mary A. Fowler
18. M. Nelson Holden
19. S. Alice Eubank
20. M. Tiny L. Whitmire
21. S. Montranella Fowler

Elisebeth P Orr
Sally Yewbank
Louiza Orr

Infant member ship
1. Florence M. McGaha 9 years old
2. Misouri T McGaha 6
3. Ellen Eubank 5
4. Nancy Eubank 2

Sept the 30th 1880
W.C. Daly Presiding Elder
F. M. Pressley Preacher in Charge

A month passes and paperwork as well as new bureaucracy in the struggling Transylvania County, along with Craf's overextended surveying work in the County, delay final deed work for the church. Yet spirits are high as the excited group meets one final time.

Craf stands at the pew he claimed so many years ago. He looks around at the other families, who have done the same and he asks to speak. "You will remember that my former idea was to tie our name to the setting. I've been struggling with what we signed up for. I was so tied to the past when we were Henderson County and now few folks remember where the 'Dividing Ridge' is. Worse yet, I have learned that there are several 'dividing ridges' in Henderson and Buncombe Counties, as well as another here in Transylvania."

Craf pauses and hears a few people sigh, "Oh my!" There is some headshaking and a few members sit like stones with their arms crossed.

"It came to me in a dream that maybe that name wasn't right for another big reason. Like the streams flowing south and north, dividing this area, our families here and this whole land was also 'divided' between North and South. The whole purpose of this worship place is to bring us together, not divide, to heal the awful wounds and unite."

Craf takes a deep breath and goes on, "So I suggest we finalize our name as 'The Little River Methodist Episcopal Chapel.' It tells where we are in more ways than geography."

Craf can almost taste the relief that spreads across the room. Everyone seems to be satisfied and they vote almost unanimously to finalize the name. The Rabbs abstain.

Summer 2012

I dangled my fingers over the edge of the dock just barely touching the top of the water. Trout Lake rippled ever so slightly as I repeated the motion until I couldn't take the sun beating down on me anymore. So, I rolled off into the cool water causing a greater ripple to disrupt even the stillest water now gently slapping the far bank. I floated for a few minutes almost wishing the sky would open up with the welcoming afternoon shower, but the blue sky promised no such relief.

I tried to empty my head, and managed to allow myself to bask in memories of summers past. At times I thought I could even hear laughter and my father's voice telling me not to swim too far out into the lake. I don't know how long I floated. Eventually I noticed I was touching the mushy lake bottom, but the trees overhead were not ones I recognized surrounding the dock. I stood up quickly, letting my toes sink into the squishy muck made of years of rotten leaves, algae and other gunk I didn't like to think about. I saw the dock, now on the other side of the lake and couldn't believe I had let myself float so far.

I sighed and then proceeded to lower myself back into the water to swim back, when I suddenly saw a water snake dart across the water in front of me. I hate snakes, poisonous or not, and I was not about to share my journey with one. I quickly backed myself out of the lake and up onto the bank. I had to grab onto the branches of a half buried tree and was pleased to find a well-worn path on the other side of the tree. My bare feet were thankful that I would be able to have a comfortable walk back.

As I headed toward the dam, I suddenly stopped and looked back at the path leading deeper into the woods. Why was Eamon so curious about this path? Why didn't he just come and walk it himself? There was nothing spooky about it in the daylight, so I let curiosity lead me. I figured as long as my bare feet could handle it, I would explore. Flashbacks of discovering the Transylvania forests with my father seemed to egg me on and a sense of belonging crept back into my soul.

The path remained worn as long as it generally followed the lake. A couple of places along the way I found wooden benches obviously placed there by the homeowners to make the lake a quaint place to take a morning stroll. At one point, as I came closer to one bench, I saw what looked like a deer trail heading off into the woods and I thought it could be the trail the Carps used to get into the neighborhood. So, gingerly, I stepped along the path and soon had to pick my steps more carefully, avoiding briars and haphazard branches jutting into the path. It didn't take long for me to realize that I wouldn't get far, but was grateful that I could blame turning around on my bare feet and not the growing fear inside.

I stopped and took in my surroundings, noticing the path took a steep turn upwards and disappeared into the heavy brush that seemed to climb up the face of a boulder, much like the rock faces that we passed on the way to Rich Mountain, just smaller. Brush, mostly rhododendron and laurel, grew along a ridge on either side of the rock face, looking much like small rising and falling mounds. I figured several other rock faces were hiding, not as lucky as the largest one which was still able to show off its beautiful gray granite. I tried to walk as close to the boulders as I could get, carefully picking my steps, when suddenly I was overwhelmed by the strong odor of cat urine. I could feel my head spin and I backed off from the boulders afraid some panther still lived in these woods.

As I turned to leave I was startled by the sound of laughter. I looked back at the row of boulders, but did not see anyone. Again, I heard a voice, but this time I recognized Junior's harsh tone, "Roy, you idiot!"

The voices were near, but I didn't wait to find out exactly where. As quickly as possible I ran back down the path trying to muffle my cries as I stepped on more than one briar.

I couldn't get back home fast enough. When I got to Mammaw's house, I locked the door behind me. Still, I just couldn't figure out why Eamon needed me to help him find the Carps. It seemed easy enough, as long as he wore shoes.

1884: Grover Cleveland is elected as the U.S. President, in spite of a paternity scandal and campaign slogan ""Ma, Ma, where's my Pa?" answered by "Gone to the White House, Ha, Ha, Ha.!" Cocaine is introduced as an anesthetic for medical use.

Teasing

It is a good year for most in the upper Little River Community of the Dunn's Rock Township. The Methodists send Rev. Pressley from Asheville to pastor the church, albeit part-time, but the people are packing the little building full, even when a preacher is not present. The little pump organ lends help with music and it is not uncommon to have the pews full and folks standing outside listening through the windows. And already folks are calling it the "McGaha Chapel" in the warm, welcoming spirit of Craf.

Fall has once again returned and Craf and Frosty Jack stand last in line as the congregation patiently waits for the preacher to have a few words with each member before they head home for a Sunday dinner. Craf stands at the top of the steps and enjoys the familiar crisp fall breeze. Finally, Rev. Pressley speaks to Frosty Jack and Craf, "What a team you two are, with you, Craf, surveying and teaching while Jack keeps peace."

Frosty Jack corrects him gently, "Now preacher, I'm not the sheriff or deputy. I'm jist the Justice of the Peace fer these parts. I try to settle disputes, resolve little cases, kind of like a local judge."

Craf chimes in, "Yeah and most of his cases are mine!"

"What on earth!" The preacher's face pales slightly. "Well, Brother J. C. McGaha, I never heard that you had trouble with the law." Confused, the holy man awkwardly wipes his forehead with a worn handkerchief he pulls from his pocket. "This shatters my image of you."

For just a moment Jack and Craf look at each other and then at the embarrassed preacher in front of them. Suddenly they burst into laughter. The preacher, not sure what is happening, just looks at the two, thankful the rest of his flock have moved on. Finally Jack explains, "Whut he means is that fer a mighty long time most disputes is over land, messed-up boundaries, lazy measuring an' paperwork. He's got to come in tu survey an' correct so many lines. We-uns even got to correct the lines twixt our own properties! So with'n his fair surveys an' reputation my job is done made easier. Folks is pleased an' feel justice is done; peace is kept."

Rev. Pressley finally smiles and feels somewhat ashamed of thinking anything less of Craf. He reaches out to shake his hand and wants to move the two men on home. But Craf sees the preacher is now embarrassed and wants to keep him engaged. He doesn't allow the preacher to let go of his hand, but leans in, pulling Rev. Pressly in close to him as if revealing a secret. Craf almost whispers, "Now, Jack, tell the preacher what else you have up your sleeve."

Jack looks around to see if others can hear. Satisfied no one can, he makes a request. "You gotta keep this under your hat 'til the decision's done."

The preacher, still gripped by Craf's hand, nods.

Satisfied, Jack continues, "I'm a-talkin' with the County Commissioners 'bout a contract to be Toll Gate Operator for both the Johnstone Turnpike and Little River Turnpike. That's what they call the Greenville or Hume Turnpike now."

"Jack!" the surprised preacher manages to free his hand from Craf's and asks, "What in the world does that mean and how can you do that with all you are already doing?"

Jack gives the preacher a hearty pat on the back. "Well, with lots uv help. My young-uns done growed up. With local fellers from old families like the Gillespies and Lances, we pretty well know ever'body here. 'Course we'll be obliged to keep the road up, and that ain't easy on Mill Hill."

Rev. Pressley looks at the white-haired man and frowns ever so slightly, "How come? It is steep with lots of curves, but clearly well built."

Jack doesn't miss a beat. Drawing a picture in the air he weaves his arm back and forth like a snake. "Well, Preacher, you hit on the hard part - the curves. If'n you look at the big size of the rocks a-holdin' the pike up in the steepest curves, and see that after a good mountain freshet a heavy wagon can either drop a wheel over the side or pry a big rock off'n the road, we got big work ahead of us. It'll take a good team of strong oxen and locust pry-bars with strong backed men to reset the stones."

"I had not thought about all that. I reckon we take the road for granted. By the way, you said 'know everybody.' "Why must you know everybody? Don't you just collect tolls?"

Jack pointed his finger at the preacher, like he had just figured out the answer to a riddle. "Haw! The idear is thet we collect jist from non-residents of the County. Locals don't pay. So, I reckin since you don't live in the county you'd be one of them paying foreigners, Preacher!"

Craf, seeing the confused look on the preacher's face, interjects, "That is unless you keep giving us some good sermons. Then they just might look the other way."

Jack, realizing that he might not understand their teasing, adds, "Well, Preacher, we ain't gonna charge toll to any man of God traveling this way on church business, whatever his church might be. His Bible is his pass!"

Craf smiles and adds, seemingly seriously, "Now, of course, that is not a license for bad sermons!"

All three are laughing by now and the preacher is finally at ease. He looks at the two men and musters up as serious a face as possible. "I got to head back toward Asheville to get home by dark and before somebody puts up another toll gate!"

Summer 2012

Mammaw nudged me off the couch and made me go to the door when she heard Kevin ring the bell. I really didn't want to, but unless I was willing to spill everything about them to Mammaw I knew I'd better answer the door. As I opened the door I saw Kevin looking at me with huge eyes, as if he was waiting for me to say the first word, but I finally just jutted out my chin and asked, "What? You're the one who rang the bell."

Kevin's eyes dropped and I felt like a creep for being so rude. But suddenly the whole day came flooding back to me; he and his brother were creeps, so I didn't feel so bad. He lifted his eyes to look at me again and this time was a little more direct, "Can we talk?" He glanced past my shoulders into the house where the TV was blasting. "Where we can be alone."

I sighed and yelled, "Mammaw, Kevin and I are just going up to the lake for a few minutes."

I heard the TV suddenly go mute. "Don't be long, hon, it's gettin' dark soon." Then full volume filled the room again, but was soon a fading noise as Kevin and I headed toward Trout Lake. Each of us sat in a swing and slowly moved back and forth in awkward silence.

"I'm sorry I didn't tell you," Kevin finally whispered.

I kept looking at the lake and the small ripples randomly appearing and disappearing, a sign of the multitude of little bugs skimming the surface. "I guess I should have known." I paused and then suddenly shoved his swing. "Stupid me should have guessed you guys were really rolling in that hay!"

Although it was getting dark I was sure Kevin's face turned bright red. "Yeah, I thought that was pretty obvious!" I turned my head to finally enjoy a laugh with Kevin, when I saw his head drop. "It was so obvious that Charlie about worked us to death!"

"Oh!" I suddenly understood why Charlie was somewhat irritated and also that Charlie must have known about them for a while. Of course this left me feeling so totally gullible and naive. "So, Charlie doesn't quite approve of the two of you?"

Kevin paused for just a minute and looked up at me. A small smile crossed his lips and gentleness appeared. "Actually Charlie is the only one who gets it. He's always watchin' out for the both of us. But . . ." Kevin's pause was longer than I could handle.

"But what?" I finally said before he totally lost his train of thought.

"But he just worries about us. He especially worries about what my brothers will do when they find out we're together." Kevin sighed and then just looked at me with an okay its all out look.

But I knew it wasn't all out, so I thought I'd push this one since Kevin looked like he wanted to be letting it out. "So, what about Junior and Roy? I saw them the other day handing off something to someone at the Allison Deaver House. I was just thinking maybe they are selling drugs. Just wondered if you think the same. . . Sorta worries me really." I tried to sound so matter of fact, but it was slightly overkill.

"What?" Kevin stood up suddenly and came toward me. He stood in front of me like a tower.

I wasn't going to have him stand over me like that so I stood right up in front of him. Although he was taller we almost stood eye to eye. "Kevin," I tried to say as gently as possible, "I was just asking you a question."

It was almost dark, but the moon was beginning to work its magic so I could still make out the very frightened look on Kevin's face. His breath was so close that I could feel its increased pace. "What do you want, Millie?"

"Kevin?" I was really confused now. He stood still and locked eyes with me. The fear remained.

"I can't turn in my brothers." A tear fell.

I wanted to touch him, but I knew I couldn't. So I just stood there breathing in his warm breath. I held his gaze. "I'm not asking you to."

His body relaxed just a little, but his stare remained. "Millie, there are some thangs you'll never understand."

I could feel a lump in my throat grow. "I guess you're right."

1884: The Prime Meridian is set at Greenwich, England; The machine gun is first introduced; Eastman introduces cheap photographic film.

The Greenville Run and Reunion

Bunyan looks around awkwardly at the ladies who seem to be staring at him, his father and then the hogs as they enter Greenville and head toward the train station. A tall, striking seventeen year old Bunyan accompanies his much smaller and aging father on one of their several weekly trips to South Carolina. Bunyan often gets bored on the long trip and is now lamenting to himself about the early warm weather which forces them to bring the load of stinky, squealing hogs to a slaughterhouse near the train station.

Bunyan speaks above the noisy hogs, "Papa, it sure was easier when the weather was cold and we could 'quieten' them before we left and deliver meat straight to the restaurants."

Craf smiles and says, "Son, yep we could kill and butcher them through th' winter months or bring salted meat. But the fact of life is that without ice, this is the best we can do. I wonder if what you really regret is not bein' able to gad about Greenville town in the summer 'cause we stink like these hogs! Not to mention the ladies who keep starin' at you. Don't reckin they've seen a handsome and stinky fellow."

Craf laughs hard at his own comment as Bunyan turns red. When he sees the look on his son's face he slaps the young man's back. "Tell you what, there is a little snack place next to the railway station where lots of railroad workers and other sweatin' folks like us go. We'll take a lunch break there."

Bunyan smiles and is thankful for his father's gesture to eat something besides their day-old cornbread and salted ham. It is not long before the two hard-working men return from the slaughterhouse to the railway station where they see a very large crowd gathered, apparently waiting for the next train from Columbia. Railway workers across the tracks are moving about to prepare the water refill for the locomotive boiler.

Curiosity over what occasion would draw such a large crowd causes Craf to lead the way to a station master standing near the platform edge. "What's goin' on? Is President Arthur or Governor Thompson coming through?"

Shaking his head the smiling stationmaster proudly responds, "Even bigger! The world's most famous outlaw, our own Lewis Redmond, has been set free, pardoned by th' U.S. President and is a-comin' home!" Craf and Bunyan forget their hunger and wait to watch, slightly overwhelmed by the spectacle.

The stationmaster orders the crowd back further from the platform edge but allows Craf and Bunyan to remain next to him as the smoking monster eases to a halt just past where they stand. He watches carefully and helps the conductor with passengers exiting but stops those without tickets from entering during the Greenville stop. He explains to Craf, "I got a wire that all along the way from Columbia, folks were crowding on the train just to shake Redmond's hand or give him a gift. He's still headin' on to Easley, but he'll be in this station 'til we get the water tank refilled."

About that time Bunyan says, "Papa, somebody is calling you from the train window. Looks like he's on crutches and might be sick." He points up and back only a car away where none other than Lewis Redmond is smiling and motioning. The station master and conductor both see it and, nodding to each other, motion for the two McGahas to go on board.

Bunyan and Craf do not hesitate to step onto the train and move into a compartment where a sickly man is standing and waving for them on to join him. Bunyan can't help touching every bench as he walks by them, feeling that it is too bad he can't ride along to see what a moving train actually feels like.

"Craf McGaha, how be ye?" an enthusiastic, yet weak, Lewis Redmond asks as he sits back on the bench holding his crutches.

"Major, I did not recognize you after all these years." Craf is startled and pleased.

"Well, just call me Lewis like when we was kids. I shore am glad to see somebody from Transylvania in these parts. I reckin I ain't too awful welcome up there. But it's where my roots is."

Craf is uncomfortable and does not know how to respond, remembering vividly the killing of another neighbor, Deputy U.S. Marshal Al Duckworth by Redmond over on East Fork not far away from his home. He simply nods.

Lewis looks away and focuses his attention on Bunyan, "And be this your boy, this strapping big feller?"

Much relieved, Craf says, "Yep. This is V.B. Sometimes we call him Bunyan. He is seventeen and is one hard worker."

Bunyan stands in silence as he stares at a man who seems more like a beaten dog than a world famous outlaw. Redmond uses his crutch to tap the bench directly in front of him. "Set down young man on that bench over there. I'm gettin' a crick in my neck a-lookin' up so far! You shore got your Mama's height an' good looks!" Lewis smiles gently and goes on. "Can I tell you some good advice?"

Bunyan nods.

Redmond clears his throat and pauses a minute. "You know what a wild man I was an' some of the bad thangs I done?"

Bunyan nods carefully, not sure where this is going.

"I'm a-thankin' God that I be a free man and not in the hands of the law. I got started out wrong in that blockade business an' thangs really got out of hand. My advice to you is to stay on the right side of the law and steer clear of moonshinin' no matter how quick you can make big money." Redmond coughs and catches his labored breath. He goes on, "I never sleep good a'nights, still feelin' real bad 'bout killin' Al Duckworth an' Amos a-gittin shot a-bein' mistook for me."

Confused, Bunyan looks at his Papa Craf who signals with his hand to not ask more right now. But Bunyan can't help himself, "So, why'd you shoot Duckworth?"

Redmond didn't miss a beat having obviously been asked the question more than once. "I never wanted to shoot Alf but I was shore that Alf had come only with the intention of shootin' me, 'cause he had threatened all over Transylvania County that he would do so."

Before Redmond could move on, Bunyan quickly added, "What led to so much of the hostility between you and all sorts of federal agents? I heard that you really intimidated and harassed agents in South Carolina."

"Well, there was a lot goin' on, son." Redmond straightens himself out some. "I did scare the daylights out of some agents and their families, a-takin' back wagons, coats and other property they done took from me. But the main reason was the killing of my best friend Amos by some agents. I know it was an ambush meant for me. I know it was murder." The noise from the crowd outside sounds like a dull banging on the windows. Redmond rests his head on the back of the bench. He pauses a moment and a faint smile appears. "I was real sweet on Adeline Ladd, Amos' sister, and finally married her. The two of them lived with their brother in a little log cabin down in Rocky Bottom with their widowed mother, Millie Cantrell Ladd. Rocky Bottom is just over the state line south of Jeptha."

Bunyan leans in to catch every word, "What happened?"

Redmond lifts his head. The smile is replaced with a distant stare. "Five or six U.S. Deputy Marshalls, as I remember, led by a man named Kane, done laid out in the woods nearby waitin' for me to visit. They watched 'bout dusk when a man come by, knocked on th' gate and Miss Millie come out to speak with him. They talked a bit then the man left. The lawmen waited all night long and the next morning -- it was a Sunday as I 'member -- the hidin' fellers seen a man come to the house, then another. It was Amos and his brother, busy 'bout chores or deliveries to neighbors or such. Amos set his squirrel gun in a corner whilst his brother started to shuck some corn, 'cording to his maw. Amos put a cow bell and plow point in his haversack and was headed out the door to the blacksmith's to get 'em repaired." Redmond shakes his head ever so slightly. "Now here is where the story's told different by Kane and by my Ladd in-laws. My wife's family says he paused by the door to pick up somethin' and the officers come from four directions a-firin' without warnin' or a-tellin' who they was. Millie Ladd done called out not to shoot whilst they was a-shootin' and Adeline yelled not to shoot 'cause it was her brother. I reckin she knew they was after me, not Amos."

Bunyan dares to ask, "What does the other side say?"

Redmond stares at Bunyan, without hostility, only admiration for this young man's need to see the whole picture. "Them officers later claimed that they did shore enough identify theirselves and that he went for his gun. But I never understood that part 'cause they done admitted that they themselves fled to the woods to hide out and figure out what to do. They laid out awhile, then one of them went to Mr. King's store to try to get a ride to Greenville. King done rented one mule to Kane, the captain of the group, and he done rode it to Easley whilst the other fellers done walked all the way to Greenville."

Craf looks out the window at the banners waving and remembers out loud, "There was a trial but they had to move the venue to Anderson because so many people were upset, especially when The Pickens Sentinel had their headlines reading "Murder in Pickens County by Revenue Officers."

Bunyan, aware that their time is limited, quickly asks, "What finally happened? Did they get off?"

Craf, aware of Redmond's growing weariness, fills in the facts. "Well, the trial went on and on and that officer Kane who was being tried for murder was found guilty of perjury and then disappeared. Word was that he fled out west and shot somebody in a stagecoach robbery -- shot one of the robbers as I read."

Redmond perks up one more time. "Ever'body wondered what I would do." The famous outlaw tries to laugh, coughing through the attempt. "The Charleston paper sent a man to search for me. After lots of tries he finally found a guide that took him an' Judge Fields from Pickens County deep into them mountains -- not far from here -- to interview me."

"Well?" Bunyan wanted him to finish.

"Ever'body thought I was hell-bent on vengeance, but the feller wrote that the visit was 'one of mutual respect.' That newspaper writer had just kind words to say 'bout me an' my treatment of them. It's all a blur now, but they might have tried to convince me not to take revenge." The outlaw leans his head back one more time and softly sighs, "I just want to git back to the cool mountain air with my wife and younguns and find some work, if'n farmin' won't provide for all them kids." The conductor slips in to tap

Craf on the shoulder that the water tender is almost ready and they should wind down. "I still cain't figure it out," Redmond declares with a puzzled look on his face.

A curious Craf asks, "What? Why the President pardoned you?"

"No, not so much that, bein' as Senator Wade Hampton and even the 'Torney General -- Brewster is his name-- was pushin' it. What throws me is how come them two fine women here in South Caroliner, Sally Taylor and Grace Elmore, organized such a big movement all over th' state of South Carliner to get me freed."

As the train whistle blows a warning for departure Craf and V.B. rush for the door. Craf looks back and asks, "What is so strange that two women in this state wanted to get you free?"

A smiling but still puzzled Lewis Redmond, declared in Northern papers to be the King of Outlaws and King of U.S. Moonshiners, throws up his hands to yell over the increasing train noise, "They be the leaders of the Palmetto State Temperance Movement!"

9

Summer 2012

"Hey, Dad!" I just needed to hear my father's voice, somebody close to tell me that everything was going to be okay.

"Hey, Pumpkin!" The familiar nickname that usually made me want to hurl now made me laugh. I was thankful he couldn't actually see me sitting in my pajama pants wearing one of Mammaw's cast-off tees or else he'd really think the name fit.

"Dad," I joked, "you know how much I hate that name!"

"Yep, just wanted to let you know I'm still here." His voice sounded a little strained.

I frowned slightly, "What is it? You sound a little weird."

I waited for what seemed forever for my father to respond. "Well, Millie, my job search . . . it's not turning up much." I could hear him clear his voice. "But don't you worry none! I'll figure something out."

"At least Mom's doing okay right?" I asked trying to sound positive, but feeling like I was going to cry.

"Yes, honey. Of course." His response was short and sweet, but I knew that it was stupid of me to think Mom was going to be able to carry all of us for very long. I could tell Dad wanted to change the subject when he sighed heavily like he was trying to clear his thoughts through his lungs. "So, how are you? Still enjoying your new friends?"

At that point I wished we were still focusing on Dad's misery instead of mine. I wasn't sure what to say. I wasn't too great of a liar, except to myself. So I came as close to the truth as possible, without having to make Dad worry about me in addition to his poor self. "I guess they aren't exactly as great of friends as I thought."

"Really? Why?" I thought it was just great that Dad had to ask the big why. I took Mammaw's shirt and stretched it over my knees until it looked like I was trying to make myself disappear.

"Not much really, just stupid girl stuff!" That was always a signal to Dad that he may not really want to know unless he wanted to talk about periods, boobs or boys.

My plan worked and he quickly backed down. "Oh, well. I guess Mammaw can help you through this one."

"Yeah, you're right!" I kissed him goodbye through the phone and then turned on the TV. I figured, like girl stuff, if I ignored my situation long enough, it would eventually all go away.

1891: The Forest Reserve Act is signed into law, giving the President the right to set aside public lands as forests; The zipper and the dial telephone are invented; Basketball is first played by bored students tossing a large ball into peach baskets on the wall at a YMCA facility.

The Picnic

The tall, strikingly handsome Volenus Bunyan McGaha arrives for worship on a Sunday, not at his home church, now commonly called 'McGaha Chapel,' but in a carriage with the equally striking Jessie Geneva Allison at the Dunn's Creek Baptist Church, one of the nearby churches Bunyan and his Dad had helped build back in the '80s. Many of the families have moved on to other churches, as the community has grown. Even some of the Raxters have moved on to several of the Baptist churches.

Bunyan is quite aware of the stares they are receiving as the gathering members glance back and forth between Jessie Geneva and himself. Everyone knows she is the daughter of none other than the beloved preacher, Rev. Elijah Allison and from one of the area's pioneer families.

Bunyan is thankful to see Walter Raxter's familiar face as he walks up to the church, but is less than grateful for his greeting. "What a shock V.B.! You see the light an' 'bout to become a Baptist?" Walter laughs, enjoying the giggles from others nearby.

Bunyan, puts on his best glare and looks directly at his old friend. "Maybe I am here to bring some light to you folks."

Bunyan suddenly smiles at the emergence of Laura, Walter's young wife. She comes right up to the new couple and reaches out to greet them. "Well, you shore brought some brightness with this pretty lady on your arm."

Suddenly the Dunn's Creek church bell rings offering a relief to the young couple. The Sears and Roebuck church bell that Laura had ordered had been the talk of several nearby communities since the preacher, for reasons no one really understood, had said the ladies of the church could not solicit funds from within the congregation. Not to be deterred, she organized several young, unmarried lasses to go throughout the neighborhood soliciting funds. More than one neighbor offered money to marry one of them!

Noting the little bell as an invitation to come inside, Bunyan quickly asks, "Can the two of you join us for a little picnic after church? We got everything with us and want to talk. Maybe down on top of Dunn's Rock if nobody is there."

Both Walter and Laura look at each other and nod approvingly. Laura leans toward Bunyan as if not to disturb the growing church silence, "We'd love that. We need a break."

As Walter follows his wife into the church he whispers to Laura, "Wonder what that is all 'bout?"

Aware that Bunyan and Jessie are awkwardly trying to find a pew where they can sit, Laura giggles. "Well, R.W. Raxter, if'n you ain't figured that out by now - him with that beautiful girl with him and us bein' a growin family -- then you ain't as smart as I thought you were!"

"Oh." Walter frowns slightly at his wife. He is quickly aware of the awkward Bunyan standing in the aisle and finally waves for the young couple to join them in the back row.

The service seems very long to the two couples. Walter whispers to Laura, "I ain't shore if'n the preacher is a-trying to impress Reverend Allison's daughter or to convert V.B."

They survive and after the service quickly hustle across the ridge and through some dense brush out to the spectacular setting on top of the rock. They settle themselves on the flat surface of a large boulder that acts as the final step before the larger rock below gives way to a steep cliff. The drop off is frightening, but the view is spectacular. The Blue Ridge Mountains rise before them casting multiple shadows. A new canvas is painted every minute as clouds pass over the French Broad River snaking its way through the valley below.

Walter and Laura are thrilled to enjoy the spread of cold chicken, yeast rolls, fresh tomatoes and leftover apple pie. Laura swallows a bite of pie and savoring the taste manages to speak, "Now boys, I reckin we'll have to go along with everybody else and call this 'Dunn's Rock,' not 'Indian Rock.' It's done called that on 'bout every map and 'sides that, below us is 'Dunn's Rock' community with a post office of that name. And that's our township name anyway."

Bunyan, loving to tease when he can, comments, "Oh, is that anything like changing from Connestee to Dunn's Rock Community down there? Folks took away references to the Cherokee when they made that change."

Laura watches Bunyan stretch out on the quilt. She bites her lip not to laugh at his attempt at showing off for Jessie Geneva. Yet Laura won't give this young know-it-all the last word. She just can't help herself. "Many folks still use th' names back-ards an' for-ards. They know this was the Cherokee Connestee village an' old-timers, especially, use that older name. And they kept the name for Connestee Road, and the falls where the mill was for years. Of course we still got Connestee Creek."

"You win," a smiling Bunyan laughs, "and I suppose since the Dunn's Creek Baptist Church is official now it's only right we give up and call this 'Dunn's Rock' since it is so close. The Dunn family will be happy we give in." Bunyan reaches for another piece of pie and as he takes a bite, looks at Walter, "So tell me, you Raxters, besides planning lots of younguns, what else are you up to here atop this mountain?"

Walter speaks up this time, "You know we got a school a-goin', though it shore is hard to git teachers up here for the three months of school. We shore cain't pay a lot and we got to fill in as we kin ourselves." Walter looks down into the valley as if concentrating on something only he can see. The pensive man finally continues, "Laura and I hope to see a U.S. post office one of these days but the gov'ment works awful slow. Looks like it'll take a few years to git it done."

Bunyan cannot resist and asks, "What will you call it? Raxter-Hogsed-McGaha-

Holden Town? Or Behind-Indian-Dunn's-Rock Town?"

Jessie Geneva can hardly believe how hard Bunyan, Walter and Laura laugh. She is actually fearful that all three of them might roll off Dunn's Rock.

Once they have settled down, Laura looks out with the others at the large thunderclouds building over the forest and seeing the green valley below confesses, "I figgered out a name already. It'll be See-Off."

After another long silence, Bunyan takes a deep breath and says, "Wow. I am moved and impressed. No explanation is needed, sitting here looking out there. From here, and much of the ridge, you can really 'see off' to the mountains and valleys and it makes you feel good."

Jessie Geneva sits as close to Bunyan as she can and whispers, "It really does."

Bunyan smiles at his sweetheart and squeezes her hand, to which Laura and Walter raise their eyebrows, but say nothing. Bunyan, not wanting the threatening clouds to end the moment, continues, "I got to confess that when I was pretty little and Papa would leave me with my cousins up here on 'See Off' while he went over Slick Rock and on to Rich Mountain, I'd sometimes sneak off secretly and sit here, feeling a lot bigger and that I was on top of the world. It was a real peace for a worried child."

Laura picks up his feeling and snuggles in close to her husband who awkwardly takes a hint to put his arm around her. Walter can't help but add his twist to the romantic moment. "I kin understand that even now. It's right peaceful here, 'cept of course when there is noise from below like the old distillery mill wheel a-squeakin' along, or somebody a-beatin' their mules tryin' to git up Mill Hill down there with too heavy a load." Walter's romantic embrace is quickly ended with Laura elbowing him in the ribs.

"I think we'll get soaked if we don't go now." Jessie Geneva is finally the one to draw their attention to the immediate urgency of the thunderclouds that are upon them. Laura and Jessie Geneva frantically throw the picnic items into the basket while Walter rolls up the quilt.

"No problem," Bunyan says as he grabs Jessie Geneva's hand and leads them all down a steep path, halfway sliding into the old Indian cave where many children had played, dreaming of other times and Indians who looked out onto the valley for enemies or game.

The party climbs down over a few larger and smaller rocks defining the interior of the cave. The ladies head for the smaller rocks at the base of the cave, but before she can sit Bunyan takes the quilt from Walter and covers up a rock for Jessie Geneva, who immediately blushes. They can hear the patter of the first drops of rain and Walter, who can hardly keep from smiling at the young couple, asks, "And what 'bout you V.B.? What are your plans?"

Laura interrupts, "Hold on a minute. We ain't give Jessie a chance to say nary a word. I 'pologize for these two old friends who'll 'catch up' forever."

"Oh, and you've not done any talking?" Bunyan teases, as Laura tries to give him a glare, but can't keep back her infectious smile.

Jessie responds warmly, "Thank you, Laura. No apologies are needed. I enjoy watching them and how Bunyan carries on. But you asked about 'plans' and, before he takes off to avoid the topic, let me share what you are probably already thinking. We are going to get married!"

Laura hugs her warmly and Walter slaps Bunyan on the back with an affectionate, "You rascal you."

The four laugh and discuss wedding plans as the rain pours. Their view is obstructed, but the cozy atmosphere brings the couples together. It is not long before Jessie admits forthrightly, "We are making plans and do have some practical questions about setting up housekeeping. Our folks tell us a lot, but we thought you are our generation and could fill in answers for some questions we'd rather not ask our folks."

The men are a little red-faced. Walter then suggests, as he pulls out all the remaining food from the basket, "When our picnic is over you girls can take the wagon back and we fellers can stretch our legs. That way you can have girl talk and we can clear up anythang we ain't already talked out."

Jessie Geneva lets the men finish off the food before she addresses her fiancé, "Bunyan, do tell them about your other plans."

By now the storm is letting up and the valley below is slowing becoming unveiled. Bunyan climbs onto a large ledge jutting out above boulders below and is careful not to hit his head on the cave ceiling. With a watchful eye looking over this part of Transylvania County and even to Haywood and Jackson Counties in the distance, he replies, "I'll be running for Sheriff of Transylvania County come fall."

Laura was not sure if it was the wind and rain or the answer, but she suddenly felt a chill. "Put your big arms 'round me, Walter, I'm a-gittin' cold."

Walter wraps both arms around the shoulders of his wife and asks his young friend, "How come? What got into your head? I mean, ain't that dangerous work? V.B. with your size, looks and brains, you could do 'bout anything you want. You've done been a good farmer an' even got a mercantile business that folks love." As he feels his wife relax he continues, "And what 'bout helpin' yore Pa with his livestock? I heard he's running at least six wagons with meat for Greenville these days."

Bunyan responds, "Don't you worry about him. He's hired plenty of help and is a good businessman. But all that is changing." He pauses. There is silence as they all look at the view, awaiting a further response. "It's good we sit here. Remember a while ago when I said as a worried child I sat here?" Bunyan gestures outside the cave. The storm is gone and water drips haphazardly around the several openings of the cave as pieces of grass and sticks willingly let go of the last drops.

All three join Bunyan and nod. "Yeah."

Bunyan points down directly below them. The sun has begun to beat down on the saturated valley and small wisps of moisture rise like smoke. "Now look down there. You see the stone building remains right down there beside the Turnpike?"

Walter and the two women awkwardly climb up to get as close to where Bunyan is sitting as possible. "The ruins of the Dunn's Rock Hotel or Hume Hotel, whatever it was called?" Walter asks. "Them bushwhackers done burnt it down in th' war but left th' slave house over th' hill,"

Bunyan nods. "Well, that destruction used to bother me, and still does. I have always worried about justice or rather the lack of it. I reckon the bushwhackers were the worst but when other crimes can go on without any stopping, how can we bring up our families in peace? I want our coming children and your children to be safe. I want folks to be able to sleep at night without fear. When people work so hard to earn an honest living, like your folks and mine, we should not have rascals running around taking property and lives."

Walter and Laura just listen while Jessie Geneva scoots in next to her man, slipping her hand into his.

Bunyan reaches up to touch the ceiling. "It's kinda like this rock over top of us. Iit's there, given by God the Creator. It protects us from the rain, or snow or even sun if we want." Bunyan takes his free hand and knocks off some of the water hanging heavily from of one large rhododendron leaf. "All those things are good things, but they can become bad things, given the conditions. It can be hail that destroys our crops or snow and ice that breaks down our roofs and trees, killing them. Or it can be hot sun and a long drought that destroys our very livelihood."

"V.B." Jessie Geneva softly whispers his name in an attempt to sooth Bunyan's growing intensity.

Bunyan squeezes her hand, but continues. "People are like that. They are basically good, like my Papa says over and over. He really believes in the best in humans and that mercy is what they need. But I also see that folks can go too far, beyond good until they, like the weather, are bad. Then we must have justice, protection, like this rock over us."

Laura smiles. "Goodness gracious! That's a lot spoke, but I reckon I can understand. You'd be a mighty good protecting 'rock' for us all. But you are so young. Like me, you are just in your twenties. You reckon folks'll hold that against you, come votin' time?"

Walter, now excited in behalf of his friend, interjects, "Actually, I reckon it'll be a lot to his advantage. Folks around here is so split up over party lines and who you be beholden to. Worse'n that, the war is still on a lot of folks' minds and whose family was Confederate and whose was Union. He is perfect because the McGahas done fit on both sides!" Walter slaps his friend on the back and is on a roll, "Besides, he's got enough relatives in

Transylvania County to put him in office, if'n they all vote."

Laura is not to be left out, "And if he'll get around the county a-speakin' and a-meetin' folks, just his good looks will get the women's hearts a-fluttering so they'll insist their men put this handsome giant in office."

Jessie smiles, winks and says, "As long as that's all they do!" She jumps down to the lower boulders, then carefully folds the quilt and tucks it under her arm ready to leave.

Bunyan is more somber as he watches the rain clouds retreat toward South Carolina over the southern mountains behind them. "Thank you, my friend, for your support and encouraging words. Just one little thing. There is only one "giant" in the McGaha family, my Papa."

"Oh dear, Bunyan," Laura adds as she repacks the picnic remains into the basket, "I meant no offense. Of course, we-uns know him real good and that he's called a 'little giant' because of his lovin' heart. And him a-bein' your Papa ain't gonna hurt your chances a bit." Laura pauses as if she's had an epiphany. A smile crosses her lips. "It's like two sides of the same coin."

Walter frowns at his wife, "You done lost me there, Laura."

Laura, excited now to explain her metaphor, pokes her husband with one finger as if telling him to listen carefully. "All I mean is that while Craf is our man of mercy, Bunyan will be our man of justice."

Bunyan smiles and nods his appreciation at Laura's kind words. The young man finally steps onto the small path outside the cave and gives the other three a hand in leaving the cave. "I know that, but I hope to win the election on my own abilities and ideas and not on his coattails. If they give me a chance I'll show them we can have a stable, safe county."

Then with a chuckle he adds, " Oh yeah, some folks say I'll do better if I just go by V.B. McGaha. I reckon too many cannot spell Bunyan. I'll sure not throw 'Volenus' at them!"

Jessie pauses a moment as Bunyan helps her on to the narrow path through heavy rhododendron and laurel. She gets closer to him and retorts, "But when we are married and you are out of line, I'll sure use Volenus to get your attention!"

Summer 2012

I really wished Mammaw wouldn't go to work. The days seemed to slow down and I felt horrible for wanting to go home. I could hear her shuffle around and make way more noise in the kitchen than she usually did making breakfast. I pulled the covers over my head in an attempt to drown out any sound or smell reminding me of a place I used to love. I felt my throat get tight and I wanted to cry so badly, but I would once again wait until I heard the Big M roll out.

Suddenly I felt my covers pulled off me with such force that I found myself practically jumping out of bed. "That's enough!" Mammaw glared at me like I was a misbehaving child being reprimanded by her mother in the checkout line at Ingles.

"What?" I gave her my best I don't know what you're talking about look and frantically looked around for something to wear. The night before, not caring to sleep in any nightshirt or even take a shower for that matter, I had thrown off my shorts and T-shirt and jumped in bed with the same underwear and bra I had watched TV in all day.

"You have done nothin' but mope and watch TV for the last three days!" Mammaw stood like a pillar. "I ain't havin' it!"

"Well, what do you want me to do?" I reached for the wadded up shorts that had somehow landed behind my nightstand. I could smell a slight odor as I unwadded them, but I didn't care.

"You stink too!" Mammaw walked over and grabbed the dirty shorts out of my hand and she huffed and puffed as she grabbed all the clothes I had scattered like trash around her guest room. "I'll tell you what you'll do!" She stopped and beads of sweat had begun to form. "You'll start by washing your clothes AND your body!" She handed me the pile she had gathered with such force that I found myself shocked. "I don't know what you're upset about, but you're starting to stink up my house."

I suddenly felt gross. There I was sitting in my dirty underwear holding a dirty pile of clothes and Mammaw was highly disgusted. "I'm sorry!" I could barely get it out. The hurting in my throat finally gave way to tears.

Mammaw heaved a huge sigh and then attempted to sit next to me on the bed. She scooted away slightly as the odor was too much to bear. "Honey, you have two and a half weeks left. I hate to see you waste them." She paused and forced herself to move in closer. I felt her warm heavy hand on my arm. "I don't know what has happened to cause you to hate bein' here. But I do know one thing." She lifted my chin so I would look directly at her. "You are one strong, beautiful young woman. You come from a long line of mountain folk who do what is right, even if it means we have to lay in bed to recover from it every now and then. But, we do get back up and," Mammaw smiled ever so slightly, "we NEVER stink!"

1892: Grover Cleveland regains the U.S. presidency from Benjamin Harrison who had won it four years prior; Immigrants flood the U.S. and Ellis Island opens to help the process; Coca-Cola, the "intellectual and temperance drink" is charged in medical studies with 400 cases of drug abuse and addiction.

The Sheriff

The fog is slowly burning off promising a warm day in downtown Brevard as opposing party leaders, Charlie and George, settle themselves on the front steps to the new courthouse. The red brick rising up behind them into a clock tower only adds greater authority to the two men's sense of importance. The town politicians do not know what to do with V.B. McGaha, the young whippersnapper from out yonder down the Turnpike in Dunn's Rock Township, not from Brevard and not known by them. He is about to marry Jessie Geneva Allison from one of the earliest founding families of the area.

Charlie looks around at the awakening streets and nods at George to sit closer so they can hear each other. As the leaders of the Democrats and Republicans, the two men have decided to meet to discuss the coming race. The men are seen in public as tough adversaries but in private actually are close friends. "George, your party done put up V.B. McGaha's name for sheriff. He scares me. And I don't reckon our Democratic feller's got a chance against him."

George snickers and gently jabs his friend with his elbow. "Now Charlie, what scares you? That he might beat your feller? Or that he's so young an' big?"

With his politician's knowing smile, Charlie confesses, "Naw, more 'cause he's plumb idealistic and has got no idea how our little county works. He's just naive."

George's teasing smile fades and he nods. "I couldn't agree more. You got no idea how hard all this is for our Republican Party."

Charlie is confused with his friend's sudden agreement on a political issue. "But you prob'ly got a winner already. He's really pop'lar."

George moves in a little closer and lowers his voice. "That ain't all. You done hit the nail on the head when you declar'd he's idealistic and naive. When we met with him and the others who woulda run for sheriff, ever' blasted feller backed out of the race to support him! We asked V.B. 'bout party loyalty and 'bout his plans for hirin' deputies. He went and said he'd hire the most competent and honest he could get, no matter what their party or family connections were."

Charlie shakes his head. "Pore feller really has got no idea how it all works does he?"

With a conspiring twinkle in his eye, the Democratic Charlie asks, "Maybe we could dig up some stuff against him. How 'bout his future father-in-law, that Reverend Allison? I understand he was not just a Union soldier but also tucked his tail in Tennessee after the war for some time, scared to come home." A fire begins to emerge in Charlie's eyes. "Well, he shoulda been. Everybody knowed he was supposed to be a chaplain for the troops but that he also led Kirk's Raiders into these here mountains! He was a guide fur them rascals! And he was supposed to pastor some churches in Tennessee."

George lowers his voice to a whisper, "Let's hold on. That'd be a big mistake, my friend, to go after that man of God. What you say is true, but don't miss the rest of the story. I seen testimony that he was forced to guide them Raiders." The fog is gone and George's denim jacket is beginning to feel warm. He feels droplets forming on his forehead as he continues, "Besides, he was so popular that people demanded that he return home, which he done did. He's served so many Baptist churches and baptized so many citizens and performed so many weddings and funerals of our votin' folks that I reckin if'n we was to attack this young man by way of his future father-in-law we'd git a popular reaction to elect him!"

Charlie stands up and moves away from his friend, slowly descending the steps to a cleared area between the courthouse and Main Street. He inconspicuously motions for George to follow him. The Republican eagerly jumps up and quickly removes his jacket as he follows his friend to the small clearing, wishing the small sapling were already a large tree casting a larger shadow. Charlie finally speaks, "Let's look at 'nother way to skin this cat then. How about this young pup with no real experience and some problems? I heard once down at Hart's store that he and a friend really did some damage whilst they was a-drinkin.'"

George throws the jacket over his shoulder. "Folks might not like that. It did happen back in '86. V.B. and W. P. McGaha had something to do with the misdeed when Jesse Cleveland's blacksmith shop was burned."

Charlie practically thrusts a finger into his friend's chest. "That's it! Let's bring out his 'criminal' background."

Gently rubbing the now sore spot on his chest, George shakes his head. "Hold on, my friend. You ain't heard the' rest of the story. They stood up for it. I seen the paper that both of 'em signed at Hart's store. They done paid $14 dollars for the blacksmith tools and $10 for the building. This was 'paid in full' and signed for by Jesse Cleveland himself. Folks is a sayin' they learnt their lesson and no charges was ever brought."

"All right, George," Charlie slaps his friend's back, making George once again wince with pain. "I reckin you're right. Prob'ly the best thang is for us to speak with him and try to educate him some." The Democrat points down the street at a tall lanky man approaching the courthouse.

"And Charlie," George adds smiling at the few women who seem to stop and glance in V.B.'s direction as he passes, "You really ought to hear him speak in some of the public gatherin's. He draws folks like flies to flypaper, includin' the women who can't even vote. Even when he speaks about some lofty 'justice' ideals way above their heads, they seem to love him."

V.B. starts to climb up the courthouse steps, eager to visit the Sherriff's office located inside. The young man is suddenly surprised by Charlie and George who seem to block his way. V.B. finds it strange to have the supposed leaders of both parties wanting his attention. He hesitates for a moment and then sits down on the top step of the courthouse. "Gentlemen, I am here. What do you have on your minds? This seems a little unusual since you two are usually at each other's throats," V.B says as he tries to break the ice.

His own Republican Party leader starts warmly, mimicking the more learned grammar of their guest, "V.B. , how kind of you to come and talk with us. We all know of you and your family and what they have done and do for this wonderful county of ours." The sweat now dripping from both men does not escape V.B. He figures they have been waiting for him.

His Democratic counterpart echoes his compliments and more formal speech, "Oh yes, all fine folks of this county know of your dad and mom and the outstanding citizen that every family member is. How often did your dad sit on the jury here! And your future father-in-law-- is he some jewel sent straight from God, with all his ministries and . . ."

V.B. interrupts, "Gentlemen, you did not stop me to talk about my family. Can you skip all this bull and say what you want to say?"

"Well," his own party leader says, "there is some concern that if you are elected, you won't understand some traditions and experiences that are important for the good functioning of our county and its businesses."

The Democrat echoes, "Yes, please understand, nothing bad about you, just that you are young and might not have learned yet how it all works here."

V.B. is losing patience and lifts his knee to rest his arm on in order to appear interested. "Get to your point, gentlemen. What is it that I supposedly do not understand?"

George sits next to him, this time using his jacket to wipe the sweat. "We've got some mighty important businesses that provide jobs and income for some really poor families."

Charlie squeezes in on the other side of V.B. and lowers his voice, "And they also help support the Sheriff's Department with extra income the county can't get from taxes. We're still a small, poor, new county, you know."

V. B. McGaha stands up from the steps to his full height and looks down at the two leaders. "So you are speaking of the bootlegging business, the moonshiners all across our county who make their poison for marketing here and in South Carolina. Unlike the legal distilleries, they pay no taxes and there is no control of what goes into their rotgut. So you think their "gifts" to you and to law enforcement should be our own local 'taxes'."

Charlie jumps up, awkwardly looking around at the curious eyes that are starting to watch the exchange. "See here, young man, you cannot talk to us that way! We are only trying to be helpful in case you are elected. You don't want to offend the people trying to help you."

"Is that some sort of threat?" V.B asks, intentionally raising his voice.

The red-faced Democrat responds, "Oh heavens no, we would never do that. We only think of our friends and relatives over in Madison County, where they lose a sheriff every so often. We surely don't want that to happen to you and your fine family. Just think about what a dangerous job it is for such a young man."

"Gentlemen, this conversation is over." V.B. brushes by the two men to head into the courthouse, but stops short of the door to turn to the befuddled politicians. "It was a threat and I don't take kindly to that. And just for your information, between East Fork, Buck Forest and Rich Mountain I have watched several moonshiners doing their 'business' when I was growing up." He turns to face not only the men, but the small crowd that has started to gather.

V.B continues firmly and loud enough for all to hear, "I was really mad when I watched some of the bootleggers hiding their goods under the Little River Chapel until somebody else picked the jars up, leaving money. And what a slick game-- pretending they were going there to pray or talk to God. I even heard some joking around, they were just 'a-listenin' an' lookin' for the spirit'. And you know what? Several of them were your relatives, both of you. So be very careful what you say or threaten!"

V.B. turns and walks into the courthouse more determined than ever to win the sheriff's job, just to send a clear message or two. He is not for sale and there has to be some justice.

After this public exchange it is no surprise to the leaders of both parties when November comes and Transylvania elects a young, tall V. B. McGaha as Sheriff. People from both parties go for this idealistic fellow who promises to be himself and to work for justice and fairness for all, regardless of party or income or which side your daddy served during the war.

Not too long after the landslide election and some months of service, the Hendersonville paper reports:

MARRIED

In Asheville, at the residence of Mr. J.J. Ritchie Mr. V.B. McGaha of Transylvania County was married to Miss Jessie Allison of the same county. The groom is the present efficient and popular sheriff of Transylvania County and the bride the charming and accomplished daughter of the Rev. E. Allison all well known in Hendersonville. The happy couple arrived in this place on the morning train yesterday on the way to Brevard which place they will make their future home. May their happiness never wane is the wish of their many friends in Hendersonville.

10

Summer 2012

The smell of fajitas made my stomach growl as I heard the door to El Capitán shut behind me. I figured Mammaw was right; spending my last couple of weeks cooped up would be a waste. Since I hadn't seen Ellie in a while I decided to eat lunch where I might run into her. Ellie's mom greeted me hesitantly, but when I motioned towards a table and pointed at the menu she grinned and repeated si, si a million times until I was finally seated next to the window looking out toward the Greenville Highway. Suddenly I shuddered at the thought of the last time I was on the other side of that window. I could still see Junior hurting Kevin and threatening Rai, but then I smiled to myself at the funny looking Rai thinking he had chased the Carps off with a broom.

"What are you smiling at?" I turned to see Rai looking somewhat sheepish and holding a half-full tub of dirty dishes. The apron he had wrapped around his waist pretended to be white, but multiple stains and a recent spill whispered that Rai was not in his element.

I smiled at Rai and half laughed, "You!" I could see him wrinkle his forehead and glance down at the tub. I quickly clarified, "Not now!" I jerked my head toward the window quite aware that Rai was starting to stare me down. Suddenly his aha moment arrived and I breathed a sigh of relief.

"Oh yeah!" He said awkwardly, but soon regained composure with his cool hair flip, which I forced myself not to laugh at. "I chased them off pretty good."

"I guess you did. But I'm not so sure if it was good or not." I looked at him, mustering up as much authority in my voice as I could, "You be sure to run if you see the Carps coming!"

"What? That's stupid!" His harsh stare returned. "I ain't runnin'. . . from nobody!"

Attempting to return his stare, I looked at him for just a minute, "What is it with you? Do you want to get hurt?"

"Rai!" His mother's sharp call told us both our conversation was over.

Rai slowly stepped toward the table covered in dishes right behind me, but he couldn't help himself and turned his head ever so slightly. He wiped a dark wisp of hair out of his eyes, but it dropped right back into the same place. "What do you care anyway?"

1893: Panic hits when the stock market crashes, as 600 banks and 74 railroads go under; Bison are near extinction with 'sports-hunting'; Over 100,000 settlers rush into the opened Cherokee land in the Oklahoma Territory.

The Feds Visit

The Transylvania Hustler, November 3

U.S. Deputy Marshal J.A. Galloway and Assistant Thomas Galloway in City on visit.

V.B. sits comfortably behind his desk reading the The Transylvania Hustler, when his door slowly opens. Two men walk in and the older one carries two cups of coffee. "Sheriff McGaha, might you be interested in joinin' us for some coffee?" Marshal Galloway asks.

V.B. smiles broadly as he folds his paper, lays it to the side and motions for the two men to sit. "Well, fellers, this is a real surprise, bein' as I am still learnin' this work."

The Marshal hands V.B. the extra coffee and settles himself in the only other chair, while the younger man settles himself awkwardly on a discarded church bench shoved up against the wall. "We really need young men like you who can learn fast and who know these mountains."

V.B. lifts an eyebrow and looks directly at the Marshal. "Or the people of these mountains?"

"Of course, that too," Marshal Galloway says warmly and quickly takes a sip of his coffee.

V.B. turns to the uncomfortable shuffling of the young man against the wall. The Marshal's assistant asks, "Do you know any U.S. Marshals, or got any contacts?"

"Not really," V.B. responds enjoying the warmth of the coffee, "but I do work sometimes with Federal Revenue Agents who might bring along a marshal or deputy of some kind to help with jurisdictional issues." V.B. pauses and reflects for a moment and then remembers, "And of course everybody in these parts knew about Deputy Marshal Al Duckworth, one of our locals, who was killed by Major Redmond. I was just a kid when he was shot in our part of the county."

"That scare you?" the assistant asks curtly.

V.B. looks at the wild-eyed assistant who is standing and uncomfortable with the way the young man speaks. The Sheriff tries to ignore the curtness. "Not really. I just know the Duckworth family, who are fine folks, and how they suffered both in the loss and in that nothing was ever done by your colleagues to get justice done."

Marshal Galloway, senior by far, shoots the assistant a look which settles the young man back onto the bench. "Gentlemen, this is not an interview for the job, just a simple checking out if you might be interested."

V.B. places his empty cup on the desk and puts his hands behind his head as he leans back in his chair. "I can save you time and energy by saying 'no, not at this time.' I have a lot to do and have promised the people of Transylvania County to do my best for them."

The Marshal stands and approaches V.B.'s desk, pulling a card out of his well-worn coat pocket. "We respect that, Sheriff. Should you want to join later, do let me know. Here's my card." The Marshal smiles at V.B. with one last thought. "Oh yes, you also might want to consider the Revenue Service, if not us. In your own time, of course."

V.B. stands to walk the two men to the door when he is surprised by the close proximity of the young assistant who is looking almost straight up into his face. "Of course you just might have heard of the John Henson murder down in the Dark Corner. Everybody knows it was the young Suddeth brothers and Goob Hinson was a-helpin' the Revenue officers against the

Suddeth moonshinin' business. Then Revenue Agent Rufus Springs, that worked these parts as well as just over the line, got hisself kilt and they never knowed who dunnit. You scared of that kind of work?"

The tall, strong Sheriff McGaha stands erect and holds his gaze over the young man who is at least a foot shorter. He then leans down a little toward the man, getting as close to his face as possible and says gently, "Glassy Mountain and Highland folks come up here across the state line too and we all have respect for one another. Anytime someone is murdered like that, there must be justice and I'm glad to hear of the fine folks who have come forth as witnesses." Aware of the growing redness in the assistant's face, V.B. continues, "I am not Sheriff of Greenville County, but Transylvania. If it had happened here I'd do all I could to find the murderers and not depend on hearsay. Murder is in my jurisdiction, not yours, unless the victim is a federal officer."

Still leaning close to the now shaking face of the young assistant, V.B. speaks clearly to Marshal Galloway, "Now Marshal, I thank you for your visit and the question. You are always welcome here, but when you come back, I suggest you not bring this smart alec unless he learns some manners or common sense about talking with mountain folks. Please get him back across the line before I find he has broken some local law!"

With an apologetic look, Marshal Galloway grabs the not-so-brave young assistant by the collar and pulls him out the door of the courthouse.

Summer 2012

The taco salad was messy, but I enjoyed the texture of the crunchy shell against the mushy beans and guacamole. I tried not to look at Rai anymore since I was sure he was secretly wishing all my hair would fall out. But when I heard a sudden crashing of dishes I couldn't keep my head from turning to watch Rai frantically picking up the pieces with his mother quickly following behind him with a broom. I thought it was no wonder he had the broom so quickly the other day. He was probably cleaning up a mess he had made. Just as I was turning back I saw Eamon. His eyes met mine and he nodded at me. I turned my head away as quickly as I could, feeling the heat rise.

"You look like you've seen a ghost!" Ellie plopped in the seat across from me. Her hands were red and wrinkled. I could tell she had just brushed her hair and pulled it back neatly into two long braids.

I couldn't believe how happy I was to see her. I smiled at her. "Hey, Ellie, I was beginning to wonder if you were gone again."

"Very funny!" She half smiled, but heaviness remained. "So didn't Rai tell you that I just had to finish with my share of the dishes and I'd be right out?"

"No," I looked briefly at Rai who continued to shoot daggers at me. "I don't think your brother likes me very much!"

Ellie started laughing so hard that I started laughing too, even though I had no idea what the joke was. Finally she stopped and took a sip of my sweet tea. "Is that what you think? I would guess it's actually the opposite."

"What?" I took my tea back and had a nervous sip. "Look he's ticked at me for telling him he was stupid to face the Carps with a broom."

"Well, Millie," Ellie leaned in across the table. "Who do you think Rai was protecting when he ran out there with a broom? Kevin? I don't think so!"

I could feel my cheeks burn and I placed my napkin on the empty plate. "But that's just weird. He's so young!"

"Not that much younger, just a year and a half . . . soon it won't matter anyway." She smiled slyly. "Unless you keep coming back here every summer and you slowly build a long distance relationship until you are both finally ready to settle down and have kids!"

"Oh, shut up!" I threw my straw with a little tea left in it at her. We both started laughing until I forgot about wanting to crawl back into my bed. But the laughter did not last long.

I saw the dark hand touch the table and heard the familiar voice speak, "Hi Ellie." Eamon squeezed in next to Ellie who comfortably scooted over. He looked at me and I just stared.

"Millie, this is Eamon." Ellie introduced the huge white smiling teeth to me. When I didn't answer she continued, "He's a regular."

"I bet he is!" Was all I could manage and wished I hadn't said anything.

"Girl!" Eamon's teeth disappeared and a confused frown began to crawl across his forehead. "I'm not so sure how come you are talkin' to me that way."

"Millie!" Ellie reached over and slapped my arm. "Be nice to Eamon. He's a big tipper." Then she gave me a what the heck are you doing look.

I shook my head as if shaking off an invisible fog and tried to fake a smile. "I'm sorry, I must be confusing you with someone else I saw around town." I saw Eamon's frown slowly crawl away, but a guarded look remained. I awkwardly gestured at the kitchen. "So what is your favorite dish? I like the taco salad." My fake smile remained plastered on my face.

Eamon was obviously keeping himself from laughing at my artificial attempt at conversation. He smiled and touched his finger to his lower lip as if contemplating the depth of my question. "The salad's good, but my favorite is their fajitas. Sometimes I like to jus' mix it up. I never know what each bite will bring. Don't cha think people are a little bit like that?"

"Like what? Fajitas?" My smile was gone and I was smirking at his silly comparison.

"Yeah." His smile returned, but his eyes narrowed ever so slightly,

Thinking I would finish the metaphor before he could, I rattled off, "On the outside everything is wrapped so neatly, but inside its just one big mess."

Eamon shook his head ever so slightly, but kept his smile, "Nah, I was thinkin' that when you look at them, you judge there's a mess inside, but once you take a bite, there's nothin' but goodness."

1894: Coal mines and railways are hit by strikes and violence; Judge Dole seizes power in Hawaii; Miss Susan B. Anthony, Mrs. Isabella Beecher Hooker and Mrs. Elizabeth Cady Stanton argue before a Senate committee for women's right to vote.

Another Church

Craf looked down at the letter from his old friend Dr. Charles Manley of Greenville. He hoped that inviting him to the celebration and dedication of the Dunn's Creek Baptist Church was a good idea. Craf looks up at the solid church structure his friends and kin built. Even though he enjoys the sanctuary of the small Methodist church that he built many years ago, he is still excited to be a part of other church celebrations. Craf reads Manley's written response.

> Dear Craf,
> Thank you for your kind invitation which was forwarded to me in Louisville, Kentucky, the location of our seminary now. I still sit on the Furman Trustee Board and as it turns out the date you gave on the envelope is a time I plan on being at the Hotel in Caesar's Head in a Trustees meeting and Retreat. I'd love to come on over the State line to join you for good food and fellowship! I may bring a trustee friend, Judge J. B. O'Neall, He wants to meet your son. By the way, as I said last time you must call me Charles.
> Your friend, Charles.

Although the letter is an affirmation to Craf that he and Manley are still friends, he does not quite understand why a judge wants to join them and meet V.B. Craf looks up from his letter to see Manley and his judicial colleague arriving by carriage. The gathering locals move out of the way of the turned up dust from the road. But once the carriage stops everyone quickly welcomes the visitors, excited they are here in time for the opening ceremonies.

The dedication is full of hymns and words of thanks. The congregation inside and those standing close to the windows outside feel pride when Dr. Charles Manley speaks a few words of theological wisdom. Reverend Billy Kurkendoll graces the congregation with a sermon on Christ's Sermon on the Mount. Once "Rock of Ages" concludes the service, tears are wiped and embraces exchanged, the womenfolk begin to prepare the food.

"Craf?" Dr. Manley pulls Craf away from his efforts to help set the tables and introduces him to the judge. Pleasantries are exchanged and Craf is thankful to have a few moments to visit. V.B. soon joins his father, amusing everyone by resting his elbow on his father's shoulder. Craf, used to the drastic difference in size, only smiles.

Seizing the moment, Craf asks, "I am curious. How come you want to see my son?"

Judge O'Neall doesn't hesitate a moment and moves in closer to address V.B., but clearly includes Craf. "I am so honored to finally meet a man in law enforcement -- part of our legal system -- who is named Volenus!"

"What?" Craf and V.B. almost say at the same time trying not to laugh.

. Not at all offended by their response the judge continues, "You see, I was so interested in history at Furman years ago and that continued through my law studies. Now I sit part time on the bench and teach law part-time." The judge's hand tries to paint a picture in the air as he describes his academic discoveries. "We must study British law to some degree as well as Roman law upon which much of Anglo-American law is based. And one of my legal pioneer heroes is the brilliant Roman lawyer named Volenus! Much of what we do today about civil law - property rights boundaries and such stuff - we owe to him!"

"Thought you might like this information," Manley chimes in as he sees the McGahas listening in silence.

"So," the judge continues, "you and your father in a symbolic way follow in the tradition of the first Volenus -- your Dad in surveying and you in law enforcement. I am happy to meet you both!"

Both Craf and V.B. are quite taken aback but proud to hear this bit of history. They thank Dr. Manley and Judge O'Neall as they head for their buggy pointed already toward Caesar's Head. Harriet has already packed a few pieces of chicken, biscuits, ham and apple pie for the journey.

V.B. thinks to himself that he wishes he had had that bit of information when he was growing up and being teased by other boys about his name. Some had even called him 'Venus,' the name of a Roman goddess of love and beauty, and some folks still love to tease him with it. As he ponders the brief visit V.B. notices a stranger shyly mingling. He looks at his father who is still standing nearby and sees that Craf has also noticed the stranger, but then he quickly moves on to join Harriet. He brushes it off as not important but thinks he might meet him later.

"Hey V.B.!" A familiar voice pulls V.B. away from his thoughts to take in the delicious sights and sounds of the celebration still taking place. The dinner on the ground is a feast for all, with food and fellowship aplenty. V.B. wishes Jessie had joined him, especially when he spots his old friend. Walter Raxter, the proverbial hard-working farmer, still feels close to his younger friend, V.B., who now towers over him and everyone else. "Well, V.B.," Walter says, "you sure take after your mama's family, the Shipmans. How big you reckin you be now?"

"Big enough to whip you, little Raxter," V.B. answers with a laugh as he follows his friend to a table.

V.B. feels a finger poke into his back and he turns to find the short but strong Laura. "First you'll have to take me on, big feller! Just take off that sheriff's badge."

"Stop!" V.B. mockingly cries, "I'll give up without a fight. I've heard how tough you are. You got to be. You married into the Raxter clan and like them, the Hogseds, and the McGahas, you'll produce many more!"

Their laughter is being observed by the stranger to the dinner on the grounds. V.B. looks at the man who is now not talking or visiting but just walking around and taking notes. The young sheriff asks those at the table if they know him and they are all baffled about the man's intentions.

It is not long before the stranger moves closer to their table and Walter confronts him kindly, "Howdy, mister. Don't reckin I've met you. You a reporter or somethin'?"

The man awkwardly responds, quickly shutting his notebook, "Well no, er, yes, you might call me that."

"You writin' for a paper in Greenville or Asheville 'bout this celebration?" Walter asks warmly. Laura continues to smile and even offers the man a biscuit from a small basket at their table. The man declines a little more intensely than Laura likes, jerking his arm away and showing a scowl, almost hatred in his face.

Both in body language and spoken words, the man is evasive, "Well, we'll see if my associates want to put it in the paper or not."

Now Bunyan stands up to his full six feet, six inches, walks closer to the older man, and says with some authority, "Just what do you want, mister?"

"I'm just wanting to know a little more about this lady here," gesturing toward Laura Raxter, who is still awkwardly holding the biscuits.

V.B. watches Laura carefully set down the basket. Laura's cheeks slowly blush and he sees Walter slowly reach for her hand. V.B. tries to be aware of his own rising temper. "Be specific. What do you need to know and why?"

The stranger straightens his back as if reaching for some sense of authority. "Fine. We heard that this lady was Laura Ashworth before she married a Raxter, and that they donated this land and are active members of this church."

"True, and . . . ?" Walter's warmth is gone.

Turning to face and point an accusing finger at Laur,a he asks, "Ma'am I aim to know. Are you kin to the John and Ann Ashworth family over in Old Buncombe County?"

Laura looks confused. "Well, there was a John Ashworth or two in the family, but how come you a-askin'?"

By now V.B. has come up alongside the man and Walter begins to stand and join V.B. So the stranger asks roughly, "Well, do you use herbs and medicines from the woods?"

By now both men have him by the arms, but Laura's curiosity and firm voice restrains them from action, "Of course I do, like all mountain folks from these parts. We got no doctors an' we learn from each other how to treat ailments an' injuries of people and animals. That's the way we survive. I learnt from my mother-in-law and Granny Crane as well."

"Let's go!" V.B nods to Walter who is more than willing to remove this man, but Laura is not done yet and she comes up to the man's face.

Laura points at the rest of the people standing around watching, "Just look 'round here. You won't see nary a woman on this here mountain that don't care for her family that a-way. Now, you ain't told us how come you want such information!"

The shaking man held just on his tiptoes by the two very strong men confesses his assignment, "Ann Ashworth was brought up on charges several times over at the Cane Creek Baptist Church for being a witch 'cause she made all kinds of medicine and treated ailments of every kind."

Laura is intense in her question, "How come they brung up charges if'n she helped folks?"

The man tries to pull away, but Walter and V.B. won't let go. Yet, he continues to speak in hopes of educating these people. "Well, she spoke all kinds of words nobody understood with her treatments. Every time the church folks would charge her and try to church her, she'd threaten to cast a spell on them and they'd back down."

There is just a moment of silence. Laura rests her hands on her hips and almost whispers her question in disbelief, "So you rode all the way up here to find out if'n I'm a witch?"

"Just a cussed minute," the angry V.B. exclaims, pulling the man around to stare directly into his face, "Just when did this Ashworth woman do her healing and spells or whatever, and why are you here?"

The stranger stumbles over his words but finally manages to rattle off memorized facts. "As I recollect, she died in 1833 and left a heap of money to her kin. Then she left a gallon of whiskey for her gravediggers. Word is out that she passed on her healing gifts to her younguns and grandyounguns, so I'm just a-checking, in case this new little church don't know 'bout the danger if she's one of them!"

"Good Lord, man, that was decades afore she was even born!" an increasingly angry Walter declares.

A hostile defense bursts forth as the stranger, "Doesn't matter! It is known that Ann Wood Ashworth passed her secrets on to her daughters and granddaughters!'

V.B. is fully in charge now as Walter steps back to hold Laura's hand and as others from the dinner are watching this strange conversation intently.

He says most firmly, "Mister, we came here for a celebration. This is a place for love and forgiveness, for helping each other through suffering and life and death. There are no witches here and Laura Raxter, like most of the women of the Hogseds, McGahas, Raines, Holdens and others all around here is a healer." V.B. feels his father move in closer and come close to the stranger as V.B. continues, "They are mothers and wives who take the roots, berries, and barks and help us all when we hurt. Now Mister, you have brought an evil spirit of suspicion into this place of love. I reckon you can go on back to where ever you came from and tell your friends we have no witches, just saints -- once you leave. Oh, you never told us your name."

V.B. suddenly hears the wise voice of his father. Craf is now looking directly at the stranger, but talking to V.B. "I finally figured out where I'd seen and heard this feller. He used to go by Schmidt, as I remember. He spied on us many years ago, before you were born. That time it was something about how white races were superior. He claimed to be a 'Reverend' back then."

The McGahas feel a commotion behind them as Reverend Billy Kurkendoll moves to join the scene and speak up to the gathered crowd to announce, "It is a good time to lift our hearts and sing 'Amazing Grace' while our visitor finds his horse. And we pray that God's grace will capture him one day!"

The crowd laughs uneasily as V.B. holds Schmidt off the ground with his feet swinging as if trying to walk. "Which horse is yours, or did you ride a jackass?" he asks.

'Reverend' Schmidt points toward a brown mare and Bunyan lifts him, not by the arms, but by the collar of his coat, and the seat of his pants, right onto the saddle. Walter unties the reins and before Schmidt has fully grasped them, Sheriff V.B. McGaha slaps the horse on the rear shouting, "I'd better not see you in Transylvania again!"

Summer 2012

"Let's go to see if Charlie's working today." Elllie slammed El Capitán's front door. Getting away from Eamon I could feel myself breathing a little easier. I was thankful Ellie didn't ask me what my conversation with Eamon was all about because I really wasn't too sure myself. I nodded and was looking forward to walking along the old Greenville Turnpike to the old camp. We didn't say much as we reached the familiar horse barn. We could hear whistling inside, followed by a sudden crash and the loudest, "Hell and damnation!" rise up before us. Elllie and I quickly ran inside to find Charlie kicking an empty pail across the barn, with its former contents of horse feed spilled on the floor.

Charlie suddenly saw us and grinned like a child who had been caught cussing. "Sorry about that! Looks like I'm getting too old for this job!" Ellie had already retrieved the pail when I grabbed a small shovel. As we helped Charlie clean up the mess he smiled. "Thanks, girls. Young fresh energy!" He sighed heavily. "I wish I had that for when the owners get here."

Ellie and I looked at each other. "What do you mean?" Ellie finally asked.

Charlie grabbed a larger bucket from inside an empty stall and turned it upside down to sit on. "In September the owners are fixin' to move up here permanently to retire. They want to restore some of the old camp's beauty. You know, clean up the old roads and get rid of the tons of dead brush." He shook his head and laughed, "That's a lot of brush for two hundred and eighty acres."

"What are you saying?" Elie looked worried.

Charlie reached up to gently pat Ellie's face. "I'm saying that I'm thrilled they're going to clean up the place and restore its beauty, but they may have to find someone younger to do the work." When we didn't say anything Charlie jumped up and headed for the door. "Come on, girls. Let me show you!"

We scrambled after Charlie who began to lead us up a gently sloping path. We could hear the noise from the Greenville Highway soon disappear as we walked along old, unkept roads. At first he pointed out the remnants of wooden structures that were used as cabins for the old camp that thrived in the 20s and 30s. "It'll all be cleared out." Charlie made a wide sweeping motion. "Then they'll build their new home right here in the middle." Ellie and I followed the old man as he led us to the edge of a beautiful lake dammed up by a wall that dared you to cross its narrow walkway with no railings on either side. Charlie waved for us to join him. I smiled as I noticed that I would only fall about ten feet instead of to my death. In any case I was more tempted to accidently let myself fall into the water lapping up so close to the edge. "This is the old swimming lake. Ellie, I'm surprised you haven't brought Millie to swim here yet.

"I've been kinda busy!" Ellie said lamely.

"Yeah, right!" Charlie snorted.

Knowing I didn't like where the conversation was going, I quickly interrupted, "That's okay. I've been swimming at Trout Lake and I still have a little time left."

"Yeah, we still have some time." Ellie smiled at me, but the guilt couldn't help seeping through. Somehow, in a weird way, that made me feel great. I didn't know Ellie actually cared enough about me to feel guilty.

"See that house over there?" Charlie pointed to the other side of the lake as Ellie and I hesitantly looked up from the narrow boardwalk. "That's a small house the owners built several years ago, and they'll use it as a guest house once their new home is completed." Ellie and I tried to look interested, but weren't really too sure why Charlie was excited about this. That's when he pointed at the chimney. "The chimney is built from the old chimney of the original McGaha homestead. You remember the place where you sat on the wall earlier this summer?"

Ellie rolled her eyes. "How could we forget."

"I just thought you might be interested." Charlie's enthusiasm was gone.

I moved on across the dam and up to the house. There was nothing exceptional about the home, except its mountain quaintness with a porch and a couple of rocking chairs. But something drew me closer. I couldn't help but reach out and touch the chimney's old stones. Their cobbled look and weathered feel gave away their age. Something stirred inside me and I could hear Ellie and Charlie stop bickering.

"What is it, Millie?" Ellie was so close now that I watched her reach out and touch the stones, but more out of curiosity than anything else. She looked at me and frowned, like she just didn't get it.

I shook my head, knowing there were no words that could describe what I was feeling. "I'm not really sure." When no one said anything I finally confessed, "It's like . . . like I'm home. Some part of me is here. Some part of me belongs." My vision blurred ever so slightly and I tried not to give in to my tears. I quickly let go, swallowed hard and turned my back to the chimney. "I'm sure it's nothing! Okay, Charlie, what else you got?"

Charlie just smiled at me like he had finally gotten the response he wanted. "Come on! You'll love this." We quickly followed him back across the dam and up an old road up behind the new building site. For the most part you could see where Charlie had managed to clear some of the underbrush allowing us to follow the old road. Throughout the hike we enjoyed heavy, tall brush that formed a canopy overhead, keeping the sun from beating down on us. More than once I stopped to breathe in the rich, cool, moist fragrance as we passed through tunnels formed by rhododendron. Then suddenly we were standing in a pine forest where we simply had to avoid stepping on mushrooms and scattered dead branches. Just as the pine forest melded into another rhododendron tunnel we found ourselves on a huge smooth rock face spreading out and downward. The heat from the sun beat down on us, but we didn't care because we could see the rolling mountains ahead of us. "Welcome to Panther Mountain!" Charlie wiped sweat from his forehead, but his ebony skin glistened as if all of him was smiling. He stretched out on the flat rock face. I thought, "He's spread-eagled like child getting ready to make snow angels. I got it though, and joined him in this sacred moment. Ellie laughed at us, but came along. Charlie whispered, "This is the same as it was ten thousand years ago."

We said very little and when we finally headed back down the path, thankful that Charlie knew where he was going, we stopped in the middle of a place that looked very ordinary. Heavy brush crawled up both sides of the bank. Charlie's childlike grin reappeared and he scrambled up the right bank through the thick brush. Ellie and I looked at each other and quickly followed him, not wanting to be left behind. As soon as we were through the wall of brush we were both shocked to see a massive rock suddenly jutting out of the gently sloping mountainside. The oblong rock created a cave-like opening surrounded by rock on three sides and thick brush protecting its mouth.

"What a perfect hiding place!" Ellie jumped around like she'd discovered a secret hideway.

Charlie sat down to rest on one of the boulders, "Actually, it was a busy place in its day for hiding a moonshine still. Many a whiskey was brewed right where you are standing."

"How awesome!" Ellie and I said practically at the same time.

Charlie looked at us, but his smile faded ever so slightly. "Not everyone thought so."

1894: Labor Day becomes a national holiday; Jacob Coxey is arrested as he leads his "resurrection of the nation" army of jobless from Ohio onto Washington on Easter Sunday under the banner "Commonwealth of Christ Band."

Outsiders

Laura grabs both men by the arm and says, "Whew, after all that I shore need a walk. 'Sides, we shore got some catching up to do. Let's step out to Dunn's Rock to set a spell in the quiet and look over the valley like we did long ago."

V.B. lets himself be pulled by Laura and responds with a laugh, "Good idea, and if we hurry we might get a glimpse of that horse and rider flying off this mountain!"

Walter's guffaw makes others look to see what the commotion is all about. "Yeah, and he'll thank that his horse has done got bewitched from bein' close to Laura Ashworth Raxter!"

With goodbyes behind them the three leave the small church and walk only ten minutes to reach the pines and laurel bushes that act as the final gateway to the top of Dunn's Rock. They carefully navigate their way to the same boulder they sat on years ago, with their legs dangling over the final flat rock jutting out with the valley below and the mountains in the distance.

The three sit as close to the edge as they dare and breathe in the gentle mountain breeze as Laura opens the conversation, "Sorry Jessie couldn't be with us this time."

"Thank you." V.B. stares ahead at the wisps of clouds ever changing the canvas before them. "Our firstborn, little Reba is ailin' but she wanted me to come on and talk with you about somethin'."

Walter is quick to joke, "Well, let me see if'n I can figger this out. It's been two years since we talked here, and two years is the length of the Sheriff's term. Laura, what on earth do you reckin he's got on his mind?"

Laura shoots her husband a critical look. "Hush up, R.W., he don't need a clown. He needs friends now. This is serious business."

A smiling V.B. lightens it up a little himself, "Well, if your post office deal with the government has not come through yet, I have a new name for your 'See Off.'"

"And what might that be?" Laura asks innocently.

V.B grins like a schoolboy. "How about a name like 'We Chased the Horse's Rear-- Both of Them – off the Mountain Town'?"

Not to be left out, Walter chimes in, "How about 'We Don't Need Your Schmidt Here Mountain?'"

Laura shakes her head at the giggling pair of grown men. "Enough, you little boys! Now tell us, V.B., just what are you a-thankin'? What does your better half thank?"

V.B. takes a deep breath, pulling his thoughts back together. "Well, I really think I should run again and Jessie believes God wants me to. Seems like I just got started and finally got a solid team of deputies, even if it's only a couple, and some part-time when I need them."

"V.B., from what I hear," Walter says, "'bout everybody appreciates what you are a-doing and trying to do."

V.B. looks seriously at his two friends. "See, even your words say that there is a lot to do and I am trying."

Laura tries to keep a serious look on her face, "Yep, we all know it's a mighty tough job in these days. But you are a big, handsome feller an' I bet you can settle a lot of disputes 'tween folks just by friendly persuasion and being so tall!"

V.B. takes a handful of pine needles and gently tosses them at Laura. "Ha! My Jessie likes to remind me that my size also makes me an easier target to hit when they start a-flingin' lead."

"Are you a-worried for baby Reba?" Laura asks, more seriously now. Walter scoots over to help her pull the pine needles out of her hair.

V.B. looks away from the couple and takes in the gently rolling mountains in the distance. "Not so much for her safety as for the world she will grow up in. I'd like to believe it will be a lot safer with less bootlegging, stealing, shooting and other lawless things."

Laura throws the last of the pine needles on the ground. "Sounds like your ideals ain't changed much in these two years. Justice is your watchword. 'Let justice roll down like waters,' I heard the preacher say. It's somewhere in the Bible."

V.B. responds, "Yeah, in several places in the Bible it is called for. I'm just trying to make it practical for everyday, common working folks. Not just some heavenly ideal for later."

"V.B., tell us," Laura asks, "What has been the best part of this first term?"

"Probably getting through alive!" V.B. laughingly responds.

But he goes on, "Seriously, getting so many neighbors to settle their differences without fighting or going to court was pretty good."

Walter finally gets a word in, "Some of your Papa's gifts comin' through, huh?"

"I guess." They notice V.B.'s far-off look, then silence. Finally, he speaks from another place inside. "You may think the hardest part of my work is trying to stop some of the more obvious criminal activities like all the violence going with the heavy moonshining and bootlegging in these parts. Well, it is pretty scary and tough to deal with. And it is the worst part since I know so many of the folks a-runnin' the stills and delivering."

Laura picks up right away something else is on his mind, "What else is it, Bunyan?"

V.B. smiles at the sound of his childhood name. "Something new, something I can't exactly put into words."

Walter stands to stretch his legs, "Well V.B., just talk about it. It'll make its way out."

V.B. jumps up to join him causing the two to step back from the edge of the boulder they were sitting on. Now that they are standing they can take in a greater view to the right. "It's like this. There are so many outside people coming in these days."

"You talkin' 'bout folks from Charleston an' Greenville?" Walter asks.

"Not exactly. They've been coming around to escape the heat for close to a hundred years. It's more of the folks who come to 'discover' us, to do some 'research' about us and our area. They go away and write articles in newspapers, magazines and books that say some pretty weird things."

"Like what?" Laura asks, slowly pulling herself to her feet.

V.B. starts moving his arms around like a mad man trying to point in every direction. "You won't believe how they paint the pictures of everybody here as uneducated, illiterate, totally ignorant and dirty. Everybody local goes around shooting his neighbors and foreigners! Did you know that?" Laura starts to laugh, thinking V.B. is joking, but stops short when she sees he is serious. "Not all of them, mind you, are so negative," V.B. continues. "We've had some really nice folks staying with my folks who were gracious, courteous and who wrote respectful things about mountain folks. One lady even called our area and Asheville 'The Land of the Sky.' How about that?"

Walter asks naively, "How come that is so troublesome for you? People write what they want to and people believe what they want to. It's a free country, even to tell lies!"

V.B. points his finger at the valley below. "Here's where the water hits the wheel. So-called 'researchers' and 'reporters' on so-called 'fact finding assignments' bring more of the same. They have 'discovered Appalachia' they say. As if we were lost!" Walter and Laura stand in silence as V.B. expounds, "And following them are the tourists who want to see a 'real whiskey still in action' or who will ride many miles into the mountains to find a 'typical' mountain family, barefoot and totin' a long gun. Often they will come back by my office in the courthouse really mad that they did not find such a 'typical' stereotype Appalachian family after riding for miles."

Walter allows a long pause before he slowly asks, "Then how come is th' writers' ignorance your fault? The readers oughter get mad at the writers that led them down such a path."

V.B.'s eyebrows seem to touch as his frown deepens. "It is a little more complicated than that. For example, a little while back we had two writers, Ziegler and Grosscup were their names. They stayed only in finer hotels like at Buck Forest and Caesar's Head. Then one of them, I don't know which, took it on himself to convince one of our bootleggers to show him a still in operation at night." V.B. stops for a moment as if remembering exactly how the story goes. "Well, he wrote all about it in their book, really glorifying it all, how they dressed him up to look like a supposed cousin of the man who took him. He, by all means, should not look like a revenuer or the moonshiners would shoot him on the spot." V.B. suddenly laughs out loud, almost forcing himself to lighten up, but Walter and Laura just continue to silently listen. "What he did not know was that I'd been watching the 'shiners for some time, from the bushes above, along with a deputy. The men working the still eventually saw his fancy shoes and almost shot him right then. Only some fast talking got him out alive. We had our guns drawn ready to shoot but our whole operation was busted and he nearly got killed. If they had shot him we would have been forced into some shooting too. And the horse they stole was another problem. I hate to think I am playing nursemaid to nosey writers."

Laura asks, "And you read stuff like this?"

"Oh yeah. And several others have done these romantic stories like dime novels, glorifying the life of the poor moonshiners just trying to feed their starving families. They write that folks in these parts here have no other way to make a living and the mean government won't let us live like our ancestors in Ireland or Scotland. And most of them think everybody here is Scots-Irish. They get mad when I say lots of our families come over from

England and Germany, Holland and Switzerland."

Walter wraps one arm around his wife's shoulder and declares, "I reckin they done got their minds made up that all whiskey-makers come from Scotland we are all the same! The way I figure it, if'n some of our local whiskey makers would work the land, the woods and animals, half of what our families do, they could make an honest livin', right?"

Laura adds, "And I read in th' newspaper th' other day that some folks in these writings talk about how good this pure whiskey is, glorifying their product."

V.B. chuckles at the comical duo, "Ha, and you would not believe it but occasionally a tourist will stop me, obviously the Sheriff, in front of the courthouse, try to slip me a couple of dollars and ask where the pure white lightening is!"

Laura is shocked. "What? How stupid can folks get?"

"Now wait, Laura, Not so stupid. In many counties here and just over the line in South Carolina that is not uncommon. The sheriff cooperates with those who helped put him in office and 'help' them when needed. He can turn an eye away or let them know if a revenuer is coming around."

Laura confesses, "I reckin I knew that and didn't want to believe it. That settles it. You got to run agi'n, big man. You need to stop some of th' nonsense."

All three friends glance at a branch suddenly swept over the edge of the rock by a gust of wind. They automatically back a little further away from the edge. Walter asks, "Just one more question. What is that 'pure' white lightning nonsense. It ain't all so clean."

V.B. nods at his friend. "Yeah, those writers do something bad when they paint it that way. We have a lot of stills where folks add all sorts of things to make the mash 'age.' Dead animals, metals, you name it. And sometimes it kills folks and lot of folks go blind. They joke about 'pure poison' when the tourists glorify it but they usually do not know it can be literally that." V.B. moves closer to the edge for just a moment to point out something below. "Funny thing is, we had two federally controlled distilleries in this county. One was the Cooper Distillery. We can see the building with its steep roof, right down there in Dunn's Rock valley. It is not so far to find ongoing, safe, licensed distilleries. The whiskey is carefully controlled, inspected and taxes paid. People can go to Greenville or Asheville or elsewhere to buy it without all the dangers."

Gently pulling him away from the edge, Laura asks, "But your writers done romanticized it so much that folks come here from Asheville, Greenville and elsewhere to try th' rotgut?" The sun is moving closer to Toxaway Mountain in the west so Laura gently takes Walter's hand and pats V.B. on the back. "It's a-gittin' late and baby Reba needs her Papa afore she sleeps. You got our blessings, Sheriff McGaha. Go git them moonshiners and bootleggers with their untaxed poison. Watch out for sensational writers and tourists with dollars in their hands."

James Crawford (Craf) and Harriet Shipman McGaha, with children, in front of home on the Greenville Turnpike

James Crawford (Craf)   Harriet McGaha

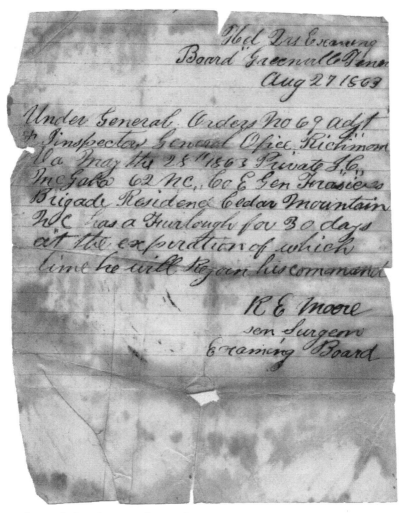

Civil War furlough paper for Craf

Fiddling Tom Fowler and dog

Ruins of Hume Dunn's Rock Hotel burned by bushwhackers during Civil War

Volenus Bunyan McGaha as Sheriff   Jessie Geneva Allison McGaha

Young Reba and Leslie McGaha

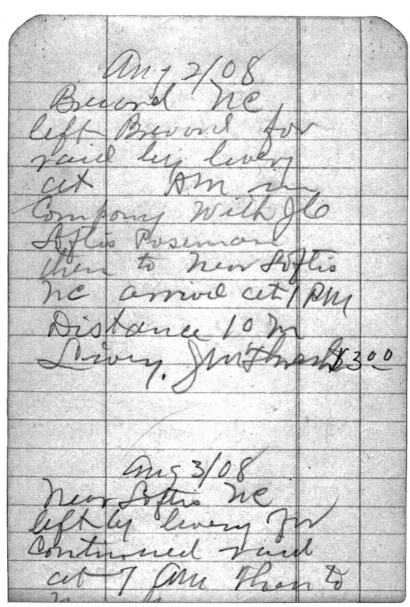

Sample revenuer diary page

TREASURY DEPARTMENT,
Office Commissioner Internal Revenue.
Form 829.

DIARY REPORT—DUPLICATE.   Page No. ....

The COMMISSIONER OF INTERNAL REVENUE:

I have the honor to submit below my diary report for the period
from ....January 11th......., 19 09 , to ....January 20th......., 19 09, inclusive.

DATE.	PLACE.	SERVICES PERFORMED.
Jan. 11	Greenville,SC.	Left 4:30 P. M. by rail for raid from Walhalla, proceeded to Seneca a distance of 40 miles, thence by livery to Walhalla a distance of 10 miles arriving 7:30 P. M.
12	Walhalla, SC.	Left by livery for raid 7 A.M. with Deputy Collector Merrick and others. Proceeded to near Longcreek PO Assisted in seizure and destruction of illicit distillery in Rabun County, Ga., 4 miles West of Longcreek, thence to near Whetstone, assisted in seizure and destruction of illicit distillery and capture of 3 gals illicit whiskey and 4 gallons found near distillery. Returned thence to near Longcreek arriving 10 P. M. Total distance travelled 40 miles.
13	Near Longcreek,SC.	Left 9 A. M. for return to Walhalla a distance of 16 miles arriving at 12 Noon.
14	Walhalla, S. C.	Left Walhalla 11 A.M. proceeded by automobile to Seneca a distance of 10 miles, thence by rail to Greenville a distance of 40 miles arriving 5 P.M. Left Greenville by livery 4 P. M. with Deputy Col. Merrick and others for raid, proceeded to near Highland a distance of 22 miles arriving 9 P. M.
15	Highland,SC.	Sick in bed, unable for duty.
16	"	Left Highland by livery 9:30 A. M. for return to Greenville a distance of 22 miles arriving 1:30 PM
17	Greenville,SC.	Sunday at Greenville.
18	"	Left Greenville 4 P. M. by rail for raid from Walhalla, travelled to Seneca a distance of 40 miles thence by livery to Walhalla a distance of 10 miles arriving 7:30 P. M.
19	Walhalla, SC.	Left Walhalla 7:30 A. M. for raid with Dep Collector Merrick and others, proceeded to near Madison, S.C. made two hours search for reported distillery, failed to find, thence to near Unity Church found distillery run out, returned thence to Walhalla arriving 8 P.M. travelled a total distance of 42 miles.

Typed IRS report

Murdered U.S. Marshal Al Duckworth

Former outlaw Lewis Redmond and family

Walter and Laura Raxter with grandson Quentin Cantrell at home in former Hume slave house

11

Summer 2012

I came for Ellie the next day. The time we had spent at the old camp and the discovery of an old hideout for moonshiners had renewed my sense of adventure and I really wanted to go for a hike back up to Rich Mountain. The path was familiar, but seemed somewhat strange without Kevin coming along. I quickly brushed the thought out of my mind and followed Ellie until we came closer to the final stretch near the opening to the pasture land. That's when I heard it, a familiar tune played effortlessly in the distance.

I stopped and Ellie stopped to look back at me with a sheepish grin. "What?" She said as if I were accusing her of something.

"Kevin's here. Right?" I said and shook my head like I couldn't believe she would lead me on this long hike to force me into being the third wheel again.

"So?" Ellie said as casually as she could possible fake. "Is that such a problem?" I just gave her one of those do I LOOK like an idiot stares. She came up to me and grabbed my arm, but I didn't let her pull me very far. "Come on, Millie, he's your friend too! We just want you to know we're sorry and want you to hang out with us." She stopped, threw my arm down, and slammed her hands together in a prayer lock. "PLEASE!"

I sighed, "Okay! On one condition."

Ellie started jumping up with excitement. "Of course. Whatever you want."

This time I grabbed her arm and stopped her from jumping. "No more lies!"

1895: J.P. Morgan profits from the government bank bailout; The abolitionist and women's suffrage fighter, Frederick Douglas, dies; Sears, Roebuck & Company begin mail order business.

The Experienced Sheriff

The cool air promises a comfortable ride between Cedar Mountain and East Fork post offices where V.B. plans to stop at the little community of Commission Springs. As he breathes in the refreshing mountain air he feels content about being Sheriff in Transylvania County. His landside reelection proves to him that the people of his county are feeling safer and that he is making a difference. The people know he can listen and is not simply a pawn of local politicians. Most of all, he has not sold out to the powerful men running illegal industries of the area.

V.B. gently leads his horse around a bend, where the forest gives way to a small meadow spotted with cattle, an indication that he is on his final stretch into the small community. The Sheriff gently guides his horse toward a general store along the road. He knows the best information on all sorts of illegal activities is found at the post offices or general stores, usually the same building. Besides, his routine visits are reassurance to the citizens as well as a deterrent to criminals. His popularity is amplified by these visits and his simply listening to people.

Before V.B. comes to a full stop he is surprised to see the store proprietor, waving him down, "Sheriff, you got to help us here!"

With his hand on his holstered gun and thinking something is badly wrong, V.B. calls out, "What is it? What's the matter?"

The balding man smoothes down the few strands of hair left on his glistening head. Eyeing V.B.'s suspicious reaction he quickly responds, "Nothing bad, Sheriff." V.B. watches a few more men wander out of the store and greet him with friendly nods.

A relaxed V.B. dismounts. "Okay, Phil, what is it then. How can I help you?"

Phil glances at the other men who nod with approval for the store owner to continue. "Well, we just got word that the government is giving us a post office for our little community here but we can't settle on a name. Give us a name and then we won't argue anymore."

The Sheriff looks at the handful of men and thinks they are joking, so

V.B. responds with the first name coming to his mind, "Reba," the name of his beloved first born.

Phil sighs, obviously relieved as he sees the other men nodding in agreement. "So it is and shall be. Reba, North Carolina."

V.B. then realizes they are serious and laughingly says, "Boy, am I glad I didn't give Reba's nickname. I'd feel funny calling it 'Bobo, North Carolina'!"

Summer 2012

"Hey, Millie!" Kevin said awkwardly as he placed his fiddle on his lap. I scooted in next to him, because Ellie made me sit between them. The flat rock we were sitting on felt warm against my bare legs, and the view made it really warming. I just nodded, at this point feeling quite indifferent about the two of them using me. I was going home soon anyway, so I might as well enjoy the majesty of the mountains.

I closed my eyes and breathed in the air. The freshness soothed my annoyance and I soon felt content to be sitting between the two new friends who were trying to prove they were still my friends. I started to smile to myself realizing they had actually planned this, which ultimately meant they did want me to be here.

"What're you smilin' at?" Kevin asked trying not to sound accusing.

"The two of you," I said as I opened my eyes and scanned one and then the other. They didn't say anything and, I continued, adding an intentional fake twang, "Now, if I understand this right, you two plan on keepin' this a secret for how long? 'Cause I got news for you, once babies start a-popping out, there ain't no one not gonna notice that."

"Millie!" Ellie jabbed me in the side. "I can't believe you just said that!"

I was starting to laugh at the whole ridiculousness of their situation. Soon I was snorting, which made Ellie giggle.

But Kevin just picked up his fiddle and started playing his familiar tune. I could tell he wasn't mad at me. His eyes glanced ever so briefly at Ellie with a glimpse of caution. I sobered and lay flat on my back as I let Kevin's music tell me that my question was not a new one.

1895: Over 300 motorcars are built, mostly steam and electric; Pope Leo XII praises the growth of U.S. Catholicism but opposes any separation of church and state; Former slave Booker T. Washington calls for education and vocational training as the better means to Negro equality.

The Raid

"Sheriff, are you sure we can trust these Fishers? And will word not get up there before we do?" lead Federal Agent Monroe, asks as he follows V.B. The sheriff is leaving Jeptha and heading up a steep grade toward the Hogback Valley Post Office. Six other revenue agents follow behind Monroe, all suspiciously scanning every corner they turn. V.B. can't believe that so many federal agents have come to break up yet another illegal still in the Whitewater area of upper Transylvania County.

V.B.'s tips as to the whereabouts of illegal operations, both big and small, come readily because of his popularity, which does not include those who run the liquid corn industries. When the tip came in about a major operation upcounty on the Whitewater River with transport down into both South Carolina and Georgia, he sent word to Greenville to the Internal Revenue Service Office. He feels frustrated because he only wanted Monroe to join him, since he is already expecting two young men from the local Fisher family to be deputized and assist them. V.B. told the Fishers to meet them at the Hogback Valley Post Office up in the day, after lunch.

"Yes, sir and no, sir," V.B. finally responds. "They are upright folks and their word is solid. As for a warning, there is only one way up that mountain from Hogback to Whitewater. We'll be on it. So if somebody sees this herd of lawmen where we meet, they would have to ride past us to warn the moonshiners. We ought to see that, unless we've been partaking of something stronger than our clear spring water!" The men continue to ride for a few minutes before V.B. finally asks, "By the way, Agent Monroe, how come you brought this herd of men? Looks like a posse. I asked for one agent due to jurisdiction questions. Nobody knows exactly where the state line is in these parts and I thought you could cover that little detail so it won't matter."

Monroe pulls his horse up as close to V.B. as possible and looks both ways before he divulges, "You may as well know, Sheriff, we think it might be the Major doin' this up here."

V.B. looks at the federal agent and frowns ever so slightly. "You mean Lewis Redmond, the one they wrote that dime novel about back in '79?"

"Yep," Monroe says looking proud to be part of such an important undertaking. "The one who killed a federal agent trying to bring him in. The one not only our agents have been looking for but also the U.S. Army tried to find."

"But didn't they catch him, as I recollect?" V.B. tries very hard not to laugh.

"Oh yeah," the agent replies, "but he got away, got some guns and then went back to rescue one of his men, a driver! Worse yet, he went around for a while after that, raiding homes of the agents who had captured him, demanding to get back his horses, money and two coats!"

V.B. can hardly believe the words he is hearing. He nods his head towards the men behind him who continue to scan their surroundings. "So that is why you brought so many men, all with fire in their eyes."

Monroe, still oblivious to V.B.'s incredulous look, continues to boast, "Yep, they want him behind bars, or, better yet, dead."

V.B. stops his horse for just a moment, letting the other agents come within earshot. He wants to make sure he is heard by all. "Look here, Agent Monroe, I want no shooting unless it is life or death. Until now, I've never had to kill a man and I hope your men are not so trigger-happy that they will cut loose. Every man deserves a fair trial." V. B. is mad. He continues, "Your information is way out of date, too. This cannot be the Major. I reckon I'll have to bring you up to date when we are through with our business. Right now just put some reigns on these men of yours and you'd better hold them back. Do you hear me?"

The fed sees that this tall, imposing sheriff has strong feelings on the subject. "Now, don't worry. We are professionals and will try to plan this so nobody gets shot."

V.B. realizes there is tension in the air and shifts the topic to be more in sympathy with the agents. "I was really upset when I saw that New York Times article referring to the Major as some sort of folk hero, a modern day Robin Hood just trying to feed his family."

Agent Monroe is taken aback. "You have read the New York Times up here?"

"Here we go again," V.B. whispers to himself. He can't believe that even the educated federal officers think the mountain people can't read or write and don't have access to outside papers.

He patiently and calmly responds to the question, "Oh yes, we have post offices all over these mountains and the mail does come through regularly. I live on the main route coming up the mountain from Greenville so we get a lot of news, not much later that you." Attempting to stay calm he continues, "Besides that, a lot of folks from Greenville, Columbia and even Charleston have summer homes all around. They see to it that they can get 'outside' news as well. In fact, I am talking with some folks about partnering with me to start a local newspaper in Brevard. We seem to be ready to start next year with the 'Sylvan Valley News'."

The fed, now feeling embarrassed that he had underestimated this mountain sheriff, shifts the topic back, "Well, I was really mad about that dime novel. I'm sure you read it too. It made him out to be a dashing hero and with a large army of five hundred men. And they anointed him 'King of the Moonshiners.' Such bull."

By this time, they have reached Hogback Valley Post Office where two young Fisher men greet them only with a nod. The two dark, lean bodies mount their horses and simply ride off together toward the Whitewater area. The locals folks hanging around for the mail stare with a mixture of excitement and fear. They have never seen so many lawmen and they know something is up.

Some of the feds are nervous, both due to the silence of the Fishers but also because of the steep road with such thick rhododendron, mountain laurel and big chestnut and poplar trees that one could not see any great distance into the woods.

Finally Monroe breaks the quiet. "Sheriff, we've never seen brush so thick. Aren't you afraid of an ambush?"

"Well, nope. I trust the Fishers. Just before that ridge up there, we'll stop and rest, eat a bite, tie up the horses real good and wait 'til dark. When the new moon comes up, we'll ease down the mountain on the other side afoot. The brush will be our protection, not just theirs. The Fisher boys know a trail leading us right through the woods." V.B. is still for a little while before he adds, "They also told me that the 'shiners get here about ten these nights, when the moon gives good light in the narrow hollow. So we need to be in place by nine at least."

"So," the agent asks, "we'll lie low and rush them when they come?"

"To be honest," V.B. confesses, "I've never had so many men. Seems to me that the risk of us bein' heard is high. I reckon it might be better if some men waited a little further back to come when needed. Besides, their dogs will smell this many men a mile away. Let's just the two of us and the Fishers spread out and hunker in the bushes for the wait."

The fed, not so sure he wants to go on without his men, reluctantly takes V.B's lead. "Sounds like a good plan, Sheriff. I'll whistle for my men when it goes down. They can circle around when the 'shiners are in so they can't get away. But watch out if the Major is there. He will shoot."

V.B. bites his tongue and thinks to himself, that this fellow must be from the moon or elsewhere and has some big need to call any moonshiner "The Major." He does remind the fed, "Now let them fire the still up to prove they are the operators. At least show they own it by doing something."

Monroe nods eagerly. "Of course."

The men take their prescribed places, with six of the agents back up the trail, over a small ridge. The Sheriff, Revenue Agent Monroe and the two deputized Fishers spread out on one side of the narrow valley with very steep hillsides. The little valley creek feeds into Whitewater River. The well-worn trail on the opposite side has a heavy-duty sled sitting in it.

As V.B. and the others slowly cover themselves with leaves and brush from the laurel, he thinks, "What a big boiler! They must have used the sled to bring it down that mountain." He notes that, as usual, standard wooden barrels are used for the primary cooker and doubler as well as the thump keg and condenser. It is a big operation and some materials for another one are being set up right next to it.

Agent Monroe is more worried about whether the main operator is the Major and whether he had included any poison ivy with the leaves he used to cover himself. He also thinks that the Sheriff's wisdom about keeping his men further back was solid after all. He himself is more experienced and disciplined than they are. He is sure he could keep from gunning the Major down. Well, maybe.

The new moon is high and they hear the men long coming. Strange to hear such noises, since moonshiners are notorious for their silence and secrecy.

A deep voice a-cussin'. A mule a-brayin'. Brush a-breakin'. Wood a-creakin' and a-groanin'. Dry earth a-moanin'.

Then they see it, a procession of comic proportion: a boy leading a mule that pulls a wooden sled carrying a massive steel boiler strapped down tightly.

Holding on to the load are two burly men trying to keep it balanced. The load is so heavy that, should it tip, the sled, mule and load are long gone down the steep ravine into Whitewater River. Behind the two men is a third with long reins and a long stick, cursing and coaxing the mule. And behind him are the proverbial dogs whose olfactory senses are undoubtedly overwhelmed by the mule and sweat of the men.

V.B. watches the scene and wonders about this new sled until he sees that the old sled ahead of them at the site has a broken runner.

Then as the boy cries out, "Pa, the old sled is in the way!" The ludicrous procession tries to stop the downhill slide of the heavily laden sled, mule, and the two men trying to stabilize it. But they have a momentum all their own, out of control.

The boy jumps aside, the mule jumps atop the old sled so conveniently blocking the trail and the new sled abruptly stops against the old, flinging the two burly men onto the ground. Only the cursing driver and his son remain standing.

The lawmen jump up quickly as V.B. calls out, "Hands in the air, all of you!"

Monroe also cries, "Federal Agents!" then whistles loudly.

The other feds tumble into the spectacle and surround the scene with guns drawn, laughing almost uncontrollably.

"Ain't nothing funny here, you-uns," the older man says wiping the sweat from his balding forehead. He scans the scene and then adds on the verge of tears, "Be gentle with my boy there."

The agents quickly frisk them all for weapons. They find only two long guns, one a ball and cap and the other a rolling block.

Agent Monroe comments, "Well for such a big operation, I'd have thought you would have better firepower, more modern guns. Did you steal these from a museum?"

The balding man looks offended by such accusations. "Mister, we just use them for gittin meat for the table. We ain't about to shoot nobody, 'specially not a revenuer!"

Monroe and V.B. consult while the other agents and deputies break up the wooden barrels and chop holes in the old boiler and new. When they start cutting apart the expensive copper condenser coil, they both note the tears in the old man's eyes.

V.B. announces to the man, "We've decided to let your boy go home and take the mule and dogs. He can take the sled back if they need it for farming."

The man looks him in the eye, and says, "You are right kind, mister. How come Oconee County sends a sheriff so far up here anyhow? I wasn't botherin' nobody."

Agent Monroe answers, "Mister, you are not in South Carolina. Best we can figure out you are in Transylvania County, North Carolina. You just met their young, but big, Sheriff V.B. McGaha." Keeping an official tone he goes on, "Now tell me, are you working for the Major?"

"Major who?" The old man looks at the two other moonshiners, each being escorted by two agents. The men just shrug their shoulders at the name.

Monroe raises his voice, slightly frustrated. "Lewis Redmond, the big moonshiner. The man who killed Duckworth, a Federal Marshal." V.B. rolls his eyes and can't believe the ignorance of the agent, yet he holds his tongue and lets the man make a fool of himself.

The balding man continues to shake his head. "Mister revenuer, no I ain't. I only works for me. Just tryin' to make a livin'."

"And these big steel barrels for boilers?" V.B. asks, trying to get back to the business at hand.

"I found 'em back when they was a-buildin' the railroad to Greenville. Reckon they fell off a flat car." The moonshiner scratches his head.

For the first time in captivity the boy speaks up, "Yeah, and when we hauled them all the way home Ma was real upset an' said he shoulda tole the railroaders. It was kind of like stealin'."

"Hush up, boy." The man sheepishly looks at V.B. not knowing what else to say.

The son, on the other hand, is not done. "Well, Pa, you got us into trouble just like Ma said. 'It'll come to no good, like a curse'."

"Well, son," the man, now weakening in spirit, says, "I just wanted something better for your Ma and sisters. This seemed like a good way to make an awful lot more money than wood cuttin' and farmin'." Then a strange thing happens. The old man changes his tone of voice like he is moving on to other matters, "Can I offer you folks some barley coffee, cold biscuits and ham afore the trip out?"

"What?" Monroe doesn't know what to say.

The moonshiner notes the immediate suspicion all around by the agents and continues. "Look, it ain't poison. I'll take some first if'n you like. We figured we'd be here a few days to put the new one up so we got enough."

Monroe responds, "Well, I never had that happen before. Most want to shoot me, not feed me! Must be the good North Carolina water here got to this man who thought he was in South Carolina!"

Still skeptical, the lawmen stand around, obviously wanting to get back to their horses and head home with their prisoners.

It is V.B. who then asks, "Is there something else you are not telling?"

The man, now shuffling his feet around, getting out the coffee can, casually answers, "I was about to git to it, Sheriff McGaha. You see, the best way to get outta here is the trail we come in on. You fellers musta heard us coming 'cause we made a lot of noise. My boy was a-beatin' the ground with a stick."

Agent Monroe, obviously a city fellow and not so knowledgeable of the mountains says, "And so? Sounds stupid to me for a moonshiner."

V.B. begins laughing and says, "Sounds pretty smart to me if you know there are a lot of rattlesnakes and copperheads that nest in here."

After hearing this comment the other six agents start building a fire and, without a vote or further discussion, the decision is made to wait until daylight to walk out.

A strange hospitality, even friendly discussion arises within the group as each one settles in for the remaining night. No one would or could sleep. After some small talk Agent Monroe carefully asks Sheriff McGaha, "By the way, I been wondering why you were so sure a while back that this could not be the Major."

"Well, Agent Monroe," V.B. responds as he watches the flames flicker. "Let me answer your question with a question since you really threw me back then. Where are you from? Not these parts, I can easily see. And did you do your homework before you left Greenville?"

The federal agent laughs and says, "Well, you are right. We've been working out in the Chicago and midwest area, chasing down all sorts of desperadoes for some time now. We just got into Greenville on the train before we heard you needed help."

V.B. tries to keep his voice steady, but a slight hint of irritation is noticeable. "And what did the boss in Greenville tell you about the raid? Did HE mention Lewis Redmond?"

The agent looks very sheepish and somewhat embarrassed as he admits, "Actually, he was not there and we saw your request posted on the board. We had no briefing and thought we'd best head on up the mountain as soon as we could arrange for horses."

"And the idea of capturing or killing a famous outlaw got your juices up?" V.B. continues to keep an eye on the captured men, who seem to be quite enjoying V.B.'s reprimanding these agents.

Monroe finally gives in. "Sheriff, I reckon you'd better tell us more."

V.B. takes another sip of coffee. "Well, in the first place, 'Major' Lewis Redmond is a right peaceable man, having served three years of his ten year sentence in federal prison up in New York State. He was transferred to the prison in Columbia, South Carolina due to bad health and then got a presidential pardon. That was back in '84."

Monroe is stunned. "You mean to tell me that that 'King of Moonshiners,' that vicious outlaw, is free now and not making booze anymore?"

"Yes and no."

"Now Sheriff, are you pulling my leg?" Monroe laughs awkwardly.

V.B. stands to stretch. "Hold on. Simply put, Lewis Redmond is a family man working to support them in legal work, not only farming but also running a federally-controlled distillery just over the line there in Walhalla, the one owned by Dietrich Beaman." V.B. points southeasterly. "In fact, he is so famous that the owners are marketing one brand of whiskey with his picture on it!"

The federal agent, oblivious to the totally absorbed audience of moonshiners sitting around the fire with them, explains his ignorance. "This is all a shock to us, Sheriff. We've been out of the loop, dealing with other bootlegging worries in Chicago."

"Where did you learn about Redmond anyway?" One of the burly men asks, as if he were somehow a part of the discussion.

Monroe does not answer immediately. He seems embarrassed and finally, confesses, "Mostly hearsay, I reckon. I did read some things in the New York Times some time ago." Then after another long pause, he mumbles that he'd read some of the dime novels about Redmond.

The burly man looks at V.B., "What about you? How come you know so much about Redmond?"

The Sheriff doesn't hesitate to answer his prisoner's question. "Simply put, I grew up in these parts and knew all the families involved in Redmond's life -- in East Fork, Cathey's Creek and Middle Fork. Since it is so close, I also know several families just down the mountain in Rocky Bottom. In addition, my Papa was our school teacher and often used different newspapers to teach us to read and keep informed about our world. As I said, the mail came up from Greenville regularly and we got an occasional New York Times, some Greenville and Charleston papers and the Pickens paper. I was about eleven when all that happened and it really captured my interest. I not only followed Redmond murdering Duckworth for trying to arrest him, but I was also interested in the agent who got away after he accidentally shot Redmond's best friend, Amos Ladd. I was fourteen when Redmond was finally captured. Then of all things, my papa and I visited with him in Greenville when he came through on the train."

Monroe slyly asks, "Now Sheriff, do I detect some sympathy for the criminals in this story? Are you really on the side of the law?"

V.B. shakes his head at the ridiculous question. "Agent Monroe, I would not risk my life and do these things if I were not on the side of the law. Yes, I am in sympathy with all folks but do not agree when they step over that line, be they moonshiners or revenue officers." The three moonshiners are suddenly aware of their transgressions. V.B. continues, "As surely you know by now, there are bad eggs in law enforcement and bad eggs in these woods doing what is not right. I really feel badly for the Duckworth family and for the Ladd family. In both cases I do not think justice was ever done. But they are trying to get on with their lives as best they can."

Seeing some light in the sky over the eastern ridge, V.B. comments, "Well, enough story-telling for this one night. As I said, the Major is a law-abiding man, married to his beloved Adeline, supporting his family and paying taxes. He had been captured over in Swain County beyond Cherokee where he had moved and repented his ways when released." V.B. can't help himself as the men ready themselves for leaving. He looks just as seriously as he can at Monroe, "Now, do you want to take the lead up the trail when day breaks? I'm sure our timber rattlers will respect federal officers!"

Summer 2012

Mammaw took me to the Co-Ed Movie Theater in Brevard. After so much time with Kevin and Ellie I was thrilled to finally have some time with Mammaw. The old theater was small, but still boasted Brevard's original decades old red and gold theater box office with window bars and a small booth fitting for a single person who took our twenty dollar bill and return a handful of change. The time we spent laughing and chomping down on butter popcorn did the both of us good. Every so often Mammaw would reach over and squeeze my hand.

Once the movie was over we stepped out into Brevard's night life. The streets were pretty much empty and at nine you could see a few restaurants finishing up with their final guests. We crossed Main Street to the parking lot on the other side and hopped into the Big M. Both of us rolled down the windows to let the fresh evening air cool the stuffy car.

She pulled out of the parking lot and turned left up Main Street to head back onto the Greenville Highway. As we passed the beautifully lighted courthouse on our left I sighed, "I'm going to miss this Mammaw."

"I know, hon." Mammaw reached over and squeezed my hand. I didn't want to let go, but knew she needed both hands on the steering wheel to negotiate the curves ahead. "But I'm sure you'll be back."

I knew she was right. I figured that one day I wouldn't leave. I just wished it were now.

We headed up the mountain cautiously taking each curve as it came. I smiled, quite aware of the growing number of cars behind us that did not appreciate her forty-mile-an-hour pace.

As we rounded the curve to the final stretch before the Sherwood Forest entrance we suddenly saw blue lights ahead of us. Police cars were directing traffic around the turnoff to El Capitán. My heart quickened as Mammaw whispered, "Oh my, I wonder what's going on there."

As we turned to the right into Sherwood Forest, I looked behind us and saw a blue Dodge Ram slowly pulling out of the gas station only a hundred yards away.

1896: William McKinley is elected U.S. President; The Supreme Court accepts a "separate but equal" principle of segregation; Henry Ford builds his first horseless carriage, following the Duryea brothers, Olds, Winton and King.

Re-election

It is a beautiful, sunny Sunday when the buggy shows up on See Off just after church with V.B., Jessie and little Reba, their own 'Bobo', who is pretending to drive. Laura and Walter Raxter have been very engaged with not only family but also with many neighborhood children who seem to be in their care. On that summer Sunday, they are all glad for the break.

"Let's picnic out yonder under that oak, not out on Dunn's Rock with these young-uns," Laura says pointing at the small herd of giggling children now eagerly running off the agony of sitting silently in church. Bobo sees them and is quick to imitate the running, but never strays too far from Jessie, who gently touches her own growing belly.

Walter watches the scene and waves for the McGahas to move to the two picnic tables under the tall oak. "Reckin it's time to talk agin."

When the food is set out, the young family joins the already set table and watches as the children stop their play and run over to the small feast. Jessie is amazed at how the Hogsed, McGaha, Holden and other children seem to know what they have to do and even gather some food for not only themselves but also for the adults. "How do you do that?"

"Do what?" Laura asks as she smiles and thanks a young girl who has just offered her a plate of fresh corn, ham and a white roll.

"How you teach them to take care of each other and themselves?" Jessie responds.

"Well, their parents do most of that and I just keep 'em a-doin' what they need to do. We are all a-learnin' lots." Laura doesn't hide her joy in each of the children as she gazes at them. "Take little Elzie there for 'xample. Nine years old and already tryin' to herd his sisters and brothers and cousins like cattle! 'Sides, we need a few more to help with all the work! "

Walter slaps his wife on the thigh, and adds, "And real soon. I ain't gittin any younger and I got this young Ashworth heifer to keep our herd a-goin'."

Before Laura can reprimand her husband V.B. adds, "And all that time you were in that saw-pit cutting planks for the chapel, I thought you were just thinking about the sawdust in your eyes!"

"Boys!" both women say together, not holding back their embarrassment.

Laura leans over to gently touch Jessie's belly. "How about you-uns?"

Laura asks trying to focus the attention away from her husband, "How soon is this-un due?"

V.B. responds, "Any time. Little Reba needs a brother or sister to play with."

"And," Jessie adds, "we are looking for land to build a home in Brevard, probably on the north side of town, somewhere near Oak Grove Church or the Siniard place. Or maybe on this side of town where East Main comes out this way."

"I can see that you'd be closer to your office at the courthouse, but people could also tell when you are a-headin' somewhere, and they shore love to talk," Walter notes.

The Sheriff agrees and qualifies, "Yes, they talk and watch my every move, trying to figure out where we are making a raid on a still. But since we usually go early enough to hide out in the woods for hours and take all kinds of round-about ways, we hope they can't figure it out and tell their kin. Sometimes they do and we get nobody, just a still to bust up."

Walter picks up on a point. "V.B., you said 'hide out.' I've heard from some deputies and even from some fellers you've caught, that you are invisible. For such a big man, how can you git invisible?"

V.B. smiles at the sudden memory. "My Uncle Tom Fowler had some Cherokee in him and I loved to spend time with him. We'd go into the woods and stalk animals and learn to hide and lie low for hours, a-waitin' for animals. We often were out there and 'shiners would walk right by and never see us."

Walter is still a little skeptical, "How come we never heard of your bringing back a lot of game if'n you were out there so much with him?"

"Well," V.B. confesses, "I said stalking, not killing. He showed me that if you don't need the meat you just watch and 'talk' with them, be their friends or neighbors. And if you do need to take them, you say some words and apologize to them and thank them for their sacrifice for you."

Now more curious than skeptical, Walter asks, "And how, by the way, do you fight the insects and keep your smell from the dogs?"

"I reckon you'll have to go out with me sometime to learn." V.B. just laughs at his old friend. He takes a bite of the roll and speaks before he has completely swallowed. "So, dear friends, to change the subject, I'll just say I'll be running for sheriff at least another term. Papa and Mama feel okay with it and the Republican Party has asked me."

"Yeah, Sheriff," Walter reaches for the last roll on the table before carefully eyeing V.B., "we also heard that they done 'lected you to be President of the Party."

An embarrassed Sheriff responds, "That's nothing. They couldn't find anybody else. What could I say?"

"Nothing?" Jessie pipes in gently patting her husband's knee, "Nothing? Ha. Remember when you first ran not so long ago and you refused to play the political games and take bribes from the so-called businesses? And they threatened you! We have come to a different place in this short time, thanks to you."

"Thank you my dear wife, love of my life." V.B. leans in to give Jessie a quick peck on the cheek, causing her to blush ever so slightly.

So for a third time Volenus Bunyan McGaha is elected Sheriff of Transylvania County by a large margin. Times are changing, however. Tourists come. Automobiles arrive. The train line has been built to Brevard from Hendersonville and has been operational for two years.

12

Summer 2012

"Stop!" Before the Big M. had fully stopped, I jumped out of the car. I couldn't let Mammaw keep driving after I saw the Dodge Ram pull away from whatever the police were investigating. Something was really wrong.

"Millie! What are you doing?" Mammaw leaned as far over into the passenger side of the seat as possible in order to see me better.

I stood still and stared in the direction of the blue lights. "I have a bad feeling about this." I looked at Mammaw and pleaded with her. "I've just got to go make sure Ellie's okay."

Mammaw patted the seat. "Get in, Millie. I'll drive you." I got in again and closed the door. We didn't speak while Mammaw turned around and headed back to the main road. After we passed the Sheriff's cars we turned in at the far end of the parking lot and Mammaw stopped the car.

We both got out and I headed for the cluster of people huddled around someone lying on the ground. I saw a broom not far from the awkwardly twisted leg. The bristles were splattered with blood. One of the deputies stopped me, "Miss, you're not allowed to go any further. We're waiting for an ambulance."

I could hear wailing and recognized Elllie's mom kneeling on the ground. I nodded at the policeman, but then simply found my way around the restaurant to come in from the backside. Mammaw stayed with me and occasionally touched my shoulder letting me know she was still there. As I came around the corner I saw two familiar figures come running out of the woods where the McGaha Chapel lay hidden in the darkness. I felt a sense of relief knowing Ellie and Kevin were not hurt, but wondered who was lying on the ground. Sirens came screaming up the mountain as I joined Ellie and Kevin who were now able to break through the small crowd.

"What's going on?" I finally asked. But my question was answered as soon as I saw Rai's long hair plastered against his bloody face. His right leg was twisted gruesomely away from the rest of his body, as if someone had tried to remove it from his hip. His arms looked intact but his bloody fingers showed he didn't go down without defending himself. He was still breathing.

Ellie came up behind her mom who immediately screamed, "Carp, Carp!" Then the mother saw Kevin and started to head for him with fire in her eyes.

A young deputy that didn't look older than thirteen intercepted the mother's first blow and held her as an older deputy with a considerable beer gut came up to Kevin. "Are you one of the Carp brothers?"

Kevin's fear showed in his eyes as he continued to stare at the mangled mess in front of him. "Yes sir," was all he could manage.

"Did you have anything to do with this assault?" The fat officer spoke more matter of factly than accusingly.

"No sir." Kevin's eyes were steady, but I could see him clenching his jaw trying to hold himself together.

The siren stopped as two medics jumped from the back of the ambulance. A young woman medic checked Rai's pulse and examined him further as the police continued Kevin's questioning. "Well, it seems Rai told his Ma that the Carps gave him a beating."

"But not this Carp." Ellie stood between Kevin and her mother. She said something to her Mom in Spanish, who then spat back words in response.

The fat deputy scratched his head and paused to watch Rai being lifted into the ambulance with a stretcher. As best I could tell, Rai's father jumped in the back with them. "How is it that you know this, little lady?" The policeman finally asked.

Ellie was quiet. She stared at her mom, the small crowd and then looked at Kevin as if asking for permission. But Kevin continued to stare at the same spot, now only marked by the bloody broom. She finally managed a lame, "Because I do."

"Sir," Kevin's voice was steady as he turned his gaze to look at the deputy. "I was not the one who hurt Rai. I would never hurt Rai because his sister is my girlfriend. In fact we were together this evening up in the old McGaha Chapel."

A flurry of Spanish exploded as Ellie tried to explain this to her mother who became more and more subdued. She shook in disbelief and buried her head into a neighbor's arms.

The siren started up again as the ambulance headed down the mountain towards Transylvania Regional Hospital.

1898: The battleship Maine is blown up in Havana Harbor; U.S. is at war with Spain; Evidence of Vikings is found in Minnesota.

Birth and Death

It is not to be a good new year. The snow is bad, really bad.

Reba is now all of four years old and her sister Leslie is two going on six. The inseparable two are excited about becoming big sisters to a coming baby, and being "real mommies" with more than dolls. They run in and out of their Momma's bedroom as she lies on the bed with their father standing close to her. The girls do not notice the sad look on their mother's face as she pulls V.B. down close to her and whispers. "I'm not so sure about this one, Bunyan. Things just don't seem right."

"It's going to be okay, my love. God has blessed us with those two and another blessing is coming I'm sure." V.B. gently touches his wife's forehead to reassure her, but is surprised to find her warmer than usual.

Jessie tightens her grip on V.B. and glances toward the door to make sure Leslie and Reba are out of earshot. "I know, but I sense something is wrong. And I know you have to go off to work."

V.B. pulls his wife into his arms and reassures her. "I'll not go. Things are covered. But I will go and fetch Laura Raxter. She has so much experience with babies." He finally kisses her forehead and stands. He is increasingly eager to get someone else here to help out. "And of course your mother will come as soon as the snow lets up. It looks like a bad January for snow and ice. Maybe Laura can bring some Hogsed help until your mother can get here."

Jessie just leans back onto her pillow and tries to smile, but the sincerity is lost in the growing dullness of her fever filled eyes.

Even though the McGahas now live in Brevard, the women in the Dunn's Rock, Loftis and Cedar Mountain communities just sense that Jessie needs them and they head to town to help, bearing food, blankets, and prayers. The menfolk get the women there, usually coming off Riley Mountain Road with sleds drawn by horses or oxen. These homemade, heavy sleds are well-built for not only the woods and snow but for "sidling" hauling on the steep mountainsides. At the foot of the mountain they catch a ride with a Hogsed or other wagon to town. V.B. is overwhelmed by their generosity in spite of the fact that the snowstorm might prevent them from getting home.

Before dark Dr. Hunt arrives and the cluster of women are excited to have a real doctor with formal schooling. But Jessie and V.B. are aware that they need their family and are thankful when the McGahas join the growing group. Jessie wishes her mother and father were not stuck at home in the snow, but is relieved when Craf and Harriet arrive to assist. Seeing the men are only in the way, Craf takes V.B. to sit a spell out on the porch, cold as it is.

The two men brush the snow off the rockers to clear a place to sit. The cold seems to help numb the growing fear somewhat as V.B. looks at his father. "Papa, you and Mama have lost so many young-uns. I'm scared. What if she loses the baby, or something happens to her?"

Craf takes a moment and a deep sadness crosses his brow as painful memories flood his senses. He finally manages to answer. "Son, it's something you never get over, but with God's help you can. You remember that we lost six of your brothers and sisters until now. One at birth."

V.B. is nearly in tears. "I'll never forget losing Wiley and Julie. The others were older and it didn't hurt quite as much. Course I never knew Mitch."

Craf rocks gently. "Of course. Makes sense as you were a lot younger when you had to lose them."

V.B. lets the tears flow. "But Papa, how did you handle it?"

There is silence for a while. "I really don't know. I tried to be there for your Mama but honestly when somebody else came to help - like here tonight, basically the same folks- I'd head to Rich Mountain to check on the hogs and cattle." More silence. "Then I'd go check on the stock." More silence. "When I got there I'd go sit on a big rock on that mountain and scream and cry my heart out."

V.B. watches tears flow freely down his father's cheeks only to be lost in his gray beard. He knows his father understands. He is not alone.

After a few more minutes of silence, the growing cold makes the men want to return to the warmth of the wood burning stove, Craf speaks again, "I don't know which is worse, seein' all the killin' and mayhem of war or losin' one of your own. You feel so helpless."

V.B. can only nod, knowing that helplessness is truly holding him captive.

Both men are startled when the front door flies open and Laura comes out on the porch, "You men will catch your death with pneumonia in this weather. Git in here to the fire, right now." The men obey and welcome the warmth the stuffy room brings. The two men are fiercely aware of the silence all around except for loud screams from the next room.

Laura guides V.B. by the arm to the bedroom door, then speaks, "First, V.B., I got to let you know the baby's a-coming. But we got some problems."

"Can I see her?" V.B. lays his hand on the hardwood door that separates him from his wife.

Laura speaks firmly, "No, of course not. The baby is a-comin' to this world the wrong way and we are all a-trying to help them both." V.B. just nods at his friend and watches her disappear into the bedroom, closing the door behind her, intensifying the feeling of being shut out.

V.B. does not move from the door as women are running in and out of the kitchen to get more hot water from the stove at Dr. Hunt's order. Each face is more anxious than the last as they step briskly by all the men trying to look busy keeping the fire going.

No words need be said.

Father and son glance silently at each other as if their conversation outside had been prophetic.

The mantel clock strikes midnight announcing that January thirteenth has arrived.

Harriet steps out of the bedroom to find V.B. still standing guard by the door. She reaches up to gently embrace him as she reluctantly whispers, "My son. I am so sorry. Your son arrived but did not make it." And the mother who herself had lost six of her own, hugs her only living son and cries in their loss. Craf is quick to lay a hand on his son's shoulder as he weeps silently.

V.B. is stunned and finally manages to ask. "And how about Jessie? How is she?"

Harriet shakes her head. "Not good."

"Can I see her?" V.B. asks his mother, but is more desperate than inpatient.

Harriet tries to encourage her son. "In about five minutes. We need to clean up some and get the others out so you and she can have a few minutes with your son." Then turning to the nervous men, she announces, "Now you men get to work. It is your job to build a box for this beautiful little creation of God. You can do that."

All the men jump to their feet, feeling relieved they can at least work on fixing something.

Tall, shaking Sheriff V. B. McGaha leans against the wall, still in shock. For once, he feels not so strong, not so in charge. But five minutes is a lifetime and he can't wait any longer, so he slowly eases into the bedroom as the women file out, all with tears in their eyes, most crying openly. They have fought the battle bravely and have lost.

Jessie lies in bed, deathly white but trying to smile. She has a small bundle wrapped tightly in her arms. She reaches for V.B. to come to her and he obeys. "I tried, Bunyan. I'm sorry."

Her husband. kneels and kisses her forehead, her cheek and then her lips, not caring whether they are alone or not. Tears flow. "Not your fault. No need to be sorry."

Jessie weakly returns her husband's affection. "I know, but I wanted a son for you so much."

"Now, now, 'twas not meant to be." V.B. kisses her once more before he sits on the edge of her bed and dares to pick up the small bundle. He lifts the blanket to find a perfectly still little face being gently washed by his own tears.

For an hour they sit there, the pale mother lying weakly in bed, the grieving father next to her holding the little boy who couldn't make the great leap into life in the outer world.

During this time Grandma Harriet brings little Reba and Leslie in for a few minutes to get a glimpse of their lost brother. She takes over the assignment of trying to walk through the "why" questions, giving the sad parents time alone.

The snow continues to fall outside as tears fall inside.

Finally, Laura comes to take the little body and wrap it in a fresh blanket.

"Where are you going with him?" Jessie asks weakly.

Laura looks at the grief stricken couple and tries to sound practical without upsetting them. "We thought we'd lay him in the shed until the coffin is ready – not long."

Jessie's voice rises in desperation as she reaches for the baby. "Can't we just let him stay nearby, maybe in the crib that V.B. built over there? Until the storm is over, maybe until tomorrow morning?" Laura hands Jessie the motionless bundle and looks at V.B. who nods approval.

As January fourteenth brings fresh snow it seems like no time before time the men have built a simple but beautiful little coffin, with "McGaha Boy" carved primitively on top already. The family shows appreciation and the baby is finally placed in the coffin and which is placed in the cold shed until they can bury it.

V.B. spends the day with Jessie, fiercely aware of her inability to leave the bed for any reason. Harriet and Laura continue to clean her bed linens as blood and other fluids continue to soil the sheets.

By midnight Jessie has become the major concern for the doctor and all the caring women. V.B. hesitantly waits outside the door once again not believing that the nightmare continues. It is Harriet once again who bears the news. "Son, she is not doing well."

V.B. looks at the doctor who has come up behind them and is preparing to leave. "How bad is it?"

Dr. Hunt shakes his head. "Really bad. I've done all I can. I don't think she can make it."

The stricken man walks into the bedroom to sit by his wife's bed and hold her hand. Sometimes they are alone, sometimes others are present. He is not aware of their presence even when they try to coax him to eat or leave.

January fifteenth arrives and Jessie Geneva Allison McGaha, beloved wife of Volenus Bunyan McGaha departs this life.

Mercifully, the snow ceases and even begins to melt as Harriet, Laura and the other women prepare the body for the burial at Oak Grove. Grief stricken Rev. and Mrs. Allison finally get through the snow, too late to say goodbye to their daughter.

On the morning of the funeral Craf and Harriet watch their son saddle his horse and put an oil slick and blanket behind the saddle. "Are you all right, son?" his worried mother asks.

V.B. nods.

"Where you headed?"

He looks at his father briefly and rides south away from Brevard.

"V.B!" Harriet cries.

Craf touches his wife's shoulder, easing her back into the house to tend to the girls. "Let him be Harriet. He needs to go."

Before the double funeral in Oak Grove Methodist Church in Brevard, neighbors near the Greenville Turnpike such as the Fowlers, Rabbs and Hogseds, reported hearing screams from the Rich Mountain area like a mountain lion. Others, like the Moores and Loftises, reported unusual, primitive howls like they'd never heard before. Was it some strange animal after stock? Was a big panther after something?

Craf knows. But he knows his son will return in time for the funeral at Oak Grove Methodist Church in Brevard. He and Harriet will sit by their sobbing son while Reverend Allison tries to comfort others in his sermon. But it will be too much for this man as well. He might be a man of God, but he is also a father and grandfather.

Summer 2012

The morning after Rai had been badly beaten I woke to the sound of frantic pounding. I ran to the front door to find Kevin's mother,

Tempy, rushing into Mammaw's arms. I peeked outside and realized it was still so early that the stars were just beginning to fade. "My boys!" she wailed.

"There, there!" Mammaw petted her like a lost puppy as Kevin's mother collapsed onto the couch.

"The law come last night and took 'em. They said that they'd done been to the hospital and took pictures of the Mexican boy. He's hurt bad."

I took in the scene, wanting to feel sorry for Tempy but thrilled to hear the jerks were in jail. Mammaw nodded for me to get the woman a glass of water. I did as Mammaw said and as I handed the glass to her I couldn't help but ask, "Not Kevin though, right?"

Tempy wailed again as if I'd pushed the wailing button. She was finally able to pull herself together, "No, not my baby. But," she heaved a few heavy breaths, "he told all of us last night when he got home that he knowed what happen and that he ain't havin' anything to do with the boys who beat up his girlfriend's brother." She swallowed a huge gulp of water.

I wanted so badly to know how they reacted to his announcement. When she didn't continue, I pushed. "Well, how did everyone take the news?"

"Millie! That's quite enough!" Mammaw shook her head at me, but Tempy patted Mammaw's hand gently.

"That's all right Maxie. She's got reasons for a-knowin', I'm shore." Tempy gave me a pitiful smile that made me want to feel sorry for her, but I wasn't there yet. "You can imagine how Roy and Junior wanted to tear into Kevin, but their Pa told them they was in 'nough trouble and better leave it be."

"What's goin' to happen to Roy and Junior?" Mammaw asked.

"Well, their Pa has followed them down to the magistrate to see if he can pay their bond, and then they should be able to come on home. At least for now."

My heart sank. I couldn't believe the Carps would be back on the street so quickly. I was hoping they would be locked up until I was gone.

1898: Theodore Roosevelt is a hero at San Juan Hill; Inventor Gatling's new gun becomes the most efficient killing machine known; Pepsi Cola is marketed in New Bern, N.C. as competition to Coca Cola.

The McGaha Family Cemetery

V.B. rocks on his father's front porch where so many travelers have found rest as they passed through. V.B. closes his eyes to take in the spring freshness that tries to sooth away the harshness of winter. V.B.'s mind continues to race back to January and Jessie. He gently shakes his head and tries to control the deep anger he feels towards God. He can't believe that after his tragic loss, the family also lost its ailing, ninety-four-year-old patriarch, Grandpa Jesse McGaha just days later on January nineteenth, just after the funeral for Jessie and the baby. V.B. recollects the brief statement of his life in the newspaper, where it noted that he was "in Capt Clayton's Eastern District of settlers and got his land grant, number 2899 for 100 acres from Buncombe County in 1830. Grandma Candice had passed on back in '75 and he'd eventually found a home and care with daughter Polly Ann and her husband, Tom Fowler." It had been a cold, harsh January indeed.

V.B. suddenly stands to shake off January's grip when the front porch door opens and Craf steps out holding two cups of coffee. The older man looks at his son, but does not address the young man's obvious agony. He simply walks up to him and hands him the hot drink. V.B. willingly accepts the mug and eagerly takes a sip feeling more than the coffee warm him. He can't help uttering, "Ahhh!" and smiles, "Thanks, Papa."

Craf simply nods and points at the tall pines that open up into the pretty piece of land they call their "burying place." Craf finally speaks. "Son, we need to make this buryin' plot more official and set it aside as a graveyard from here on out. Can you get a couple of other folks to be trustees with you?"

Slightly overwhelmed by his father's choice of topic V.B. stumbles over his words, but manages to get out, "Of course, Papa. No problem."

Craf goes on further as if thinking out loud, "Sorry we did not think of this a while back before my Papa and Mama died. Orr cemetery is not so far away. But our McGaha family is really a-growing and a-going. When

Papa Jesse signed this land over to me back in '62 it was one of the first books of deeds when Transylvania became a county. I reckon he'd say this is a good family use for the little plot."

Patting his dad on the back, feeling thanks for the old man's timing, V.B. nodded. "I reckon so."

And so on April 22, 1898, James Crawford McGaha signs the document giving one acre to Trustees V.B. McGaha, H.L. Hardin and Silas McCrary "for purpose of a graveyard." The McGaha family cemetery is official.

Summer 2012

"So now I get it." Mammaw looked at me as she handed me a warm biscuit. The stars had finally faded, giving way to the promise of a hot day.

"Get what?" I asked as I spread Mammaw's homemade apple butter on my biscuit.

"Why you were so upset." She sat down across from me at the small table and heaped apple butter on her own biscuit. "You're upset about Kevin and Ellie being a couple."

I frowned slightly. "Actually, not really. I'm just upset they didn't let me know. They hid it from me and used me."

"Kinda like you don't let me know what's goin' on?" Mammaw's words stung.

"No! That's not the same." I said lamely as I felt it harder to swallow the biscuit that just seemed to grow in my mouth.

Mammaw didn't yell at me, but just looked at me sort of sadly. "Is it not the same, Millie?" When I didn't answer she added, "Honey, I can't help you if you won't let me."

1898: Treaty of Paris concludes the Spanish American War. The battlefield death toll in the War is only 289, but over 4,000 die of diseases and from consuming "embalmed beef". A Negro postmaster is appointed to Lake City, South Carolina resulting in a riot in which the postmaster and his family are killed.

Healing Change

The squealing laughter of Reba and Leslie is heard all the way to Craf's barn. Summer finds V.B. and his two little girls spending more time in the refuge of the hospitable home of Craf and Harriet. V.B. especially loves Sundays when a simple worship at the McGaha Chapel seems to relax him, especially after many of the long days and nights he puts in at work.

On this Sunday Craf has managed to get V.B. to help him in the barn, but before they close the door V.B. peeks one more time around the corner to see his mother and the girls chasing each other. He is grateful that the girls cling to their grandmother who can give them much knowing love that few women could quite grasp. The benefit is mutual, for Harriet can somehow regain something of what she had lost in the deaths of her own children. These girls and she need no words, just lovin' time together.

"Sure is good to hear your girls laugh again, son." Craf's voice pulls V.B. away from the picturesque scene.

V.B. follows his father into the cool musty smell of the old barn. "Yeah, Papa, I'm afraid I'm not the best dad for them in these days."

"It must be really hard for you without Jessie." Craf heads to a shelf where he stretches to reach a tin.

"Yeah." V.B. comes up behind his father and grabs the can before Craf can retrieve a wooden step stool.

"Thanks." Craf shakes his head at his tall son for showing off. A few minutes later Craf has gathered a couple of hammers and laid them out on a low bench near an old wooden table with two broken legs. Craf finally continues, "It sounds like you don't think you can do right by your two little girls."

"That's right. I'm gone so much in my work. And when I am with them I don't think I can give them what they need." V.B. picks up a hammer and places himself in front of one of the two broken legs, realizing his father is going to have him fix this table, although he is quite aware of his father's abilities to do it himself.

Craf smiles at his son's willingness to jump in and help, so he holds out the tin can for him to reach in and grab the needed nails. "First of all,

Bunyan, it has only been a few months - weeks really - since you lost Jessie. You got to have some healing time."

V.B. grabs a handful of nails and places them on the barn floor. He picks out the least rusty ones he can find. "I know. By the way, I sold my part in the newspaper my partner and I started in Brevard."

Craf searches the can himself and picks out his nail preferences. "That was probably right. You do need more time for your girls and bein' Sheriff of Transylvania."

"Papa, I'll not run again this year. I can't do it." V.B.'s first blow with the hammer drives the nail completely in place.

Craf picks up his hammer and begins to nail the broken leg on his side of the table. "Not a fourth term? How come? Has Jessie's loss made you decide this?"

V.B. picks up the next nail and places it strategically on the broken leg, "Admittedly, it has been part of the decision. Jessie was such a supporter of me and my work. I felt I could face almost any obstacle or criticism out there with her to come home to. She made me feel at peace inside when I was hidin' out in the woods about to catch some criminal. I felt strong with her encouraging me." The hammer falls, but this time two blows are needed. "But I need to move on. I don't want to have to go through another election with all the politicking, and pressures to answer all the questions - why did I arrest this one when everybody knew that one was worse and so on." V.B. continues with one more nail. He pauses a moment and looks at his father who is watching him. "Now I am so embarrassed when I am at the courthouse in court or some public meeting. I feel like I'm the one on trial or watched more than the defendant or speaker."

Craf frowns and is not sure what his son is saying, "You mean that folks are more critical and staring at you more now?"

Suddenly V.B.'s face reddens and he fumbles around for another nail. "What I mean is that women are botherin' me!" When his father continues to stare at him V.B. elaborates. "They come to court and look just at me, smiling and gigglin'." Craf continues to stare and V.B. sees his father is trying to keep from laughing. "They bring cookies to the office and try to hang around and flirt. They bring some made-up problem to get my attention. It's awfully embarrassing. I can hardly get my work done."

Craf can't hold back anymore and asks, "They haven't started making whisky to get you to capture them in the woods have they?"

Craf and V.B. laugh hard and long, the first time in months for the Sheriff. "Whew, I guess I needed that. Good for the soul."

Craf wipes tears from his eyes and resumes hammering his end of the table. "And for a hurting heart."

"I reckon." V.B. examines the broken table leg and decides it would really be overkill to add any more nails.

Craf adds one last nail and looks seriously at his son. "Well son, jokes aside, you're a young man at thirty-two and those girls may need a new mother someday."

V.B. throws his hammer on the bench and waits for his father to flip the table right side up. "I know, Papa, but I'm not ready to think like that."

"Absolutely. You need more healing time and by all means don't marry too soon. It is always a mistake." Craf nods and the two men turn the table to standing position.

"On account of what people think?" V.B. tries to jiggle the table to see if it is sturdy or not and is satisfied to find there is very little give.

Craf, satisfied, begins to gather the hammer and nails. "Heavens, no. When your heart is broken you are vulnerable. Some people will take advantage of that."

V.B. watches his father walk over and grab the footstool to replace the nail can on the high shelf. "Like the cookie ladies?"

Craf puts the stool away and comes to sit on the top of the table and lean in real seriously toward his son. Craf gently caresses his beard. "But you can also mess up if you jump too soon. You see that the girls need a mother and you feel lonely and horny and you could jump into the wrong relationship."

V.B. laughs at his father and punches him on the arm. "Well, Papa, if somebody looks interesting down the road, I'll sure bring her over for you to check out. You sure did a good job picking Mama!"

Craf laughs as his son's playful punch almost knocks him off the table, "Bein' as she picked me, you'd best have her and the girls check out anybody who catches your eye and heart - whenever that comes."

As father and son walk slowly back to the house, the children are playing on the tree swing while Harriet watches from the porch. "So, what mischief are you two up to out there in the barn?"

As they join her on the porch, Craf answers, "We fixed that old back porch table and Bunyan will not run again for sheriff."

"Concernin'that table, it's about time. I'm needed a place to put my canned goods here before long." Harriet continues to rock " As for runnin' again, I kind of figured that out already." Sitting down in his adjoining rocker, Craf asks his wife, "How come you know such things before I do?"

Harriet reaches out and pats her husband's hand. "Women's intuition. We just know some things." She looks at her son who has settled himself on the top porch step and is looking out at his girls. "So, did you two men talk about what you will do, if'n you're not Sheriff?"

V.B. smiles, "Well, Mama, we didn't get that far. Besides, I thought I'd best tell the two of you together." Craf looks surprised, but says nothing since it was something they both should hear together. "Well, you both know that I've busted a lot of stills through these mountains, along with all the other stuff." His parents nod knowingly. "And in many of those busts we were with federal agents."

"Revenuers," both respond.

Craf doesn't hesitate. "They've been after me for some time to join them."

Craf stops rocking and becomes almost giddy as a child, "Goodness gracious! My son working as a federal agent. My little boy who was always worried about 'justice' now has an even bigger chance to help bring it about."

Harriet reaches out to pat her husband's arm again. "Slow down, husband. Not proud are you? He said he is looking into it. And he is not your little boy, he's our grown man and we are both proud of him!"

V.B. quite enjoys his parent's excitement, reaffirming the direction he is considering. "Like I said, I'm looking into it for the future. My business seems to be enough right now to keep me going. I need a break for a while from the law. Maybe a little later."

"And which business, son? You got your hands into a lot," Harriet asks seriously.

"I'll probably work on the mercantile business in Brevard. I did okay with the timber work in Vanderbilt's forest and got along with Dr. Schenck. He was good to answer my letters, let me work the timber, and even trout fish from time to time." V.B. pauses to look and listen to the giggles coming from the swing. "But I need to be closer to my girls. You folks are helping out so much but I don't expect you to raise them for me."

Summer 2012

The drive to Transylvania Regional Hospital seemed longer than normal. I just couldn't shake Mammaw's comments at breakfast about me hiding information from her and noticed that my loving warm grandmother was more distant than usual. So, I simply leaned my head against the cold glass window pane and watched Transylvania County whiz by; mountain curves soon straightened to pass sod grass fields hungry for more rain. I glanced at the pick-up soccer game in front of Brevard Elementary as we entered town, suddenly wishing I could jump out and join the group of carefree, sweaty kids not thinking about what happens next.

We bypassed down town and took a curvy road through neighborhoods proudly displaying cut lawns and blooming daylilies. Some yards even had stalks of corn waving, identifying small fresh vegetable gardens.

Once we hit the main road again neighborhoods gave way to drug stores and gas stations until we finally turned right along a short road leading us to the hospital parking lot. It wasn't too hard to find Rai's room since the volunteers kindly guided us down a few sterile halls. The door opened after we knocked on it and Ellie embraced me and then Mammaw waving us into the small room. Sunlight poured into the room from a small window in the corner, attempting to combat the fluorescent glow. Kevin stood quietly in the window nook and nodded at us. There were two beds, and Rai's mom was sitting on the empty one looking at her son as he was propped up trying to eat some Jello.

"Hey, Millie." Rai smiled as he sat up a little straighter, seemingly proud to have his bare chest showing off his abdominal muscles.

"Hi, Rai." I walked a little closer examining the cast around his leg all the way up to his thigh. Thank God he had a sheet covering his lower extremities, although I could tell he was on enough drugs that he wouldn't have been very embarrassed if he were completely naked. "I hope you're not in too much pain."

"Nahh!" Rai slurped the Jello and smiled with chunks of red still clinging to his lower lip.

"I guess he's feeling pretty good." I looked at Ellie. Mammaw had joined Mrs. Alverez on the empty bed.

Ellie rubbed her brother's hair, careful to avoid the obvious scrapes and bruises on half of his face, where it looked like he may have been held down face first on the concrete. "Yes, it looks like the medicine is working. He was in pain early and it wasn't a pretty sight." She nods over toward her mother. "Mom is worried that he'll get hurt again." She briefly looks at her boyfriend in the corner.

Kevin doesn't move, but tries to finish filling us in. "The Sheriff tells us that even though Junior and Roy are able to get out on bond, they still have to face assault charges in spite of their claim that Rai came at them with a broom. It's just that they can be out while they wait to face the charges. The whole thing can take a while."

Mrs. Alverez said something to Ellie who nodded and helped Rai sip some water from a huge plastic mug.

I didn't know what to say and looked at Mammaw who spoke up, "What happens next?"

"We'll bring Rai home in a couple of days and he'll eventually get better like everyone does with a broken leg. AND we'll just hope the Carps stay away, or get arrested for something else. Apparently," Ellie's voice suddenly took on a harshness I had never heard, "assault is not a big deal. They have to get picked up for a greater offense to actually do any serious jail time."

Kevin and I looked at each other, but neither of us said anything.

1898: The U.S. takes over Guam, Philippines, Puerto Rico and Hawaii; The Supreme Court upholds an eight hour work day; Thirteen Negro scabs hired by coal mine owners to break up a strike in Illinois are killed.

A New Face

"Hello, Miss Thrash." V.B. nods at the young lady who glances his way as she enters the court room.

"Good mornin', Sheriff." Rose Thrash smiles briefly at the sheriff as he continues to greet everyone who enters the now very crowded and stuffy room. She wonders if she perhaps saw a lingering glance from the handsome widower.

V.B. makes sure he doesn't look Rose's way again. He is highly aware of her affections, along with all the other young women. He just cannot entertain the thought of courting again, although Rose would be at the top of his possibilities list. He shakes the thought from his mind as he watches in surprise as the courtroom fills up for a simple county commissioners meeting.

"What is all this about, son?" Craf pulls off his wool cap as he adjusts from the winter cold to the body-heat driven warmth.

V.B. walks with his father down the aisle to find their place in the front row where he had already draped his jacket over two of the wooden flip-down seats. "Remember how I told you sometimes outsiders come to 'discover' or 'research' or 'find' some typical mountain family and end up stereotyping us all? And how sick and tired I am of how they make us all out to be ignorant, backward, illiterate, gun-totin', drunken, incestuous barbarians?"

Craf nods as he settles into the seat. "Damn idiots they are!"

V.B. sits down next to his father and leans in, "Well, a couple of weeks back there was one really feisty reporter from New York came in on the train and all but called me a liar when I told him that most folks can and do read and that some families, like the Hamiltons, even had classical books and Greek and Hebrew books."

Craf, highly aware of his own rising temperature, simply asks, "And why did HE get so mad?"

With a mischievous look in his eye, V.B. responds, "Maybe it was because I told him that most folks here could and did read their Bibles about judging others hastily!"

Craf lets out a laugh, "That's my boy!"

V.B. quickly adds, ""You won't believe this, but that angry, but ignorant, 'smart' fellow hung around for some days doing some questioning about our family and then went to the courthouse deed books."

"Our family?" Craf is baffled, "Deed books! What on earth for?"

"I guess I made him so mad that he wants to expose me as a liar and make out that even our McGaha family fits his preconceived notions." V.B. points at a young man who had already thrown his frock coat over a chair at one of the two large oak tables usually used as the prosecutor's table. He looked like a carpetbagger with his long sleeved blue striped shirt under a tight-fitting vest accented by a black bow-tie. "It seems he plans to write a magazine article and can't wait until he gets home to do it. So he thinks he is 'smart and informed' that he is showing up at this County Commissioners meeting, having passed the word around Brevard that something big is to happen."

Craf shifts awkwardly in his seat desperately trying to recollect any family business worthy of such notoriety. "What on earth did he do?"

"Just watch! He is slick but not as smart as he thinks." V.B. slouches down in his seat and crosses one leg over the other and lets it dangle ever so slightly, as if to show this cocky reporter he has no worries.

As the meeting commences, with all its pomp and circumstance, it is finally time for the reporter to speak. His growing pools of sweat, now slowly soaking into his vest, show the audience that this man may not be as confident as he is leading them to believe as he begins to hold a piece of paper in the air. "I have discovered out information that Volenus Bunyan McGaha's Uncle Tom Fowler and Aunt Mary, Polly Ann, as you remember, had 'indentured' themselves way back in seventy-five and could not write!"

The crowd remains still except for several shrugs of confusion. Finally the one of the commissioners asks, "Mister, what in tarnation are you tryin' to prove?"

V.B. suddenly stands and speaks, "Apparently he is trying to prove that the whole McGaha family was illiterate and so poor they had to hire out as servants to others, implying I have become Sheriff for something less than honorable reasons."

"That's only partially true." The aggressive reporter is defensive.

The County Commission Chairman, now quite enraged, tries to steady his voice. "What part might that be?"

"Just that the Sheriff claims literacy in his family and I have proven otherwise. Whether he is an honorable Sheriff or not is for you to decide." With confidence the man stands with his head held high.

At this point the county attorney gets the nod from the Chairman to stand. "Please educate that young man."

The lawyer, comfortable with his surroundings, places his papers on the table. He manages to look official enough with a starched white shirt and navy bow tie. "Sir," he addresses the reporter, "Have you read the entire document?"

"Er, yes." The reporter awkwardly holds the sheet up as if to examine it closely. "I think so."

Remaining very formal, the lawyer proceeds, "Sir, you are confusing 'indentured servants' with an 'indenture' that was the long-standing word for a deed in a land sale. The Fowlers sold some land to David Syms up on Cannons Creek. This was simply the registering of the deed."

Craf leans toward V.B. "How in the heck did the lawyer know that so fast?"

V.B. whispers back, "Somebody in the Deed Office tipped off the County Lawyer where the reporter had been snooping around and he did some looking himself."

The reporter manages to pull himself together to ask the lawyer, "Why did they use that word 'indentured' for a deed?"

The lawyer speaks, clearly interested in his own discovery, "In the old days when a contract or deed was made they wrote it down twice, at the top and bottom of the paper. Then they cut the paper in two with a jagged or curvy line like a giant teeth bite. Each party kept their half of the document and they could be proven to be authentic by fitting the giant-like 'teeth marks' together. Hence, the name 'indenture'."

The Commission Chairman stands and looks sternly at the young reporter. "Mister. We do have some folks in these parts who do not write and some who do not read. We have some who cannot do one or the other due to an affliction and some by choice. We have many folks who put their 'mark' on a document because they are embarrassed by their writing, but they can read their Bible and do basic math and basic writing. The document of a deed is so important some are too anxious to put down a name."

The reporter's vest is now thoroughly drenched. He begins to speak, "But . . . "

The Chairman cuts him off, "As I understand it, you came here from New York City. I do not have to ask you if there are any folks there who cannot read or write, either in English or their own original language."

The red-faced reporter attempts to speak once more, "Sir, I . . ."

The Chairman of the Transylvania County Commissioners stops him. "It appears you have a personal agenda that is not on our County business agenda. We do not take too kindly to having our residents talked down to, or about." The Chairman simply looks at V.B., "Sheriff McGaha, help this misguided young man find the way to the train station and if he can't read the timetable any better than a deed, help him figure out when the next train heads back toward Hendersonville and beyond."

13

Summer 2012

I pushed up the window pane very carefully and climbed into the cool dampness of the McGaha Chapel. I figured some time alone to clear my head would do me good. I loved this little well-kept secret nestled under the tall pines on the small hilltop, yet only a few hundred feet from the highway. I loved the thought of the thousands of people zooming by who never once saw the piece of history, seemingly untouched since the 1800's.

I carefully pulled the window back down as I found myself safely inside. I felt a peace overwhelm me as I plopped down on the closest wooden pew, stretching out on the broad seat, staring up at the slowly deteriorating ceiling.

"It's peaceful, ain't it?" The voice made me almost pee in my pants. I sat up quickly, but saw no one.

"Hello?" I shakily called out, feeling my heart race.

"I love to come here to think too." The voice was clearly recognizable this time. I jumped up and charged down the aisle until I saw him tucked between two pews.

"Kevin! You scared the crap out of me!" I slid into the pew behind him and leaned my arms on the back of his pew. Kevin didn't move, but just kept staring up at the ceiling. His eyes were red and the skin around his lips was blotchy. He tried to smile, but the attempt just gave way to another tear finding its way down the side of his face only to disappear into his ear. "You okay?" I felt the question was lame, but I had to ask.

Kevin laughed, but it was more like a sarcastic bark. "Let's see, my family hates Mexicans, yet my girlfriend's Mexican and my brothers almost killed her brother. And . . ."

"And?" He knew I knew what the and was but he couldn't finish the sentence. I watched Kevin suddenly sit up in his pew and wipe his nose with the bottom of his t-shirt. For just a moment I caught a glimpse of bruises on his very white stomach. "Where'd you get that?" Before I could catch myself I had already blurted it out.

Kevin frowned at me a little. "What? You think Junior and Roy'd let me get away with lovin' Ellie without a beatin'?" He saw the look of horror on my face and he added. "Don't worry none. I reckon I left 'em each with a bruise or two of their own. Hey, I may have broken Roy's nose all over again."

"Good!" was all I could say. I realized there was so much of Kevin's life I could never understand or even accept as right or good in my book. Although I saw Kevin with tears and bruises, I could honestly say I didn't see a boy, but a growing, young man.

I leaned back and stretched out in the pew to look up at the ceiling again. "I guess sometimes we make choices and they hurt, but it makes us stronger and somehow we begin to find out who we are."

I could hear Kevin stretch back out on his pew. "Millie?"

"Yeah?" I barely whispered.

"You are from here." Kevin didn't say anything else, not for a long time. We both lay there in silence breathing in the moist, cool, healing air of the McGaha Chapel.

1899: President McKinley is the first U.S. President to ride in a motorcar, a Stanley Steamer; The U.S. Supreme Court rules that the West Virginia Hatfields were arrested legally by the Kentucky McCoys after family members were murdered by the former in their feud; The Samoan Islands are divided between the U.S. and Germany.

Renewed Life and Loss

V.B. often chafes at being in town with all the social pressures and politics. His Brevard businesses are prospering and his house in town is a block away from the courthouse, just off East Main Street, yet he finds as many reasons as possible to escape. He prefers the open countryside and woods to this confinement. The paperwork seems to grow in the sheriff's office in the courthouse. He hears noise outside.

"Sheriff, I am so mad!" Luke Osteen bursts into V.B.'s office. The sheriff calmly looks up to the young man with red curly hair with a few wood chips caught in it. V.B. puts down his pen, thankful to take a break from the huge pile of paperwork.

V.B. motions for Luke to sit. "That I can see, Luke. Something wrong at the Osteens?"

The young man begins to pace. "Just 'cause they's filthy rich don't mean they kin run over us-uns."

"Calm down some so I can understand what your problem is. Have a cup of coffee and spell it out for me." V.B. hands him a cup and puts a calming hand on his shoulder.

Finally, Luke calms down enough to take a seat. He gulps the coffee and then takes a deep breath. "Well you know we got land next to the Vanderbilt land where that German feller is a-runnin' a crew for timberin' and plantin' more trees. Some kind of school I hear."

V.B. is gentle in response as Luke sips his coffee. "Yeah. It is a school for training folks a better way to do forestry instead of just cutting and destroying everything to wash the land away. Dr. Schenck was brought in here by the Vanderbilts to help us learn. It is the first such school in all of America."

V.B. realizes too late he has gone a little too far in his clarification when Luke jumps up and asks facetiously, "Well, are you a sayin' they got the right to tear down my fences and start a-workin' my timber?"

V.B. raises his hand. "Calm down. Of course not. They have to obey the law like everybody else. How do we know which piece of land it is?"

"You can ride out with me and see. Your Pa done the survey some time ago and I got his readin' right here." Luke carefully sets down his coffee on V.B.'s desk between two gingerly balanced piles of paper and pulls out a piece of folded paper from his overalls.

V.B. takes the paper and reads the survey carefully. He looks at his desk and then looks at Luke. "Why don't we go right now to look at the lines and fence? My deputy has just come in and can cover."

V.B. enjoys the fresh air as he follows Luke out to assess the damages and is somehow surprised that he is already back in his office by early afternoon. His deputy follows V.B. into the office where the piles of paper haven't disappeared. The deputy leans up against the back wall and casually crosses his arms. He is curious about how V.B.will handle the sensitive nature of the situation. "Sheriff, they's the biggest employer we got. More families work up there, aside from them that is students in the Forestry school. I shore wouldn't want to make Dr. Schenck mad!"

After some thought, V.B. says, "I have an idea."

"What's that?" The deputy watches V.B. begin to shuffle through the papers.

V.B. is preoccupied with looking for something and answers without looking up. "Well, I've got to serve papers and they usually go through our Clerk of Court to the Buncombe County Clerk of Court and then the Sheriff's office serves them on the folks in question."

The deputy finds V.B.'s behavior is annoying. "And your idear?"

"Well, I reckon that Dr. Schenck is a gentleman and being a good German, will appreciate order and tact. Since both he and George Vanderbilt have such high profiles, it's bound to get out, maybe hit the papers." Suddenly V.B. pulls out a single clean sheet of paper and holds it up. The deputy can't quite make out what letterhead is printed at the top.

The young man, moves in to take a closer look at the paper, but is still confused. "Come on. What's your idear?"

V.B. smiles and points to the top of the paper. "I'll just write it on my business letterhead and send it privately, not through the courts."

Calming down the deputy crosses his arms again and resumes leaning against the wall. "And you reckon he'll accept it as legal?"

V.B. begins to look for his pen and is quick to find one sitting on his closest pile. "I've met him and rest assured, he will. Once, when I had to go up to his school to stop a fight between some big fellers, he was more concerned for the mess they made than their beating on each other! He said over and over, 'Ordnung ist alles'."

"What's that mean?"

"I asked and he said, with a heavy accent, 'Order is everything' - here in our cabins, out there in the woods, everywhere!"

Sheriff V.B. McGaha waves his deputy out the door and quickly gets to work writing a tactful letter on his business stationary:

V.B. McGaha   **J.E. Neill**

V.B.McGaha & Co.,

Dealers in

General Merchandise,

GREAT BARGAINS IN EVERYTHING WE HAVE IN STOCK

Brevard, N.C., Mch 27 1899.

Mr C A Schenk
Biltmore NC

My dear sir

I hold Capias against yourself, Mr Foster and others, for tearing down the Luke Osteen fence. Will you please be here next Monday to answer the charges. I have instructed the Clk of Court not to send my Capias to Buncombe as I felt sure you would rather not have it sent down there. So I hope to see you next Monday April the 3rd

Yours truly
V.B. McGaha Shff

V.B. is not surprised when Monday, April third comes and a dignified Doctor Carl Schenck arrives with his assistant, Mr. Foster, to meet with V.B. and Luke. The men stand before Judge Gash in the sheriff's office, which was obviously straightened up from the previous week.

Schenck shakes V.B.'s hand and immediately gets down to business. "I am fery sorry fur our mistake. Ve vill replace de fence und pay fur de damages." The German forester looks at the judge who has made himself quite comfortable in V.B.'s chair. "Your Honor, I am fery sorry to bring dis trubble und take your time." Then he turns to Luke who stands quite dumbfounded by the presence of the distinguished man and his sincerity. "Herr Osteen, ve want to be gut neighbors. I am fery sorry." He reaches out his hand to Luke who willingly accepts the gesture of good will.

Judge Gash, having simply observed the brief but sincere transaction, is pleased. "The case is settled and all damages will be paid as promised."

V.B. nods at his deputy as the men all file out of his office and the deputy smiles at V.B.'s ability to distinguish between justice and vengeance, leaving both parties of a dispute satisfied. As they go out the courthouse door, Schenck says to V.B., "Danke, Sheriff. Very gut. Remember, ven you vant something - fish, cut trees or vatever, let me know."

"Thank you, sir," V.B. says, smiling warmly, thinking of fishing for trout again in Pink Beds.

Summer 2012

My last week was going to be one of joy; that's what Kevin, Ellie and I decided. We were going to spend as much time as possible swimming and hanging out together. I got my wish and jumped into the small lake at the old Piedmont Camp. I couldn't get enough of climbing up on the small dam and falling back into the lake behind me. The cool water and the secluded feeling seemed to tease the three of us with a sense that there was nothing in the world for us to worry about.

When we had enough of being wet, we would lie on the small floating dock that had once withstood many campers feet climbing and jumping from its wooden surface. At times we were so quiet that the water lapping the sides of the dock, the crickets, and a gentle wind rustling the tree tops was all we could hear. I knew it would all be replaced next week with bustling street sounds and endless texting.

"You want to see something fun?" Ellie sat up and her dark skin glistened. Kevin and I were game so we jumped into the water after her and swam to the dam. We climbed onto its edge and walked to the left where we quickly stepped through a hedge of bushes. We suddenly found ourselves surrounded by trees and rhododendron and a huge rock that was resting on a smaller rock, both jutting out into the small clearing surrounded by brush. "It's a whale!" Ellie giggled.

"It sure is!" I laughed when I realized the rock's resemblance. Kevin proceeded to climb to the top of it and pretend he was riding it. Ellie and I joined him and the three of us were ten years old again.

I stood up and looked as best I could through the bushes to see the lake, but it was sort of hard, so I turned my head to look in the other direction. "Hey guys I can see the barn."

Kevin and Ellie stood up to look at the familiar horse barn. "Hey, there's Charlie!" Elllie squealed. We all watched Charlie lean against the barn door as if waiting for someone and then he suddenly waved.

"Who's that comin' up the road?" Kevin's voice was sober.

We all stood still and watched a white truck pull up. My heart raced. "Is that a 1999 Ford F-150?"

"What?" Kevin looked at me like I was wacko, "How can you tell from here?"

My eyes lit up and I looked at my two friends. "It looks like my Dad's truck!"

1899: The Anti-imperialist League is formed in light of multiple U.S. overseas acquisitions using an 1821 quote of John Quincy Adams, "She might become the dictatress of the world; she would no longer be the ruler of her own spirit."

Careful Courtship

V.B. is attempting to engage in a business conversation with Mr. John Thrash, father of Rose. The Thrashes had moved over from Hominy Valley in Buncombe County and had done well for themselves, not only in business in town but also in local land investments. John and Sarah Thrash are one couple whose mercantile store is a place of respite for the sheriff, especially when court is in session and everybody wants a piece of his time. They also encourage him to stay in the bustling merchantile business in the rapidly growing Brevard. Where others saw farms as useless, John saw potential, especially in the Little River Valley. He had hired good help for the store and farms and that, along with good supervision, meant success. The six Thrash sons and daughters were given an education and encouragement in business.

"How are your girls doing, Sheriff?" Rose asks as she walks by.

"Okay, I reckon. They sure miss their mom. I am away a lot with my work but their grandparents do a lot with them." V.B. walks over to stand next to Rose while John becomes distracted by a customer. He smiles at the young Thrash woman. "By the way, I'm just V.B. or Bunyan. I'm not 'Sheriff' to you."

Rose blushes and manages a shy smile. She asks sweetly, "And what do all the young women in Brevard call you?" She pretends to straighten goods on a shelf.

V.B. follows behind her as she slowly walks down the aisle, straightening cans that looked just fine before she touched them. He smiles at her obvious nervousness. "Mister McGaha, Miss Rose. For some I am still called 'The Sheriff.'"

She pretends to be aloof, knowing how the talk of the town, and county, is about this tall, strikingly handsome widower and which lucky lady might get "arrested" by this sheriff. "Well, I guess I should be honored, V.B. or Bunyan."

V.B. spontaneously touches a can she is already holding in order to catch her gaze. "How would you like to meet my girls Sunday, say ride out to church at McGaha Chapel and eat with my folks in the old home place?"

The sheriff is suddenly aware of John and Sarah who are standing in the store taking in the whole scene and V.B. turns red. Embarrassed, he turns to them and starts to ramble, "But I didn't speak to you about . . ."

"Young man," John breaks in beaming, "you do not have to ask our permission. We know you and your family. Rose is a grown woman now and we think she can decide such things herself. Most of all we trust you. Have a nice buggy ride Sunday and greet your folks for us." V.B. looks at Rose who nods, but can hardly speak.

V.B. staggers out the door trying to regain his balance going up Main Street to the courthouse and he beats himself just thinking, "What have I done? Why did I do that? What got into me?"

Thankful that his mother is spending the week in town, he turns to her that evening after he helps put Reba and Leslie to bed. His mother, ever the wise old woman, asks, "What's ailin' you my boy?"

"I did something stupid today, Mama, and I can't figure it out." He sits next to her at the kitchen table where she is holding a mug with both hands.

"And what might that be, Bunyan?" Harriet takes a sip of warm tea and then pours her son a cup.

The sheriff buries his head in both hands, trying not to look at his mother. "Without thinking, I asked Rose Thrash to church this coming Sunday and to your place to lunch. She'd asked about my girls and I told her she could meet them. I don't know what got into me."

Harriet reaches over and gently pets the top of her son's head. "My dear boy. You were thinking too! But with your heart and not just your head! I'm proud of you." He looks up at her and she can see relief in his eyes. She hands him the second mug. "She is a fine young woman and we'll all welcome her to our hearth there. I know the girls will love to meet her."

V.B. takes his mother's hand and squeezes it. He smiles, and takes a sip of hot tea from his mug, and an automatic "Ah," slips from his slips. "Now, Mama, you make it sound serious. It's just a date, not marriage!"

Harriet takes another sip. "We'll see."

Summer 2012

I ran back to the lake Ellie, Kevin and I had been swimming in to grab my flip flops and throw on my jean shorts and white T, not caring that I might still be a little wet, and then raced down to the barn as fast as I could. Kevin and Ellie laughed at me and said they'd meet me there, but weren't planning on killing themselves in the process.

I think Dad must have wondered what the heck was making all that noise, because he looked a little shocked when I came barreling over the old rock wall. His face lit up when he recognized me and opened his arms just in time to embrace his wet daughter. With my face buried in his shirt I muffled, "Dad! I missed you so much!" I breathed in Old Spice, which flooded my senses and made me suddenly feel like everything was going to be okay.

"Hey, Pumpkin!" I could feel him hold on to me and sigh deeply. "I missed you too."

I suddenly came to my senses and looked up into his face and saw he had aged over the summer. I didn't remember quite as much grey hair and he felt thinner than usual. "You're early. I thought you weren't coming until Sunday."

"Well, you're right." Dad pointed at Charlie, but managed to keep his arm around my shoulders. "Charlie here suggested I come up and talk to him."

Charlie was grinning at us, thoroughly enjoying the show. "Hey, Millie. Looks like you three been swimming in the lake." He nodded up the dirt drive where Ellie and Kevin were walking toward us hand in hand.

"Yep. And it was awesome!" I waved at Kevin and Elllie and yelled, "This is my Dad."

Kevin yelled back, "We figured!"

"So, what're you talking about?" I asked, very sure that weather, horses and old times would be the answer.

"A job." Dad smiled at me. "Charlie thinks I may be perfect for taking over as groundskeeper and could help out with restoring the camp to some of its original beauty. . . since I am from here and all."

I couldn't believe what I was hearing, and I tried not to scream with joy, although I really wanted to. Kevin and Ellie came up next to me as I blurted out, "That would be great!" I immediately changed my tone as I realized that it wasn't that easy. "But what about Mom's business? Where would we live?"

Dad tried to smile, but I saw he was also still working it all out, "Well, Mom said she could get back with the old hair salon where she started in Brevard years ago, they always said they'd love to have her back, but it would take time to rebuild her clientele." Then he smiled, an honestly happy smile. "We'd live with Mammaw. I know it's small, but I'll eventually add on a back room and bath for her to have some privacy."

"I know Mammaw would love us living with her." I pictured my lonely grandmother finally having her son home again.

"So you're stayin'?" Kevin punched me in the arm. Ellie hugged me and gave me a huge kiss on the cheek.

"I guess I am." I smiled.

"Wait a sec." Dad's voice was slightly nervous. "This is why I didn't tell you I was coming early. You weren't supposed to know this until it is a sure thing. First we have to wait and see if I even get the job."

1899: Butch Cassidy and gang rob a train of $60,000; The New York Times uses the word "Automobile" for first time; First Buddhist Mission comes to San Francisco.

A New Start

Craf grabs little Reba and Leslie as they run to him yelling, "Pappaw. It's okay. We miss mama too. But God sent us a new mama. It'll be good. We'll help her!"

Craf smiles at his two granddaughters and is thankful that the lovely, twenty-five year old Rose A. Thrash has become Bunyan's bride on this May 28, 1899. The wedding in the little McGaha Chapel is beautiful and there are more folks standing outside the open windows than can sit inside the little building. "I know you girls will be great helpers, if you stop throwing flowers in each other's hair." Craf begins to pick the small pedals out of the girls' hair. "Looks like you had more fun throwing them at each other than on the floor as you walked down the aisle."

Reba and Leslie grow wide-eyed. "Sorry, Pappaw."

Reverend Allison came up behind the girls and pulled them into his arms. "Don't worry. Everyone enjoyed a good laugh!" Craf is pleased that Rev. Allison had accepted the invitation to perform the ceremony, both in support of his son-in-law but mostly for his two granddaughters. He sees how they all had suffered in the loss of his daughter and knows that Bunyan had loved her deeply. He knows that the girls really need a mother and feel this decision is from God. As the most influential minister in the county, his blessing is sure to still most wagging tongues.

It all seems like a new start for Volenus Bunyan McGaha and his two little girls. A new, strong feminine presence in the person of Rose, 'Mommy,' seems to stabilize them.

For some months, they all adjust well and the other McGahas, Fowlers, Hogseds and assorted kinfolks quit worrying about Bunyan and his girls. Craf and Harriet especially are relieved and grow most fond of their daughter-in-law to whom they relinquish the care of Reba and Leslie.

Late one September night as they sit on their Brevard porch rocking gently, Rose reaches over to hold V.B.'s hand. He smiles at her, waiting for her usual questions about his work, his business, and how the customers are responding to him. But instead, Rose bluntly asks, "And are you makin' enough?"

V.B. stops rocking and wrinkles up his brow as he leans in towards his wife to figure out what she's wanting. "I reckon so. But why this question? Are you askin' something else?"

Rose sighs and tries to keep a straight face as she looks into her perplexed husband's eyes. "Just want to know if you could support another youngun!"

Bunyan jumps up and sweeps her into his arms. "We're pregnant!"

She holds on tight as she tries to answer him, knowing perfectly well he's not listening to her, "I think so. I've missed my time of the month now a couple of times and other signs are a-comin' on."

Although V.B. can hardly believe he will be a father again, he can't seem to cling completely to the joy. It is at the Christmas family gathering where Harriet draws her son aside, asking him to help get water from the spring and eggs from the chicken house. "Son, it does my heart good to see you a-glowin' when she is a-showin'. And showin' she is. I reckon it'll be a fine spring baby for you two."

V.B. follows his mother to the spring house carrying two empty water jugs. "Thanks Mama. Are you a-trying to say more?"

She takes one jug and begins to fill it with fresh mountain water before she looks at her son. "I been a-wantin' to ask but don't want to stick my nose into your stuff."

"Ask what?" V.B. hands her the second jug.

Harriet fills the second before finally asking, "Well, what's a-ailin' you? I see you happy and, like I said, a-glowin' about this baby. But sometimes you look downright worried, sad -even scared. I thought it might be this new business work you got and all the worry of building a new home. But I cain't get over the idea that ain't it. Is your old mama worryin' too much?"

Looking around to see that no one else can hear, he is assured they are both alone in the cold December air. "Now Mama, how come you can pick that up? No my work is fine, even fun sometimes. I've never been happier than when I feel that baby move in her belly. But then that awful thought comes - that memory of what happened before, how I lost the love of my life and our baby."

V.B. carries two jugs of water as he walks with his mother to the chicken house. She stops and she looks up to her son, gently cradling his face between her aging hands. "I wondered if that might be a botherin' you. Just last week Laura Raxter and I talked about how good Rose is a-carrying that youngun'. We both decided it would be a healthy one and agreed that it would be a girl, on account of the way it's a-ridin'."

V.B. is quiet, watching his mother walk into the coop and skillfully gather some eggs to place in her apron. Tears are pouring down his cheeks. Nothing more needs to be said.

Summer 2012

Dad encouraged me to walk on home with my friends since he needed to stay and talk shop with Charlie. I reluctantly kissed him and said I'd see him at home.

As Kevin, Ellie and I walked along the old turnpike that wound back around behind El Capitán we slowed down as we came to Ellie's house. We could see an old lawn chair stretched out under a pine tree off to the right of the house. Rai was stretched out with his leg slightly raised.

"Hey, Rai." I ran up to him and Ellie and Kevin slowly followed. "You look like you're doing better." I could see the bruising on his face was clearing up nicely.

"I guess I can't complain." He flipped his long dark hair, but most of it fell back into his right eye. "I guess this is one way to get out of sweeping and bussing tables."

"Hey Rai!" Kevin spoke, but obviously kept his distance. Rai just gave him one nod.

Ellie laughed and ruffled her brother's hair. "Aw, you guys still getting used to each other?"

"Shut up Ellie!" Rai snapped at his sister.

"Well. I got to head on home." Kevin lied, but was obviously trying to excuse himself.

Ellie ran over to him and linked arms. "Okay, I'll walk you to the river at our usual crossing."

"Oh! I get it." I laughed. "So the first day I met you, you were waiting for Kevin?"

"Yep!" She smiled and Kevin turned a little red.

Rai made a gagging sound. "I don't really want to hear this!"

"Milllie, I'll be right back!" Ellie took off with Kevin before I could say a word. Kevin just gave me a quick wave and let himself be swept away. I stood for a moment before I realized I was alone with Rai, not my favorite situation to be in. When I turned I saw that Rai seemed to be staring down the road after the disappearing couple.

"Weird, huh?" was all I could manage.

"Understatement of the year!" Rai waved his hand to force his hair to stay behind his ear.

I looked at Rai and could see a harshness I had only had a glimpse of before. I couldn't help myself. "It wasn't Kevin, you know!"

"Duh!" Rai glared at me. But I didn't back down from him and just glared back. When I didn't say anything he finally took a deep breath and gave up, replacing the look with one of complete defeat. "I don't care anymore!"

Suddenly I saw a boy before me, one I had never seen. "What's that supposed to mean?" I came in closer and plopped down on the ground, the soft pine needles acting as a cushion.

Rai just looked straight ahead and I could tell he was trying not to cry. "Look at me. I got beat down. They won."

"So? The way I see it, you took on Roy and Junior and lived to tell about it." I gently punched him in the arm, "That's like in Finding Nemo when Marlin takes on sharks, and still comes out on top."

Rai smiled. "Yeah, I liked that movie."

"Me too." I enjoyed watching Rai finally smile. I think I hadn't ever seen it until that moment. He wasn't some tough boy trying to prove anything - he was just a kid.

1900 : Republican William McKinley is re-elected as U.S. President defeating William Jennings Bryan; U.S. population swells with over one hundred people an hour passing through Ellis Island; U.S. Troops assist international force in putting down the Boxer Rebellion in China.

A Tough Birth

She is silent - too silent, he thinks.

On May 1st, 1900, Sarah Jacksie McGaha entered the lives of Rose, Bunyan, Reba and Leslie. But the joy of that event was dampened greatly, for the baby's grandmother and namesake, Sarah Thrash, passes on from this life.

V.B. feels blessed that his wife and baby are alive, "Rose, my love, I'm so glad you and little Jacksie are doing so well. I'm awfully sorry about your mom." Rose remains silent.

"What are you a-thinking?" He asks carefully. Silence is her response, but not as if she is ignoring him or didn't hear. The look in her eyes is far away, yet empty.

He feels helpless. He holds little Jacksie to Rose's breast to nurse, but cannot seem to move Rose to engage in more than simply allowing herself to be a wetnurse. V.B. would have asked her mother what to do to fix it, but it's too late for that. He cannot understand her withdrawal and wonders if maybe it is just the death of her mother that has sent her away in spirit for a little while.

Harriet does not hesitate to move in for a while, "to help with the baby and other girls" theoretically. She plans on helping while V.B. goes about the thriving businesses he has going now in addition to being sheriff. The first evening, after Reba and Leslie finally go to sleep with their little sister in a crib next to her sleeping mother, Harriet is quick to address her son, "Bunyan, I'm worried about Rose and I can see that you are too, though you do not say so."

V.B. sits down in the living room in one of the straight backed chairs closest to the window. He looks out at the empty Main Street. "Ma, you could always see things when none of us could, and see right through me. Yep, I've been worried ever since the baby came. She never seems to get back on her feet. I figured it was because of losing her mom so soon."

Harriet walks over to stand next to her son. "The way I see it is that that's only part of the problem. This was her first young-un and sometimes us women-folks have some troubles for awhile after th' baby comes."

V.B. looks up at her. "What do you mean? Did I do something wrong?"

Harriet shakes her head. "I talked with Laura Raxter and Nancy Guice McGaha about it. I think it was Nancy that said that it sometimes happens that a woman's spirit slips out with the afterbirth and it can take a while to get it back."

V.B. frowns at this seemingly superstitious explanation. "I really do not understand but tell me what I can do to help her!"

Harriet just sighs. "Love her. Be patient but not pushy. Give her time. Be with her and the baby."

V.B. stands, slightly irritated. "I'll try, but I'm a right busy man with many irons in the fire."

Harriet shakes her head as she follows her son into the kitchen and watches him take a glass down from the cupboard and fill it with tap water, a luxury she still does not have. "Son, I was not going to say it but I must: you have too many irons in the fire. Pull some back. Move out of the middle of town. Build you and her and the girls a smaller, more quiet place on the edge of town or come out of town."

V.B. looks surprised. "You mean close the livery and blacksmith shop and feed store?"

Harriet sits down at the kitchen table as if trying to find some relief. "I did not say that. Why not sell them? Your mercantile store goes well. Just take care of your wife and baby." When V.B. doesn't answer she continues, "She needs some time and some hope. Give her something to look forward to."

With a nod, V.B. reluctantly agrees with his mother, "I'll do my best." Then he looks at her and lets loose, "I've worked awfully hard these years, not just for my family. I have wanted to prove to those politicians and moonshiners that a sheriff can pay his own way without being subsidized and compromised. I have not sold my soul, but has all this work been too much on my family?"

Harriet just watches her son return to the window in the living room. "Bunyan?"

V.B. stares out onto Gaston Street and Harriet has to strain to hear him, "How stupid! Of course we've got the best place so close to the courthouse with so many businesses all around our house. We get more traffic than a railway station." He looks at his mother. "Okay, we'll move!"

His decision is clear.

Sylvan Valley News, Nov. 30, 1900

Another real estate deal was consummated yesterday morning by which the Bunyan McGaha property, reaching through from Main to Jordan streets, on Gaston, becomes the property of Van Whitmire. This included the V.B. McGaha residence, corner of Gaston and Jordan streets, the old livery stable building on Main, now occupied by T. L. Snelson, and the old shop and stable between. This is very desirable property and the price $3,000 was reasonable.

A store and house on the outskirts, away from the Brevard bustle, does the trick. Rose begins to perk up when he asks her help in planning the house and the store right next to it so he can be close if needed.

Summer 2012

"When is Mom coming?" I asked with my mouth full of pizza. It was great to have Mammaw, Dad and me sitting around the same dinner table. As small as the table was, I knew it would have to be replaced with a bigger one if we were all going to live here.

"Don't know yet, depends on if I get Charlie's job or not." The sparkle in Dad's eyes made something inside me jump. I could see Mammaw soaking up every bit of her son's explanation. "I'll meet the owners the day after tomorrow and Charlie thinks I have a really good chance. At that point your mom will head on up here."

"Great!" I took another bite.

"Robert," Mammaw looked a little concerned, "don't you think you need to get Millie enrolled in school?" Mammaw watched Dad nod before she added, "Then there is taking her home before school starts so you can pack."

I suddenly realized how serious this whole move was. I would be going to Brevard High and Ellie, Kevin and I would actually walk the halls together. Would our friendship continue? Would I make new friends? I suddenly realized that I never thought I would actually have to give up my old friends and home. Transylvania County just always seemed like an impossible dream. Now reality didn't seem as easy as I had always thought. Yet, I knew this was where I belonged, I always had.

1902: President Teddy Roosevelt is injured and a Secret Service agent is killed when a streetcar hits their carriage in Massachusetts; A new, nutritious gelatin desert named "Jello" is introduced; Helen Keller publishes The Story of My Life.

Double Tragedy

Sitting on the porch one afternoon Rose enjoys the giggling sounds of Reba and Leslie as they 'baby' little Jacksie as if they were grown mothers. Reba pushes the swing as Leslie carefully holds the toddler. Rose turns to V.B. who is standing nearby, staring off in the other direction. He is slowly twisting the small mustache that has become a defining characteristic of his appearance. "What are you a-thinkin' about? Something else is a-cookin'."

"Well, you caught me." V.B. reaches out his hand for her to get up and join him.

Rose enjoys the warm touch and lets herself be pulled to stand next to him. He wraps his arm around her waist. "Yep. Some other business idea is rolling around in your noggin. Tell me about it."

V.B. does not hesitate. "Well, I stand here and see how much traffic we have back and forth to Greenville, our main connection to the outside world. The mail comes up every week. Folks go down to shop. Folks come up for the cooler weather."

"So, what is your business idea?" Rose is aware of the growing excitement in his voice.

"I think I'd like to start a bus line between Brevard and Greenville someday."

Rose tries not to be shocked and fumbles for a response to her entrepreneur husband. "How on earth could you do that? Take a buggy or your freight wagon with benches in it?"

V.B. pays no attention to Rose's slight sarcastic tone. "Nope. Enough of them on the road now. Someday, I'll have me a car, a good big solid one."

"One of those noisy horseless carriages that scares the poop out of our horses in town?"

"Exactly!" V.B. almost shouts. "That is where the future is." He pauses and waits for his wife's response. When there is a little more than a moment's pause he coaxes her, "So what are you thinking my little love? I've told you my crazy thoughts."

Rose tightens her arm around V.B.'s waist as if giving a quick squeeze. "Do you reckon that carriage can haul us two and four younguns?"

V.B. does not catch on at first, but suddenly her meaning hits him and he turns too quickly and falls off the edge of the porch, jumping up and screaming "You're pregnant!"

Seated again, the smiling Rose reaches off the porch to embrace the tall man of hers and says, "Looks like we'll be blessed again." Reba and Leslie run over to the rejoicing couple with Jacksie clumsily following behind squealing with delight, unconcerned about the reason for the joy.

V.B. is speechless and tearful with all his girls surrounding him.

Rose is happy and reassuring, "Hopefully that awful sickness that hit me after Jacksie came won't come again. I hear from Dr. Hunt that there may even be some medicine to help fight it. It's some kind of depression that can come after a baby is born. Something to do with women's 'chemistry'." V.B. is happy to hear that she will talk about it now and has even been studying about it to try to prepare for it.

The moment of joy soon melts into fear and sorrow. V.B. cannot believe it when Laura Raxter announces, "She ain't carrying that young-un right." Even with Dr. Hunt's hope in the new young nurse, Miss Sadie North, and her training, V.B. plummets into desperation when even they confirm that the "Baby does not sit right."

V.B. feels like he is walking back into a nightmare, one he never imagined would be replayed. This time the nightmare is in a different house, but the same people come and walk in and out of his door. The same women hustle and bustle about with sheets and hot water and send the men to get the doctor. Craf and Harriet arrive too with a wagon for the overflow of people and food, but V.B. only sees a fog and endless mumbling that brings no peace or reason, so he does not respond. He moves to his bedroom and speaks only once. "Can you ladies leave me alone with Rose a little while?" He sees in their faces the same worried look the doctor had, but they obey and leave.

Rose speaks weakly, "I'm sorry, my love. They say something is not right."

Sitting on the edge of the bed, Bunyan puts his arms around Rose and just holds her a while. Finally he asks, "What can I do?"

"Two things," she quickly answers. "First, bring the girls to me for a little while. Second, stay with me as much as you can and as they will let you."

"I'll always be just outside the door during the delivery and right here as soon as those angels deliver our new blessing." V.B. tries hard to sound cheerful but they both know it is hollow.

In the next hours, the house is inundated with food, firewood and offers of help. Word has passed around that it is no normal birth, but V.B. only has eyes for his wife. He lets Reba, Leslie and Jacksie stay as long as possible, listening to their mother as she tries to sing their favorite lullabies, until the pain sets in. She kisses them each gently and urges V.B. to hurry them out the door. Once the girls are gone Rose finally gives in to the looming torture.

V.B. runs into the living room to hasten the nurse, doctor, Laura and his mother to return to help. As he turns to reenter the room he is stopped by Nurse Sadie. "You really ought not go in now."

With haunting memories he pushes her aside and saying emphatically, "I'll be with her until the doc or she says to leave!"

The women on one side of Rose's bed move aside to let the big man sit by her side and hold her as best he can. She is twisting, jerking and convulsing, calling out his name, obviously in horrible pain. He and they try to hold her and keep her from falling off the bed.

At one point she passes out and when she comes to, she looks at V.B. and says, "I'm sorry."

V.B. unabashedly kisses her all over her face. "Nothing to be sorry about, my dearest love, my darling, sweet wife."

She smiles and whispers, "I love you Volenus Bunyan McGaha," before the violent convulsions start again.

"And I love you, my wonderful Rose," V.B. stands up as the doctor nods to him that it is time to leave. Harriet helps usher him out the door. She finds her terrified granddaughters and takes them out to the wagon for some comforting food and nurturing Grandmother lap time.

Walter gathers folks outside into some heartfelt prayer for Rose and the baby, mostly silent prayer so as not to disturb those inside. He watches V.B. go to the end of the porch holding the porch post so tightly, he fears the grieving man will pull it down. "Come on big man, step off th' porch an' don't be a-pullin' th' porch down on everybody 'a prayin'."

"It's not right, not fair!" V.B. cries out. "They've got to come through this."

One of the would-be helpers, a neighbor from Brevard, says, "Now V.B., I'm sure it's all a- goin to be . . ." as Walter stops him with a disapproving scowl and a raised hand.

Craf, silent until now, speaks, "Now Brother Orr, I know you mean well but we ain't sure of anything 'cept'n God's love."

The screams inside subside and are replaced with gentle sobs which turn into open weeping.

The sad-faced doctor comes out with blood still on his hands, shirt and trousers. "Mr. McGaha, I'm truly sorry. I did all I could." With a pale, grave face, Laura appears beside the doctor. She can barely speak. "We lost them both."

V.B.'s old nightmares of the loss of his wife Jessie just after childbirth come back as he collapses on the porch in shock.

Harriet swiftly moves over to her sitting son and grabs his arm with a firmness that shoots physical pain up his arm making him look into her eyes. "I've got the girls. Do what you have to do."

Walter and Laura herd the crowd away so those "Job's Comforters" will not bother him. Laura clears the women out after Rose is cleaned up and the baby is beside her.

He is alone a long time with his beloved bride and baby. No one knows what he says to them.

Craf has already prepared one of the horses from his wagon for his son and hands him the reins when he finally comes out of the house. The dwindling crowd watches their grieving sheriff ride south. They know he'll be back for the funeral. Craf watches and understands, as no one else can.

Once again cries and screams are heard on Rich Mountain.

14

Summer 2012

Kevin and I had been Trout Lake all morning, listening to the occasional car sounding like a jet plane disturbing the stillness as it zoomed up Robin Hood Lane. Once in a while someone would stop, park, and walk their dog around the lake. One little old lady still wearing a bathrobe waved at us while her poodle did his thing, but the other people came and went generally ignoring us.

"Too bad they need Elliie today at the restaurant," Kevin was all stretched out on the dock at Trout Lake. His fair skin had definitely darkened since the beginning of summer and I could see his bruise was beginning to fade. I guess in some way I was happy to have a little time alone with Kevin. Deep down I still hoped he would rise up and turn in his brothers for selling drugs.

"Yeah, she'll come up a little later," was all I managed. The dock wasn't very long, so I settled for sitting on the end with my feet dangling into the water, cautiously watching for the water snake. I thought I saw someone walking on the other side of the lake, but figured it was just one more homeowner walking a dog.

We sat there quietly for a very long time before I could tell the silence was killing Kevin. He finally asked, "What are you thinking?"

"You don't want to know," I said honestly.

"Sure I do." Kevin propped himself up on his elbows.

"I was thinking about your brothers and their illegal business." I tried to sound light about it, not wanting the same reaction as last time.

Kevin lay back down and covered his eyes with the crook of his arm. "Oh, no. Here we go again." When I didn't say anything he added, "I thought we had an understanding."

I noticed his voice wasn't as ticked as last time so I didn't hesitate to shoot straight, "Yes, I guess we do. I understand that you understand that something is going on and I understand that you made me understand that you won't do anything about it."

Kevin sat up again and looked at me. He wasn't mad, just really intense. "Almost! You need to understand that I cain't do anything about it."

"I guess I don't see the difference," I said, calmly letting my toes draw circles in the water.

Kevin sat up completely and scooted over to sit next to me. He dropped his feet to touch the water too. "Millie, Junior and Roy are assholes and mean sons of bitches, but they're my brothers. We've played pirates together in this very lake and eaten turkey dinners together."

"But they beat up Rai?" I whispered.

"And the law will make 'em pay for that," Kevin answered. "Not me."

"I guess I can't expect you to turn them in." I saw the water snake return and lifted my legs up to the dock. Kevin let his dangle a little longer.

"Why ain't you done it yet?" Kevin's question surprised me.

"What?" I asked watching the snake come awfully close to Kevin's toes before he splashed the water chasing the poor creature away.

"Why ain't you gone to the Sheriff's Department yet?" Kevin leaned back on his elbows again, but let his feet keep dangling.

I could feel my cheeks turn red and I didn't quite know what to say. I finally stammered. "I guess I don't really have any evidence," I confessed. "I only saw them once and I was far way. And then I saw this guy, Eamon, who keeps hanging around."

"Did you just say my name?" Kevin and I turned our heads to see Eamon sitting on one of the swings.

"How long you been sittin' there?" Kevin jumped up defensively. I jumped up too; staying close to Kevin was my goal.

Eamon's smile was a little too friendly. "Just a few minutes. Enough to hear my name."

"What do you want?" Kevin walked up off the dock towards the swing set. I followed close behind.

"I was just wonderin' why you said my name." Eamon stayed seated, not too worried about Kevin's defensive stance.

"I was just telling how you've been hanging around," I stammered. "That's all."

Eamon slowly swung himself back and forth. "And that's a problem how?"

Kevin and I just stood still and couldn't really answer that question without incriminating him, so Kevin just repeated, "What do you want?"

Eamon sighed and I saw a glimmer of weariness as he glanced across Trout Lake, "So, I had me a good walk aroun' the lake. Nothin' much but a cool path." Kevin and I listened as he kept talking in a casual tone, like family sitting around the dinner table sharing our day's adventures. "Then I saw this small path leadin' off into the woods. I took it and ended up in the middle of the woods with just a bunch of big rocks."

"Boulders," I corrected.

"Oh, so you been there too?" Eamon smiled and Kevin looked at me in disbelief.

"Not really! Just took a stroll like you." I looked at Kevin and Eamon, "So? What's the big deal?"

"You shouldn't go into the woods by yourself!" Kevin fussed at me and I could see Eamon's smile grow.

"And why is that, Carp?" Eamon knew who Kevin was and it gave me the creeps.

Kevin's cool and detached look that I hadn't seen since the beginning of summer suddenly returned. "I don't know," He slowly drawled. "Maybe some mean black bears might get you."

Eamon's smile faded. "Funny boy!" He stood and turned his back to the lake. "Maybe all Carps are the same." He looked at me and barely whispered, "Be careful, young lady. I think maybe there's somethin' more dangerous than bears in the woods."

He turned and walked away leaving Kevin touching me shoulder to shoulder. We didn't move until we saw the van spit gravel and take off down Robin Hood Lane. After a few minutes of deeper thought and lots of feeling, I was able to say, "That's why."

"Why what?" Kevin moved away from me and walked back over to the dock. He picked up a handful of stones and started chucking them into the water.

I walked over, but kept some distance so I wouldn't get hit. "Why I haven't said anything to the law," I sighed. "I really didn't find anything when I went snooping. I could hear Junior yell, but I couldn't tell where it came from, nor did I care to find out." Kevin didn't say anything. I watched him throw more forcefully with each handful of stones. I finally said, "And I really don't get Eamon. I don't understand why he's trying to figure out where your brothers are when he meets them all the time to buy his drugs."

Kevin suddenly stopped and looked at me. "You saw him buying from Roy and Junior?" His face was slightly pale.

"Yeah!" I could feel my cheeks warm. "So?"

Kevin shook his head and chucked one last rock into the lake. "That don't make one lick a sense!"

"Why?" I watched Kevin come up to me and get as close as possible.

He almost whispered, "'Cause he ain't from around here." When I looked confused he explained, "Junior always brags about not messin' with people from out of town, 'cause he cain't be sure about their loyalty." Kevin shook his head and sort of laughed. "Stupid! That's what they are! Stupid!"

1906: San Francisco is ravaged by an earthquake; Violence erupts in Atlanta with calls to disenfranchise Negroes and to revive the Ku Klux Klan; Coca Cola replaces cocaine with caffeine in its sodas after legal threats.

The Interview

The chair feels stiff and unforgiving as Volenus Bunyan McGaha, , successful businessman, entrepreneur and former Sheriff, awkwardly shifts his weight to get comfortable in front of a door with a sign that reads

"U.S. Treasury Department, Bureau of Internal Revenue." He is in the modest waiting room of Captain R.C. Merrick, Agent in Charge located in Greenville, South Carolina.

Having worked with so many revenue agents, U.S. Marshalls and other "Feds" over many years, he should feel comfortable, but he is as nervous as a schoolboy. The tall man shifts again and catches the eye of the secretary who is watching his every move. He is not sure if she is evaluating his behavior or enjoying his good looks.

V.B. gives up on getting comfortable and quickly stands to lean against the only blank wall next to the office door, but a little too close to the secretary. The young lady, with her blouse cut low enough to make a man look, smiles sweetly and finally breaks the ice, "I am so sorry that the chief is delayed. I'm sure he will be through with this meeting soon. He really does want to see you and has been talking excitedly about your meeting."

Relieved by her words, V.B. says simply, "Thanks." He hopes she is not like the "cookie ladies" who will want to make conversation to "get to know him."

Her warm, professional side comes forth, however, as she points to some books and brochures on the shelves across the room and suggests, "There are some items you might want to peruse while you wait. It seems to help me when I have to wait. It turns my frustration into thinking about something else. Also, that literature tells a lot about the Bureau and its long history."

V.B.'s curiosity is aroused and he is relieved to have a reason to move and keep his back to the young lady. As he turns to reach for a few brochures and books he quickly remembers his manners, "Thanks. I read a lot and always need to know more, especially about the Bureau."

V.B. tries another chair and as he settles down he is captured by some brief historical information, especially noting that the Department of the Treasury goes back to the days of the U.S. Constitution in 1789, thanks to Alexander Hamilton, the first Secretary. The first purpose, he learns, was to collect taxes on imports, especially spirits. But then he is pleased to read that the Revolutionary War debt that could have crippled the young nation was quickly paid by those import taxes.

V.B. skips over the paragraphs on the short-lived Whiskey Rebellion of 1794 but is caught up in how the import taxes collected had paid for most of the government buildings and operating budget of the U.S. for generations. As a businessman, political leader, and citizen he could appreciate that.

Back during the Civil War, in 1862, Congress set up the Office of Internal Revenue under the Treasury Department and then, in 1863, authorized the hiring of "three detectives to aid in the prevention, detection and punishment of tax evaders." By 1877 the official name was "Bureau of Internal Revenue."

V.B. steps outside into the hall to take a bathroom break and becomes a bit more skeptical about what he has been reading, wondering if the writers are balanced in their stories.

"Will they tell the dark side?" he wonders.

When he returns, he is pleasantly surprised to read further that in fact they tell of the great national scandal of 1875 when agents broke up the "Whiskey Ring," a conspiracy of revenue agents, dealers and politicians. Millions of dollars had been stolen from the people and finally Congress reformed the system.

V.B. is so absorbed in his reading that he does not hear the door to the inner office open, but is suddenly aware that someone is standing close by.

"Mr. McGaha. I am Captain Merrick. Please forgive me for keeping you so long." Captain Merrick stretches out his hand.

V.B. jumps up, startled, and drops the book, but shakes the captain's hand. "Okay. No problem, I was learning a lot a-readin' here."

Merrick laughs, picking up the book and says, "Well, didn't you already know most of that stuff? I heard from Agent Monroe some time ago that you had to educate him."

Ignoring a flirtatious giggle from the secretary, V.B. remains focused on the captain. "Well, sir, I was Sheriff then in Transylvania and he did not know much about these parts or what had gone on."

"Well, you did a good job and made a good impression on him and his men. Probably prevented some unnecessary shooting, too." Merrick motions V.B. into his office. Once the door is closed and the two men have settled into more comfortable chairs the Captain comes to the point, "How about working with us in the Bureau? Your reputation as an honest lawman is known far and wide. There are some skeptics who cannot believe that any sheriff in these mountains is not on the take from at least some bootleggers or politicians. We have watched how you worked your own businesses to help pay your own way. It is a pity that so many mountain counties are so poor that they cannot pay a decent wage to their main law officer."

V.B., quite aware that he is being flattered, still takes offense. "Sir, I can understand why some of my former colleagues were forced to accept money to support their families. I don't judge them for that."

Merrick remains impressed with V.B.'s loyalty. "No, but you have not done that, is that true?"

"Yes, of course. But I am thankful that I have a big family that supports me - I mean we had a big farm and have done well in some other enterprises."

"Yeah, I reckon many of us here in Greenville have enjoyed good McGaha beef or pork from off that mountain!" Merrick laughs and is at ease with this big mountain man.

The feeling is mutual and V.B. asks, "What would I have to do?"

"Well, you know most of it since you have worked with many of our agents in the past. Basically, you help see that taxes are paid on spirits, tobacco and a few other things. That means inspecting several federally approved distilleries through these mountains regularly."

V.B. responds, "And finding the other 'distilleries' that are not approved?"

Captain Merrick laughs. "Of course, as you are aware, that is your main work and most dangerous."

"And what about paperwork?" V.B. can't help a slight look of disdain that appears.

"I've heard that when you were Sheriff, you fought paperwork. Unfortunately, since the 'reform' of our department, we all are required to file full accounting for our time and travel. We have a form for you to fill out for weekly reports. It's not so much. I know from your business background you can do it easily. And I have seen your writing which is better than mine. But the good news is that the government provides you with a typewriter and carbon paper!" Merrick watches V.B. slowly twists his thin mustache as he broods over the proposal. Hoping to continue the dialogue the captain says, "The time has flown and lunch time is here. How about if I invite you to lunch?"

V.B. snaps out of his thoughts. "I reckon that would be a good idea, bein' as I'm right hungry."

At a nearby restaurant Merrick lets the former sheriff order his food and a coffee. He attempts small talk, but once coffee is poured the captain can't help himself. "I do not want to push you. I know how mountain folks respond to being pushed. But how are you leaning?"

V.B. takes a sip of his coffee and can't help but express its goodness, "Ahh." He savors the caffeine lift and then smiles at Merrick. "To shoot straight with you, I'm a-leanin' your way."

"Good. Then I'm required to 'orient' you even though you probably know more than most who sign up. Some details and swearing in we can do back at the office. Right now let's talk about a couple of items and call it interview and orientation."

"Okay with me. What do you want to talk about?"

The waitress arrives with V.B.'s fried chicken and mashed potatoes.

Merrick waits for the young lady to hand him his plate before he continues. "Religion and trust."

"Can you be more specific?" V.B. asks as he swallows a mouthful of potatoes.

"How might these two topics affect you when you are working as a revenuer?" Merrick begins to meticulously cut his ham.

After another sip of coffee V.B. answers, "I reckon you know about my Papa and our upbringing."

"Yes, of course. We heard about him at Furman and folks have heard about his hospitality and the Little River Chapel." The captain finally takes a bite.

V.B. enjoys a chunk of his chicken and then wipes the grease off his mouth with a napkin. "Well, then you know I try to help keep the little Chapel goin' and help out others as well, both in my business and as hospitality when needed. But what has that to do with revenue work?"

Sensing he may be rubbing V.B. the wrong way, the Captain quickly clarifies, "Let me be specific. How much do you trust religious people?"

"Oh! Good question. My answer is short- as much or as little as anybody else." V.B. manages another mouthful of potatoes while he speaks. "Even when I was little and so many folks stayed over with us, I quickly saw that some preachers and teachers could be trusted and some who claimed to be men of God were rascals and not to be trusted."

"And folks who are not preachers?"

"Oh yeah, we had plenty of them. They could talk religion, use the language of Zion, but I learned to look out for what they did. For example, even as a little feller, I would hear big 'spiritual talk' after church or at the post office. Somebody would talk about 'listenin' for the spirit' or a having a 'little talk with Jesus' and then announce a day in the week."

"And?" Merrick stops eating and is curious and completely engaged.

V.B. leans in a little. "Well, on that day I'd hide behind the rhododendron bushes or the outhouse at the Chapel and see them 'visit' at that time all right, leaving jars of bootleg under the chapel or pickin' them up and leavin' money."

"How long did it go on?"

"It sure stopped when I was Sheriff and after. Word got out, I reckon." V.B. signals to the waitress to fill up his coffee again.

Merrick resumes eating his meal. "So what have you learned about trust and religion as it relates to the blockade whiskey trade?"

Thanking the waitress, V.B. takes another sip of fresh coffee, "Ahh!" He looks at Merrick and lifts his cup. "That the proof is in the pudding. Or as my Papa would say, 'You know them by their works, not their words!'"

Merrick puts down his fork and presses V.B., "And what if you had a well-respected pastor of a local church, even someone as respected as your father-in-law, Reverend Allison. Could you suspect him if his people loved him, but you heard rumors? Could you check him out objectively?"

V.B. turns pale at the mention of his late wife's beloved father, thinking how he had stood by him and the girls when she died. He puts down his coffee cup and leaves his food alone. "Well sir, that one takes me back. It's a theoretical question so I'll give a theoretical answer, but then I have a question for you."

"Fair enough." Merrick is aware he may have crossed a personal boundary, but he needs to know.

"If anybody close to me is a-breakin' the law I'd really look into it - very carefully and discretely - to prove or disprove my information. None of us is above the law." Pushing away the pain V.B. is in complete professional control. "As Sheriff, I most often knew the moonshiners and bootleggers. I never had to gun one down because we could talk. They didn't want to shoot me and I didn't want to hurt them, just stop their trade. Same for theft and so on."

"Good answer, McGaha. What is your question?" Merrick sips his coffee, wishing he could relish it like his guest.

V.B. still does not touch his food. "Why on earth did you ask me that? Is there something more behind it than testing me?"

Merrick puts down his cup. "As a matter of fact there is." He smiles, pleased with V.B's intuitive and observant behavior.

"Can you tell me what it is?" V.B. asks.

"There are preachers that choose to use their positions to have 'spirit-filled' churches with a little more than God's spirit and even their members will go to lengths to support them. One of the most successful moonshiners that we finally caught was a Baptist preacher named Bayless not too far down the mountain from where you live who had the best disguised distillery in his basement that we've ever found and he was giving his flock more than the Holy Spirit." Although Captain Merrick has a good laugh, he is aware V.B. only politely smiles. The Captain sobers quickly and continues, "And what sort of work questions might you have for me?"

V.B. reflects a little and then asks, "What about my territory? What are you thinking?"

"Well, you will be a federal agent and we all have to go where and when needed. But what we had in mind is mainly in Western North Carolina, upstate South Carolina and maybe in the Georgia mountains as well. We need a mountain man like you."

"And that territory includes the Dark Corner as I hear it." V.B. states.

"Of course! Upper Greenville County, South Carolina, leading over into lower Polk County, North Carolina and bordering on your own Cedar Mountain is part of the geography. But I reckon you are not asking a question of geography when you speak of the infamous 'Dark Corner.'"

V.B. responds, "To be honest with you, I know about a lot of the shootin', stillin' and bootleggin' in those parts. My family is worried that I'm somehow supposed to stop all that and that I might get killed in that rough place."

Merrick and V.B. let the waitress take their plates. "V.B., let me put you, and them, at ease. No, we do not plan to 'clean out' the Dark Corner. Most of the shooting has been between families or for informing about stills to local authorities. No federal officials have been shot in there and I do not expect it. There is more than enough to keep us busy elsewhere!"

V.B. realizes his host is glancing at his watch and asks, "So what do I sign and where do you swear me in?"

A pleased Captain says with a big smile, "Follow me back to the office. You can be on your way in minutes, Revenue Agent McGaha!"

Summer 2012

It felt weird heading out to the Rich Mountain pastures with Ellie and Kevin knowing that I was no longer counting down the days until I'll be gone. When Ellie wanted to know why we weren't swimming and were hiking instead, Kevin and I just said it was getting boring. I mumbled something lame about the water snake, but really we just wanted to get away from the morning's memory of our meeting with Eamon.

We followed our usual path leading away from the restaurant towards High Rocks, our gateway to the last long stretch up to Rich Mountain. As we approached the large boulders loomimg up in front of us I couldn't keep the memory of the boulders behind Trout Lake out of my mind. The boulders I had seen were smaller and covered with so much vegetation. Studying High Rocks I smiled to myself at the possibility of vines and rhododendron also covering this entire rock face and draping down to the ground leaving large cavelike spaces accessed by simply pushing the vines away like a curtain. I found myself wishing we could stay a few more moments to explore the possible secrets of High Rocks, but Ellie and Kevin were already heading up the final path.

The hike seemed longer than usual since we didn't do much talking, but an occasional whistle from Kevin showed me he was just in thought and not pissed off.

Once we reached our favorite smooth rock we settled on it and pulled out some Gatorades and leftover quesadillas. The chewy cold cheese and black beans felt rubbery, but the taste was perfect. In fact we ate them so quickly that my stomach hurt, so I leaned back and let the warmth of the smooth rock slowly cook me through my T-shirt.

Giving Ellie and me a quick glance and a sly smile, Kevin pulled out his fiddle and announced, "I wrote this." At first when he started playing, I expected the usual, since he always played his sad song and several hymns, but, this time, both Ellie and I looked at each other and grinned. He was playing something new. I suddenly recognized the tune as the same one he'd been whistling as we walked up here. His eyes were closed as he let his fingers race, but his cheeks were relaxed and the corners of his mouth were turned slightly upward. I guess the only way I can describe it was like we were hearing a huge smile emerge from inside Kevin's soul.

1906: President Teddy Roosevelt is the first American to receive the Nobel Peace Prize for his mediation in the Russo-Japanese War, but not for his "Big Stick" policies in Middle America; President Roosevelt uses the term 'Muckrakers' from John Bunyan's Pilgrim's Progress against writers who only dig up trash.

The Revenuer

The initial trust between V.B. and Captain Merrick proves to be a good indication of the ongoing working relationship. Months fly by as he becomes the experienced federal officer. His experience as sheriff and a mountain man pay off.

Before he starts his car V.B. returns a small diary to his coat pocket. Its leather binding is already wearing thin from his weekly entries over the past several years. He can hardly believe that he, "Inspector" McGaha, has traveled by train, by livery, by auto, by streetcar and by foot over hundreds of miles, mostly in the mountains of the Carolinas and Georgia. An occasional special trip to Pine Mountain, Georgia or Columbia, South Carolina to assist other agents in larger raids has carried him far afield.

His diary reports indicate most trips, however, have been to areas around Walhalla and Seneca, South Carolina and various remote areas over the line in North Carolina. And the "Dark Corner" of upper Greenville County does demand multiple raids.

His time away from home has come with a cost as his girls are mostly being raised by their grandparents. Loneliness too must be battled, but he finds solace in his usual helpers, Special Employees Hendricks and McCravy and sometimes neighbor J.C. Loftis, who assists as as a posseman when V.B. is closer to home in Transylvania County. His immediate boss, Deputy Collector Merrick, goes along on many raids but usually defers to the skills of V.B. to take the lead.

It is awkward for him to once again pursue folks he knows or at least bust up their stills so close to home, especially in nearby Loftis, an area he'd cleared out as Sheriff some years ago.

Nearby East Fork, with unclear state line boundaries, is no longer the problem when V.B. was sheriff, for his area of jurisdiction is no longer an issue. But there, and the Cedar Mountain/Jones Gap areas are difficult areas in that he knows about everybody and is kin to many. The good side of that was that he could stop the trade, even if only for a while, without blood spilling.

Even the raids just over the state line in remote South Carolina communities of Pumpkintown and Rocky Bottom are constant, with illegal stills popping up like mushrooms. The matters in the Transylvania County area become more intense, however, for with increased industry including massive tourism, it seems the demand for the famous and highly romanticized mountain dew is rampant. With timber business including logging, lumber production, tanning and multiple related businesses, jobs are plentiful, so the population is growing.

Trains now transport not only logs and lumber, but also a very wealthy class of people to Lake Toxaway, a high mountain resort hotel that draws America's rich and famous. And the booze flows.

V.B. drives his brand new horse-drawn buggy, only dreaming of those new horseless carriages, down the final hill into Rosman, the former Jeptha, which is a boom town. The enterprising industrial family, the Silversteens, have transformed it and, to some degree, Brevard, into bustling business communities. This also seems to motivate the blockade runners, both the moonshiners and bootleggers. They are emboldened by the increased demand and act almost oblivious to the legal need to be approved, inspected and taxed. V.B. is forced to arrest many more to make the point, even some of his friends.

The revenuer's buggy does not stop as it passes through Rosman on this daylight raid. V.B. breathes in the beautiful Saturday afternoon as he heads about a half-hour from the middle of town. Once the he reaches the familiar hill he pulls up on the reins and leaves the buggy parked on the side of a dirt road. He climbs up a heavily wooded slope to look down into a small creekbed where a still is running strong. He sees John Dodson, a friend for many years.

As he carefully climbs down the hill, V.B. raises his voice with a heavy heart. "John, this is Bunyan a calling out. Now don't you try running or go for a gun. Just stand where you are."

A friendly, fair-headed John turns to greet his old friend. "V.B., you know I'd never take a bead on you, like I know you'd not either. What kin I do for you?" John tries unsuccessfully to look innocent and calm, as if nothing is wrong. He walks over to the stream and rinses off his dirty fingers, quickly wiping them on his trousers, and extends a hand to his friend.

V.B. shakes the partially dry hand. "John my friend, just what are you doing making bootleg whiskey?"

John does not hesitate to explain, "Well, times is mighty hard and this feller from up at Lake Toxaway done come all th' way down here and told me he'd pay real good for some. He says when them rich folks ride the train up there, they ask 'bout our pure white lightenin'."

"You know it's against the law!" a pleading V.B. notes.

John scratches his head. "Shore, Sheriff. But them fellers told me the law wouldn't bother to catch me. 'Sides I oughta make more money in two or three runs than in a year of farmin' and loggin'."

"John, you know I'm not Sheriff anymore, but even as a revenuer I've gotta take you in," an apologetic V.B. responds.

After the still is rendered useless, John reluctantly, but without resistance, follows V.B. out of the woods to his buggy. The two drive back to Rosman without speaking, anticipating the up-coming hearing.

The hearing before U.S. Commissioner Ford in Rosman takes place in a small back room of the post office, the only federal building in town. John and V.B. sit in the sparsely furnished room, wishing the windows had been opened more often to clear out the musty smell. The two friends wait patiently for the commissioner to shuffle through his notes strewn across the only table, shoved up against the far wall to give room for the few spectators to stand. The commissioner finally shifts his large physique in the small wooden chair to ask V.B. about the details of the raid and what evidence he has as to the guilt of Dodson. Since John had not run or resisted arrest, V.B. considers him cooperative.

Commissioner Ford leans back and reaches his hands behind his head, uncaring of the beads of sweat blatantly running down his own face. "Mr. McGaha, I note some hesitancy in your report. Is he guilty or not?"

V.B. does not hesitate. "Yes, your honor, he is guilty of making illegal whiskey. No doubt there." He can feel John shift awkwardly. The brief whispering from the spectators reminds V.B. that Dodson relatives are present to witness V.B.'s supposed 'betrayal.'

The commissioner frowns slightly. "Then what are you doubting?"

V.B is reluctant, but aware of his friend's rapid breathing he finally speaks. "Your honor, I have known this man all my life. He is a good man, honorable and kind to his family and neighbors. To my knowledge he's never been doing any of that vengeance stuff like down in the Dark Corner some years ago."

The Federal Commissioner is clearly frustrated. "Agent McGaha, are you saying I should let him off the hook? You arrested him and brought him in!"

V.B. remains calm and collected. "Oh, no sir. I'd never do that. What concerns me is that old larger issue of supply and demand that is not dealt with. As former Sheriff I know that such issues land within local jurisdiction, not ours."

The heavy set man drops his arms into his lap. "So you are saying that the demand for more and more whiskey up at Lake Toxaway for 'real mountain booze' forces these local folks to make it?"

"Your honor, I'd say 'tempts' rather than 'forces.'" V.B. glances briefly at John, now increasingly pale. "In one week, John told me, he could support his whole family for a year the way the market demand is right now. I just think his motive is good, but his method is not."

V.B. steals a glance at the Dodson family, now in fear and in tears. They cannot understand what is going on or what will happen.

V.B. is surprised by his own words and wonders if he himself will be in trouble with this federal judge for speaking his mind.

John Dodson is in shock, wondering now if his family will now starve during the boom time because of his stupid decision to make white lightening instead of farming and logging. He regrets he ever listened to some of the newcomers from the Toxaway rich who convinced him and some of his neighbors to make big , quick money by providing them with 'real' mountain booze.

Commissioner Ford sits silently for some minutes, writing on a pad of paper. Finally, he asks John Dodson to stand. V.B. stands with him, gently bracing his friend so he will not faint. "Mr. Dodson," Commissioner Ford begins, "you have broken federal law. You must be punished." A cry from the family is quickly muffled as the commissioner waits for silence. He continues slowly, "You do not fit the usual pattern of rascals I have had in my court, according to the witness of the very man who arrested you.

Your family is here in your support. They did not leave you on your own during this hearing." The heavily sweating official pauses momentarily to glance at V.B. "If Agent McGaha is to be believed, you could go back to your work or get a job at the lumber works or tannery here and not make illegal liquor again." Without emotion or enthusiasm the commissioner concludes, "Therefore, I fine you $100 which is about what the tax would have been on that liquor and I give you a sentence of there years to be suspended. That means you are on probation and to report your activities regularly. If you fail to walk the straight and narrow and leave the distilling business to licensed firms, you will see a very long time in federal prison. Do you understand?"

A weak John Dodson says, "Yes, sir, and thank you." He looks at V.B. and can't speak for fear of crying.

V.B. just pats him on the back as he looks back at Commissioner Ford who finally smiles and gently shakes his head at V.B.

Summer 2012

When I walked through the door I felt sweaty and gross and wanted a shower after our hike up to Rich Mountain. I didn't expect Mammaw to have company. "Hi Honey." Mammaw waved me over to the couch where she and Dad were sitting with an older lady. "This is your relative, Jeraldine Paxton." Jeraldine wore a sweet yellow summer pant suit and had her white hair neatly cut into a bob. Her modest amount of makeup, modern black rimmed glasses and golden loop earrings gave no hint of her age. Later I found out that, in her eighties, she was still driving and living at home.

"Hello," I said politely, half expecting to be dismissed so the grownups could talk.

"Hi, Millie, it's so good to see you again. I remember when you were a baby." Jeraldine smiled and I had to move in closer to sit between her and Dad on the couch. There was something about her that made me want to listen. "I remember your Papaw playin' his fiddle down the halls of the hospital. The nurses hated telling him to stop, but encouraged him to step on outside." She looked at Mammaw. "Maxie, do you still have Great Uncle Tom's fiddle?"

"Shore do!" Mammaw stood up and disappeared into my bedroom and brought out the fiddle, not touched since Kevin played it at the beginning of the summer. Mammaw handed it to Jeraldine who touched it like a long lost treasure.

"Did you know," Jeraldine looked straight at me, "your's Pappaw's great Grandfather, Tom Fowler, married Polly Ann McGaha, my great-grandfather's sister."

"Who was your great- grandfather?" I asked, slowly letting myself be surrounded by my ancestors.

The lady in yellow carefully handed the fiddle back to Mammaw after one last caress. "Craf McGaha." Jeraldine squinted at me as if trying to figure a way for me to make a connection between her memories and my present. "You know, the McGaha Chapel?" I nodded reliving all of my own memories of the sacred chapel. She continued, "Well, he built that!"

"Wow!" Was all I could squeeze in before she began examining the contents of her large green handbag.

"I brought something to show you." White hair gently fell to her cheeks as she shuffled through the contents, pulling out odds and ends, folders with loose black and white pictures peeking from their corners. "Here it is!" A small leather bound booklet appeared, its rough edges and deep scratches in the leather showed heavy use. Mammaw, Dad and I watch her carefully open it up and show us the first page. "V.B. McGaha, Greenville South Carolina." Jeraldine's voice was very matter of fact as she briefly explained to me who V.B. was. "He was my grandfather and this is his pocket diary for the IRS revenue work he did. Oh, the stories he used to tell me."

"Now that is something else!" My Dad reached out and Jeraldine let him take the diary and gently thumb through it.

"Why haven't you shared this before?" Mammaw asked, carefully closing up the fiddle case.

"Well, I didn't have it. My mom, Reba, had given it to my sister Maud, who had it all these years, but after she died her daughter Eva Jo found it and gave it to me." I could see pain in my distant cousin's eyes, and unfortunately I didn't avert my gaze quickly enough. She touched my hand gently. "You never really get over the death of family."

"I'm sorry," I whispered.

1906: Football rules to allow passing the ball are approved to cut down on deaths in the game; Grain is accidentally overcooked to produce corn flakes and Kellogg's Toasted Corn Flakes gives competition to other cereals; Writer Upton Sinclair exposes Chicago's unsanitary meat packing and abuse of immigrants in his book The Jungle.

Quaker Beer

V.B. doesn't complain, but leaving his cooler mountain home on a hot summer day for the sweltering streets of Greenville still vexes him. He comforts himself by remembering that he is at least not escorting rank hogs.

He reports in to the office in Greenville expecting the usual conference with Captain Merrick, but finds his boss rather acting strange, if not strained. "Bunyan, you are a good agent. I've been out with you and have seen firsthand how you work."

V.B. settles in his usual chair facing Merrick's desk and wondering what is coming on. Has he done something wrong? Will he be fired? What is it that his boss is not coming directly to the point about? For lack of knowing how to answer he says, "Thank you."

Small talk is forced until Merrick finally leans forward, placing both elbows on his desk, and comes to the point, albeit awkwardly. "You are my best field agent right now and I can be sure you will come back alive and there will not be a lot of moonshiners out there dead. Now I have a very different assignment for you."

Relieved that his boss is finally shooting straight, V.B. sighs, "And that is?"

"Quaker Beer. Here in Greenville." Merrick pauses, he knows V.B. reluctantly comes to Greenville, and that asking him to stay for some time is asking for a favor. Merrick continues, "I am under a lot of pressure from locals, from influential congressmen and thus from Washington."

A very perplexed V.B. blurts out, "What the - oops sorry - just what is 'Quaker Beer' and why is it our problem?"

Smiling, Merrick tries not to be a condescending boss but rather a teacher and asks, "Have you tried the popular so-called 'root beer'?"

"Oh yeah," V.B. replies, "Good to the taste and innards. But it is not made with alcohol, right?"

More relaxed, Merrick leans back in his chair. "That is correct. A Quaker man up in Philadelphia named Charles Hires put it together in his pharmacy. With wild roots, berries and other good things. He actually introduced it at the 1876 U.S. Centennial Exhibition and today he sells millions of bottles a year. He was active in the temperance movement and wanted to make something as an alternative to alcoholic drinks."

V.B. is still confused. "Then why is it our problem?"

Merrick stands and comes closer to V.B. Leaning against his desk Merrick continues, "Well, here is the rest of the story and why it is our problem. For years the name "root beer" stuck, but many folks called it 'Quaker beer' because of Hires and his faith family of the Society of Friends. When someone is harmless, peaceful and simple, folks tend to use the term 'Quaker' because of their peaceful beliefs."

"I still do not understand." V.B. shakes his head.

"Well, there was another real beer from Pennsylvania with alcohol in it, brewed by none other than William Penn himself."

"Wasn't he Quaker too?" V.B. asks.

"Yes, but early Quakers did partake moderately for some years until the onset of industrialized distilleries and increasing misuse of alcohol. Because they were so active in social matters the Society of Friends basically supported the temperance movement because of alcohol abuse."

V.B. stands and walks over to the one window. He hopes to catch a cool breeze, but is met by more heat. "So why is it our problem now and why are all these folks putting pressure on you?"

Merrick joins him at the window as they both look down into the busy street. "Simple. Many coffee shops, street vendors, and soft drink merchants are selling 'Quaker Beer' without quality control, alcohol licenses or taxes.

They are playing on the confusion these days between the so-called 'Quaker Beer' of Hires and the marketed alcoholic 'Quaker Beer' brewed and bottled in several places with or without the name."

V.B. looks at Merrick. "So you want me to hit some places here in Greenville to help stop the selling of the alcoholic type?"

Merrick tries to sound like this is a great opportunity. "You got it. You'll ride more street cars than ever and arrest quite a few vendors who 'innocently' sell these bottles to a lot of young people who also claim they 'thought' it was root beer." He watches V.B. begin to twist his thin mustache. Hoping he is not being too pushy he continues, "Your federal badge will be your ticket since you are on official business. Besides, we are running out of travel funds this fiscal year and this will help us get through."

"Have I been spending too much?" V.B. is suddenly concerned.

"No, of course not." Merrick is quick to respond. "And your record keeping is perfect. I just wish some of your colleagues were as thorough. But for this assignment a horse or auto would not be good on Greenville streets!"

A smiling V.B. heads toward the door., "Guess I'll drink a lot of coffee and ask a few questions to check this out."

"Hold up just a minute." Merrick, relieved that V.B. will stay, quickly clarifies. "Yes, drink some coffee but mostly observe the proprietors in action. That is the best approach. I hear their businesses are booming with teenagers and others. Catch them actually selling the stuff."

"And what shall I do if I don't know if it contains alcohol? Do you want me to drink some? I reckon I wouldn't be worth much after a few stops!" V.B. is laughing now.

A laughing Merrick responds, "No, but it is appropriate for you to confiscate samples to bring to our lab here in Greenville for testing."

As he departs, V.B. calls back, "Off to the sober streetcar patrol!"

V.B.'s sister, Sally Sarah, is thrilled to give her baby brother a room in her home. Having married a Hardin she willingly moved to Greenville to be with his family. The revenuer figures that spending some time with his sister and the Hardins would be special compensation for agreeing to work in Greenville.

V.B. is quick to get started. His thoughts center on the new task. He reflects on how simple the occasional checks on tobacco sales and taxes in stores had been. Most folks had kept good records and had not tried to deceive anybody.

He rides the car down Main Street and sees his first target, a coffee shop with sidewalk tables. It is most popular on this hot day.

"Good morning, sir. How may I help you?" the waiter asks after V.B. sits at a table on the sidewalk.

V.B. is inspired by his new assignment, so very different from raiding stills in the woods. "Well, young man what do you recommend on this hot day? What are most folks ordering?"

Looking around, then over his shoulder, the man says softly, "Some have Quaker Beer- you know called root beer. But if you want, we might find some real Quaker Beer in back."

A sly V.B. says, "Sure, why not."

Shortly, the man reappears smiling and opening a bottle with "Quaker Beer" written on the side and even a picture of William Penn with the name "Society of Friends."

V.B. asks, "Are you the owner of this neat business?"

"Well, yes," the proud young man responds, his chest swelling with pride.

"And your name?" V.B., engrossed in his new acting role, gently twists his mustache.

"Wagner, Will Wagner." The owner unsuspectingly shares. But his smile quickly disappears as he watches V.B. raise the bottle toward his mouth, but then on up to his nose where the scent of alcohol is most clear. The young man is at first puzzled, then falls into a panic.

"Well, Will Wagner, let me introduce myself." V.B. displays a caught-you smile, "I am V.B. McGaha, Federal Agent with the Revenue service. I'd like to see your permits, your taxes paid on this alcoholic drink, and your supply."

Wagner's shoulders droop in defeat. From joy in service to a customer to being busted as a criminal in seconds, leaves Wagner with little more to say except, "Sir, you know I have no papers and paid no taxes."

By now all the other customers are quickly departing for fear of being included somehow or even questioned about their potential complicity.

Over the next days, Bunyan carries a shoulder bag as if he were shopping. The bag, however, is for the purpose of carrying confiscated "Quaker Beer" back to the lab while various shop owners wait in fear, usually claiming innocence. They have supposedly 'not been told' by their supplier that Quaker Beer had any alcohol.

He hauls in John Frawett, J.P.James, Thomas Shalenky and several others for selling "Quaker Beer" which he confiscates. His diary records some of those but his investigation in downtown Greenville cannot last long, for word gets around about this tall, striking agent "visiting" so many street vendors, coffee shops and other popular soft drink places.

Finally, Merrick tells him at his weekly report time, it is enough. "The people who had brought the pressure are now jumping on the other foot, saying it is enough. Business downtown is hurting, they say."

V.B. slightly confused looks out Merrick's office window at the now very familiar streets of Greenville. "But are they okay with the reduced Quaker Beer trade?"

Merrick once again joins him and they both watch a stray dog sauntering cross the street. "No doubt. But they also fear folks will not come to shop downtown and they are embarrassed by your arrests."

Gently twisting his mustache he snickers, "So now they sing a different song."

"So it is with business and politics." Merrick shakes his head.

V.B. sighs, somewhat relieved. "I really understand as a businessman myself. I've sent the message and they got it. Time to move on. Time to head back to the woods and mountains where I belong!"

Summer 2012

Dad managed to convince Jeraldine to let him keep the diary a few days for us to look through. Mammaw was sitting in a recliner dozing on and off after a long day at the Dollar Tree while I was snuggled close to Dad on the couch as he thumbed through the small leather- bound book. Some of the revenuer's handwriting was hard to read, but we could generally make out where he went and what he did. Dad read, "June 20th Confirmed with Deputy Marshal Alexander as to reported still; found information false, left for Greenville at 9a; arrived at 12:30 pm; Traveled 20m; livery at Wyatts Stable $1.00." I couldn't help but soak the old time, sure he wasn't reading Clifford to me anymore, but somehow it was just as exciting. He turned the page. "He's written down everywhere he went and what it cost." He stopped and pointed at another entry, "July 20th; Near Loftis, left by livery; continued raid at 8AM; Made search for reported Disty; failed to find; Livery S&R $1.89." Dad stopped for a moment as if recalling something important. "That's around here."

"What do you mean?" I leaned my head against his shoulder.

He thought for a minute. Dad said, "This place, where Sherwood Forest is, used to be known as Loftis. It even had its own post office."

"Cool!" I smiled and then asked, "What do you think disty means?"

"Distillery for sure," Dad explained. "V.B. McGaha would go around busting up illegal distilleries, where they were making liquor without a license."

"Bootleggers?" I asked.

"Yep." He turned the page. "I guess here's one he didn't catch in Loftis."

"I guess not." I yawned. I looked over my dad's shoulder and listened to him read entry after entry. Soon my eyes felt heavy and I started to doze. Each entry began to sound just like the one before. Suddenly Dad elbowed me.

"Look at this!" He waited for me to be fully awake before he continued. "Looks like he did find it. Here, read."

I took the diary and read, " Septemper 30th; Loftis; left by livery; assisted with raid at 7AM; Disty report confirmed in cave under heavy overbrush; note hidden mounds; Livery $1.30." My face paled.

Dad looked at me and touched my forehead. "Pumpkin are you okay?" Mammaw stirred and suddenly paid attention.

"Not really," I answered truthfully. I looked at Mammaw who saw right through me. She knew I was holding something back.

"Millie, what is it?" Mammaw's eyes begged me to let her in, to stop trying to handle it all on my own. When I didn't respond, she gently shook her head and leaned back again in her recliner.

"Millie? Mom?" Dad closed the diary and looked between his mother and myself. "What's going on?"

Mammaw didn't move, but just sighed, "I'm not really sure. Millie can't seem to understand that we are on the same side. She likes to hold it all in and push away those of us who love her more than anything."

"Millie?" Dad touched my arm.

I began to cry. Tears flooded down my face and until I could taste their saltiness. Dad handed me a tissue while Mammaw waited. I could see a few tears roll down her cheek, but she remained calm.

After I finally stopped sobbing, I cried, "I'm sorry." Then the gasping started all over again. It was pretty embarrassing. I felt like a young child who had been reprimanded and felt like was the end of the world.

I finally went to the bathroom to blow my nose really well and wash up my face. I looked in the mirror and told myself what an idiot I had been to hold back from Mammaw. We were going to live together and things had to change. I needed her, but she needed me too.

As I walked back into the living room I headed straight for Mammaw and sat on the edge of her recliner, leaning into her and hugging her as best I could. "I love you, Mammaw, and I promise I won't hold back anything from you anymore."

Mammaw's tears flowed more freely but she smiled. "I know, sweetheart."

That's when it all came out, I mean everything: the hostile encounters with Roy and Junior, the suspicious exchange at the Allison-Deavor House, Eamon's constant appearances, Kevin's unwillingness to go against his brothers, and my stupid solo hike in the woods behind

Trout Lake where I saw those same "hidden" mounds.

"Well, let's go." Dad stood up and walked to the kitchen, where he carefully tucked the diary into Mammaw's purse.

"Where?" I looked at him as he grabbed his car keys.

He looked at me and then looked at Mammaw who nodded in silent agreement as he said, "To the Sheriff's department."

I looked at the clock. "Now? It's late and you have your meeting in the morning."

"Millie's right, Son." Mammaw joined him in the kitchen. "We'll go tomorrow after your job interview. Nothin's gonna change between now and then."

1906: San Francisco Board of Education orders segregation of Oriental from non-Oriental students; President Roosevelt visits the construction of the Panama Canal, the first sitting President to travel abroad.

The Bushwhacker

Revenuer V.B. McGaha is glad to have some time off with his girls and folks. Just walking with them down the Turnpike to the Chapel for worship is more healing than he imagined it could be. Although the deaths of Jessie and Rose still haunt him, he still feels the women's spirits live through Reba, Leslie and Jacksie, who are now looking more and more like young ladies.

There is a special evangelistic meeting in the Chapel and V.B. is in a deeply reflective mood as he sits looking at the little mourner's bench in the front. He reflects back on his childhood questioning Papa Craf and Frosty Jack about justice in this place.

Even though the preacher is talking about forgiveness and repentance in pretty harsh terms and all those present have very serious looks on their faces. Much to the discomfort of the poor preacher, V.B. is lost in his own thoughts and smiles as he lets the memories surrounding this chapel flood his senses. He realizes that right here so many years ago, his own pilgrimage had in so many ways begun as a little boy.

His smile is shattered and thoughts broken, however, as a stranger steps forward to the front toward the mourner's bench. The preacher is obviously taken aback because he has not yet made an altar call asking for anybody to come forward to repent, or pray.

The fellow reaches the front, barely able to breathe, as if the trip from the back to the front has exhausted him. He carefully sits down on the bench facing the crowd. No one recognizes him, but it is clear he is trying to look his best in an old wool suit, two sizes too large, and graying hair slicked down with some heavy grease. He looks up and says in a shaky voice, "Folks call me Billy Boy and I've done some awful bad deeds and seen bad stuff. I've got the consumption and they say I'm about to die." After a long pause to find air he continues, "I was a-runnin' with some bushwhackers for some time."

The preacher approaches him to try and lead him back down the aisle, but the stranger grabs his arm and looks at him with eyes popping out, and repeats, "I seen things and done some really bad things."

The preacher backs up and decides to let the man purge himself. As he begins to softly list some crimes, folks start slipping out the door, not knowing what to do with what he is saying and worried about him bringing the contagious consumption into their little chapel.

Finally, the preacher regains both composure and control of the situation, stopping him tactfully, assuring him of God's forgiveness, salvation and grace. He quickly walks over to V.B. and asks him to stay awhile to hear the rest of the man's story since it is filled with criminal substance. Sending a final blessing towards the mourner's bench, the preacher hurries down the aisle and out the door to join the others outside the chapel.

V.B. feels very awkward since he has missed most of the sermon while reflecting on the question he had asked his own father about bushwhackers and forgiveness in this very spot as a four-year old. He is aware of the stillness and the labored breathing in front of him. He is alone with the fellow.

V.B. is sitting on the first pew facing the dying man. He does not move, but looks directly at Billy Boy. "I'm here just to listen. What do you want to tell me?"

Billy Boy looks a little puzzled, and glancing toward the door where the preacher has left, and back to V.B.

With a softer voice, V.B. tries to assure the man. "I reckon the preacher thought you'd feel freer talking to a lawman about your past. I was sheriff here and am now a federal officer. Maybe you'll get your load lightened easier that way. Everything the preacher said about grace and forgiveness is still good."

With tears running down his face, the stranger replies, "Oh yeah. I shore do feel right good a-talking to a real law feller, since I done all them things."

V.B. listens to stories of stealing and selling cattle, of robbery and other crimes as the man continues to cry, making his breathing even more difficult. Finally V.B. asks, "I am wondering, how come you happened to come to this place - here in Transylvania to confess all this? You said you last lived near Greenville and did most thefts there."

Billy Boy pauses and breathes in deeply as if the chapel air will heal his lungs. "Well sir. I was still young an' a-runnin' with the fellers that shot that Deaver feller here. But that was at the end of the War and I run off from 'em after that. It were awful and I hope God can forgive me."

V.B. is wide awake and his heart is beating fast. "Anything else here in our county?"

Billy Boy feels a weight begin to lift as he confesses, "Well sir, they was this hotel just down the mountain, mostly stone, right under that Dunn's Rock by the Turnpike. We done set fire to it after we loaded up 'bout three wagons with plates, silver, linens and other things."

V.B. is on full alert, finally getting some word about the Hume Hotel whose ruins still grace the community. But he feels something is missing and asks a question that surprises even himself, "Was anybody from around here part of that?"

Surprised by the question, Billie Boy responds, "Shore. For that big load, the feller that led us-uns lived not far from the hotel, right above the Turnpike, past the big Cooper 'stillery. He paid us good and we stuck all them things out behind his house, some of it buried. I think the road was called Riley Mountain Road."

V.B.'s is by now so angry he struggles with keeping some professional poise to get more information. "And do you know what he did with the loot?"

"Oh yeah, sometimes he'd hire us-uns to haul it by dark to Greenville and tell folks his fine family had hit hard times and he was forced to sell family heirlooms."

V.B. remembers the man, strange in looks and behavior, not at all sociable and always nervous when he, as Sheriff, met him in town. Papa Craf did not like the man and folks in town said he told tall tales about his Confederate service, although no one remembered seeing him in any outfit either."

"Bunyan," Harriet's voice interrupts from the chapel door, "here are two jars of cold spring water for the two of you. We'll be taking the girls on home."

"Thanks, Mama. Wait just a minute, I think we're about finished here. I'll go with you." V.B. stands and steps over to Billy Boy, leaning down to help him up.

Billy Boy depends heavily on the lawman as he gets him to his feet and they walk down the aisle. "Yes, sir. Thank you, sir. I ain't never talked to a lawman and I shore feel a heap better a-gittin' this off'n my chest. I reckon now I can die in peace." He slowly makes his way out the door to his horse. V.B. helps him up and watches him ride away slowly.

It is a long weekend and V.B. has to wait for Monday to find a judge to make a case for a warrant to search the man's place. He gets the current sheriff and some of his deputies to go with him.

The ride out the Turnpike to the foot of Riley Mountain road is ominous for everybody. Investigating ghosts from the past never sits well with young deputies. The men leave their horses at the foot of the road and, with guns drawn, carefully climb the hill to a an ordinary old wood frame house. With the sheriff's deputies watching the back, V.B. and the sheriff walk past a front porch swing blown back and forth rising winds promising a storm. They slowly enter the unlocked front door. The house is silent.

A rank smell causes V.B. to step outside to pull off his jacket and wrap it around his mouth and nose. Returning to the front room he sees the sheriff, with his bandana around his face, staring up at a body hanging from a rope, dead for some days.

From outside a deputy calls, "You fellers oughter come back an' see this." After letting the body to the floor, they step out back to an empty root cellar, mostly underground with fresh digging marks inside and out. A few pieces of fine linen and silver are scattered. They immediately conclude that his remaining loot has been stolen, after all those years.

Once V.B.'s presence is no longer needed he rides up to his parents' home as fast as the rising winds allow. By the time he reaches his mother's kitchen table he quickly grabs a cup of her coffee and sits down with his aging parents, each enjoying a piece of warm apple pie. Since they were fully aware about the confession in the Chapel and his planned joint raid with the local sheriff, they asked, "Well, how did it go? And how was it for you?" He tells them what they had found.

Finally, he takes his first sip of coffee and lets out his traditional "Ahhh," and looks very seriously at his father and confesses. "I reckon the biggest problem for me was the fact that here was a man who was supposed to be a neighbor but was really the Judas amongst us, betraying all the loving folks around him." Craf and Harriet listen and let their son take another sip of coffee before he continues. "We liked to think that most of those evil people were from elsewhere, deserters from one side or another. But it shook me up to realize the enemy was us."

Harriet interrupts, "Oh, how much I remember your papa worrying about the bushwhackers that they chased in the War, and whether our family was safe from them. Also, he did not want to come to the Confederate Reunions in Brevard, not just because of the glory and gory war stories but because he did not trust some of them. This fellow must have been one he did not trust."

Craf sighs and slowly speaks, "I believe in mercy, but I also know there's bad in us all."

Harriet reaches out and gently pats her husband's arm. "And that Billy Boy fellow confessing there in the Chapel was just what your papa always hoped for." Craf smiles at his wife and places his hand over hers.

V.B. goes back to the question that has always been with him. "That whole episode even raised up inside me all my old anger about justice and fairness. How many more folks like that man got away with murder, rape, pillaging, and other destructive actions and worse."

Craf asks softly, "Did he?"

Harriet adds, "We don't know what went through his mind before he tied that rope around his neck do we?"

V.B. pauses, twisting his mustache between his fingers, "Part of me thinks it was only because he lost the rest of his loot and he might have to go to work as an old man. But then I think, maybe the guilt finally caught up with him and he punished himself for all his deeds, that maybe there was just a little bit of humanity under all that evil."

Harriet raises her voice ever so slightly, "We'll let the preachers decide if he's burnin' in Hell. I reckon he had his own hell here, a-livin' like that."

With a heavy sigh V.B. feels himself become the child from so many years ago, "I'd love to have arrested him and had tried him in court, to prove there is some justice in these parts."

Craf smiles at his son, "There is, Bunyan, there is."

Summer 2012

I didn't sleep well and was up before everyone else and decided to make Mammaw and Dad some breakfast. They were surprised and Dad blamed it on my guilty conscience. I swallowed hard guessing he was probably right, but Mammaw gave me a big kiss and thanked me saying she'd clean up.

After Dad took off down the road toward the old camp I decided to take a quick dip in Trout Lake to knock the heaviness out of me. When I got to the dock I looked around for the water snake and then dove in, letting the stinging cold send an icy rush through my body. I couldn't get out fast enough and hurried to the sunny spot at the end of the dock. I sat there with the towel wrapped tightly around me.

"Are you trying to punish yourself or somethin'?" Kevin's familiar voice made me smile. He plopped down next to me.

"Nah." I smiled. "Just trying to wake myself up. Didn't sleep well."

"Really?" Kevin pulled off his T-shirt and stood up on the edge of the dock. "Why?" I just sat in the sun and watched him dive off. He didn't come up quite as frozen as I did, but he did hustle out of the water. When he realized that I hadn't answered his question he looked at me a little more seriously. "Why didn't you sleep well?" He asked again, coming back to sit next to me, a little closer than normal as if he was hoping I'd share my towel with him. I handed it to him and let him dry off. He tossed it back at me and put his T-shirt on, but he didn't move away any. "Well?" He almost begged.

"Kevin," I looked at him, so close that I felt I could actually see into the blue of his eyes. "What if I told you my dad and I are going to the Sheriff today?" He didn't say anything. "What if I told you I had something that showed where an old cave is that your brothers are using for something?" I kept talking for fear of what he might answer.

"What if I told you this something could show the Sheriff where that cave is and they could maybe bust your brothers?"

Kevin didn't move his eyes away from mine. I could hardly breathe and I knew tears were starting to force themselves to the surface. I tried not to cry, but it was useless. He reached up and caught the first tear falling down my cheek. He finally whispered as if relieved, "I would say it's about time."

1908: The National Conservation Commission is established by President Roosevelt in order to conserve U.S. national treasures; William Taft, Teddy Roosevelt's choice as successor, wins the U.S. Presidency.

The Gentle Giant Departs

It is a freezing January twenty-first when Craf and Harriet hear a horse coming down the Turnpike at breakneck speed and assume that it is some emergency when the rider stops at their gate. Reverend R.G. Tuttle dismounts hastily, appearing confused and anxious. They normally see him on an occasional Sunday at church when it is his rotation time to preach at the McGaha Chapel.

"Come in from the cold, Brother Tuttle." Craf and Harriet have prepared well for the cold winter of '08 at home with plenty of firewood in the shed, as well as canned goods in the root cellar, meat in the smokehouse and hay in the barn.

The Reverend shakes the snow from his coat and moves close to the fire, asking how they are doing. Craf and Harriet eagerly share how their three granddaughters, Reba, Leslie and Jacksie, at ages fourteen, twelve and eight, are living with them, Jacksie sharing time with the Thrashs, while their Papa is often away on Revenue business. The Reverend sees only joy in the old couple's faces as they explain how V.B. has also moved in with his folks at the home place and love for his girls to grow up where he did, with the richness of love and mercy ever preserved.

Craf hands the Reverend a cup of coffee. "I'm sure you didn't come to check up on our family, but I reckon ye came with something else on your mind."

After letting the coffee warm him, the holy man speaks, "Yes, Brother Craf, you can always see things right away. I'm sorry to have to say that your neighbor Jane Rabb passed away."

Harriet finds herself suddenly holding Craf's hand before she manages to utter, "So sorry. How is Felix?"

"It's hit him pretty hard. They'd been married forty-eight years. He sent me to ask you a couple of things."

Craf does not hesitate. "Of course, Brother Tuttle. What can we do?"

"First, she wanted to put in her obituary that she was a founding member of the Dividing Ridge Church." The Reverend steals another warm sip.

Craf, noticing Harriet's questioning look at him, responds quickly, "You do not have to ask anything of me. She and Felix helped all of us in founding our little group. We struggled with the name for some time. Of course they should use that name."

The Reverend is obviously relieved. "Thank you. That little Methodist chapel meant so much to both of them. When she left her Presbyterian church home in Tennessee to come here all of you really took her in." He pauses to finish his coffee. "The second request may be a bit tougher. She wanted to be buried in the McGaha family cemetery right near your house. I know you watch after it for the family."

Again, Craf is quick to respond, "I see no problem. They are family. In fact I'll hustle up some men to help dig the grave. We may need several to work through this frozen ground."

It is not long before Rev. Tuttle refuses a hot meal to be on his way. As they stand in the doorway, feeling the bite of the cold wind, he comments, "It sure is a tough time to die."

Once the girls have been fed and tucked into their beds upstairs, Harriet and Craf sit by the warm fire to have some hot soup and cornbread, giving thanks for their long years together. The death of a close friend and neighbor prompts their thoughts about their own mortality.

"Harriet, I reckon none of us knows when our time comes, but I hope mine is not dragged out as with poor Jane. She suffered so much this last year."

Harriet gently sweeps the cornbread crumbs from her skirt and tosses them into the fire. "Poor soul, she's at rest finally. You're right, we do not know our time or place, but let's hope not so soon! My little man, I still need you around this farm and in my arms!"

For the next three weeks the weather stays cold with little snow. As Craf comes from the barn where his cattle and sheep have been fed and bedded, he notices the smoke from his chimney crawling toward the ground like a mystical snake slipping down the roof. He stomps into the warmth of the kitchen. "Storm's a-comin' Harriet."

Passing her husband a cup of hot cider she answers, "I reckon so. I feel it in my bones and got a headache. I don't have to read your signs outside anymore -- this old body tells me!"

They both laugh. Harriet then asks, "What are you a-thinkin'? I see some worry on your face."

Putting down his cider to take off some layers of clothing, he tries to sound as matter of fact as possible, "My hogs are out a-rangin' on Rich Mountain. If we get much snow they'll not find mast enough. I've got some corn stored over there."

"Let's see what tomorrow brings." Harriet says calmly, although her insides suddenly feel more than just the weather.

Wednesday arrives with a fury. The blizzard lets up a little after the noon hour and they could only see a little of the Turnpike in front of the house and some trails through the woods out back.

Craf finds Harriet in the living room with the girls where they are doing some long overdue mending. He announces, "Harriet, I got to check on those poor hogs. I know you worry, but I'll go by Tom Fowler's place to ask him to come help me out Friday. If the storm gets bad, I'll go back by their house to spend the night."

Harriet pretends to be more concerned about the hem of Reba's red dress. "Craf, I reckon there's no changin' your mind when it's set. I do worry, but it sounds like you have a good plan. But you won't try to cut across Panther Mountain will ye?"

Craf walks a little closer to the gaggle of women. "Nope. I'll head straight for Cannon Creek to the Fowlers' place then to the field and shed where the hogs ought to be. I'll be careful, my love."

Suddenly Harriet stands and walks over to a peg on the wall near the door. She returns with her hands full, "At least let me wrap my long wool scarf around your hat and neck and you've got to put my long winter coat over yours It will fit okay and cover more of your legs. This is one time our size difference helps. And thank goodness you have those new lace-up boots from your last trip down to Greenville."

Craf smiles at his dear, protective wife and indulges in a long, warm embrace from Harriet, with the girls giggling in the background. Kissing each of his granddaughters' foreheads, a bundled-up Craf finally trudges out into the snow toward Rich Mountain.

It is slow going with the snow becoming ever deeper and showing no sign of letting up. He can find the way to Tom and Polly Ann's house.

Stomping the snow off on the small front porch Craf is not surprised to see his sister throwing the door open, "Craf, what are you a-doin' out in this?" Polly Ann asks pulling him into their home.

A laughing Tom Fowler comes up behind and answers her question as Craf steps over to warm at the hot stove. "He's your brother and after all these years a-carin' for man and beast, what do you reckon he might be up to?"

Craf removes his gloves and rubs his hands together above the stove. "Well, I aim to check on my hogs on the way home but I really came by to ask if you could come over to help me on Friday, Tom."

"Of course, Craf. Ain't much I kin do here in this weather but play my fiddle and your sister gets tired of that after awhile." Tom scratches his bushy white beard before he suddenly bursts out in laughter at the look on his wife's face.

Thankful for the quick warm-up Craf puts his gloves back on and heads towards the door. "I'd best get along if I'm to get home by dark. See you Friday, Tom." Craf steps quickly out into the cold closing their door with a thud.

His thoughts are mixed as he heads on toward Rich Mountain. He wonders how badly the hogs are scattered and if he can find them all. He feels his feed for them should be secure but as the snow gets even deeper, he wonders if they can be rounded up. Hopefully they will know some food is in the shed.

Craf also wonders if he is doing the right thing remembering the long embrace from his Harriet and the worried look on his sister's face just now. Should he have stayed the night or asked Tom to come with him?

Bundled as much as he is, he begins to realize with some humor how his small size helps him move about with agility but on the other hand he does not have fat to burn or to keep him warm. He laughs as he thinks that he'd never been able to put on the "winter fat" that bears and even his hogs sometimes did, as well as some of his human friends.

His laughter continues as he remembers how his size had worried his parents, but how they had seen him grow into a respected man, a Civil War veteran and most of all, a beloved man in the community.

Although he had scowled or frowned for the photographs folks had made of him, he now is free to laugh as he trudges toward his beloved mountain grazing land where he had spent many hours throughout his lifetime.

It was here he and Epi had watched their animals, eaten many a meal and he had peppered his papa, Jesse, with so many questions.

It was this holy ground where he came to scream and cry when a loved one died and where Bunyan had come to pour his heart out with his losses. He smiles as he thinks of how that tough man of justice, this respected lawman has such a gentle spirit and a heart of gold. He is making at least a three-state area a safer place for everybody as a federal lawman. Craf feels joy and security in that.

As he moves along, carefully grasping rhododendron branches for support, he finds himself remembering so many things, about how blessed he has been with family and friends, for that little church community and the chapel they'd built.

It was here he could escape the horrible memories of that awful war and think about his living children -- what joy they brought to him. How pleased he was that two daughters, Bertha and Sally, had married Hardin men, one of whom followed in his own steps as a surveyor in the county, another just over in South Carolina. And Julia, their other daughter, had gone off to Indian Territory with her man, Steve Keith. His correspondence with them over the years had helped keep the family close. His heart is warmed with the many thoughts of his family.

As his steps slow more and more, he cannot feel his hands and feet. Strangely, he wants to rest by a large oak for a few minutes. He bends to scoop out a hollow in the drifted snow at the base.

Sitting under the mighty oak he looks up at the barren limbs and feels the trunk against his back as well as some exposed roots under him. He remembers something from the Bible about the mighty oak growing from a tiny seed, or was it a mustard seed? But he feels the oak is really his family for whom he lived.

He thinks, they were like that tree, his family. Not just the many McGahas and their kin, but also that little faith community and the neighbors and hundreds of visitors who had been at his home over the years.

As sleep slowly comes, he feels a strange warmth inside and a special closeness to his beloved Harriet. He re-experiences her embrace, not just the one a few hours before, but a lifetime of being embraced by her love and support, so symbolically captured in being wrapped up in both his coat and hers. Then, he sees a pair of eyes watching. They are gentle, warm, loving eyes nearby.

The curious doe moves closer, blinking the falling snow from her eyes, watching this small human creature, sensing no harmful intent. She turns to listen to the last earthly whisper of the little giant, Craf McGaha, "I love you forever, Harriet."

Summer 2012

"I got the job!" Dad slammed through the front door while Mammaw and I were finishing off some macaroni and cheese for lunch.

"Yeah!" I jumped up and hugged him. Mammaw joined in and just about smothered me as her big arms embraced both of us.

"I can start whenever I'm ready." He sat down and took a few bites of the best quick lunch in the south. "I told them I have some loose ends to tie up, but I should be able to start next week." I couldn't believe what I was hearing. It was actually going to happen. We were really coming home. Dad rushed through the rest of his lunch and grabbed Mammaw's keys. "First loose end we need to tie up is a visit to the Sheriff's Department." I could feel my stomach suddenly drop again.

Mammaw made herself comfortable in the passenger side of the front seat so I crawled into the back seat of the Big M. Dad didn't hesitate to give me the rundown on how dangerous my behavior was and that I could have gotten hurt, but I let him do his fatherly thing and just said, "I know," every few minutes.

Mammaw would occasionally throw in a, "Now, Son, Millie's already said she's sorry."

Soon the lecture died down and a peaceful silence filled the car, one with no secrets. As we hit the bottom of the mountain and I could see Dunn's Rock high above me on my right, Dad suddenly said, "I'm proud of you."

Of course, this shocked the crap out of me after his whole lecture. "What?" I wanted to make sure I heard him right.

"I said I'm proud of you, but I'm not saying it again," Dad's voice joked.

"Okay," I said really slowly and leaned forward to get closer to him. "But why?"

Dad eased around the final sharp curve before the Greenville Highway straightened out and glanced at me briefly. "Because you really do want to do what's right and just." He paused, "You simply don't have a clue how."

I punched him lightly in the arm. "Thanks a lot!" I teased.

"Careful now, Millie, your dad is in the driver's seat." I thought I heard Mammaw giggle.

"He sure is!" I leaned back and sighed.

1908: Henry Ford builds the Model T and William Durant forms General Motors to market a wide range of motorcars; Westinghouse Company introduces the electric iron and toaster to reduce labor for the housewife.

The Reunion

Eight months have passed since the February blizzard and autumn has returned. V.B. notes how much warmer the fall weather in Greenville is, at least ten degrees higher than up the mountain in Transylvania. The warmth is a stark contrast to the cold when they had lost their beloved Papa Craf. Now he is meeting his distant sister and her husband at the train station, finally coming home after all those years away.

Staring at the train tracks he wonders, "Will I recognize her? How should I greet him? When will the train ever pull in? Will she be angry with me?" He feels guilty that he has not kept up with Julia and her husband Steven except through her letters to their parents. They had been faithful in writing and sharing with him news from the Keiths in Oklahoma. He had left the communication to them and now realizes he has neglected his sister.

It is different with the two nearby sisters, Bertha and Sally, and their Hardin husbands, W.B. and A. L. He visited with them on his work-related travels and they had been able to come right away to help with local funeral arrangements for their father.

Only an hour late, the mighty engine pulls its load of precious people and fragile freight into the Greenville Station. As the crowd emerges and trudges down the platform one couple heads straight for the tall lawman.

"Bunyan?" The graying woman standing before him, with a light brown sweater gently draped around her shoulders, holds out both arms.

"Julia? Steve Keith?" Bending deeply to embrace the little old lady, V.B. asks, "And how is my little big sister?"

Still touching his face and mustache and hugging him once again, "It's been so long," she mumbles amidst tears.

Fighting his own tears and with a long arm around his brother-in-law, V.B. asks, "How was your trip?"

"Long, but much easier than in the wagon a-goin' the other way so many years ago!" Steve's white hair reminds V.B. of how long it has been.

Picking up their carpetbags, V.B. leads them outside to the street and declares, "We'll see now if modern times here a-gettin' up the mountain are easier than in a wagon like we did when we were a-growin' up!"

"Oh my God," Julia exclaims, "You 'spect us to ride in that?" pointing to a new Model T Ford where V.B. is depositing their bags.

Steve adds, "You must be a-makin' good money by the Feds if you can afford this."

The two visitors cautiously get into the back seat of the car with Julia gently caressing the shiny black leather while V.B. adjusts the spark and throttle and steps to the front to turn the crank It fires on the third try.

In the driver's seat he pulls out into the traffic, trying as best he can not to scare the many horses. "Naw. I don't make all that much. This Model T is on loan from a dealer here in Greenville who has been after me for some time to drive it for nothing for a while."

Letting his arm hang out over the door and inspecting the smooth black finish, Steve inquires, "Now how can he afford that? What's in it for him? What's the catch?"

Carefully weaving through town V.B. raises his voice so they can hear him above the engine noise. "I asked him all that. He says it's the best tool to market his cars, especially to have a lawman driving one of his wagons." He tilts his head slightly to one side to project his voice behind him. "I tried to tell him, I could not really surprise any moonshiners in it and am not sure if it's even going to get up the mountain to Jones Gap. We'll try the new road by Caesar's Head."

Steve laughs, leaning forward he yells, "So! This is your trial run and we are your pushers if it don't!"

"That's one way to look at it." They all laugh.

Small talk dominates until Traveler's Rest where they rest their voices for a while from all the yelling. All three travelers almost hold their breath in awe as the Model T easily takes the curves and steepness of the new mountain road. When they finally reach Caesar's Head Julia begs for them stop and see the majestic view of South Carolina. The break is good for all of them and gives V.B. a chance to continue the small talk. "And how are things in Indian Territory?"

Steve Keith breathes in the cooler mountain air. "Now Bunyan, you know we've been a state since last November. Or do you not get news up in these mountains?"

V.B. follows his sister as she leads them to the Caesar's Head overlook. "More than we need sometimes. I hear through my office that it's still pretty dangerous out there -- more U.S. Marshalls killed in Oklahoma than anywhere in the whole land."

Standing on the edge of the mountain looking down into South Carolina Julia sighs deeply, "Oh my. Thought I might never see the beautiful fall colors in these mountains again." Julia finally looks at her brother and focuses on the subject they have avoided until now, "Bunyan, I'm so sorry we couldn't make it home for Papa's funeral or his dyin'."

V.B. walks over and puts an arm around his sister's shoulder as she quickly uses her sweater to wipe away a stray tear. "Well, it took us all by surprise and none of us was there for his departure. Not quite like when Grandpa Jesse passed on back in '98. We knew his time was comin' for the longest time. That snowy night in February it just seemed to be Papa's time, like the death angel was a-waitin' for the cold and ice."

Julia keeps looking straight ahead. "Yeah, but Grandpa was nearly a hundert years old, Bunyan."

Wanting to get home before dark V.B. guides the two guests back towards the car. "That's right, but for those last twenty years after Grandma Candice died he never seemed to be with us."

Reluctantly, Julia follows her brother after one last look at the brilliant fall colors painting the valley below. Once she is settled back in the car she continues, "Bunyan, tell us how it was with Papa. We appreciate the letters a-tellin' us, but I need to know more."

Before V.B. pulls out into the road he reaches into his coat pocket and hands Julia a small envelope. "Julia, we've a little piece before we hit home, so why don't you and Steve Keith read these three newspaper articles I brought. They give three different perspectives on him and his passing. We can talk after."

He hands them the articles. There is a long silence as they read and exchange the articles several times to re-read them.

Finally, as if to help in her grief, a tearful Julia reads aloud from the Sylvan Valley News issue dated February 14, 1908:

"J. Crawford McGaha, better known as "Craf", died under sad and peculiar circumstances Wednesday of last week. He left home last Wednesday morning to look up some hogs that were out in the range without food, and the snow made it a duty to feed them. He told his family when he left that if he did not find them he would probably spend the night at Tom Fowler's and hunt farther the next day, so when night came and he did not return there was no uneasiness at his home. He was at Fowler's house in the afternoon and made arrangements for Fowler to come over and work for him on Friday, and left for home before dark. This was the last seen of him alive."

Julia stops and weeps uncontrollably as a tearful Steve simply puts his big arm around her shoulders. Finally she says, "I got to do this. At least try." She continues,

"Friday morning Fowler went to McGaha's according to promise and the discovery was made that Mr. McGaha was missing. A searching party was organized and the body was found near the trail where it had lain for two nights and a day undisturbed. The find was a terrible shock to neighbors and friends who were in the searching party, as well as to his many friends in all this mountain country."

V.B. drives in silence, but makes out bits and pieces of his sister's voice over the noise of the engine. Steve watches his wife patiently, holding his breath as she works hard to maintain her composure and is obviously determined to read the paper article aloud as if it will bring some catharsis. She goes on.

"Mr. McGaha was 76 years old, was born, married, and had lived a long and useful life on the waters of the Little River. His house was known far and wide for its hospitality, and there are few citizens of the county but have participated in its cheer and shelter. He was a good neighbor, a true friend and an honored citizen. Mr. McGaha was a liberal member of the old M.E. church, and was the prime mover and principal contributor in building the Little River chapel, near his home, as a place of worship for his denomination. His house has always been the home of the Methodist Episcopal clergymen who have visited this country since the war, and his donations have kept up the semblance of life and interest among the few who worshiped at Little River chapel."

Julia seems more focused now on what she is reading and observes, "Well, this writer did grasp what a gracious, loving man he was in his merciful treatment of others -- both people and their stock."

Steve adds, "And you can see what a role he played in the building of that chapel. I hear that many folks call it 'McGaha Chapel,' is that right?"

V.B. suddenly realizes that the question is directed toward him and that he must respond. Fighting back some suppressed tears, he says, "Oh yeah. Actually for some time now, much to his embarrassment, folks refer to it that way."

With a nod, Julia continues her reading pilgrimage,

"He leaves a widow and four children to mourn their loss. V.B. McGaha, his only son, was for many years sheriff of the county. The daughters are all married, one of them being the wife of A.L. Hardin, our efficient county surveyor. W.B. Hardin, who lives over in the edge of South Carolina, married one, and Steve Keith, now living in the Indian Territory, married the third."

Steve breaks in, "How come they'd mention my name and not Julia's?"

A frown is on V.B.'s face. "I don't rightly know. Reporters can be quirky. We didn't have a say in that and were so shocked by Papa's death we didn't ask to see it. Sorry, Julia."

Julia shakes her head and gently tucks a loose strand of hair behind her ear. "I'm pretty used to it. If women can't vote, why should our names be listed?"

Both men swallow hard at her obvious and appropriate anger. After a heavy silence she goes on reading.

"No visible cause for his sudden death is known. He left home last

Wednesday morning in his usual health, and the exertion of walking over the mountains in the snow must have been too great and heart failure resulted. His sudden death will be regretted by a large circle of friends, and the News joins them in sympathy for the immediate family."

"Nice, I guess." Julia says as she reaches for the other two death notices.

With a gentle hand V.B. reaches back for her outstretched hands and says, "Why don't we let the others be? I reckon that it was good for us all to read that one, but I'm not sure I can take more right now."

"You're right, brother. Thanks for indulging me." Julia smiles and reads the other news articles in silence, passing them on to her husband.

Bunyan feels their silence and waits on their further questions, not really knowing himself what else to say.

Julia shifts back to the articles, realizing her hurt is still showing, "I was tickled to see an article by his Methodist pastor and by a Baptist preacher bein' as most McGahas are Baptist." She leans in closer to make sure her brother can hear. "Bunyan, I know that Elijah Allison was your father-in-law and . . ."

V.B. interrupts, "Julia, he will always be my father-in-law, and my children's 'Grandpa Allison.'"

She puts her hand on his shoulder. "Of course he is, little brother. He is a gracious, loving man and really wrote not just kind, but also accurate words about Papa."

Steve leans in for a moment and adds, "Yeah, and I felt like he never sat in judgment on your Dad for being a Methodist. That came through in his article, too."

V.B. practically yells, "On that point, he is head and shoulders above many of the other uneducated, jackleg preachers who come through these mountains trying to tell us how wrong we are, or how God only speaks through their church or dogma."

"We have our share of those in Oklahoma too!" Steve adds and then leans back, still admiring and scanning the intricacies of the Model T.

Julia plunges forth, "I never knew this Methodist pastor who wrote the other letter but was impressed by his words. It seemed like he knew

Papa well."

V.B. carefully passes a horse pulling a wagonload of hay. Both drivers exchange waves before he continues, "Yeah. He knew how close Papa was to my Reba, Leslie and baby Jacksie; how he and Mama helped so much when their own mamas died. They really did a lot of the raising of the girls."

Steve leans in again to state, "I noted the dates- - how he gave such details on life events so carefully. I could not help but notice that the pastor wrote that your Papa became a Methodist in 1877. As I remember that's five years after they built the Little River Chapel!"

V.B. is thankful to finally reach Cedar Mountain Community as he guides the car down the final stretch to the McGaha homestead. "That's right. I'm not really sure that anybody other than A.J. Loftis was a Methodist when they built the Chapel. Certainly Walter Raxter and his whole family were Baptists. But it did not matter back then."

Julia takes in every tree and building as they pass by her old stomping grounds. She catches herself and remembers to finish her thought, "And as you said, most McGahas up on See Off were -- and I reckon still are -- Baptists." As she continues to let the familiar surroundings flood her senses Julia suddenly allows more prevailing feelings of anger to burst forth, "How come at Papa's age he had to go back out on Rich Mountain- - and in a snowstorm?"

V.B. slows down the Model T. "Dear Julia, I reckon you answered your own question. He had to. That's who he was. Like the preacher wrote, when man or beast needed help it was his God-given nature to check and help." Julia can see her brother's shoulders rise and drop as if releasing a heavy burden, "For months now we all asked ourselves that same question and tried not to beat ourselves up with it."

Julia sees her father's famous stone wall come into view. "And Uncle Tom Fowler -- how did he handle it?"

"He and Aunt Polly Ann took it pretty hard as you can imagine. They were so close for so many years. I hear they cried long and hard."

"And at the funeral?" Julia feels Steve encourage her to sit back and relax. She takes his hand and lets him pull her in close.

V.B. slowly pulls the Model T onto the dirt road, the old turnpike, running parallel to the new Greenville Highway. "Well, Big Tom Fowler brought his fiddle to the house for that service. The first couple of hymns he had us all in tears and speechless. His great beard cushioned that fiddle and absorbed many tears." V.B. suddenly laughs, "Then at the end, he did something that might not have gone over well at the Chapel."

"Something from his Cherokee tradition?" Steve asks.

"Nope. Mama asked him to cut loose with some lively numbers that Papa loved as a kind of joyous celebration." V.B. glances back at his sister for a moment. "You can remember what they said even when you were still here, Julia -- that Big Tom's fiddle can make the mountain roll." V.B. paused before he concluded, "The mountain rolled that day, cold as it was. It echoed and reverberated all through our world. Our merciful giant had fallen. The death angel had come. And we celebrated Papa's life."

Silence. Tears.

After a long pause, Steve Keith comes back in less than a tactful way with a well-intended detail, "I am thankful that his body was intact, bein' down in the wilderness so long." Julia gives him a frown and, realizing his timing might have been off, he defends his thought, "We read that in one of the articles. I'm just thankful."

V.B. assures him, "It's okay, Steve. We are all thankful that none of the hungry animals in that blizzard found him. That is a blessing. It's interesting, though, that we found signs of a single deer, probably a doe, next to him."

As they pull up to the old homestead Julia smiles. "I reckon he wasn't really alone. At least one of the beasts he loved so much gave him company in his last moments."

Summer 2012

"How may I help you?" A young lady spoke to us from behind a massive reception desk at the Sheriff's Department that doubled as a barrier to the waiting room.

"We would like to speak to a detective please." Dad spoke briefly and did not seem to think it necessary to spill the whole story.

The woman pulled open a drawer and checked a piece of paper. "Looks like Detective Soldate has detective duty today. What is your name?" Dad answers her and she picks up the phone. Skipping any greeting she gets straight to the point, "The Fowlers are here to speak with you." She listens for a moment and then hangs up. With one hand she grabs three visitor tags and with the other a clipboard. "Please sign in and you will each need to wear one of these. Have a seat in the lobby and Detective Soldate will be out shortly."

As Dad signed us in, I hung the bright red visitor tag around my neck with visitor printed all the way up and down the cord. "You think they know we're visitors?" I whispered to Mammaw.

"Shh, Millie!" Mammaw fussed at me. We made ourselves comfortable in the lobby that boasted a beautiful cathedral ceiling with windows flooding the room with sunlight. The waiting room was hotter than I expected, although the receptionist continued to enjoy her warm sweater. I was impressed with the new facility and knew the community was proud to finally move out of the outdated building in the middle of town.

We were alone, a little disappointing I think. I expected at least someone else to make the silence a little more entertaining. I was relieved when a very young woman came in with two little kids who ran all the way to us and sat on the benches closest to me as their mother signed in at the front desk, obviously knowing what she was doing. With a red tag around her neck she settled in next to me and apologized, "Sorry about my boys. They always get excited when they get to visit their daddy."

"Oh." I tried to be nice. "So they actually get to visit with him?"

"Just through the video monitor, but it's better than nothin'." She smiled and I could see her top teeth had decay deep into the gum. It took all I had in me not to show the sadness I was feeling, not knowing if it was abject poverty or drug use that caused such decay.

Mammaw reached over and touched my hand before she spoke to the woman, "Well, we wish you a right nice visit."

We could suddenly hear a door behind us open. "Fowlers?" I recognized Detective Soldate from his visit to our house at the beginning of the summer. He came over and shook our hands, even mine, and invited us to follow him. He used his tag, definitely not red, to open the door and we followed him through a complicated maze of hallways.

"Did they build it this way to make sure anyone trying to escape quickly couldn't find their way out?" I asked before I figured it wasn't really the best way to make a good impression.

Soldate laughed and added, "You'd think that was it. But really we have no idea what anyone was thinking. You can quote me on that!" He guided us through another hallway until we ended up in front of a sign with "Conference Room A410" neatly engraved on opaque glass mounted onto a nicely finished oak slab. "Let's head in here." We quickly sat in the new leather chairs around an oval table with a telephone acting as its centerpiece.

"How can I help you?" Detective Soldate reached behind him to a desk in the corner of the room and pulled out a legal notepad.

"My daughter would like to share with you some of her observations," Dad said suddenly feeling a little awkward, "but it's up to you to see any relevance or not."

"Always is," Soldate stated and then looked straight at me, "Shoot."

I pulled V.B.'s diary out of Mammaw's purse and laid it on the table. I didn't hand it to him yet; I had to explain first. I told him of my experience at the Allison Deaver House and how I watched Eamon buy something from Roy and Junior. I explained that this Eamon kept bothering me and I was sure he was looking for more pot or whatever he was buying. I told them of my visit into the woods and how I took off because I heard Junior yell, and, of course, I was worried about my feet in the briars and then there was the horrible cat-pee smell.

"Excuse me?" Soldate interrupted and looked up from his legal pad, "Did you say cat-pee smell?"

"Yes, sir," I answered and looked at him slightly confused.

He wrote something down and then got up and walked to the door. "I'll be right back." Within minutes he returned and my heart stood still as I saw a familiar head of corn rows following behind him. Eamon smiled so big I could see every one of his teeth. "This is Federal Agent Todd Williams." He introduced Eamon to us and Mammaw and Dad shook his hand while I just sat there staring. "He's been undercover for some time and working with the ATF out of Greenville." Looking at my blank stare he continued. "That's stands for Alcohol, Tobacco, and Firearms, Millie."

"You can close your mouth now." Todd laughed and reached out and shut it for me.

His touch repulsed me and I suddenly came alive. "What does any of this have to do with alcohol, tobacco or firearms?" I could feel my face get red. "And you could have been a little less criminal acting, freaking me out like that!"

Todd sat down and lost his smile. He suddenly became very businesslike and pulled out his own notepad. Even his voice was more professional. "I'm sorry Millie if I upset you, but I was trying to find out where the Carp brothers are producing their methamphetamines." He looked at our stunned faces and continued, "Six months ago the Sheriff's Department found meth in a car on a stop for a routine traffic violation. The young boy was terrified and immediately spilled that he traded his grandpa's shotgun for the meth. He'd heard his other friends were able to trade their guns for meth, so he did it too." He looked straight at me. "Since firearms are involved they pulled me in to help. We suspect the Carps sell the guns as well as the meth."

Soldate continued, "We have suspected meth production taking place somewhere in the woods, but have not been able to locate it. Even our drug dogs are trained to identify the end product, not the production stages. However, one side product of meth production is an intense cat-urine type of smell. Looks like Millie happened to be there when the aroma was strong."

"Meth?" Mammaw almost cried. "I thought we were dealing with marijuana. Oh, no not meth. Tempy will be devastated."

G. Keith Parker and Leslie Parker Borhaug

"As in Tempy Carp?" Detective Soldate asked.

"Why, yes," Mammaw looked confused. "She knew the boys were up to somethin' but handn't a clue it was anything more serious than the marijuana her husband dabbled in years ago." As she watched the men take notes she suddenly started crying. "Oh, I should never have said that or come here!"

Dad reached out and touched her hand while Detective Soldate tried to make her feel better. "Mrs. Fowler, its good you did come. You just confirmed our suspicions that Mrs. Carp was not a part of the illegal activities, so you just helped her." Mammaw tried to smile, but was still not convinced. She tried to settle herself by searching in her purse for a tissue.

"And Kevin." I spoke quietly.

"Excuse me?" Soldate looked at me.

"Kevin had nothing to do with the meth." I spoke clearly and mostly looked at Todd. "Eamon, I mean Todd, knows it too."

"I do?" Todd put down his pen and leaned back in his chair, "Please explain."

I took a deep breath. "Well, you saw that Kevin, Ellie and I hung out most of the summer together. He also always stood up to his brothers when it came down to it."

"Not when it comes to the meth," Todd simply stated.

I started to sweat and realized Todd was right. Kevin had known something, how much I never knew. "But," I stammered, "he couldn't have possibly been part of it!"

Todd looked at me and suddenly looked much older, probably his real age. "How can you know, Millie?"

Suddenly it hit me. "He asked me to turn his brothers in, sort of. He said he couldn't because they were family, but he didn't understand why I hadn't done it yet. And then I told him this morning what I was going to do and he said it was about time." There was some silence. "He didn't try to stop me. Isn't that the same thing as asking me to do it for him?"

Soldate and Todd looked at each other and nodded ever so slightly, one of those maybe nods that promises nothing, but shows there is thought taking place. Soldate looked at the tabletop in front of me. "So what do you have for us?"

The diary seemed to grow in my hands as I remembered its importance. I swallowed hard. "One reason I didn't come to you earlier was I didn't know exactly what to tell you. But I do now." I told them about how my cousin Jeraldine Paxton had let us borrow her grandfather's diary. I opened the leather-bound booklet to the page where V.B. describes the still bust in Loftis. "Sherwood Forest is where Loftis used to be. You see how he describes the heavy brush and the hidden mounds? They have got to be in a cave under those large boulders."

Soldate reaches for the diary and reads it. "Well, what do you know! The Carps are using an old moonshiner hiding place. I bet there are some crevices where they've got piping shoved up through to let the cave ventilate."

Dad looked at me and gave me an I'm proud of you look. I just nodded, not sure how to feel. I was relieved that none of this was up to me anymore, but was not sure if this would be one more thing Junior and Roy would only get a slap on the wrist for. So I couldn't help myself and blurted out, "So, will this be like when they beat up Rai? Will they be out on the streets the next day and maybe never see jail time?"

"Millie!" Mammaw reprimanded me.

"Excuse my daughter! She's had a lot on her mind." Dad smiled a bit embarrassed and then gave me a glare.

Soldate smiled and leaned back in his chair. "It's okay. I understand how things may sometimes look." He stood up and walked over to a little side table displaying a jug of coffee, Coffeemate and a Styrofoam cup with 25 cents per cup written on the side. He grabbed an old mug and poured himself a cup, conveniently forgetting to drop a quarter in the cup. "You see, Millie, the Carps have dug themselves a hole that will be pretty hard to dig themselves out of any time soon." He sat down again and handed the diary back to me. "You give this back to your cousin. We have all the information we need and as far as we're concerned this conversation never took place." Todd nodded as well.

I could feel my father sigh, "You mean Millie doesn't have to testify?"

"What for?" Soldate smiled, "She never really had any proof and the only hard evidence comes from a lawman who's been dead for years. We'll take care of the rest."

1908: Doomsday prophet Lee J. Spangler and followers sit atop a mountain dressed in white, awaiting the end of the world; The International Paper Company introduces the Dixie Cup, the first one designed to be thrown away.

Home Again

"Julia! Steve Keith!" Harriet hurries to embrace her daughter and son-in-law as they walk through the front door. Harriet can't stop touching her daughter's hands as she pulls her into the kitchen where her sisters and their husbands, A.L. and W.B. Hardin, are eagerly waiting. Sally and Bertha jump out of their chairs to hug Julia while the men all shake hands and slap each others' backs. V.B.'s girls and the Hardin children all run in to make the kitchen unbelievably crowded as they greet an aunt and uncle they do not remember. The reunion is a mixed one, with many tears and much laughter. Harriet takes in the scene of her remnant children and her beloved grandchildren gathered into her domain. She's sharing the famous McGaha hospitality once again, but this time all the travelers are her own kin.

It is not long before Harriet has all the grownups around the kitchen table and the children at two small tables in the living room eating her cornbread and chicken soup. Julia can't get enough molasses and butter spread over her mother's cornbread and keeps finding herself having to check her chin. Finally she wipes her mouth one last time and looks once again at V.B. "How long you bin back here with Mama?"

V.B. swallows his last spoonful of soup before he answers, "Pretty well since Rose died. After I could sell most businesses in town and got on with the Feds, it seemed the right thing to do. Mama is really raising the girls and this is much closer to Greenville where my headquarters are."

Julia doesn't seem to care that they are not alone at the table. "I'm really glad you came home, Bunyan. Mama needs you."

V.B. looks across the table at his mother who is pretending that she isn't listening, but her concentrated effort at emptying an already empty soup bowl tells V.B. otherwise. He smiles and says intentionally, "Yep, I reckon. And I need her too." His mother looks up for a moment and gently nods at her son before she begins to clear the table.

Steve moves in to change the subject, very much interested in the adventures of his brother-in-law. "Tell us a little about your work, Bunyan. How is it different from bein' Sheriff?"

V.B. is more at ease talking about his work than the deep grief he has been carrying for so long. He watches his mother hurry the grandchildren to help clear and clean while her own children do some catching up. V.B. leans back in his chair and twists his mustache. "Well, it sure is easier for jurisdictional issues -- even funny at times."

"How so?"

"More than once I caught somebody over the line in South Carolina who knew me and quickly called me 'Sheriff.'" V.B. chuckles for just a moment as he recalls, "Just last week, one man actually laughed when he did that and announced, 'Joke's on you, Sheriff. We be in the great state of South Car'liner. You shore be out of your territory!'"

"What happened?" Steve asks.

"I flashed my federal badge and said to him and his two buddies, 'Well, gentlemen, I'm not out of state but you are out of date! And you are in my territory as a federal agent!' Never seen faces fall so far. They could have stepped on their own jaws a-hanging so low."

"Did they resist?" A.L. is easily drawn into the conversation as the women become sidetracked and move to help their mother over her objections.

V.B. ignores the women and continues. "Nope, they were so shocked they just handed me their rifles and put out their hands for cuffs. Then they sat there and cried as my deputy and I cut up the beautiful still, their own 'work of art!'"

Steve continues to press V.B., who is thoroughly in his element. "And back in Brevard. How do the folks see you there now?"

Briefly, V.B. is distracted giving Reba a quick kiss as she hands her daddy a large piece of apple pie. He grabs his fork and does not wait for the others to be served. "Kind of crazy. Lots of folks don't know what do with me, being as they have another sheriff now. Brevard town struggles with their local enforcement."

"What do you mean?" A.L. asks as his wife sits down next to him with two plates. He thanks her. Everyone returns to the table to enjoy their pie. V.B. puts his fork down for a moment. "Well, they struggled a long time with giving out whiskey permits and folks either watering it down or adding bad stuff to it. Then one judge put out an order forbidding bad whiskey. That helped some." As if trying to remember correctly, V.B. begins to twist the other side of his mustache. "After whiskey makin' and sellin' was outlawed, even the governor wrote the sheriff after me to crack down on it in town and the county. Since I've been a revenuer the folks in town keep trying to get me to help out there, but I tell them it's up to their own Brevard police and county Sheriff."

"Help out with what?" Julia is finally relaxing now that her mother is sitting still.

"With 'Blind Tigers' after different powerful speakers from the Anti-Saloon League came to Brevard tryin' to get the officials to stop them." V.B. states as a matter of fact.

Steven Keith sighs, "V.B., we've been out in Oklahoma since it was just Indian Territory. What on earth is a 'Blind Tiger'?"

V.B. quickly clarifies, "It's a store or restaurant that has a back room where booze is available. The police turn a blind eye, usually with some payoff in money or booze."

"How do folks know about it? Word of mouth?" Sally quietly asks.

"Don't have to. The store will simply have a little stuffed animal -- a tiger -- in the window." V.B. waves to Reba to grab him another piece of pie. She rolls her eyes, but obliges.

"It's a shame!" Harriet suddenly speaks. V.B. assumes she is commenting on the 'Blind Tigers' and not his second piece of pie.

Steven adds, "I've read about the 'Blind Pig' out in California and up north, with the pig meaning the police. Sounds like the same thing."

V.B. responds, "Yep. And 'speakeasy' in New Orleans and elsewhere."

Julia breaks in, "Our quiet little town of Brevard doing like the big cities!" Harriet shakes her head and gets up again to clear the last of the dishes. Reba and Leslie are quick to follow without needing any reminding this time. Julia continues, caught up now in the experience of her 'little' brother. "How about tax collection?"

V.B. smiles and says, "Yep, as sheriff I had to collect taxes for a while and now as revenuer I check to see that proper federal taxes are paid on booze, tobacco and the like."

"Was or is it hard?" Julia continues, aware that Bertha and Sally have joined their mother. She compensates for staying seated by stacking the loose plates and silverware left on the table at the end for easy pick-up.

V.B. quickly finishes his second piece of pie and tops off the dishes with his empty plate. "Naw, not as Sheriff. Everybody knew me and that they ought to pay. I had very few problems. They knew that if they were really in a bad way, I'd stand up for them in county commissioners' meetings to ask for a reduction. Many folks, for example, were not able to do their required road work due to some infirmity. Or were destitute and had to go to our county poorhouse. So tax time could be a time to help folks and hear their problems, maybe even get rewarded with whispered news about a still somewhere!"

"You mean neighbors a-squealin' on neighbors?" Julia asks, somewhat shocked.

"Oh no." A broad McGaha smile reveals something more to come. "Those whisperin' tips in my ear were usually from a wife who was worried sick about her man and what he was teaching the young-uns. They always asked for me not to hurt their man, just stop his whiskey-making and the life of tension."

Harriet encourages her girls to sit back down and enjoy visiting. She has enough help with her grandchildren. Sally and Bertha finally join their sister and the men as Stephen queries. "And now in this job as revenuer -- is it similar to the sheriff's job?"

V.B. twists his mustache a moment. "Not really. I reckon it is about as far on the other side as possible. Down in South Carolina where most of my work is, the folks were already mad enough that a tax was required, and they were saying it was their God-given right to make whiskey, but then, in 1890, their state was the first in the Union to prohibit alcohol sales, led by the temperance movement."

Bertha breaks in, "So folks can't make it and can't sell it and you revenue officers are the targets for their anger!"

"Along with the county or state lawmen who work with us."

Julia asks, "How about your working here in our home area? Is it easier than down the mountain? Folks know you."

"A lot easier. I work best alone, without a big posse of lawmen. I calculate folks are more likely to panic and haul off a-shootin' if they see lots of lawmen with guns drawn. When a moonshiner or bootlegger is a-lookin' down the barrel of a Colt 44 pistol or Winchester rifle or shotgun it is bad enough, but if there are 10 or 12 pointed your way with trigger-happy deputies a-grinnin' and shakin', you'd panic too!"

Steven jumps in, "Looked like a Remington revolver you were a packin' on the way here. That right? I thought you got your Papa's 1860 Army Colt."

"Yep. Papa's was good for its day and pretty accurate but I need a double action these days. I also have a Winchester model 1887 lever action shotgun. Never had to fire it at a human, thank God."

Steve pauses a moment and then, feeling very much like a school boy, asks, "Did you ever get shot at yourself?"

V.B. smiles at the frequently asked question, always seeing some disappointment in response to his answer. "Well, just in June this year, Merrick and I were raidin' and bustin' up stills near Walhalla when we caught some lead a-flyin' our way. Killed Merrick's horse right under him. Neither of us got hit, thank God." V.B. knew people wished he'd been shot at more and expected it in his years of working as a lawman, but he was proud that he had not. He smiles to himself at the memory of his father's sense of mercy and reckoned that some of his father's reasoning actually flows in his own blood and impacts his enforcement of justice.

"Did you catch the fellers who did that?" Steven Keith pulls V.B. back to finish the story.

"Nope. But we put them out of business for a long time."

Julia notes his calm nature in telling the story and asks, "Do you have a lot of your 'business calls' in that area of South Carolina, not far over the line from here?"

"Oh yeah. If you study my journals you'll see many train ticket and livery costs for regular raids from Seneca to Walhalla, to Merritsville to Tigerville to Gowensville to Pickens to Venus, Highlands and on and on."

"You mean our Highlands, beyond Toxaway?" Steve asks.

"Actually South Carolina has one too, but I work both places called 'Highlands' along with Table Rock Mountain in between."

V.B. stands and encourages the rest of his family to join him in the living room. A.L and W.B. quickly fold up the two small children's tables and pull up some chairs, letting their wives take the rockers. Julia, sitting in her father's old rocker gets her brother's attention once more as he lets Jacksie climb up in his lap. Even as an eight-year-old she still tries to get some snuggle time with her father when she can. "It sounds pretty boring, more so than the travel and raids. Is there ever anything funny?"

With a big smile V.B. remembers, as he holds his daughter tight, "Oh yeah. Once as I waited my turn in the Asheville Courtroom some feller from over in Haywood County came to court to say that a man owed him $300 for moonshine he had sold him."

"He did what? What did the judge do?" Steve asks.

"Well, the judge did order the man to pay the moonshiner the money owed. And then he threw the moonshiner, money in hand, in jail for making moonshine whiskey!" Jacksie giggles along with the adults.

The room is silent for a few minutes as A.L. decides to start a fire. Although the extreme cold has not arrived, the family is eager to feel the cozy glow of a small fire. Julia brings V.B. back to the original concern about his local raids. "And now, pray tell brother, is it safer for you to go alone in these parts?"

"Simple. They know me and that I won't pull a gun on them for no reason." V.B. answers without hesitation, "There are more ways to get the job done than playin' Wild West. For example, right across Little River, down there at Loftis." V.B. points westward and Jacksie actually follows his finger to find she is staring at the wall next to the front door. "I busted up a lot of stills and poured out a lot of mash in a few months. There was one especially big operation in a cave with the rhododendron and ivy so thick I could hardly locate it."

"How'd you find it, Daddy?" Jacksie looks straight into her daddy's eyes as if he is telling her a bedtime story.

"Well, I'd been climbing all over the big boulders when I come upon such a crevice in a big rock I was standing on. I had to be careful not to fall through into a cave below. I hardly saw the opening and accidently knocked a rock off into it. That's when I heard a splash and a whole lot of cussin'."

After the group stops laughing, Steven adds, "And so close to home!"

"Yep. I reckon some folks could see every time I left the house and got scared I was headed their way. Local Loftis business pretty well dried up shortly."

"Of course, some of them just moved their operations on over to Reba but mostly to East Fork. As you know, there has always been lots of 'stilling' in these mountains."

Rocking in front of the fireplace, Julia reflects on her childhood, on long lost siblings and especially on her beloved Papa. "You know, Bunyan, Papa was so good to write to me in those years, ever the teacher. One of his favorite topics was what you were doing and what concerned you. He was so proud you went into law work since you were always looking at justice and fairness. He once wrote that you were the other side of his coin."

"What did he mean by that?" V.B. suddenly finds he is speechless.

Julia continues to stare at the growing flames. "He never clarified that but I reckon he meant that mercy and justice go together. And everyone knows what a compassionate, merciful man he was. He would never give himself credit for anything special, though." Julia is silent with gentle tears slipping ever so slowly down her cheeks.

Summer 2012

"Let me show you the way out." Detective Todd Soldate opened up the door to lead us out of the Sheriff Department's conference room.

"Millie?" Todd stood and walked toward me, not even looking like Eamon anymore. He held out his hand and after only a moment's pause I took it. "You done good!" He smiled and I returned his smile, suddenly seeing a man who was just doing his job.

"Thanks," I whispered as I followed him out the door. We wound our way through the intricate passageways until Todd stopped and opened a door to the right instead of leading us out into the lobby. "I thought we were going out the door?" I asked.

Todd smiled as he led us into a wider hallway. "I want to show you something." He pointed to a wall where portraits hung in several rows. "These are all the Sheriffs Transylvania County has ever had." He pointed to the center of the top row. "Do you recognize him?"

"Volenus Bunyan McGaha. Well, I'll be!" Mammaw smiled. We all moved in a little closer.

"Wow!" was all I could manage. The young man staring back at me had a dark vest neatly gathered under a jacket with wide cut lapels that spread out like pointed butterfly wings. His white collar was held snugly to his neck by a wide tie that looked gray since the whole picture was black and white. His short hair was neatly cut with one small strand of hair falling a little onto his forehead. His dark eyes seemed so intense that it looked like he was thinking deeply about something. I guess he was handsome in a sort of old-guy way. "I can't believe I'm holding his diary in my hands." I looked around feeling somewhat childish, but no one seemed to find my comment lame. They seemed to be thinking the same thing.

"It's pretty amazing that an old Sheriff is still helping us today." Todd Soldate sounded almost as childlike as I did.

"Yes, it is!" Dad gently reached for my hand and looked at Soldate, "I guess we better head on out. We don't want to keep you any longer."

As we walked out the door, I glanced back at V.B. I don't know if it was his neatly cut moustache or what, but it sure looked like he was smiling.

1908: Erich Weiss, aka Houdini, son of an immigrant Hungarian Rabbi, becomes known as the world's greatest magician; Thomas Edison's film entitled "The Widow Jones" brings about censorship due to a twenty-second kiss.

Coming Home

Julia wraps her warm sweater around her shoulders as she joins her brother on the porch with two cups of coffee. The cool fall evening floods her memory as she carefully sits on the top step of the porch next to V.B. She looks at her brother who is deep in thought. "Bunyan, what are your plans? Any changes?"

"Well, Julia," the soft-spoken lawman answers, reaching for one of the cups, "after my contract ends next year, I'm thinking about hanging up my badge and gun."

"And do what?" She gently leans in against him for just a moment.

"Well, Mama needs me now and the girls really need their Papa. They are growing up so fast."

Julia looks out into the darkness, but can still see the outline of the barn in the moonlight. "Would you be helping around th' homeplace?"

V.B. takes a sip of the steaming coffee. "Ahh." He savors the taste as Julia laughs at her brother's habit that he has taken with him into adulthood. "Of course, I'd be helping a lot. I still have some business ventures that are easier for a man my age and some ideas. I'm a-getting too old to chase folks all over these mountains."

Julia sips her own coffee. "What sort of ideas? Newspaper business again? Didn't you start The Sylvan Valley News back in '95?"

V.B. responds, "Not papers or a desk. How'd you like that Model T Ford ride up the mountains? Don't laugh, but I am a-studying about starting the first automobile bus line between Brevard and Greenville." V.B. can still see the funny look on Rose's face when he first mentioned the idea years ago. "South Carolina is already improving their roads trying to bring tourists to the hotel on Caesar's Head. As soon as North Carolina works on our side up Mill Hill to the state line, it'll be perfect for a heavy motor car."

"But," Julia queries, "can't folks just take the train from Brevard to Hendersonville, then to Greenville?"

"True, but it takes a long time, you probably have to spend the night and it costs a good bit. I figure I can haul folks to Greenville and back in a day for a lot less money and in much less time, once the road is ready."

Julia responds to her brother, proud that he has remained the entrepreneur in the family, "We wish you all the best. Do let us know when it is a-goin' so we can plan another trip up the mountain in more style than that little huffin' Model T!"

Harriet comes out onto the long porch to sit with her talkative adult children and settles into a rocking chair. "Well, will we talk all night until mornin' milkin' time? The three girls have been asleep for hours."

V.B. responds, "Well, Ma, as you could hear, we got a lot of catching up to do. I'll have to go back to Greenville to report in soon. And they'll have some days to catch up with a lot of other relatives."

"Looks like the house is pretty booked for sleeping an' meals over the next weeks," Harriet proudly responds as she smoothes out her apron. "You-uns know your Papa would be happy for you all, a-gettin' one or the other together, renewin' family bonds."

V.B. verbalizes deeper feelings, "Well, Mama, he taught us well, right here in this place of peace and mercy. I reckon his spirit will live on here in many ways. It feels like he's up yonder a-lookin' down on us and saying he's a-fixin' up heaven for folks and their beasts."

Harriet slowly speaks with tears flowing, "The headstone for his grave is being carved now. We decided on these words being pretty close to your Papa, 'WEEP NOT FOR ME DEAR LOVED ONES. I AM GOING TO BE WITH JESUS WHERE I SHALL BE WAITING AT THE BEAUTIFUL GATES TO WELCOME YOU INTO THE PARADISE OF GOD'."

In spite of the wording, Harriet begins to weep with Julia who only nods her approval. V.B slowly stands. "I reckon everybody felt that expresses who he was and will always be." He swallows hard to hold his tears and says, "I'm hoping to help out more here in the spirit of what Papa would have done. Nobody could replace him." V.B walks up behind his mother and embraces her gently, "As soon as I can finish up with the feds, I'll be right here to try to put into practice some of those things we all learned from Papa. We'll keep the home place fixed up and when I get my auto-bus I'll help haul you and other folks to the chapel."

"Young man, I am still perfectly capable of walking!" Harriet retorts in a feigned indignation.

They all laugh and laugh beyond the humor of her comment. It seems to be a healthy catharsis from so much grief.

Volenus Bunyan McGaha breathes in a deep breath of the cool mountain air and realizes it is time to come home, to Transylvania County and to a peaceful, secure part of the world. Mercy and justice are here.

16

Summer 2012

The three of us sat on the familiar smooth rock in the middle of the cleared field. Ellie sat in the middle and I was closest to the woods. I occasionally glanced back to the path we had followed, but as we sat in the crisp mountain air I felt my body finally relax. We had nothing to say, but somehow we were finally at peace.

As Kevin pulled out his fiddle and began to play he drowned out the sounds of sirens off in the distance. As we three studied the view, I figured the mountains staring back at us had seen more than one child grow up.

1940: France falls to the Nazi Troops; The Battle of Britain continues; Franklin D. Roosevelt is elected for an unprecedented third term as U.S. President and calls for America to be "an arsenal of democracy" in light of the coming war.

The Departure

January, 1940 is a very snowy, cold winter month in the Appalachian Mountains of Western North Carolina. That cold is very harsh for an older V.B. McGaha, who is now suffering with severe pneumonia. The former Transylvania County Sheriff and Federal Revenue Officer lies in the home of his daughter only a few yards north of the imposing Dunn's Rock in the See-Off community of southern Transylvania County.

Breathing heavily, he calls from his borrowed bed for his daughter, "Leslie, is it still snowing?"

"Yes, Papa. Don't you worry 'bout it. We got plenty of wood and a warm enough house."

He asks further, "Can you see off the mountain toward Pisgah Forest or down in the valley across th' river to Reba's and Elzie's place?"

"Nope. Just snow in the air and on the ground."

He worries on, barely able to speak, "I'm such a bother and takin' up space here on See-Off. Maybe I shoulda stayed in Brevard in my house."

Leslie tries to comfort him, "Papa, you're plumb sick with this pneumonia and got no business bein' by yourself in town. We got so many Hogseds an' Raxters an' McGahas on this here mountain who are close kin and that love you, that nary a one is gonna let you go back while you are ailin'."

He responds weakly, "Well, with your gaggle of kids right around here, and Reba's flock down th' mountain and Jacksie's nearby, I reckon I got enough Grandkids to watch out. But I just don't want to be a burden."

"Papa," Leslie tries to encourage him. "Speaking of Reba's flock, her man Elzie and their boy Perry are hangin' round here right now, a-waitin' on this storm to go by." She does not want to tell him that they have actually been on See-Off Mountain with their horse, Lady and a sled helping to ease the body of a deceased neighbor off the mountain. Roads up to See Off are impassable for motorized vehicles due to the snow.

A still weaker voice eases from V.B., now barely audible, "Is it about the middle of the month now?"

Leslie tucks the cover carefully around him and assures him, "Yes, Papa, it is. Now try to rest."

But V.B.'s inner thoughts are not just about his being a burden to the family, but rather about the storm and his vivid memory of almost forty years ago when his beloved Papa Craf had died in a similar snow storm on nearby Rich Mountain. He had been alone, that great man who had provided hospitality for man and beast alike. And it was mid-January four decades ago that his beloved Jessie and their baby had gone on.

His thoughts bring a smile to his face as he reflects on his own life in these local communities and how his grandchildren, the visiting camp children, the summer residents and others loved to hear of his experiences as sheriff and as a revenuer, a man of justice. He has become a popular story-teller and that pleases him. He can still hear his granddaughter, Jeraldine, asking, "Grandpa, please tell me another story." She would snuggle under the covers with him promising, "You know I'll remember them forever."

Leslie slips away to fix a meal as she notes his pensive face. V.B. hears her tell grandchildren, "He's just a-restin'. Let him be for a while." He remembers the words that that he and his Papa Craf had been 'two sides of the same coin', mercy and justice. He stops coughing and feels an inner warmth. He feels even warmer when he thinks his time may be near and he might be reunited with his beloved Jessie Geneva, his precious Rose and their babies, his babies.

On January 14th Volenus Bunyan McGaha passes from this earth, but the snow does not. In the yard, the grandchildren ring the loud brass dinner bell for several minutes and they hear the snow-muffled responding bells from down in the valley, across the river and on out the See Off ridge beyond Dunn's Rock. Everybody knows now.

HISTORICAL EPILOGUE

Volenus Bunyan McGaha retired from law enforcement to help raise his daughters and help Mama Harriet until she passed on in 1912 and was laid to rest next to her beloved Craf in the McGaha Cemetery.

The home place was sold to a textile mill, Piedmont Manufacturing Company from Greenville, and eventually became the Piedmont Camp with the McGaha family home becoming the popular 'Wemar Lodge' and with occasional visits from none other than Bunyan to tell stories about the good old days and to correct stories the children made up about the Lodge or Chapel. The Elks camp followed, after which private families have owned the property. The old house is gone but the wall for the yard remains.

Bunyan bought a touring Packard for his bus line between Brevard and Greenville and for picking up older folks for services at the McGaha Chapel. He carried some grandchildren such as Reba's little Agnes around with him for such pick-ups as well as to look for, and transport, multiple ministers when needed.

When he sold the home place, he moved into a modest house in North Brevard, on the corner where the Asheville Highway and Hendersonville Highway split. It was property his gracious Father-in-Law, Reverend Allison, had given to V.B.'s and Jessie's girls, Reba and Leslie.

Walter and Laura Raxter left the See-Off homestead above Dunn's Rock where she had been the first Postmistress and they had donated the land for the Dunn's Creek Baptist Church. They settled on a farm in the large bottom land under Dunn's Rock and moved into the former slave house associated with the Hume Hotel which had been burned by bushwhackers during the Civil War. With multiple children, grandchildren and nearby relatives, they cleared the many acres of bottomland of trees, sold to pay for the acres of land. Most locust trees, however, were kept for building drainage canals in the cleared fields.

One of Walter and Laura's sons, Elza, married V.B.'s daughter Reba and they settled to farm the land across the river on 137 acres of land with the help of their extensive tribe of twelve children. (They lost two in birth, or shortly after.) Other children of Laura and Walter received plots of land in the Connestee/Dunn's Rock valley on the south side of the French Broad River.

Bunyan was also married a third time to a local widow, Nancy Bishop. The marriage did not work out and he lived alone his last years in his house in North Brevard, spending some time with the families of his daughters Reba, Leslie and Jacksie.

A letter from V.B. to one Hardin cousin, Hubert, dated December 20, 1938, indicates he was still running his bus line and in fact had a break down and was detained for nearly 6 hours, arriving in Greenville only at 10 p.m. at night. He told of driving on to Rock Hill, S.C. to talk business with Mr. Rice, one of the Moore heirs about buying some Rich Mountain property from him and other Moore heirs. No offer was made but it appears that V. B. and Hubert were into some property purchase venture. Of interest also, is his mention of visiting his ailing sister Sarah daily apparently in Greenville where she lived and he drove. His engagement with family history is indicated as he notes in that letter that Vardery, his nephew, Sarah Hardin's son, knows where the grave of Hubert's Great-Grandfather is located and will help mark it.

V.B. died of influenza and pneumonia in a snow storm on January 14, 1940 while staying temporarily with his daughter, Leslie Hogsed on See Off Mountain. Sons-in-law, Carmen Hogsed and Elzie Raxter, as well as grandson Perry Raxter, strapped him to a sled and slid it down Riley Mountain Road to the Greenville Highway, the former Turnpike, for transport to Brevard in a hearse driven by his cousin Ed McGaha with Osborne-Simpson Funeral home. V.B.'s sister Julia Keith died that summer. Her husband Steve had passed on in 1912, the same year Mama Harriet McGaha had died.

Volenus Bunyan McGaha was buried in the old Oak Grove Cemetery next to his beloved Jessie Geneva and their baby. Somehow his name and date of birth were incorrectly carved onto his tombstone. The first name given there was "Venus" and the mistaken birth date was 1872 rather than the correct 1867 which is listed in several government documents and census papers.

It mattered not, for the legacy of the Sons of Mercy and Justice remained and they had done their work on this earth and gone on to meet their own peaceful mercy and justice.

ACKNOWLEDGEMENTS

The story of this book began when I (Keith) helped transfer ownership of the well-preserved little McGaha Chapel from the First United Methodist Church of Brevard to the Transylvania County Historical Society of which I am a Board Member. My great-grandfather, Walter P. Raxter, helped build the Chapel in 1872 and some of my Raxter cousins, who were also McGaha descendents, began to show me old family documents. Then they began to entrust long-kept papers to me for use and preservation. Pictures followed along with genealogical records. A letter from the Civil War and personal letters, legal documents and a diary, plus official reports from Bunyan's Revenue service came forth. Old records from the little church and many valuable items were given. Then those who remembered their Grandpa Bunyan shared their stories about him as a grandparent, what he said about being Transylvania County Sheriff and a Federal Revenue Officer.

Public records were also helpful, in the Transylvania County Courthouse, in the Rowell Bosse Room Archives of the Transylvania County Library where the help of Marcy Thompson and, previously, Betty Sherrill has been invaluable. Copies of all documents obtained for this work will be housed in that local archive. The Biltmore archives graciously provided, and gave permission to use, copies of correspondence between Sheriff Bunyan McGaha and Dr. Schenck. Special thanks go to Sue Dempsey Brewer for her extensive work compiling both court documents and newspaper articles from early Transylvania history. Those have been most helpful.

Credit is given for use of several historical facts from specific years used in this work from *Chronicle of America*, edited by Clifton Daniel (Dorling Kingsley, LTD).

In any work this extensive where so much community effort has been contributed, any writer has anxiety about not listing everybody who has helped. I have such anxiety but wish to apologize ahead of time; so very many folks have helped, some in small but important ways, others in profoundly vital ways.

I note first some direct descendants, mostly grandchildren, of Bunyan McGaha. Jeraldine Raxter Paxton has been the keeper of most documents and graciously shared them and helped in ongoing ways. Her sister, Nadine Raxter Ashe, has given help in typing, chasing down information and many other ways including deciphering her grandfather's revenue service diary with help from her daughter Melanie. It was their brother, Perry (along with Helen) Raxter, who first showed, and copied, some family records that got us started in this collection of old records. He also granted permission to use his witness of his Grandfather Bunyan's final trip off See Off. Interviews with their sister, Agnes Raxter Henderson, and brother, Calvin Raxter, before they passed away, helped fill in the story as did the interview and help from their cousin Lula Hogsed Johnson.

Another of the McGaha cousins, Martha Jay Johnson, loaned me her massive copy of the McGaha history and genealogy files and was most patient with my use until their cousin Duane J. Dean graciously provided a personal copy and granted permission to use the information and pictures from those records. Duane and his wife Stacey have given ongoing support in research. Those within the McGaha clan who helped either directly or indirectly with their research should be noted: Gene McGaha, Mary Elizabeth McGaha Stiles, Josephine McGaha McCrary, Edward McGaha, Jack McGaha, Stan McGaha and many, many more. Clifton Fisher, a direct descendent of "Epi" McGaha, was helpful in researching family tradition as was Marshall Loftis who assisted with his ancestors.

During the research for the book and the Chapel turn-over, many folks provided other documents and guidance both from the First United Methodist Church of Brevard and Transylvania County Historical Society. I am deeply grateful to the entire Historical Society for their long standing individual and collective support as well as for their permission to use the image of the McGaha Chapel on the cover. Society President Eugene Baker also had an ancestor, Jackson Gillespie, who worked on the Chapel and served as Trustee.

Randy Carter, retired NCIS and U.S. Customs officer, provided valuable background information on the history of both customs and the Revenue Department. Frank Duckworth provided the only known picture of, and showed the grave of, his relative, the murdered U.S. Deputy Marshal Alfred Duckworth, a figure in the "Major" Lewis Redmond part of the story. Sheriff David Mahoney has been supportive as well as Chief Deputy Brian Kriegsman and Ricky McCall who have assisted in modern information on law enforcement and drugs in Transylvania. Our own cousin, Milford Hubbard, who served the longest of any sheriff in Transylvania County history, also assisted and provided information about the Duckworth murder which occurred near his family home on East Fork.

The Furman parts of the story could not have been so effective without the help of my old colleague and friend Dr. Glen Clayton, retired Archivist for the Furman University Library. Our two close Swiss family friends, Gerhard and Gerdi Stutz, are to be thanked not only for their decades of undying support but also for the setting for some writing in their Alpine house in Soerenberg, Switzerland.

Special thanks go to the Transylvania County Genealogical Group, especially Michael Allison, Virginia Green and Wylene Alston for leading in genealogical research and, along with many others, putting together The Heritage of Transylvania County, Volumes II and III. The Transylvania Genealogy Group has been influential in ongoing stimulation on line and probably made many unconscious contributions. My sincere thanks go to the more than eight hundred members of that group.

For the quiet, peaceful, wooded campsite setting of Cascade Lake on the lower Little River, one setting of the book, thanks go to the supportive staff of the Cradle of Forestry in America Interpretive Association. For the exceptional editing assistance of Anne Wanicka we are both truly grateful.

This has been a family affair, with much love and support and patience for the long pilgrimage it has taken. In addition to their encouragement, my wife, Jonlyn, and our children have helped with reading the manuscript: Paul Parker, co-author Leslie Borhaug and Kym Sebranek. Paul's work on map-making and on rescuing old pictures from the world of antiquities into the digital world has been crucial. Leslie's daughter, Sarah Borhaug, designed the photo illustration on the cover. The touchy recovery of the hundred thirty-plus year old photo of Alfred Duckworth is thanks to the skills of nieces Kara Beth Brunner and Scharme Brunner Price at the Brunner Studio in Berea, Kentucky. Niece Gwen Brunner Hensley has done the remarkable task of structuring, formatting and finishing the technical work in text and pictures.

Others who have contributed in multiple ways would include Mac Morrow, the centenarian Vera Jones Stinson and other Jones family members, David and Maria Fleshood and the Word Became Flesh Foundation, Bruce and Jacquelyn Rogow.

Several sites in the Dunn's Rock, Rich Mountain and Cedar Mountain communities have been crucial settings for this story. Our deep thanks go to current owners of those private properties who have allowed us access to them and their encouragement in this research, especially Billy and Gail Hagler, as well as Debbie and Rod Parrish. In addition, a special thanks to Jose Luis Gonzalez, Benjamin Gonzalez and Rogelio Gonzalez, the owners of The 3 Caballeros.

Leslie has worked extensively in co-authoring the work, especially in bridging between the past and present through the creative present time story as well as bringing life into my historical narratives. Although Leslie and I are co-authors of this work, she acknowledges that the original impetus, major research and historical writing are mine. However, the development and completion of the final product would never have happened without her. No father could be more appreciative of his talented daughter. Leslie wants to thank her husband, Tore, and her children, Sarah, Amy and Maya, for their endless support.

Above all, my thanks cannot be said enough or be expressed strongly enough for my loving, most encouraging, very patient wife of over half a century, Jonlyn Truesdail Parker. Truly, this could not have happened without her multi-leveled support.

Bunyon McGaha, Brevard, Dies

Former Sheriff and Revenue Officer Here to Be Buried Today.

Brevard, N.C., Jan 15- V. Bunyan McGaha, 73, well- known citizen of Transylvania County, N.C. died at the home of his daughter, Mrs. Leslie Hogsed, near Brevard, Sunday at noon following an illness of one week.

Mr. McGaha was Sheriff of Transylvania County eight years and was revenue officer several years with headquarters in Greenville, S.C. In the revenue capacity, he served with Capt. R.Q. Merrick, now with the Alcohol Tax Unit in Atlanta.

At one time he was interested in journalism publishing in Brevard and established the Sylvan Valley News in 1896.

He owned and operated the first bus lines between Greenville and Brevard, a period of four years. He was a son of the late J.C. and Harriet McGaha and was affiliated with the Little River Methodist Chapel at Cedar Mountain.

McGaha had been married three times. His first wife was Miss Jessie Allison of Brevard; his second marriage to Miss Rose Thrash of Davidson River, NC and his third union was to Mrs. Nancy Bishop, Cedar Mountain.

Surviving are three daughters, Mrs. Elzie Raxter, Brevard; Mrs. Leslie Hogsed, Brevard; Mrs. Jacksie Wolfe, Davidson River.; three sisters, Mrs Sarah Hardin, Mountain Lake Colony, SC; Mrs Ellen Hardin, Brevard and Mrs. Elmina Keith, Oklahoma. A number of grandchildren survive as also do the following step- children: B. C. Bishop, Charlotte; W.B. Bishop, Cedar Mountain; J.B. Bishop, Greenville and Miss Jennie Bishop, Greenville.

Funeral rites will be conducted Tuesday afternoon at 2 o'clock at Oak Grove Methodist Church near here. Interment will be in the adjoining cemetery. Rev. Harvey Smathers of Pisgah Forest and Rev. J.R. Bowman, pastor of Oak Grove, will officiate.

In Memoriam

J.C. McGaha

Brother J.C. McGaha, one of the stewards of the M.E. church, dies suddenly near his home, a few weeks ago. His death is a severe blow to his church and family. He was always regular in attendance at church and Sunday school and a leader in the prayer meetings and maintained an exemplary Christian character. He was a useful member, having professed faith in Christ when quite young. He was loved and esteemed by all who knew him. Though afflicted many weary days he bore his affliction with Christlike submissiveness, calmly awaiting the summons of Him who doeth all things well, to cross the mystic river with the boatmen cold and pale.

He would spare no pains to make peace, settle difficulties and allay strife among his neighbors. He was kind to the needy, attentive to the sick, a friend to every good enterprise and an enemy to all kinds of vice. His family,

his church and the whole community will miss him. To the bereaved wife and children we extend our deepest sympathy in this dark hour. Fain would we offer words of comfort to them but we can only point them to one who has promised to be our burden bearer, and who was a "man of sorrows and acquainted with grief." He alone can brighten the shadowed home and heal their broken hearts. Weep not dear wife and children. While you so sorely miss your dear husband and father here, he is done with troubles and afflictions of this life and is sweetly resting in the pure beyond and when your frail barque shall have drifted to the other side he will be standing with outstretched arms to receive you and welcome you into that beautiful home of the soul, where under the protecting light of your Savior's smiling face, you will live in divine peace forever.

E. Allison

Our Friends Gone Before

McGaha- J.C. McGaha was born in Transylvania County, N.C. June 12th 1832 and ended his earthly pilgrimage February 5th 1908- being 72 years, 7 months and 23 days old.

He was converted in the year 1853, and united with the Methodist Episcopal Church in 1877. Brother McGaha was a loveable character and his friends were numbered by his acquaintances. He loved the church, delighted in the fellowship of Christian people and, so far as he could, aided in every enterprise set of foot for the social, intellectual, moral and religious interest of the community. His home was a Christian home, he adorned his profession by a godly walk and chaste conversation and exerted in him family and influence which was a savor of life unto life. The writer as his pastor has known Brother McGaha for some time and has been often a guest in his home where a cordial welcome and generous hospitality greeted him whenever he entered it. Here we found the Methodist Advocate-Journal, our Church paper, and other good religious literature and also were cheered by the kind words and manifest sympathy with us in our work for the Master. At a meeting held last year in his home church Brother was richly blessed and comforted in the conversion of two

grand-daughters, who were largely brought up in his home and for whose salvation he was deeply interested. May they endure unto eternal life!

In the lonely mountain near the place where he experienced the saving grace of God in his conversion experience more than fifty years ago he ended his life on this earth. He went into the mountains in search of some hogs which had strayed and for two days and nights he remained alone, his family not at first apprehending any danger to him. When found life was extinct.

Funeral services were conducted in the home amidst the sobs and tears of loved ones after which the casket was tenderly born to the family burying ground on the hill overlooking his home which his presence had made so bright and joyous, now sad and lonely and there we deposited his remains to await the resurrection of the just.

He will be greatly missed, not only in the home but in the church and in the community; but we are well assured that our loss is his eternal gain. Sorrowing one follow him as he followed Christ and you will meet him again in the mansions of the blest whither he has gone before you. Yes, meet to part no more.

Rev. M.A. Matheson, Pastor

Relentless Hand

It gives us much pain to announce to our readers the sad and unexpected death of Mrs. V.B. McGaha which occurred at her home in Brevard Saturday evening. Her illness was very brief and no one was dreaming that Death was so near, and had such a firm grasp upon the thread of life. Many friends and relatives visited her during the day Saturday and were hoping for a change that she might be relieved. Dr. Hunt was at her bedside constantly, but medical skill availed nothing, and about 12 a.m. it was discovered that she was in the very throes of death. Mrs. McGaha was a daughter of the Rev. E. Allison and was most always very hale and the prospects for a long life seemed promising indeed. She married our genial sheriff shortly after his election to that office, and we are not saying too much to say that a more happy family could not be found. It was one in which the sunshine of welcome always beamed and joy, peace and plenty always abounded. Two bright-eyed little children graced their home and the pleasures of this life seemed complete. How uncertain is life, how certain is death.

Death of Wife of Sheriff of Brevard

Brevard, N.C., Jan.19- Mrs. McGaha, wife of Sheriff McGaha of this county whose death has been mentioned in the columns of your paper a few days ago was only thirty years of age, and greatly beloved by all who knew her. She was a daughter of Rev. E. Allison, and was married in Asheville November 18, 1893. Mrs. McGaha was the mother of three children, two of whom are living. She was an active member of the Baptist church and was a power for good in the community. She was a sufferer for some time before her death and received every possible attention from friends and physicians. Her death is a blow to her devoted husband and family, a loss to this community and church. The people of this county deeply sympathize with the sheriff in his bereavement.

APPENDIX B: THE WALTON WAR

The Southern Transylvania County communities of Dunn's Rock, See-Off, Cedar Mountain, East Fork, Cathey's Creek/Selica and surrounding areas were part of the so-called "Orphan Strip" over which militias of North Carolina and Georgia fought, some sixty years before the Civil War. This is also the area in which the story of this book had its major setting.

The conflict arose over confusion first between early settlers in the late 1700s as to where the state line was between North and South Carolina. Were the settlers in the land South Carolina deeded to the Federal Government? Several early settlers filed their land claims with South Carolina. Some families petitioned to be brought back into the jurisdiction of that state in order to have a governmental authority. The plea was rejected and the term "Orphan Strip" was applied to the area considered by many to be part of Buncombe County, North Carolina. Many settlers had land grants or claims with North Carolina and attended militia musters and court in Buncombe County.

In 1802, Georgia claimed the land up to the North Carolina line, the 35th parallel. The Georgia survey was highly inaccurate, following a former one and was far north of the 35th parallel. In 1803 Georgia named the area Walton County, Georgia and some settlers of the area shifted allegiance to that state. The governors of the two states were to try to ascertain the exact location of the 35th, and thus the exact boundary, but because there was no assurance that land grants and titles from North Carolina would be recognized by Georgia, it fell through. The situation became very serious with claims of authority from both states. The "orphan" now had conflicting parents.

The constables and tax collectors from Buncombe County were threatened with trial for usurping authority. The disturbances increased with riots and multiple disturbances. In 1804 Walton officials accosted

Robert Orr, off Wilson Road at the current Glen Cannon property, in order to remove him since he had a North Carolina grant, not one from Georgia. When he promised not to interfere with Walton County officials he was allowed to stay. A similar challenging visit was made to Will Raxter in the Cathey's Creek area. The Waltonians then visited John Havner at his home on Wilson Road at McGaha Branch. Havner was a Buncombe County Constable and a fight occurred. Havner was struck in the head with a musket and died by the next day.

The Buncombe County Militia was called out within four days led by Major James Brittain and 72 men plus 24 local residents arrested the Walton County officials, taking them to Morganton for a murder trial. They escaped and were never caught. Most Waltonians moved to Georgia and some tried to set up a government in exile. Georgia submitted the dispute to Congress but North Carolina recommended the two states resolve it. All agreed the line should be the 35th parallel and multiple readings were done to locate it. Georgia refused to accept the joint survey and appealed to Congress. By 1811 they hired their own survey who confirmed the 1807 joint survey. When Georgia named another new county Walton County, they had finally given up their claim. In 1971, however, a Georgia Legislator tried to raise the territorial claim, again to no avail. Many current residents in this area of Southern Transylvania County are descendents of the "Walton War" participants and most of the families in this story were affected by the conflict.

A more detailed account may be found in the article "The Walton War" by Martin Reidinger in The Transylvania County Heritage Vol.2-2008, pages 8-10.

APPENDIX C: McGAHA CHAPEL AND HISTORICAL NEIGHBORING CHURCHES

McGaha Chapel was finished in 1872 but it took until October 8, 1883 for the legal action to be finished with the purchase price of five dollars being given to A.J., "Frosty Jack," and Margaret Loftis for the Deed for the Little River Methodist Church. The Trustees receiving the Deed were J.C. McGaha, Jackson Gillespie, R.W. Raxter and F.M. Pressley who replaced A.J. for the turn- over of the property and building.

The Deed reads: "The parcel of land lies within the Dunn's Rock Township, Transylvania County, N.C., on the north side of the Little River on the Johnstone Turnpike Road to be used, kept and maintained as a place of Divine Worship for the use of the ministers and membership of the Methodist Episcopal Church."

Most of the same families were actively engaged at the same time with the building of the nearby Dunn's Creek Baptist Church on See-Off in 1876 and with the Deeds in 1881 and 1884. The Holdens had obtained permission for a church and school but that building burned down. Walter and Laura Raxter of this story gave the first fifth of an acre for the current church.

In nearby Cedar Mountain, Baptists also built the Rocky Hill Baptist Church in 1875, shortly after the Chapel was finished. The neighboring communities in East Fork and Carson's Creek had Baptist churches dating to 1840 and 1863 respectively. Well beyond Cedar Mountain down Reasonover Road, almost in today's Henderson County, the Blue Ridge Baptist Church had started in the 1850s or 1860s.

In the turn of the century from the late 1800s, many folks moved from See Off and upper Dunn's Rock community into the valley of Dunn's Rock/ Connestee, also starting churches. Carr's Hill, at the foot of Becky Mountain and Rich Mountain started about 1882, meeting in various places in Dunn's Rock community before building on land donated by Carr Landreth. Part of that same group also started the Dunn's Rock Baptist Church a little later on Connestee Road.

There was also for some years a little Methodist church at the intersection of Connestee Road and Island Ford Road. The story is that the ministers of that Methodist congregation and the Dunn's Creek Baptist Church on top of See Off worked together, taking turns meeting in one church one week and the other the next. When folks were invited to join a church both ministers stood at the front so folks could decide also which congregation they would enter.

The story includes the story of the St Paul's in the Valley Episcopal Church, also in the midst of Dunn's Rock Community. After their hotel in Dunn's Rock was burned by the bushwhackers, Robert and Mary Hume moved to Brevard and were instrumental in relocating the church to become St. Phillips Episcopal Church in Brevard in the 1880s.

The least known church activity in Dunn's Rock, and possibly the first in the County, was the Mamre Meeting House started by the Presbyterians, probably about 1790. That group and ministry moved to Davidson River to be part of that Davidson River Presbyterian Church. Recent research has shown that Mamre was located alongside the Turnpike in the Rockbrook curve of the Greenville Highway, next to where the Dunn's Rock Bridge once crossed the French Broad River and just a short distance from where the Old Federal "Cooper" Distillery now stands.

APPENDIX D
A LETTER HOME AND A NEWSPAPER ARTICLE

The Home of the Tourist and Commercial Traveler

HOTEL BERKELEY

PATTON AVENUE,
BETWEEN PUBLIC SQUARE
AND POST OFFICE

FRANK LOUGHRAN,
PROPRIETOR

Asheville, N.C.　　Feb 11th 9 PM　1895

My Dear Wife Jessie,

I got through all OK. It was so late I just thought I would stay up town to night.

I will go down to see Doug tomorrow. I hope to be home Wednesday night. But if I don't come don't be uneasy. I hope you and Bobo is all right. Kiss Bobo for me and take good care of yourself Sweet heart.

Lovingly your husband

Bunyan Mc-

The Brevard Clipper
The Sheriff of Transylvania County

No other office within the gift of people requires (or receives) more personal attention of man eternal vigilance than the Sheriff. A man to hold this position must be possessed of firmness and utter fearlessness. Volenus Bunyan McGaha, Sheriff of Transylvania County is just this kind of man. Duty is his watch-word, and on that line he continues, never swerving from the most difficult tasks. He is a safe and reliable guardian of the peace and a terror to the evil doers.

Mr. McGaha is a Transylvania County boy, born and raised. He was brought up on a farm, which he followed until 1889, when he established himself in the merchantile business, which he continued until 1893 to the satisfaction of a large patronage.

No man hereabouts is wielding a more potent influence for the enforcement of law, order and security than Sheriff McGaha. He always, however, has a hearty greeting for one and all, and in his office will always be found due absence of "red tape."

He was elected Sheriff of Transylvania County in 1892 and reelected in 1894 and 1896, and has ever served the people in a most conscientious and deportable manner. He holds the mystic ties of good fellowship with the odd fellows and is a man held high in estimation of county folk.

APPENDIX E: FACT OR FICTION?

Essentially, all stories, characters, reports, paper articles, government reports, etc., in the historical story are factual. Creative dialogue and a few characters have been used along with old, unconfirmed stories about the community.

The following are notable "fiction:"

1. All dialogue, including interviews.

2. Visits of Drs. Judson and Manley as well as the Judge. All were actual figures with Furman.

3. "Reverend" Joseph Schmidt.

4. Names and number of slaves. The family story is that Craf did convince his Papa Jesse to free theirs.

5. Gerda Sumi from Switzerland.

6. Repairman at Cooper Distillery in Dunn's Rock.

7. Bushwhacker gang characters. The murder of Deavor, however, did occur.

8. Party leaders who interview V.B. for Sheriff.

9. "Upper Transylvania Raid" including Agent Monroe. However, the Major Redmond story told therein is factual, including the characters named.

10. Rose's post-partum depression.

11. Will Wagner.

12. Billy Boy.

13. The feisty New York "investigative" reporter before the County Commissioners.

14. The "present time" parallel story. Except for Jeraldine Paxton, who is a grandchild of V.B. McGaha and who did share the contents of V.B McGaha's diary and much other material.

15. The death and burial of Epiphroditus (Epi) McGaha is an unsolved mystery. Some records indicate a date of 1860 but his family oral tradition is that he died in the Civil War. Several searches of those records give no mention of his service. His accidental death in the story is thus fictional.

Made in the USA
San Bernardino, CA
19 November 2013